STEELTOWN

James Grady

STEELTOWN

BANTAM BOOKS
TORONTO · NEW YORK · LONDON · SYDNEY · AUCKLAND

*Each character in this novel is entirely fictional. No reference
to any living person is intended or should be inferred.*

STEELTOWN
A Bantam Book / January 1989

All rights reserved.
Copyright © 1988 by James Grady.
Book design by Nicola Mazzella.
*No part of this book may be reproduced or transmitted
in any form or by any means, electronic or mechanical,
including photocopying, recording, or by any information
storage and retrieval system, without permission in
writing from the publisher.*
For information address: Bantam Books.

Library of Congress Cataloging-in-Publication Data

Grady, James, 1949–
   Steeltown.

   I. Title.
PS3557.R122S7   1989   813'.54   88-47841
ISBN 0-553-05328-0

Published simultaneously in the United States and Canada

---

*Bantam Books are published by Bantam Books, a division of
Bantam Doubleday Dell Publishing Group, Inc. Its trade-
mark, consisting of the words "Bantam Books" and the por-
trayal of a rooster, is Registered in U.S. Patent and Trademark
Office and in other countries. Marca Registrada. Bantam
Books, 666 Fifth Avenue, New York, New York 10103.*

PRINTED IN THE UNITED STATES OF AMERICA

O   0 9 8 7 6 5 4 3 2 1

for Stacey and Josh

Stranger
in Town

ONCE UPON A TIME, STEELTOWN worked big magic in the great
American dream, but on the May morning the man flew into
that city, he saw empty smokestacks rising into a clear sky.

A jam jar of Japanese flags stood next to the cash register at the airport newsstand.

"What are those for?" he asked the clerk.

"Chamber of Commerce's givin' 'em away," she said.
"Want one?"

"No, thanks."

He gave her a quarter for the local paper with its front
page stories about beautiful spring weather and a local
labor leader who'd blown out his brains, exited to the
sidewalk and tossed his bag into a battered cab.

"Where to, Mac?" asked the cabby, who wore a Mets
cap. He sized up his passenger in the rearview mirror: a
good-looking guy in a classy suit who'd made it through his
thirties the hard way. Too thin. Gray eyes like nails driven
deep in the wood.

"The city," answered his fare. "Any good downtown
hotel. Not too good, though."

"Easy," said the cabby as they glided away from the
curb.

The airport sat on a plateau ten miles from town, where
the smog from the factories hadn't been as thick and the
right people had owned the land for the airport authority to
buy. Set off-center in a state of amber waves of grain and

■ 1 ■

purple mountains' majesty, Steeltown was surrounded by mine-scarred, jagged hills. Scrub pines and yellow bunch grass were the only vegetation; less hardy foliage died during the boom days before World War I, when smelter owners claimed that Steeltown women were envied worldwide for the ivory complexion given them by the arsenic in the city's air.

The taxi rolled peacefully through the hills for five miles. Then the cabby glanced in the mirror.

"Shit!" He shook his head. "Look, Mac, I'm sorry about this."

Behind them, a police cruiser's red lights flipped on as it nosed up to their trunk. The cabby pulled off the road.

"Whatever it is," said the passenger, "don't lose your head."

The cabby rolled down his window, stared straight ahead, stony-faced. The passenger kept his hands on his knees.

The black and white cruiser had *SHERIFF'S DEPART-MENT* and a gold star painted on its doors. A shotgun poked up from the dash. The deputies wore khaki uniforms and utility belts weighed down with Magnums, handcuffs, and blackjacks. The driver sauntered toward the cabby's window while his partner leaned on the roof of the cruiser. The partner yawned, but his eyes never left the cab.

"My, my, my," said the cruiser's driver. Through mirrored sunglasses, he scanned the men in the taxi.

"Hey, Joe!" called the driver to his partner. "What do you think? Think we got some violations here?"

"Most likely," answered Joe.

"Most definitely," said his buddy as the taxi passenger rolled down his window. "Most definitely we got some violations."

"What's the problem, Deputy?" asked the passenger.

"Could be anything, couldn't it, Joe?" said the deputy.

"Sure," yelled Joe. "Anything. Low tire pressure, bad shocks. Lights too dim."

"It's daylight," said the fare.

"Hell," said the first deputy, "we really don't know what's wrong. We'll have to make a thorough investigation, pull the cab in—you with it, you un'erstand. Might need to search you, see what else comes up. Could take a couple hours."

"Could take all day," said Joe, swaggering over to join his partner.

"Could take all day *and* all night," said the first deputy. "They still got Crazy Eddie in the lockup, Joe?"

"I dunno," said Joe. He smiled at the passenger. "What do you know, buddy?"

"I don't know why you want to tie me up in any beef you got with the cabby," he said.

" 'Cause it's your cab, man!" said Joe. He stuck his head inside the cab window. He smelled of whiskey. "You hired it, you're responsible."

"I've never heard of any law like that," said the fare.

"You know what they say," Joe told him, "ignorance of the law is no excuse."

"I can see that," said the stranger with eyes like nails.

"Besides," said Joe, "we ain't got no beef with the cabby. He's a good boy. He's already made his ice."

"You know what else they say?" said the first deputy. The stranger shook his head, and the first deputy leaned closer while Joe moved back. "When in Rome, do as the Romans do."

"What do the Romans do in a situation like this?" asked the stranger.

"I like you!" said the deputy. He looked at Joe and said, "I like him!"

"Hell of a guy," said Joe. He beckoned to the cab's passenger. "Let's see some ID."

The man took a billfold from his suitcoat, passed the deputy a New York driver's license in the name of Walter Mathews. The deputy examined the laminated card, then handed it back.

"Well, Walter Mathews," said the first deputy, "seeing as how we're all friends, Romans, and countrymen, how 'bout we say we stopped you so you could buy a ticket to the Sheriff's Posse's Ball? On second thought, a guy like you has a friend: two tickets."

"How much?"

"Twenty bucks," said Joe. "A ticket."

The passenger opened his billfold wider, and the deputy nodded at the flash of green bills.

"One other thing," he said. "Lay twenty on the cabby now. That's what the ride in plus a decent tip comes to. We don't want to worry about him getting stiffed. You wouldn't want us to come looking for a stranger who stiffed some local boy, would you, Walter?"

"I'm not here to give anybody any trouble," said the stranger as he passed a bill to the cabby, who stuffed it in his shirt pocket. Joe took two other twenties from the stranger's hand.

"Real good, Walter," said the deputy. "Have a nice day and a pleasant stay in our fair city."

"Where are my tickets?" he asked.

The deputies laughed as they sauntered to their cruiser.

"I'm sorry, mister," mumbled the cabby. "I don't have any choice about what happens. I'm just trying to make a living."

"Forget it," said his fare.

They rode silently to a nationally franchised hotel on the edge of downtown, one that the cabby said "still isn't too bad."

"Where can I rent a car?" asked his fare as he climbed out.

"There's a place down the block," he said. He hadn't looked his fare in the eye since the cruiser pulled them over.

"Thanks."

"Hey, mister!" the cabby called out as his fare started to walk away. "Mind if I give you some advice?"

"I take all the help I can get."

"We call this slag heap Stealtown," said the cabby. "Only we spell it with an *ea*. As in thief. This never was a straight city, but it used to be a great place to live—if you didn't mind a little excitement and a lot of hard work. When they shut down the Pit and the rest of the mines, when they closed factories and smelters and mills, all the great hit the road.

"Some of us are stuck here, but you're just passing through. Keep on going—and get there fast. There's no business here worth doing. Go rent your car. Get in it, and get out of town."

He put the cab in gear, tugged the bill of his baseball cap.

"And drive careful," he said as he chugged away.

The hotel's electric glass doors slid open. A wispy old man in a black suit sat asleep on a couch, his mouth open. The blast of fresh air woke the old man; he frowned as the new man in town walked past.

The startled desk clerk quickly flipped off a TV game show.

"Hello, sir!" he said, face beaming. "Can I help you?"

"I'd like a room," said the man with gray eyes.

The desk clerk pushed a white card and a pen across the counter. "How long will you be staying with us?"

"Depends," said the stranger.

"No problem," insisted the clerk. "No problem whatsoever."

He pulled a key at random from a cabinet of slots full of keys and spun the registration card around.

"I think you'll find room 1015 quite comfortable," said the desk clerk. "Quite a view of the city, Mister . . ." He glanced at the card. ". . . Mister Reston. How will you be paying?"

The man passed the desk clerk an American Express card in the name of John Reston.

"Our bellhop has the day off," said the clerk. "If you'll let me switch on the answering machine, I'll grab your bags and . . ."

"That's okay," said the stranger, "I can handle it myself."

Elliot Kimmett III lived on an estate surrounded by a city park. The park had once been the Kimmett family's private preserve, but Elliot Kimmett II had donated the land to the city in exchange for permanent relief from property taxes on the remaining estate. The Kimmett homestead now covered an area only the size of a baseball stadium. A twelve-foot iron bar fence encircled the estate.

The man with gray eyes drove his rented car along the

black iron fence. On the other side of the bars, a pair of great Danes loped after his car. When he turned onto a driveway leading to the gate, they disappeared into the shrubbery.

Two TV cameras were mounted on the gateposts, another atop a pole inside the trees. He leaned out the car window and pushed the button beneath a speaker box on a white column.

"Yes?" said a disembodied male voice.

"I'm here to see Mr. Kimmett," said the man in the car.

"Who are you?"

"Tell him the man from New York has arrived."

"Put your driver's license and company ID in the box," said the voice. An aluminum box slid out from the column. "Face up."

The box carrying the demanded IDs slid back into the column, reemerged a minute later.

"Drive all the way to the house," said the voice as the iron gates swung open. "Don't get out of your car until you stop at the front porch. The dogs are loose."

The Kimmett mansion was built in the twenties, when no architectural excess was unthinkable or, for the Kimmetts, unaffordable. The visitor crossed the Dixie front porch and rang the bell beside the steel-reinforced oak door. A TV camera was mounted above the entrance; another hung from the porch rafters.

The butler who answered the door wore a black tux and kept his eyes lowered as he bowed the visitor inside.

The husky, middle-aged man striding toward them across the carpeted entryway wasn't as diffident. He wore a banker's three-piece blue suit and had a cop's glint in his eyes.

"I'm Raymond Nelson," he said, "Mr. Kimmett's executive secretary. Mr. Kimmett is expecting you. Do you have any matches?"

"I don't smoke," said the visitor.

"That wasn't the question," replied Nelson. "Mr. Kimmett lives in a delicate environment with a high oxygen content. No matches, no lighters, no combustibles of any kind, are allowed in his rooms."

"I don't play with fire," was the reply. Over Raymond

Nelson's shoulder, the visitor spotted a man by the grand piano whose business suit contradicted his flattop haircut and Marine Corps stare.

"Don't you want to know if I'm carrying a gun?" the visitor asked Nelson.

"We know you're not," he said, nodding to a glowing red light on the wall by the door.

Somewhere upstairs a door closed. Heavy feet trod over the ceiling toward the stairs behind Nelson.

"Are you healthy?" said Nelson. "Any cold symptoms? Flu?"

"Don't worry," he told the secretary. "None of my problems are communicable."

A giant wearing a tuxedo lumbered down the stairs. He stood almost seven feet, had a barrel chest as round as most men are tall. His hands seemed the size of basketballs.

"This is Judson," said Nelson. "He'll take you to Mr. Kimmett."

Judson swept his hand toward the staircase.

"Aren't you joining us?" the visitor called down to Nelson as he climbed the stairs.

"I know what I need to know," said Nelson.

"Lucky man."

Judson led the way up three flights of stairs to a desk outside a set of double mahogany doors. A sign warned that oxygen was in use, fire was dangerous. A shrewish-looking nurse sat behind the desk, reading a paperback.

There was a *click*, and one of the double doors swung open. The visitor entered the room alone. Behind him, Judson shut the door.

The guest's first breath inside the room made him light-headed: the chamber had the atmosphere of an oxygen tent. Beneath the crisp purity was a perfumed tang.

He'd stepped into a jumble of time. To his right was a mahogany four-poster bed crafted when the Civil War was yesterday's news. The wall opposite it was an electronics center that belonged in space launch headquarters: a six-foot screen flanked by three television sets, slots for cassette and VCR tapes, and a compact disc system.

On the bedside table, a black dial telephone sat next to an electronic remote control.

Half a dozen overstuffed chairs were scattered through the room with the effect of a nineteenth-century British men's club. A wet bar jutted out from one wall; closed doors led to bathrooms, closets.

The paintings on the walls ranged from gaudy nudes appropriate for a Wyoming saloon to surreal masterpieces the Louvre would cherish. One wall held black and white photographs of factories and mines.

"What's your name?" called out a raspy male voice.

An old man sat by the windows. Sunlight streaming through white gauze curtains made him a silhouette in a chair beside a round table.

"Mr. Kimmett?" asked the visitor.

"What's your name?" called out the old man again.

"Jackson Cain," he said.

"Is that your real name?"

"What difference does that make?"

"Come closer," said the old man. "Come closer."

Cain walked deeper into the room. The tang in the air grew stronger the nearer he drew to his host, a sweet, orchid smell.

"Do you know who I am?" said the master of that room.

His features were still shadowed, but Cain saw he wore a terrycloth bathrobe, pajamas, slippers. His elbows rested on the arms of the chair, his trembling hands dangled over his lap.

"I assume you're Elliot Kimmett the Third," Cain said, "though we've never met."

The old man laughed, a cackle like dry leaves blowing through a skeleton.

"Come closer," he said. "I like to see what men like you look like."

The orchid smell was an unhealthy perfume in Kimmett's sweat. White hair lay matted on his skull. His body looked as if a vampire had sucked away his blood. His hooked nose was flanked by green eyes that glowed like the core of a blast furnace.

Cain started to pull out an empty chair when he heard a growl.

In an alcove to his left, curled up beside a rolltop desk,

was a black great Dane. He growled again. Kimmett spoke a command. The dog lowered his head to his paws—but kept his eyes on Cain.

"I keep him hungry," said Kimmett as his visitor sat down.

"I'm a light eater, too," Cain told him.

"You're going to do a job for me," said Kimmett, "you and your company."

"That depends on the job. And whether we can come to terms."

"Don't tell me about terms!" snapped Kimmett. "I know how to make a deal! As for the job . . . Well, your company and my family go back to the beginning. Don't tell me about mergers and new names and your modernized services. I know your company. They know the Kimmetts."

"But we don't know what you want."

"Why did they send you?"

"The director knew I was the best man for this job. For you."

"I know him," Kimmett said. "From long ago. From when he was what you are now. My father had some union trouble. Your firm sent your boss and I met him. He got the job done. We tried to hire him. He said no. Said he was a company man, *your* company kind of man. What kind of man are you?"

"Adequate."

"We'll see, we'll see."

"What job do you want us to do?"

"Recover something that's been misplaced."

"What?"

"This town," he said. "*My* town."

They stared at each other for a long time. Finally, Kimmett laughed.

"I like you," he said. "You know when to let the other man make his play."

"You're a charmer, too, but I'm here for business."

"And I've got plenty to give you."

"What?" Cain asked again.

"I already told you: reclaiming this town for me."

"My firm doesn't provide psychiatric help."

"You think I'm crazy." Kimmett chuckled. "I'm too rich to be crazy. I know what I want, and I can afford to get it.

"Do you know where you are?" he asked abruptly.

"Steeltown."

"How do you spell that?" he asked.

They both smiled.

"I'm thinking of revising my map," said the visitor.

"That's why you're here, Jackson Cain, or whatever your real name is. What do you know about this town? About me?"

"I've kept my eyes and ears open."

"Good, because this town eats men who don't want to see and don't want to hear.

"My grandfather and men like him built this city. He beat everybody—other families, the rabble, the Reds, unions, big-money boys from back east, weak-willed do-gooders, and know-nothing bureaucrats. We owned half the mines, smelters, and factories, called the tune for the downtown businesses. We controlled the unions, ran the city and as much of the state as we needed to, kept Washington out of our hair. We grew rich, the town boomed, and everybody was happy."

"Everybody?" asked Cain.

"Everybody who mattered," said Kimmett.

"My father succeeded his father," he continued. "I started taking over in the war, when our copper and steel got us a lot of gold from beating the Germans and Japs.

"Then . . ." he shook his head. "The world was different after the war. We were big business. Our interests became corporate. We sold stock, divested and diversified and . . .

"We opened up our hand to reach for more and Steeltown slipped through our fingers. We watched it happen—the companies' stock going to banks and trust funds, getting picked up in mergers we paid little attention to. The family made millions, of course, but . . ."

He shrugged.

"My father died. Then mining bottomed out. The steel mills, the factories . . . The Europeans and damn Japanese built their own Steeltowns. Now this town is just a rusted shell."

"Why do you want it back?" Cain asked. "Rebuilding the empire—if it can be done—might cost you most of your fortune."

"Better to reign in hell," he said, smiling, "than to be merely rich anywhere else."

"I don't buy that," Cain said, shaking his head. "You don't either. You're too old and sick to enjoy the crown long enough to make it worthwhile."

"Yes," he said. "I can see why they sent you.

"Do you believe in death, Mr. Cain?" he asked.

"So do I," he said, after his visitor didn't answer, "but there is a way to beat death."

"Not for guys like me," said Cain.

"I am not like you," answered Kimmett. "I have a son." He shook his head. "A grandson too, but from what I've seen, he might be worse than his father. An unfortunate mingling of blood.

"My son ... He is not yet himself. I will see to that before I die. Steeltown belongs to our family, it *is* our family. It is me, and as long as it is tight in my family's grasp, I shall live. I'll reclaim Steeltown before I die, and ..."

"Legacies don't always work out the way we want," said Cain. "What does your son think of all this?"

"My son is a man who goes along. He married a woman beneath him. She's irritating, but of no consequence. I neglected raising him properly, just as I neglected Steeltown. But I shall rectify everything.

"Do you still think I'm crazy?" he asked.

"That's never mattered much," said Cain. "Tell me about this town and what you want me to do in the real world."

"There is no real world, Cain. We invent the world every day, and the ones who win are the ones who do the inventing.

"First, the Kimmetts traded away Steeltown, then the corporations wrote it off. A man named Olson grabbed the city in the 1960s when the big firms started their retreat. He was a back-street boy who wouldn't settle for factory work. He used gangsters to get him the city garbage contract, pilfered that with the political machine, then started a national dry cleaners franchise, bankrolled shopping malls that broke the downtown merchants. He bought his way into politics. He courted America's presidents and they courted him. For the last twenty years, he kept Steeltown as his personal fiefdom, his safe haven.

"Olson ran this town like a spider. You had to be in the center of the web with him—or have been there—to see how everything linked together. Most people only knew he was rich and powerful. Most people can't see the webs of their world—and wouldn't dare look even if they could.

"Olson died two months ago, a heart attack in his sleep. No children. Two ex-presidents came to his funeral, the governor, a congressional delegation. I stayed home.

"Do you know how history works, Cain?"

"I've seen some," he said.

"History gives us moments when, if we act boldly, we can change the course of time. We have such a moment now.

"This isn't a city anymore. Steeltown has no head, no brains, or heart, no fire in its belly. Three dogs are eyeing each other over Steeltown's skeleton. Of all the dogs, they are the only ones who count. One is a cop, one is a crook, one is a politician."

"That could be one man," Cain told him.

"Those three dogs rule this town together," said Kimmett. "They're waiting for my body to fall on the bone heap. The dogs think they'll outlive the lion, so why challenge him now? They know my son will be easy prey. You and your company will tame these dogs, get me this town back so I can pass it on properly."

"And not die," said Cain.

"Yes," he replied. "Now will you do it, or do I need to hire other help?"

"I don't know," said Cain. "I need to think about it, check with the home office."

"But you could do it," Kimmett insisted.

"I could try. But it would cost you."

"I'm used to paying," he said.

"Give me today," his visitor told him as he stood. "I'll look around, get back to you. Your consulting fee buys a carefully considered answer."

Kimmett's laugh followed Cain to the door.

The River

CAIN FOLLOWED THE STREAM that flowed away from Kimmett's estate. The further he drove from the park, the smaller the homes became and the more blistered their paint. Most of the houses had 1900-style front porches. Even the biggest and best of the homes were at least twenty years old.

The stream emptied into the river at the city line. Once a vein of Steeltown's wealth, the river flowed out of the western horizon, snaked a wide canyon through the town, then rolled on to the distant sea. Factories, steel mills, and railroad tracks weighed down the flat levees in the river's gorge, seven miles of smoke-blackened corrugated steel buildings, slag heaps, assembly plants, power plants, and smokestacks, with chain link fences marking the borders of industrial empires. One stadium-sized gutted building was the main smelter for Bushmaster Copper; between the open pit mine and its smelting facilities, Bushmaster once employed 7,200 workers in this city. Now, Bushmaster's Steeltown payroll comprised a dozen watchmen. The coke plant for American Steel loomed beyond Bushmaster's fence. American Steel's plant was a maze of empty catwalks, motionless conveyer belts, and dismantled blast furnaces housed in ten-story brick boxes with thousands of book-sized panes of glass. American Steel once employed eleven thousand men in mills along the river; now no one worked in its rusted behemoths.

In the glory days, the river ran bright orange and

smelled of poison. The companies sucked in its water and spit out steam and waste. Factory whistles and clanging machines echoed over the water day and night. Barges ferried tons of ore, I beams, rolled steel, copper and steel tubing, and finished railroad spikes over this liquid orange highway. Now the river was a muddy blue-gray, its rippling surface burdened only by the sky.

The city's retail center was a mile north of the river, six blocks of ten-story stone and glass buildings. Cain drove down Main Street, under the banner reading WELCOME HIROSHIMA AUTO WORKS! past the boarded-up shoe store, the Roxy movie theater's chained doors and empty marquee, the department store with its GRAND SALE! sign faded from a year's exposure to sunlight. In the window of what had once been a Ben Franklin dime store, Cain saw a man-sized white wooden cross next to a hand-painted butcher paper sign proclaiming Big Screen TV for American Evangelical Hour, Weds.—8 P.M. Rerun, Sat. Morn., 9. Sermon: "AIDS—The Devil's Due?" Textbook Purification Committee, 8 P.M., Thurs. Cain counted twenty-four people on the downtown sidewalks.

Main Street led to a town square. At the far end of the square was City Hall. On each Fourth of July of years past, miners and factory workers paraded from the river to the square as their cheering families and friends jammed the streets. As many as twenty thousand workers marched in the parade. There were beer and hot dog booths, cotton candy and lemonade stands for the children. The parade ended at a bandstand in front of City Hall, from which politicians and giants of industry praised Life, Liberty, and The Great American Way.

The streets Cain drove through had names like Zinc Road, Smelter Street, Gold Drive. A legend of the 1930s claimed that two cops found a dead dray horse on Aluminum Avenue and dragged it to Iron Avenue because they couldn't spell the true scene of the crime for their report. Some streets were named for local politicians who'd seen to their own immortality. Others bore the names of hometown heroes whose deeds were footnotes to poorly remembered wars. Some streets were named for geography that no longer existed: Montenegro, Croatia, Saint Petersburg. Cain drove past a dead-end back street once famous as Venus Alley, a walled-off business district forbidden to males under twenty-one where women displayed their wares in picture windows or waited in ruby-walled suites. Venus Alley was now an urban gulch of garbage cans and rats.

In the city the well-off lived on the West End—upwind from the river. South of the river were warehouses and truck depots. Before the civil rights battles of the 1960s, the Southside had also meant Little Harlem. Now those houses were inhabited by refugees from Latin American, Southeast Asia, and Newark. On the Southside, skid row, with its grain alcohol cribs and crack houses, awaited the weak.

Cain's rented car shook as he turned east from Main Street. Every few feet he'd hit another pothole. He drove into the old neighborhoods that formed a crescent moon curving from east of downtown through the city's northern border.

Once the crescent held ethnic pockets: Bohunk town, Little Italy, Jew town, Mick town, China block. There was a Teepee town for the few hundred Indians who'd fled the state's reservations. There were Walkerville, Meaderville, and Dingham, "independent" communities on the curve of the crescent that were gerrymandered in and out of the city limits to suit the whims of political machines and mine owners. The old borders of the ethnic neighborhoods were as strong as barbed-wire fences, although one block looked much like another: clapboard houses, neighborhood stores, corner bars big enough for forty customers on a Saturday night. The public halls provided clues to a block's history: the Serbian Orthodox Reform Church, the Polish Community Center, Mount Zion Synagogue, the Greek Orthodox Church.

But the old neighborhoods had dissolved. As Cain drove past old Detroit dinosaurs rusting at the curb, the people all looked, walked, talked, and lived the same. Instead of the babble of a dozen tongues, the sounds of daytime television and country and western radio stations drifted into his car.

He motored past two high schools, three hospitals, and one "Center For Permanent Care," where miners coughed out their days and factory veterans stared at their mangled bodies and watched the water stains on the ceiling grow year by year.

Cain turned north, toward Steeltown's soul.

When Elliot Kimmett I and his contemporaries invaded this peaceful high country valley, they discovered "the richest hill on earth." The iron ore came out first, and spawned the steel mills along the river. When that iron played out, the tycoons fed their mills ore from Minnesota and Pennsylvania. After the iron era, geologists found silver, zinc, and finally copper. Thousands of miles of shafts punctured the hill and zigzagged beneath the city. In the 1950s, the copper that could be economically won by deep-shaft mining played out at the same time the Bushmaster conglomerate swallowed the neglected Kimmett companies and lesser foes. Bushmaster owned the richest hill on earth, but it was a plundered prize. But Bushmaster also possessed technology, so in 1954, the company changed the way mining had been done since the city's birth. Instead of digging into the richest hill on earth, they dug it up.

The richest hill on earth became the world's biggest man-made hole, an open pit mine a mile and a half wide and twelve hundred feet deep. Smelters digested the hill. Trucks carted the discharge to huge slag heaps the wind eroded each year. As the Pit grew, it swallowed not only the hill, but parts of the city. Walkerville fell into its mouth. When the wealth in that hole finally played out, the north edge of the pit was against the mountains, the south end against the lawns of unlucky citizens Bushmaster hadn't seen fit to dispossess.

Cain parked his car in front of a weathered gray house with broken windows. A wooden wall blocked the end of the street. From one nail in that fence dangled a sign that read Keep Off! Danger! An empty oil drum lay on its side beneath the sign. He turned the barrel over, warily stood on its rusted bottom, and peered down into the Pit.

Nothing, he thought. A rock-walled, dynamite and dozer-scarred crater. Empty dirt roads zigzagged up the opposite slope. A pool of stagnant water darkened the bottom of the Pit.

He went back to his car, drove away.

Ten minutes later he found a pay phone on the wall of a boarded-up bowling alley. He pushed the buttons for a long distance number and credit card billing.

"Hello?" said the man who answered.

"Where's Kirby?" said Cain.

"Who's calling, please?" said the man.

"Red Rider," said Cain.

After a pause, the man said, "We show this line as secure."

"This is Cain. I want to talk to the director."

Since he hadn't signaled an emergency, he had to wait on hold, then talk to a second-level aide, then wait on hold again. When that electronic deadness ended, Cain heard the calm tone of the man who approved his pay.

"Yes?"

"I've just seen Kimmett," said Cain.

"What does he want?"

"To run Steeltown again."

"Why?"

"Because he thinks he can. Because he thinks he'll get something more out of it than a rusted-out city."

"Explain."

"Fathers and sons."

"I don't understand."

"What's important," said Cain, "is that he's serious."

"But he's not Howard Hughes. Is this something we can profitably undertake?"

"Don't you want to know if I can do it?"

"The issue is the earnings we can get compared to losses we might sustain."

"We can make our money."

"Has he told you what the job entails?"

"What little he said matches what we know."

"Do you think the client's objective can be achieved?"

"We can do our part."

"You know, Cain, I was reluctant to give you this assignment."

Cain said nothing.

"Your insistence did not sway my judgment; your experience in similar matters and years of loyal service with the firm did. In sum, I had to assume you were acceptable."

"I appreciate your vote of confidence."

"Do you appreciate my intolerance should you fall short of our trust?"

Cain said nothing.

"Do not forget who you are," said his boss.

Neither man spoke for several seconds.

"So you recommend we accept Kimmett's contract?" the old man finally asked.

"Yes."

"Very well. Our fee will be a minimum of five hundred thousand dollars. Plus expenses. Overruns at our premium rate."

"Cheap enough, for a whole town."

"Half a million wouldn't have bought you a square block of Steeltown in the old days."

"Kimmett remembers you."

"And I him. How many people do you need?"

"You gave me the job, let me do it."

Silence filled the line.

"Very well," said his boss finally. "What do you want?"

Cain told him, then said, "When I need more, I'll send for it."

"Be sure you do," said his boss, then he hung up.

Cain checked his notebook for the second number he called. Again, he had to work his way up a chain of command.

"Well?" snapped Kimmett as soon as he came on the line.

"I'll take this town away from whoever has it now," said Cain. "But it will be up to you to grab it then."

Allies

"THIS IS WHAT YOU'LL DO," Kimmett told Cain later that day.

"That's not the way we're going to work," was his reply.

Raymond Nelson leaned back in his chair. Sunlight streamed over the three of them as they sat at Kimmett's bedroom table.

"Get this clear!" snapped Kimmett. "You work for me, and I've got a plan. You're . . ."

"You've got a plan, all right," interrupted Cain, "and I'm it. You got half a dozen thugs roaming around the house, you've got Nelson to ramrod them. Maybe you got some good ideas, but you're smart enough to know you can't make the play yourself. Quit trying. You called us. You want me on the line, I call the shots."

Kimmett glared at him. Cain stared back.

"Be very careful, Cain," said the old man.

"I know my work. And we've got a deal."

Kimmett grunted, settled back in his chair. Nelson grinned.

"I need a reason to be here," said Cain, "That will take some time to figure, but if I wear your uniform or your son's . . ."

"Leave my son out of this," said Kimmett.

"That might not be easy," said Cain. But he shrugged, nodded, then asked, "Can you control him?"

"He sits where I put him," the father replied.

"For now, that may be enough," said Cain. "If he's

■ 19 ■

going to wear a crown, we may have to reshape his head, but that's tomorrow's business. Tell me about today."

Kimmett nodded. Nelson pulled three manila file folders from a briefcase by his feet. He dropped them on the table in front of Cain.

"Newsclips," said Nelson, "credit reports, FBI memos . . ."

"Nelson was with the Bureau," said Kimmett.

"Just a retreaded public servant," said Nelson. "Like the gentleman in the top file:

"Harry DiCarlo, formerly of the FBI. The political machine, with Olson's blessing, made DiCarlo chief of police. His role was to stand between the smart guys and the Bureau. The bet was the Bureau wouldn't embarrass itself by exposing one of its own as a crook.

"Is that how DiCarlo saw it?" asked Cain.

"DiCarlo is a pig," said Kimmett. "Always pushing for more."

"Harry grew so blatant the Bureau couldn't ignore him," said Nelson. "They videotaped him accepting hundred-dollar bills from a mobster in a Bureau sting. They figured Harry would cop a plea and fade away. Harry fought back. He claimed he took the money as part of his secret plan to end corruption, that he was setting the mobster up, not the other way around. The jury bought it . . ."

"Did Harry buy the jury?" asked Cain.

"Whatever," continued Nelson. "What we have now is a police chief who is officially innocent—and therefore, almost untouchable."

"So much for the city cops," said Cain. He frowned, remembered his morning: "What about the sheriff's department."

"The sheriff is a puppet, an elected official," said Nelson. "Elected officials here are part of the political machine, and Mayor Richard Nash drives the machine."

"In this town," said Kimmett, "the party organization chooses the candidates for the party members to ratify in the primary. Since it's a one-party city, elections are decided before the public vote.

"As a lawyer, Nash used his union clients to get picked ward boss. He exhausted his opponents, made it to the city council at thirty-seven. He took everybody's bribes so he was nobody's property. Nine years ago, Nash levered himself into the mayor's office.

"Mayor Nash lives with his mother, a miner's widow. No mansion for him, no fancy suits or flashy women. He doesn't drink, doesn't smoke, works late, and goes to church on Sunday. There's hardly a funeral, wedding, baptism or bar mitzvah he doesn't attend. Nash always wears a gray suit, white shirt, and a black tie."

Kimmett shook his head.

"All of us thought he was too unimaginative to be dangerous. Too drab. We mistook his austerity for timidity and the voters mistook it for selfless dedication. Nash uses all his energies to hold his city tight."

"And himself," muttered Cain.

Kimmett and Nelson glanced at each other. Nelson continued:

"All the money he skims goes into his war chest. The backroom boys woke up one day to find themselves taking orders from the man in the gray suit."

"Except for Olson," said Cain.

"Olson *owned* the backrooms," said Kimmett. "As long as Nash didn't cross him, Olson didn't care what the mayor did. Hell, having Nash take over the political machine made it easier for Olson. He only had to deal with one man instead of a dozen. Besides, Olson could have swept him into the gutter with a blink."

"Mayor Nash played the heroic reformer at first," said Nelson. "He hung the old guard's civic stooges with their own corruption, then stuck his people in their slots and resumed business as usual. You don't sell the city paper clips unless you buy the nod from Nash's boys.

"He owns our district's congressman, and a piece of both U.S. senators. The governor and he are rivals, but the governor knows he can't run Steeltown. This valley sends three representatives and two senators to the state legislature. The mayor owns two of the reps and one of the senators. The other two legislators have been in office since Christ was a corporal. Nash doesn't hold their leashes, but they don't cross him. He's waiting for them to be history."

"Just like he's waiting for me," said Kimmett. He laughed. His eyes were bright. As they talked, it seemed to Cain that the old man grew stronger, younger.

"Who runs those other two legislators?" asked Cain.

"I hold some sway with them," said Kimmett.

Nelson continued: "Here ambition requires an army. While Olson lived, Chief DiCarlo obeyed the mayor. After Olson died, DiCarlo used his own 'reform' campaign to fire all the mayor's loyalists in the police department and create his own goon squad. The mayor then organized the sheriff's deputies as his mercenaries.

"The mayor cut Chief DiCarlo out of the machine's payoff loop and keeps the police budget as low as he dares. DiCarlo bleeds off money the machine used to suck from the streets.

"So far," said Nelson, "it's a stand-off. They take political potshots at each other but nobody's been badly bloodied."

"Yet," said Kimmett.

"What about other law?" asked Cain.

"Look in the phone book," said Nelson. "You won't find any. The U.S. attorney for this district is the same one who blew the case against DiCarlo. His spirit is shattered. Even if it wasn't, he's only got enough budget to pay his secretary."

"FBI?" asked Cain. "Drug Enforcement Agency? State troopers?"

Nelson shook his head to each question.

"Funny," said the ex-federal cop, "neither Congress nor the state legislature can get funding bills passed for outside enforcement agencies in Steeltown. In the old days, the mining and mill czars saw to it that no mine inspectors, labor investigators, or pollution control monitors had offices here."

"Business regulates itself!" snapped Kimmett. "That's why you're here, Cain."

"So much for the cops," said Cain. "What about the robbers?"

"Your third folder contains a *New Yorker* article from four years ago," said Nelson. "The reporter called Steeltown 'Bomb City, U.S.A.'

"Rackets are *the* big business in Steeltown," said Nelson.

"We love our fun. Drugs, prostitution, plus our numbers game called *the bug*: it's $16 million worth of nickels and dimes a year in this burned out smokestack city. Guys bet ten cents a day of their unemployment check to feel like they're doing something. You want bigger action, there's a private casino in a windowless warehouse across the river from the Mills. Players get shipped in from all over the country. There's a sports line run out a couple private homes tied straight into Atlantic City. The IRS figures Steeltown for $27 million a year in illegal gambling business.

"Chicago, Detroit, Cleveland, Philly, New York: all the old line Mafia families chewed a piece of Steeltown one time or another. Every few years, there'd be a war over who owned what. As long as they killed each other, nobody cared? Until Bloody Sunday."

"Which was . . ." said Cain.

"Four years ago. Olson was alive, Nash was mayor, DiCarlo was police chief, and there was a gang war. Seven hoods whacked in two months. In Steeltown, ninety percent of mob killings never get solved.

"Joey 'The Blimp' Machino was the local *capo* for a Philly family demanding more of the bug from Detroit and Cleveland families.

"Joey loved waffles. He and two of his boys went out to breakfast one summer Sunday. They ate at a pancake house with a parking lot. Across the street from the parking lot is St. Anne's Church. Should have been safe. The cafe was crowded, they were close to God, he could see if anybody tried to monkey with his black Caddy.

"They ate a huge breakfast. Waddled to the car as church was letting out. They got in their car.

"And somebody pushed the remote control button for the bomb in the car parked next to them. Maybe twenty sticks of TNT.

"There was a roar and the fireball thirty feet high from the gas tanks, smoke and chunks of both cars flying like shrapnel. . . .

"Three little girls in white dresses skipping down the church steps were shredded into hamburger and bloody cloth."

Nelson shook his head.

"By sunset, everybody in town knew the crooks were killing kids. Next day, shotguns started appearing in the racks of pickup trucks. Foremen said they saw pistols under the shirts of guys working the lines. A couple cop cars got hit with bricks. Bars where the bug is sold got their windows smashed. Somebody spray-painted *Vigilante* on City Hall. Steeltown was nasty during integration, but the mood then was mild compared to what was festering in the streets after Bloody Sunday.

"Tuesday night, six o'clock local TV news. A dippy blond woman reporter is doing a live stand-up from the church steps, babbling 'bitter twist of fate' pap, when a wild-eyed guy with jet black hair bullies his way into the TV picture.

" *'Fate's got names in this town,'* he says, his act playing in every living room and corner bar. *'We aren't stupid and we got the guts to say nobody kills kids in Steeltown and walks. That's the truth, or my name ain't Johnny Maxx!'* "

Kimmett tapped the file folders in front of Cain.

"He's Number Three," said the old man.

"Johnny Maxx talked his way out of reform school by joining the Marines," said Nelson. "He'd charmed a couple women into whoring for him, sold grass to college kids, pulled a couple stickups, a few burglaries. He'd free-lanced for connected guys—strong arm stuff for a loan shark, wheel man on a dope smuggle out of Kentucky—but he hadn't thrown in with any faction, nor has he ever been busted. After his Tuesday night TV debut, he dropped off the map.

"Wednesday morning, the head of the Detroit faction and two bodyguards were standing in the entryway of their office building headquarters. Through the glass doors, they watched two of their guys check their car for bombs.

"A white male walked toward them, bold as you please, shot the boss smack through the forehead, drilled the bodyguards in the chest. The killer vanished before anyone made his face.

"That left the man from the Cleveland outfit, a creep named Tenelli who had started in the porno rings. His bulletproof picture windows faced the college across the street. Tenelli had binoculars permanently mounted on a tripod right by his living room window so he could scan the women's dorm and the grass field where the coeds sunbathed.

"One o'clock that Wednesday afternoon. Eighty-five degrees. The Detroit guys were cooling on the coroner's slab. Tenelli and his boys were snug in his air-conditioned fortress.

"A gorgeous girl with a flat tire stopped her car opposite Tenelli's picture window, got out, and slammed the door. She had long, naked legs. Her thick wavy red hair hung down to her shoulders. She pranced to the back of the car, flipped open the trunk, and bent over, showing the guys her black bikini bottoms.

"Slowly, she unbuttoned her red shirt. Tenelli headed for the binoculars. She spread her arms wide, shrugged off the shirt and flounced around for a few seconds, then leaned against the car and gave them a three-quarters profile as she glared at the jack and the flat tire. Tenelli put his eyes against the binoculars.

"*WHAM!* A softball-sized hole exploded in the picture window. Tenelli flew backwards with his chest blown to red mush."

"But . . ." Cain tried to interrupt; Nelson kept talking.

"The cops found the sniper post in a fourth-floor girl's dorm room. Remember the exploding bullets Hinckley used on President Reagan? They didn't work because John Boy was too nuts to acquire quality. Our sniper used an old M14 semiautomatic rifle. The rifle was stolen from Quantico. A vise kept the gun locked on a preset firing line. The clip was packed with explosive bullets. The cross hairs of the telescopic sight were lined up at chest height, right beneath where the binoculars stood. The first bullet blew the bulletproof glass out of the second slug's path.

"The woman in the black bikini vanished, leaving the car with the flat tire that had no puncture. The car turned out to be stolen.

They never found her—or the sniper.

"Thursday they buried the murdered kids. And a funny thing, the funerals also seemed like a victory celebration. Didn't matter which hood ordered the hit on The Blimp that also killed the girls. Both deserved to die because their war killed kids. Nobody got away with nothing. Steeltown justice."

"Where was Johnny Maxx all this time?" asked Cain.

"According to Bureau phone taps and turned guys' secret testimony," said Nelson, "Johnny badgered his way into seeing New York's Five Families. The Steeltown hick made an offer to those big boys: let the Mafia profit from Steeltown *as a whole* rather than through whatever individual families could claim and keep. A Vegas operation, only instead of Steeltown being wide open, Johnny wanted it locked up, with him holding the key. Any other plan, Johnny said, would cost them blood and money."

"And they bought it," said Cain.

"A month after the funerals," continued Nelson, "Johnny Maxx opened a vending machine company that quickly won municipal and union contracts. He visited the casinos, the dope houses, the bug runners and bankers, had friendly chats about what was what. Pimps started paying street dues. Big-time heists got cleared with his boys. Nobody bucks him. Besides, the sniper killing was sneaky but smart, which made him dangerous. The one-on-three shoot-out was pure balls. Steeltown loves pure balls. Hometown boy Johnny Maxx becoming the new big man is Steeltown justice."

"Are we sure one of the dead men whacked The Blimp?" asked Cain.

Kimmett laughed.

"You've got a devious mind," said Nelson.

"Isn't that what you're buying?"

The three of them smiled.

"Johnny loves to get his name in the paper," said Nelson, "see his face on TV. His fronts include movie theaters and bars. His vending company rakes in millions in quarters and dimes, but who can check? He finagled a special deputy's badge, so legally packs a gun.

"Johnny bribes DiCarlo for protection," said Nelson, "he pays Nash . . ."

"Ice," interrupted Cain. "In Steeltown, bribes are called ice."

The other two men stared at him.

Cain shrugged. "This town is a quick teacher."

"Yes," said Kimmett, "you'll do."

"At any rate," continued Nelson, "besides *icing* the police department, Johnny Maxx feeds Mayor Nash's machine."

"You think Johnny is tired of shelling out," said Cain. "You think he wants more than running the streets."

"I don't think," snapped Kimmett. "I know. DiCarlo and Nash are squeezing him. Johnny Maxx isn't the kind of guy who takes the squeeze. He's got turf they want, so even if he doesn't want theirs—which he does—he has to take over the whole damn town to keep any of it.

"What you have here," said Nelson, "is the Balkan states of America."

"Who owns the press?" asked Cain.

"Radio is just noise," said Nelson. "We have two TV stations. One of them only does sixty-second news spots. The other station has the dippy blonde. She's as smart as they come over there. Bushmaster once owned the paper secretly, kept news of mine accidents, factory problems, and incorrect politics from bothering the citizens, but they sold it when they pulled out. The current publisher carries on their tradition: don't rock the boat with bad news. The press is no problem."

"Except for one little shit reporter," Kimmett added.

"A guy named Josh Hammond," said Nelson. "He's savvy enough to get a juicy story, but his publisher keeps him on a short leash. Hammond wants a ticket to bigger things. He survives because the mayor and DiCarlo use him to lob grenades at each other. Hammond's stories about Johnny Maxx make him sound like a shady but colorful folk hero."

"Hammond has no respect," said Kimmett. "If he were worth it, I'd jerk his chain and he'd end up on the next train out of town."

"Passenger trains quit running here ten years ago," said Cain. "What about the unions?"

"In a town with twenty-one percent real unemployment, where only three small factories are still open and all the mines are shut down, what about the unions?" Kimmett countered.

"The steelworkers' and miners' unions are organized into one giant governing body called the Steeltown Industrial Coalition," said Nelson. "The SIC is part of the Teamsters, although the individual trade unions are also tied to their own nationals. When this was a company town, the money czars and the corporations played one industrial work force off against the other. An umbrella union with city-wide power was the only way labor could counter the bosses' oligarchy. There are still a few rambunctious individual unions, some activity below the SIC umbrella level, but nothing with real power.

"As for the SIC, everybody owns a piece of it: Nash grabbed reins dropped by the corporations, Maxx squeezes it through the Teamsters, and DiCarlo bullied his way in. All that didn't matter when the mills and mines were open because the member unions had enough clout to work in SIC's shadow to take care of the workers. Now that everything is shut down ..."

"So much for organized labor," said Cain. "What else is out there? Churches? Civic groups?"

"Last year," said Nelson, "a law professor at the college organized some accountants, academics, a crazy minister, a few federal bureaucrats. They called themselves the Citizens' League, and make noises about civic corruption and organized crime. They uncovered some phony contracts, published a few flyers. The professor went to Washington and testified to a Senate subcommittee hearing that the city was 'trapped in the iron grip of a criminal dictatorship.'"

"Hammond did one story on their crusade," Kimmett said. "And four paragraphs appeared on the testimony in the second section of *The Washington Post*. Nobody else noticed. Nobody else cared.

"The crusaders' money ran out," said Kimmett. "The professor lost his tenure. I understand some of the reformers met Johnny Maxx 'accidentally' in the street. Mayor Nash fostered the idea that the League was pure politics, and therefore sleazy. Their leafleteers got police tickets for littering. Most of them lost interest. I don't think they even hold their quaint living-room meetings anymore."

"You told me to keep your son out of it for now," said Cain. "To do that, I need to know where he is and what he's doing."

"My son," Kimmett said, "avoids everything of substance. I pushed him through law school. His natural inertia and the tramp he married . . . Do you understand women, Cain?"

"Not enough." Cain shrugged. "They're not my business."

"You're lucky," grumbled Kimmett. "The only good thing abut my daughter-in-law is how she made it convenient for my son to return to his home town. He writes wills and contracts for the middle class, shuffles paper for fools who think knowing him might prove useful. An inheritance from his grandfather made him wealthy by the city's standards. He plays tennis, serves on charity committees. Lately his major effort has been to head the Chamber of Commerce group hustling a Japanese car manufacturer for a factory in Steeltown."

"Steeltown's last true hope," added Nelson.

"Hah!" said Kimmett.

"Here's how it goes," said Cain. "First, nobody can know I'm working for you. Second, I'll tell you only what you need to know."

Nelson and his boss glanced at each other. Nelson shrugged.

"Be sure you make no important omissions," said Kimmett.

"I never do," said Cain. "I'll start when I get confirmation that you've paid our half million retainer. Plus I need thirty thousand dollars in untraceable expense cash."

Nelson frowned, started to speak, but Kimmet cut him off.

"Of course," he said. Then smiled.

"It will be properly accounted for," said Cain.

"Of course," repeated Kimmett.

"Nelson can bring it by my hotel," said Cain.

"It will get there," said the ex-FBI agent.

"I expect results," said Kimmett.

"I'm here," answered Cain.

Nelson escorted Cain from the room. Near the bottom of the stairs, they met Judson on the way up.

"The mountain going to Mohammed?" said Cain.

"Perhaps," answered Nelson.

"What's his job?"

Nelson smiled. "Among other things, he's here in case Mr. Kimmett decides I'm overstepping my bounds."

"Are you?"

They stopped, faced each other.

"I like the quiet life of a good soldier who's chosen his army carefully," said Nelson. "My salary increases each month Mr. Kimmett lives. I serve at his whim, and he requires absolute loyalty—which I suggest you never forget."

"What about Judson?" asked Cain.

"Mr. Kimmett hired him when Judson was quite young. He came from a destitute family. No one else wanted him."

"He's probably more fun than the great Danes."

"I wouldn't know."

"Would you know where a fellow might be able to buy some cocaine from a connection of Johnny Maxx's?"

"Yes," Nelson said, "I'd go after Maxx first, too. He's the most vulnerable. And the most dangerous.

"Go to the Cairo. Maxx is a silent partner. Deal with a man named Frank Peterzell."

"Thanks," said Cain as he opened the door.

"Good-bye," said Nelson as he swung it shut.

Work

CAIN ANSWERED THE KNOCK on his hotel room door.

"I got a wife," said the grim man in a maroon nylon jacket and blue jeans who stood in the hall. He carried a black briefcase.

"She's not here," said Cain.

"I think I got something for the man in this room."

Cain's eyes flicked to the briefcase, glanced down the hall. The man was alone.

"Come on in," said Cain.

His visitor had bristly gray hair, broad shoulders, and steel-toed work boots that carried him into the room like it was a mine field. He was born handsome, but his face was lined and tired. His frown pulled the corners of his eyes down to an unblinking squint. One hand fidgeted at his side. The other gripped the briefcase handle so tightly his gnarled knuckles were white. The man seemed covered by invisible dust.

"I got a wife," he told Cain.

"So you said." Cain leaned against the writing table.

"Got a son about to graduate high school," said the man, not relaxing. "Daughter going to be a nurse."

Cain nodded.

"I own my house," said the visitor, thrusting his jaw forward. He looked at the floor. "Twenty-one years, never missed a payment come rain or shine or strike or . . .

"Man come into McGuire's, buys me a beer. I've seen

him around. I don't know who he works for or who he knows and I don't want to know, so don't tell me."

"Okay."

"Nineteen years and four months I worked the power plant at Bushmaster. Never late, never lunch-boxed so much as a nail out of the place. Never shagged that or any job in my life. Never filed no phony claims neither, and I got the scars to show it. Nineteen years and four months. Six months shy of the pension line, they lock the gates.

"Guy in McGuire's says he knows all that. Says that's why he's offering me a chance for some easy money. My mouth fixed itself to tell him no offense but no thanks. Words didn't come out.

"You know what a hundred dollars is to my family?"

Cain shook his head.

"Two weeks."

He held the briefcase toward Cain.

"The guy gave me a hundred to bring this to the man in this hotel room. I don't know your name, I don't want to know it. I don't know what's in here, and I don't want to know."

"Just toss it on the bed," said Cain.

The man flung the case there as though it burned his hand. He turned to go.

"That ain't the whole deal," said Cain.

Those gnarled hands at the end of the maroon jacket closed into fists; the man faced Cain and stepped backward toward the door.

"Deal was," said Cain, pushing away from the writing table, sticking his right hand in his front pants pocket, "a hundred up front and another hundred when you delivered."

Cain pulled a money clip of bills from his pocket. All business, he counted out five twenties, stuffed the clip in his pocket, and held out the hundred.

"The guy in the bar never said that was part of it."

"Must have slipped his mind," said Cain. He kept his outstretched hand with the money steady.

"I don't take charity," whispered the man.

"I don't give it," said Cain.

Still, the man hesitated.

"A deal's a deal," said Cain. "A job's a job."

The man blinked, nodded. He stuffed Cain's $100 in his jeans, walked to the door, then stopped. He didn't look back as he spoke.

"I don't want to do this work no more," he said.

"Okay," said Cain.

The man left.

Cain looked out his window. The setting sun threw shadows on the city. The streetlights turned on. Car headlights drifted through the streets.

The black briefcase held $30,000 bundled in stacks of twenty-dollar bills. Cain put $600 in the billfold he carried inside his jacket, another $100 in the money clip in his pants. He closed the briefcase and hid it between the bed's headboard and the wall.

The Firm's Chicago office had sent a suitcase filled with his requests on the afternoon plane; had it taxied to Mr. Reston's hotel as though it had been a bag lost in transit.

Wonder what Chicago wondered? thought Cain as he checked the bag's contents. He looked inside a small manila envelope, nodded, and slipped it into his shirt pocket.

He darkened his hair with a shower-out mixture from Chicago, brushed and sprayed it into a different style, glued on a matching-colored mustache. Heel lifts raised him two inches. Tinted but nonprescription glasses distorted his eyes and changed the shape of his face. He put on a baggy sports jacket Jackson Cain would never wear, then contemplated himself in the mirror.

Like a Watergate Warrior, he thought. He stared into the glass until he felt himself blend into what he saw. Then he turned out the lights and went into the night.

The Cairo nightclub was sandwiched between a topless bar and a liquor store. Cain parked out of sight of its off-Main address, then walked through the cool spring darkness.

She stood beneath the blue neon sign in the doorway of the white stucco Palace hotel. A black velvet band circled her throat. Her red dress had a plunging neckline and a mid-thigh slit. She wore black stiletto high heels, had brown hair teased and sprayed off her shoulders, rouged cheeks and slick crimson lipstick. Small town eyes were her best feature: widely-spaced, large and clear, diamond blue and still alive.

"Where you going, Honey?" She smiled, slow-stepped to Cain. Her lilac perfume surprised him.

A dyed blond woman in purple—stockings, miniskirt, and fake leather jacket—smoked a cigarette in front of the adult bookstore next to the Palace. Cain smiled at the brunette.

"Nowhere," he said.

"That's not very smart," she said. "Sure ain't no fun."

"A man's gotta do," he said, smiling so she knew that old saw was a joke.

"Yeah, but he don't have to do it by *himself*." She pursed her lips. "You know what you need?"

"Let me guess."

She laughed.

"You know what you need!" she said, licked her lips. "Come on, Honey, spend some time with me. It'll be *real* special. And it won't cost nowhere near what it's worth."

"I'm not in the buying mood."

"Sure about that?" she said. She ran her finger down his chest, over his stomach, let it fall away as she brushed his groin.

"How's business?" he asked.

She rolled her eyes up for the *pity me* look, truly noticed him, and shrugged. "Hard for a girl to make a buck in this town."

"Leave," he said.

"Nowhere better to go, Sugar," she said. Grinned for real.

"Then I hope your luck changes," he told her.

"Me too," she said as he walked away. She called to his back, "Don't forget me, Honey!"

The Cairo was a piano bar without a piano player. A black Steinway waited on a platform surrounded by round tables. A raucous Rolling Stones song two decades old blared from a juke box. Glassed candles on the tables in the piano pit and the wall booths filled the cavern with flickering shadows.

Two couples sat in booths. At the tables in the piano pit were another couple cooing and holding hands, two men in factory worker's clothes nursing beers and saying nothing, an animated trio of hard cases in flashy suits, a thin fidgety man in a gaudy sports jacket, who stared over his candle at the piano's motionless ivory and ebony keys. Two elderly men and a woman wrapped in the blues sat on alternating bar stools. Smoke from the woman's cigarette spiraled to the ceiling.

The cocktail waitress strolled through the room in a costume that looked like a red one-piece bathing suit with a skirt. She wore black mesh stockings. A young latino in a white jacket washed glasses at the end of the bar under the watchful gaze of the hefty bartender, whose blue shirt showed half-moon sweat stains in his armpits.

Cain picked an isolated stool in the middle of the bar. The barkeep filled his brand-name scotch order, then went back to his corner post where he could watch the busboy and the front door. Cain waited until the trio of suits marched out.

He beckoned the bartender, draining his glass as the man came his way.

"Another?" said the bartender.

"Yeah," said Cain. He dropped a twenty from his wallet next to his glass, and made sure the bartender saw the bill's many brothers. "Go slow about setting it up. That back door lead to the alley?"

"Why?" said the bartender.

"I feel like a smoke."

"We got ashtrays."

"That's nice," said Cain. He sauntered out the back door.

The alley was a brick tunnel lined with battered aluminum garbage cans. The rotting stench was strong, so to be sure, Cain walked a few steps away from the Cairo's cans before he leaned against the opposite brick wall. From his jacket pocket, he fished the manila envelope Chicago supplied and shook out one of the joints. He lit it, blew smoke through the alley.

Thirty seconds later the Cairo's door opened. The latino

busboy nervously stepped into the alley clutching a crumpled paper bag.

"Oh!" stammered the young man. *"Perdon, senor."*

Cain shrugged, raised the joint to his lips, and took a
deep drag as the busboy lifted the lid of the garbage can and
dropped the paper bag inside. Cain exhaled. The boy had
trouble getting the lid back on. When he finally succeeded,
his eyes darted toward the man leaning against the brick
wall.

"Garbage," he explained softly, "I take out garbage."

"De donde eres?"

Cain's words nailed the busboy's anxious feet to the
alley pavement.

"San Salvador," the busboy whispered; hesitated, then
asked, *"Lo conoces, senor?"*

Cain nodded. He extended the glowing cigarette toward
the young man in the white uniform: *"No quieres?"*

"Gracias, no." He shuffled backwards toward the door.
"Con permiso?"

Again Cain nodded. The boy scurried inside.

Give him a minute to make his report, thought Cain. He
flicked away the half-consumed joint.

"So," said the bartender as Cain sipped his second scotch,
"How was your smoke?"

"Great alley," answered Cain with a smile that was sly
and maybe stoned but definitely not stupid.

"To each his own. What brings you to town?"

"Business."

The cocktail waitress walked to the end of the bar,
caught the bartender's eye.

"Back in a minute," he said, and after making two
drinks for her, he was. He put his elbows on the bar, leaned
closer to Cain.

"What business you in?"

"I'm a facilitator."

"A facilitator, huh? That a good business?"

"I do fine."

"Why did you come to Steeltown?"

"Wise guys know this is a great town for business."

"You looking to move your business here?"

Cain shook his head. "I'm bringing it through town, juicing up the local economy. Everybody ought to like that."

"This . . . facilitation. You buying or selling?"

"My associates are in the process of establishing their business in an underdeveloped and unclaimed distant market."

"How come you came to the Cairo?"

"People told me this was the kind of place I'd feel at home."

"Yeah," said the bartender, gesturing to the darkness, "it's a great place. These fans of the Cairo, they got names?"

"Everybody's got a name."

"Of course, we ain't been introduced."

Cain stuck his hand across the bar: "Walter Mathews."

"Mack Jensen," said the bartender. The two men shook hands and each one knew the other was strong.

"I never heard of you, Walter. Maybe I know your friends."

"I got lots of friends. New Orleans, Texas."

"Texas is a big place."

"One of my buddies there likes to be called Snake."

"That's real Texas. Never heard of him, though."

"I'm surprised. He has a rep."

"Not here. Who else you know?"

Cain rattled off half a dozen names.

"Don't know any of them."

"Too bad," said Cain. "But maybe you know a guy they told me about here. Guy who might want to plug into my associates' business. Guy who might want to help me out."

"Who's that?" asked the bartender.

"Peterzell. You know him, don't you."

Jensen shrugged. "It's a big town."

"And he hangs out here."

"Maybe he does, maybe he doesn't. If I see him, maybe I could pass on what Walter Mathews wants from him—if I knew."

"Tell him I want to do some business."

"What?"

Cain smiled. "You let him and me worry about that.

But tell him maybe he can help me out with a related situation."

"Un-huh."

"I been on the road a long time. I'm real tired. I could use some energy to wake up. I wake up, maybe I can do *real* business."

"Stick around," said the bartender before he walked away. "You never know."

Fifteen minutes later, the cocktail waitress strolled back to the bar. Jensen spoke before she could open her mouth.

"Time for your break, honey. I'll catch your tables."

The waitress shrugged, perched on a stool and lit a cigarette.

Cain watched Jensen in the mirror as he went from table to table, talked with all the customers. He returned to his post, made three drinks, put them on a tray and shoved it toward the waitress.

"Pass 'em out, Linda," he told her. "You know where they go."

She sighed, stubbed out her cigarette, went back to work.

The thin, fidgety man in the gaudy sports jacket who'd been staring at the piano got up from his table and came over to Cain.

"So you're Walter Mathews," he said in a hoarse whisper.

"What is it with you guys?" snapped Cain. "You all got a case of the cutes. This is supposed to be a wised-up city, where a guy doesn't have to game around what he's about."

"Don't tell us how to run our town," hissed the thin man. "And you're the one playing games."

"Not with strangers," said Cain.

"I'm Peterzell, you're looking for me, remember?"

"So maybe you are and maybe we can finally stop dancing."

"So you don't exactly check out a hundred percent either, Bub. Maybe I know a couple of those names you been dropping, but if I do, they sure as shit never mentioned you."

"You're playing me like you think I'm the law. You want to know what I want? I'll tell you, which means if I'm law, I've got no case 'cause of entrapment. You're supposed to be connected. I'm looking to score some blow."

"Maybe that's possible," said Peterzell. "How much?"

"Let's start with a gram, and if you ain't got it or can't come up with it fast, fuck it, I'll take my business to guys who live up to their rep."

The two men stared at each other for thirty seconds.

"You come on tough," said Peterzell.

"I don't have the time for hearts and flowers."

"But you're lucky. Go to the bathroom. There's a towel dispenser above the sink with room inside it for six of those twenties in your wallet."

"Or I could flush my money down the toilet, same difference," said Cain. "Don't play either of us for a fool. And street price is a hundred dollars a gram. Plus, I'm not buying anything unknown."

"If you're that hinky, we got a back room you and I can go to and . . ."

"And who's waiting for us there, me all boxed in with a full wallet? There's a great alley out the back door."

Peterzell glared at him—then laughed.

"Yeah," he said, "I heard you seen our alley."

"We going to visit it or what?"

"Lead the way," said Peterzell.

Cain shook his head.

Peterzell laughed again, and led Cain toward the back door.

"This is dynamite stuff!" said Peterzell. They stood in the alley where Cain could watch both entrances and the Cairo's backdoor. Peterzell handed Cain a thimble-sized brown glass vial whose screw-off black cap was also a tiny folding plastic spoon. "You don't use test kits like narcs, do you, *amigo*?"

Cain tossed the vial back to him.

"You first—just in case this really is dynamite."

"You are a trusting son of a bitch," said Peterzell. He smiled. "Don't mind if I do. After all, it's your stuff."

He used the vial's spoon to snort powder up each nostril.

"No discounts for what you shared!" He grinned broadly, shook his head. "Wow! That's great!"

Peterzell handed the vial back to Cain. The drug dealer shook his head as the stranger backed up three steps so he'd be out of jumping range while his hands were full and his eyes occupied. Cain snorted two spoonfuls.

The powder burned his nose, numbed it briefly. His pulse raced with a disquieting charge. Mild euphoria hit him, vanished.

"You stepped on this too many times with speed and dental anesthetic and baby laxative and bullshit," said Cain. "Skimmed too much of your product for personal use."

"Hey, asshole . . ."

"Don't asshole, me. Can you deliver real stuff?"

"How much you think you can handle?" sneered Peterzell. "Ten grams?"

"Six kilos," said Cain, "spread over three weeks. First two keys soon. And none of that shit. Wholesale quality, bagged in bulk. I will test, and not by nose. We pay ten grand a key."

"You're nuts. Twenty or no go."

"Twelve, and you're overpricing the market."

"Sixteen flat, or walk."

"Okay," said Cain, "for now, sixteen—for the *real* stuff. After we do business this round, my people will expect a discount."

"This is a city of possibilities, my friend."

"Yeah, well it isn't my turf."

"So?"

"So I don't take delivery in your backyard. Walking into gamey guys' action with my people's money in one hand and my dick in the other is not what I get paid for."

"I don't travel."

"There's traveling and there's traveling," said Cain. "The road goes in and out of this town. There's got to be a rest stop over the county line on each side."

"Why over the county line?"

"Like I said," said Cain. "This is your turf. I believe in doing business in a neutral zone."

Peterzell laughed. "I don't get paid to take risks."

"No balls, no bucks," said Cain. "Put it together. Be at the Cairo every noon for a week. When I'm ready, I'll call.

You tell me which rest stop. Any place out of the county where a car can park in the lonesome and a fellow can see who's there and who's coming."

"How do I know you won't try a rip?"

"Bring a friend to hold your hand—if you have to. I might do the same. Remember: if I get ripped, my associates know who I was looking for and where, and they don't give a damn if this is Steeltown or Hell."

"The business don't work on credit."

Cain handed five twenties to the dealer.

"As a sign of my good faith, I'll pay for that shit you tried to unload on me." Cain dropped the vial in his pocket. "As for front money . . ."

Cain counted out five hundred dollars in twenties. He fanned the bills in front of Peterzell's smile, then neatly stacked them in his own hands. He ripped the stack in half.

"What the . . . !"

"Here," he said, passing half of the torn bills to Peterzell. "Five hundred in twenty-dollar half bills isn't worth hassling through a bank for either of us, but it's too good to waste. I'll bring the other halves with me. A bonus for you just to show I'm a stand-up guy. To show you're a stand-up guy, you ice any heat out of your end. If you can't do that and can't front the goods yourself, you probably can't deliver them."

"You're crazy!"

Cain smiled; he left the alley.

The Match

THE RINGING TELEPHONE WOKE Cain at seven-thirty the next
morning.

"Yeah?" he answered, his startled heart pounding as he
cleared away his chemical and sleep fog.

"Hold on," said Nelson, then Kimmett came on the line.

"You don't waste time, do you?" snapped his raspy
voice.

"What are you talking about?" said Cain, fully awake.

"What kind of stunt did you pull last night?"

"Nothing big. Nothing you want to know about."

"Hah! I wonder. Have you read this morning's paper?"

"No."

"Somebody murdered that snoopy reporter last night."

"What!"

"Wake up, Cain! Josh Hammond, our would-be hero of
the free press, got himself shot. It's front page news."

"Who . . ."

"Person or persons unknown," hissed Kimmett. "So the
paper says. What do you say?"

Cain said nothing for thirty seconds.

"If it's in the newspaper," he finally told Kimmett, "he
had to be killed *before* the last press run. Even stretching
deadlines, they'd had to have the story set by midnight. In a
town this wired, word that Hammond was shot spread like
wildfire. One of your stooges would have let you know long
before the presses ran. I was back here by eleven, but you

waited until now to call me and pretend you read it with the weather report. Why?"

"Maybe to see what the news meant to you," Kimmett told him.

"So you ran this riff, risked compromising me by calling my hotel . . ."

"Our machines show your line clear, *Mr. Reston.* Your switchboard wouldn't recognize Nelson's voice. We're not fools."

"What do you know about Hammond's murder?"

"The paper printed everything we know. What are you going to do about it?"

"You didn't hire me to investigate random murders."

"But . . . !"

"I'll get back to you," Cain told the man who'd hired him.

Cain hung up. He sat on the edge of the bed, ran his fingers through his hair. Luckily, he hadn't showered the dye out. He shaved and dressed quickly, glued on the false mustache, wore the glasses and heel lifts.

As he had the night before, Cain exited the hotel by a side door. The spring morning was crisp—clear skies and clean air. He bought a newspaper from a vending machine and walked to the only sit-down restaurant downtown, a cheap cafe not far from City Hall.

The coffee shop had been open since seven. By the time Cain got there, all the booths were taken. He took one of the three empty counter stools. The waitress brought him coffee and the cream can, took his order for bacon and eggs, then left him with his newspaper.

The boxed story on the front page told him little: At ten-thirty the night before, an unnamed citizen found the body of *Tribune* reporter Joshua Hammond on the floor of an underground parking garage four blocks from where Cain was having breakfast. Hammond had been shot once in the head. No weapon had been found.

Hammond was divorced, with no children. His parents were dead, his ex-wife lived in Akron. He was twenty-eight.

Cain glanced at the rest of the stories—war in Afghanistan, confusion in Congress, local union officials planning a major rally, baseball's spring season. As the waitress cleared away his dirty plate, he cradled his coffee cup close to his lips and kept his head down. He worried that his mustache might come unstuck.

"More coffee, mister?" The waitress held the pot in front of Cain.

He shook his head, paid, and left, carefully looking at no one and letting no one look at him.

The bank opened as Cain walked past it. He changed a $5 bill for silver, walked to a pay phone, and punched in a credit card number for a phone call to Washington, D.C.

The firm's D.C. office ran him through the standard security checks before connecting him.

"Hey, Jack!" said a man he'd known for years. "How are you?"

"Great. Working."

"Yeah, I saw the memo from the old man."

"You got somebody high up in DEA?"

"There's a regional supervisor looking at the pension he's due to get in a year who's been floating balloons about needing a second career. Off the record to me as an old friend, you understand."

"You think the firm will sign him up?"

"He's not brilliant, but we can always use another old boy."

"And he'll give you a hand now?"

"What makes a good old boy good?"

They both laughed.

"I need the name of an agent in their field office at the state capital out here," said Cain. "Somebody who's clean, mean, and hungry. He's got to have clout and savvy, too."

"How soon do you need it?"

"Can you call me back in five minutes?" Cain rattled off the pay phone's number.

"With it or without it," said the exec.

Cain waited in the shadows. Two shiny sedans pulled to the curb across the street. The cars disgorged a dozen Japanese men in identical blue suits. They wore name tags and smiles. They clustered together. Three affable Caucasian men led the Japanese farther down the street, pointing to this, explaining that.

"We're in luck," said Cain's colleague when he called back. "The agent you want is Bill Wood. Here's his private line."

He rattled off a number, then added the agent's work address.

"That do it for you?" he asked Cain.

"We'll see."

"You know, I was surprised to hear you were on a big job so soon after . . . I thought you were on leave."

"This was too good a job to turn down," said Cain. He made his farewells, hung up.

For his second call, he fed the pay phone quarters he'd gotten at the bank. He also pressed a handkerchief over the mouthpiece and spoke in a deeper than normal tone.

"Yeah?" said a man who answered on the fifth ring.

"Bill Wood?" asked Cain.

"Who's this?"

"I'm a comrade in arms and your new best friend. I'm calling from Steeltown."

"You one of Nash's boys or did DiCarlo give you your badge?"

"Never mind," said Cain. "Let's just say I got my limits and a public-spirited heart."

"Un-huh."

"This is a pay phone, so don't waste time tracing. I'll give you the number so you can verify the call."

"Why would I want to do that?"

"Maybe so you can build a justifiable and reasonable record for future activities."

"What are you talking about?"

"You'll figure it out. Meanwhile, I'm mailing you my bona fides. It should get there tomorrow. You want it sent to this address?"

Cain rattled off what he'd been told by Washington.

"That'll do. But I never trust any gift from Steeltown."

"You *are* smart, Wood."

Cain read him the number off the pay phone, then hung up.

He wandered toward his hotel. A transaction at an office supply store was accomplished with minimum effort and while his mind was elsewhere. When the hotel elevator jerked to a stop on his floor, his focus returned. He moved quickly, confidently.

In his room, he donned surgeon's gloves from the bag sent by Chicago. He addressed the padded mailer he'd just bought to DEA Agent Wood. In the mailer he put Peterzell's glass vial of cocaine, after carefully wiping the glass. The money he'd torn was old and impractical to fingerprint. He stuffed the torn bills in the mailer, sealed the mailer with tape, stuck on twice as many stamps as were probably needed.

When he was done, he showered the hair dye away. The mustache, glasses, and heel lifts went back into the Chicago suitcase. To check out of the hotel, he wore the same clothes as when he checked in. He was careful to leave certain clothes at the top of his travel bag. The briefcase full of money came out from behind the bed. He transferred twenty thousand dollars to the Chicago suitcase, then closed the briefcase on the rest.

Cain checked the hotel room one last time. No trace of him remained in its anonymous neutrality. He picked up his bags, and walked out the door.

"I told you I needed a reason to be here," Cain said to Kimmett and Nelson as they sat in Kimmett's bedroom three hours later.

Kimmett wore his bathrobe and pajamas. Nelson had on a dark suit. Cain wore worn work boots, blue jeans, and a denim, snap-button shirt. A battered brown leather jacket was draped over his chair; his original suitcase and the briefcase of cash waited by his feet.

"But I needed something else, too," continued Cain, "something I'd planned to manufacture as I went along. I need a match."

"What?" asked Nelson.

"A match," said Cain. "To light a fuse."

"Matches aren't allowed in this room," said Kimmett.

"It isn't this room I'm looking to explode," answered Cain. "This town's been ready to blow since Olson died. You know it. Mayor Nash, Chief DiCarlo, Johnny Maxx, they know it, too. Trouble was, whoever lit the fuse would probably go up with the bang. So all of you waited.

"That's why you hired me," said Cain. "If I lit the fuse and blew up, too, no loss, because you and Nelson would still be there to fight for the pieces. Well, we all got lucky.

"Hammond's murder is the match—and if it isn't now, it will be by the time I'm through with it. Plus we're going to use the murder to give me my reason to be."

"What are you doing here?" snapped Kimmett. "You show up looking like . . ."

"Looking like another Steeltown guy out of a job," answered Cain. "Mr. Reston checked out of his hotel, returned his rental car, went into a public bathroom and vanished. The guy who came out dressed like this didn't get noticed as he walked here."

"Which public restroom?" asked ex-FBI Agent Nelson.

"We don't have much time," said Cain. "You're going to have to do a lot, fast. Those two state legislators the mayor doesn't own—can you influence them?"

"Possibly," said Kimmett.

"How about the governor?" asked Cain.

"He's available to listen."

"And none of them are marked as your men," nodded Cain. "Perfect. What's going to happen is this:

Somebody gunned down a crusading member of the fourth estate. Doesn't matter how good our opposition is about containing messes in Steeltown, I'll make Hammond's murder explode all over the *country*, and that blast will blow the lid off this town. We'll get our political friends to call for an independent commission to investigate Hammond's murder and *all other related matters*. Maybe we'll make it a legislative body, maybe something from the governor's staff, I don't care, as long as it's got clout. And me.

"We pack the commission with clean people—not our guys, but *clean* people. Pull some members from that Citizens' League you told me about, people everybody knows aren't owned. A couple legislators from far away. Make it big and impressive and so cumbersome it won't control its own clout."

"Who will?" asked Nelson.

"Me," said Cain with a smile. "Which, of course, means you."

"Of course," said Nelson.

To Kimmett, Cain said: "You must know nonowned people in this town with bucks to spare, the heirs of the families your grandfather beat. Can you pressure them for cash?"

"For what?"

"Civic good. Which you can sell them as their own hides. They can't be so stupid they don't know that as soon as Nash or DiCarlo or Maxx becomes sole dictator, their quality of life will sink.

"As good citizens of Steeltown, you can be appalled by the murder. You can cough up money to pay for the commission—which marks you as white knights and gets the commission money to kick ass right away.

"You should be the biggest white knight of all. You organize the fund drive, you contribute your experience and the suggestion that the Commission immediately hire my firm to provide an investigator."

"You," said Nelson.

"Me," answered Cain.

"Sounds like I'm paying twice for your services," answered Kimmett. He smiled, nodded toward the briefcase by Cain's feet. "Or should I say three times?"

"I don't care how you run the books," said Cain. "Why don't you handle the funding? Nobody needs to know you already gave."

"This . . . commission," said Kimmett, shaking his head. "I don't like it. Suppose it's not so tame as you say?"

"Why does that worry you?" asked Cain.

"It doesn't, if you do your job," said Kimmett. "And if I'm on the Commission to—"

"Forget it!" snapped Cain. "If you're on the Commission, then everybody knows it's just your baby. The only way for you to claim this town after the war is for you to have spotless armor. If you're on the Commission, your armor will be covered with blood."

Kimmett scowled.

"You're right about the Commission, though," Cain
said. "It'll have to be carefully watched. There'll be me, of
course . . ."

"Of course," said Nelson.

". . . but there should be someone else. Some inoffensive
shadow of you—just to be on the safe side and pave the way
for your ascension. And his own."

"My son will never do it," said Kimmett. "He's spent
his life avoiding combat and politics. The closest he's come
is his damn development committee for the Japanese."

"You said he'll sit where you tell him," argued Cain.
"That's all he has to do: sit. If you're right, he's been so
innocuous nobody will distrust him. And it will be good
practice for his throne, whether he knows it or not."

"There are other ways to do this," hissed Kimmett. "I
can get you a badge to go hunting Hammond's murderer
from . . ."

"From who? I need a badge that's trusted and clean."

"You don't need a badge to hang a murder on a man."

"We're gunning for *three* men," said Cain. "Not one
frame job."

"Frame? One of them must be guilty, you just need
to . . ."

Cain shook his head.

"You didn't wait to call me so I could get my beauty
sleep," he said. "As soon as you heard about Hammond's
murder, you started scheming. When are you going to get it
through your head that you put *me* in charge? I've already
figured all those other ways and they won't work. You keep
moving us back to square one, where the score's always the
same: we do this my way or you go it alone."

Cain paused for a minute. When the other two men
didn't speak, he said, "It would be a shame to waste Hammond's murder."

"The little shit was never worth so much," said Kimmett,
and Cain knew he'd won.

"Why did you come here this morning?" said Nelson.

"To work all this out," said Cain. "This has to be in
place by tomorrow night, or it'll be out of our hands. We

also have to pray that nobody hangs the murder on some guy and puts out the fire."

"Don't worry about efficient law enforcement in this city," said Nelson.

"I worry about luck," said Cain.

"What are *you* going to do?" said Nelson. "In your clever scenario, you're not supposed to exist yet."

"I'm going to hide right here, helping you guys put this together. The big risk is somebody from the hotel or car rental agency or on the street later might recognize Jackson Cain as Mr. Reston or Walter Mathews . . ."

"Who?" asked Nelson.

". . . but maybe a haircut and keeping my picture out of the media will take care of that," said Cain.

Kimmett shook his head.

"This wasn't how I had it planned," he said. "This isn't how I like it."

"This is what you got," said Cain.

Rain

RAIN BEAT AGAINST KIMMETT'S window that night as Cain stared out at the storm. He was snug and dry in his fourth-floor guest room. The rain streamed through the pale glow of floodlights mounted on the roof, fell to the manicured lawn surrounding the mansion. In darkness beyond the electric illumination, Cain saw the shapes of trees swaying in the wind. Lightning flashed; thunder rumbled. He touched his fingertips to the glass; it was cool, smooth, and trembled.

Cain turned away from the outer world and a burning knife stabbed his right knee. He stumbled to his bed. The pain hit him again as the mattress sagged beneath his hips.

Damn weather! he thought. He swung his left leg onto the bedspread. With both hands, he cupped his right knee, then lifted that leg beside its mate. His head sank into the pillow.

It'll pass, he told himself. Always does. Just lie quiet. Relax. Don't push it.

Damn, damn weather!

Someone knocked on his door.

His eyes flicked to the right, to the oak bureau and his suitcase standing in the open closet. He angled his face up, focusing past the nightstand and reading lamp to the room's heavy brown door.

Someone knocked again.

"Come in," he said, as casually as he could. He forced

his heaving chest to normal breaths. And don't ask why I don't get up.

The door swung open. When Cain didn't move, Judson lumbered toward the bed. His giant shadow rolled over Cain.

"Mr. Kimmett asked if there's anything more you want," said Judson.

"I'll be damned," said Cain. "I didn't know you could talk."

"There's a lot you don't know."

"Why don't you tell me?"

Judson slowly shook his head from side to side. He grinned.

"You're supposed to be the smart one," said Judson.

"So they say," answered Cain, torn between coaxing more words from this monster and getting him out of the room.

A rolling bass laugh escaped Judson's mouth. His blockish face turned this way and that, his eyes scanned the comfortable bedroom. He nodded, walked toward the door.

"What's on for the rest of the night?" asked Cain.

From the doorway, Judson turned. He pointed down the hall.

"I sleep down there," he said. "Close."

His huge forefinger swung back into the room, aimed itself at Cain.

"This isn't your room to keep," said Judson.

"I wouldn't want it," Cain answered.

Judson nodded. His mouth gaped in a semblance of a smile. He stepped into the hall, pulling the door softly shut behind him.

Cain cupped his hands over his exhausted eyes; his brow was damp. No doubt Judson saw its sheen. Cain's knee ached but he didn't care. He looked at his wristwatch: nine minutes to midnight.

All that afternoon, Kimmett had worked from his bed, Cain from the round table by the window. Nelson kept notes and juggled dozens of calls on extra phones they'd plugged in. They heard snatches of each other's conversations, yelled news back and forth, cajoled unseen conspirators, and complained aloud. Kimmett's bedroom became a newsroom on deadline, the Pentagon's war room, Tammany Hall. The butler fetched sandwiches and pots of coffee. Maids cleared away dishes and crumpled sheets of yellow legal pad paper that only minutes before had been covered with scrawled intelligence rendered obsolete by the next phone call.

As the day wore on, editors and publishers and air-time kings in the national media received calls from people they trusted, owed, or feared, people who could be reached by Kimmett or Cain's firm. Sometimes the callers were fellow titans of the fourth estate, sometimes they were politicians, sometimes they were golf buddies with legendary good judgment.

Sometimes the call went to journalists in the trenches from men like Cain, perpetually unattributed and effective sources. Often Cain discovered that the questions: What are we going to do about that Steeltown murder story? and What is everybody else going to do? had been asked before he had a chance to insert them into the daily flow of intellectual commerce. Such unprompted interest sometimes came from genuine concern for the great moral issues; more often, it came from the press's imperative for conformity: if everybody else is treating this as important news, it must be, so our coverage can't be any less than theirs.

Reporters, columnists, and those who gathered words for pretty faces to speak to the TV cameras needed little encouragement to become excited about Hammond's murder; often, however, they needed hints on how to turn their excitement into activity. One of their own had been murdered, but what could they do about it? Thousands die each day. Journalists have deadlines and budgets and partitioned priorities. The man—what was his name? Hammond? Like the organ?—died in godforsaken *Steeltown*. It wasn't like he was a movie star or sports celebrity.

But this is a big story, said trusted sources. And it's tangible: a gunshot victim is easier to write about than how the gun and the killer came to be. Sometimes the sources whispered a suggestion of bigger things than mere murder.

We've seen it all before, said the warriors of truth.

Yes, said the whispers, and it's always sold papers.

Reporters pestered editors who'd been prepared to be pestered. Leashes were loosened. Make some calls, chase it down, get back to me, and we'll see what we got.

So calls went out to Steeltown—to the mayor, the police department, the sheriff's office, to the publisher and editors and reporters of the local paper: What was he working on? Who could have killed him? What's being done? Give us something to feed the news machine. The governor got calls, phones rang in offices of federal cops. Airplane tickets were bought. By midafternoon, it seemed the whole world wanted to know about one Steeltown murder.

"We've got to do something," Kimmett ventured to half a dozen citizens who had the money and mind to think that they could. Kimmett eventually heard his arguments relayed to him *before* he made them. Then Kimmett simply said, "Well, *somebody* suggested that . . ."

The governor, already harried by calls from reporters demanding to know what he was doing about a mess that wasn't his business, started hearing from his allies and campaign contributors.

The state senator and state representative who weren't controlled by Mayor Nash's machine had neighbors and friends calling them with genuine fears. In the best chambers of their hearts, the legislators wanted to fix the mess splattered in their backyard; in the darkest chambers of their hearts, they feared doing *anything*, for action generates reaction, and God knows where that chain stops.

All the politicians were happy to hop in the back seat of whatever bus someone else would drive forward—or at least away from this disquieting crisis.

"The trick," Cain told Kimmett, "is to make them so uncomfortable they must do something, then give them the something you want them to do all dressed up in a package that looks like the easiest, most painless choice."

"Not that I'm sold on this special commission idea," the state senator told the governor the second time they talked that day, "but I keep hearing about it and it doesn't sound so bad."

An ambitious young lawyer on the governor's staff discovered an obscure law that allowed the governor to create

a special commission to oversee emergencies between legislative sessions. The state's legislature had just adjourned.
The law allowed the governor to pay for such a group with
general revenue funds. The governor could create a commission only at the request of at least six state legislators. The
governor's lawyer found no provision barring the commission from utilizing private monies or unduly limiting its
powers.

At 4:00 P.M., neither of the independent city legislators
would ask the governor to exercise his option.

Said the senator, "Might not be a bad idea, but I can't
see my way clear to demand a leapfrog over the way government works every day just because of one more murder."

The senator wanted one more reelection. Kimmett
couldn't convince him that a bold solo move would not
make him vulnerable to Mayor Nash's machine.

Said the representative, "This is a complex question
with jurisdictional issues requiring study."

The representative was paralyzed with inertia.

At 4:11, as the close of official business neared, the
governor took yet another phone call, this one from a state
senator whose district lay two hundred miles from Steeltown.
The senator was a farmer who represented those few surviving American farmers, a mortal who fought drought and
hail and acts of God.

"I'm sick and tired of Steeltown and it's pissant messes!"
he yelled into the phone mounted on the wall of his machine
shop. "I've been riding tractor all day, listening to the radio
'bout this murder. Nash and his no-count cops can't find
killers, but every year they strut their way to the state house
and demand more money for roads and relief and pay me
this so I can grease Sam that and the hell with it! What the
hell are we going to do about that damn town?"

While the farmer paused for breath, the governor told
him about the commission idea, about the good citizens
who'd offered to bankroll it and save taxpayers' dollars,
about how he shared the farmer's concerns but his hands
were tied—unless the legislator was formally asking the
governor to create a commission: Was he?

"Goddamn right I am," said the farmer, "if it'll clean up the goddamned town!"

Within sixty seconds, the governor had the two independent Steeltown legislators on a conference call; they agreed to accede to their colleague's request and join his effort for civic betterment.

"Shit," said the farmer. He spat tobacco juice and went back to his tractor, wondering what nonsense he'd stepped in now.

Three other legislators anxious for good press as white knights were quickly found.

At 4:25, the governor called the law professor who had long before formed the reform group and been ostracized for his efforts. The two men had never spoken to each other. The head of state reached the state-salaried teacher in his academic office, where he was boxing his books and contemplating his uncertain future.

What a shame the loss of tenure was, the governor let him know. No doubt some twisted mistake of imponderable academia.

Un-huh, replied the professor.

The governor abandoned all talk of personal problems; they clearly were not important. He told the professor the truth in this order: Hammond's murder greatly upset him. A legislator had asked the governor to create a special investigative commission. Steeltown's prominent citizens had volunteered their time and money. The professor was the best choice to head the commission—and should bring a couple of his League's members on board to serve with the farmer, two other legislators from distant corners of the state, and a few others the governor might appoint. The governor would assign the lawyer from his staff who had researched the law regarding the commission, and, "there's already a crackerjack investigator we've signed up for the nuts and bolts work."

An *independent* commission? the professor wanted to know.

Certainly, the governor informed him. Within the standard legislative rules of operation.

Oh, had been the professor's reply. For a full minute,

neither he nor the governor spoke. Finally, the professor said:

"If I don't take this chance, I mock my work."

The governor didn't care about the professor's logic; he had his eyes on the clock and his ears keyed for a yes.

"So you'll do it?" he said.

"What choice do I have?" replied the professor.

The governor congratulated him, hung up, and hurriedly prepared for a five-o'clock broadcast live press announcement. He courteously called Mayor Nash with the news at four-fifty, and learned, as expected, that His Honor knew his political associates had been busy. Mayor Nash officially thanked the governor for his concern, and pledged the full cooperation of his administration. He asked for and was not promised a seat on the commission. The two men bid each other cordial farewells. As an afterthought, the governor had an aide relay news of the commission to the city's police chief.

By six-thirty, the media machine was eagerly digesting its latest fare.

Sunset swamped Kimmett's bedroom with rose light. The old man lay propped up by a mountain of pillows. Cain faced him from a chair pulled close to the bed. At the window table, Nelson whispered quiet encouragement over the telephone to a timid ally. The nurse unwound her blood pressure cuff from Kimmett's arm.

"Better than I expected," she declared.

Kimmett laughed.

"I haven't felt so good in years!"

"Well," she said, returning her equipment to a black medical bag, "be careful not to feel any better."

She stalked out of the room as Kimmett laughed again.

"One more thing," said Cain as daylight faded.

The old man frowned.

"Your son," said Cain.

"Can't that wait?" His voice took on a pleading whine.

Cain shook his head.

The old man sighed, shook his head, and stared toward the wall of blank television screens opposite his bed. The room darkened. Cain waited like a sphinx.

Finally, Kimmett snapped on the bedside light. He dialed a number he needed to look up in a black address book. Both hands cradled the phone against his face. As he talked, he kept his green eyes shut.

"Hello, my dear," Cain heard Kimmett say. A razor replaced the whine in his client's words. "Lovely to hear your voice. . . . Nothing that concerns you. . . . Well, we both know that's a mistake you often make."

The old man forced a dry, cackling laugh from his chest.

"Now I need to talk to my son. Get him for me, please."

Kimmett's lips curled in a sweet smile, then quickly straightened to a serious line.

"Hello, Elliot . . . fine. How are you? . . . Ah yes, the Japanese . . . That's good, Elliot, I'm sure . . . Do I need a reason?"

The father laughed at what the son said.

"And I thought you learned nothing from me!

"Actually," he continued, "I'm calling on *your* business. You know this Hammond murder? . . . Yes, and it can't be ignored. Many of our friends feel the same way—as, I'm sure, do your Japanese. . . . Would they invest in a city whose streets are covered in blood? . . .

"Did you hear the news that the governor appointed an investigating commission? Not what *I* would have done, though I support it with our friends. . . . We're picking up the tab. . . . The governor wanted me. I can't. But since Kimmett money is bankrolling this group, he insisted that a Kimmett should serve on it. He'll appoint you. . . .

"You want to do the right thing, don't you Elliot? . . . And convince your Japanese our city is safe for them? . . . Yes, that's right. . . . No, not much. They've already hired the workhorse . . . that law professor from the Citizens' League. . . . What you have to do is say yes.

"It's not a favor to me, Elliot. . . . Yes . . . I'm sure she will, but remember, her loyalties and sense are not to be trusted. . . . All right . . . Of course . . . Good-bye."

Kimmett hung up the phone. Looked at Cain and nodded.

"Now I rest," said Kimmett. "Nelson will take care of you."

Cain, settled in quarters above the outside world, was

invited to shower in his private bathroom. An hour later, the butler phoned him.

"Dinner is served, sir," said the servant.

Cain ate alone at a dark wooden dining room table that reflected the twinkling crystal chandelier. Fifteen empty chairs waited on each side of the table, an empty chair stared at him from the far end. To his left were serving sideboards and china bureaus. As Cain ate, the butler stood by the kitchen's swinging door. The curtains were open on the floor-to-ceiling windows to Cain's right. Flashes of lightning and thunder's low rumbles punctuated his meal; the rain began before Cain finished. He dined on Kimmett family china, with heavy antique silver utensils: prime rib, baked potato, fresh asparagus, a ten-year-old French red wine. The hot apple pie came from a widow's kitchen two miles away. He declined Jamaican coffee from the steaming silver pot, told the butler he never smoked and especially never smoked cigars, but accepted a tumbler of Napoleon brandy.

"One for the road?" Cain asked as he rose from the table.

"As you wish, sir," replied the butler, refilling Cain's glass with amber fluid.

With a sated man's easy tread, Cain toured the mansion. The ceilings were high, the walls were beautiful wood hues. When not carpeted by lush Orientals or thick pile, the floors were darkly stained oak. An aroma of old wood buffed with lemon polish filled the house. He found a library full of first editions. He ran his fingers along their spines and wondered who had last searched them for wisdom. Cain found two sitting rooms, each overly decorated with stuffed chairs and expensive paintings. One portrait showed Steeltown's sire and another his son; a third showed the manor's present lord. The walls had space for succeeding art. Cain found a music room with a grand piano, a billiard room, a grandfather clock. From behind a closed door came murmurs of televised drama and male conversation. An open door showed him an office where a black great Dane sprawled before the desk. As Cain passed by, the dog barked and leaped up. Cain froze. From the room's corner, one of Nelson's tough young men snapped his fingers. The beast dropped to his haunches, snarled, then relaxed.

"Move slowly," said the dog's boss. "They have to get used to you being around."

Cain nodded, walked on.

The doors on the second floor were closed. More bedrooms or offices. He didn't want to risk finding out then.

A casually dressed guard sat at the nurse's station outside Kimmett's third-floor door. He and Cain exchanged nods.

The fourth-floor hall was empty. One door was Judson's; perhaps another belonged to Nelson. Cain went to his own quarters.

Whoever had searched his gear had been thorough.

Do they suspect something is wrong or are they just paranoid? Cain wondered as he lay on his bed, his watch ticking toward tomorrow. He flexed his knee: the dull ache of aftershock had replaced crippling pain. He swung his feet to the floor, gingerly raised his weight off the bed, and stood.

And didn't collapse.

He opened the door to the deserted hall. The banister was three gentle steps away. He risked vertigo gazing down at the stairwell's boxlike shaft. Rain drummed on a stained glass skylight above his head. From below came the tolling of the grandfather clock counting down midnight.

The faint tinkle of a woman's laughter floated through the mansion like a ghost.

Command Performance

SUNDAY EVENING, TWO DAYS LATER, Cain concentrated on the closet door's full-length mirror as he flipped the big end of the tie around, dropped it through the loop, and pulled the knot snug.

He'd chosen a dark blue suit from clothes shipped to him by a colleague Cain trusted enough to send to his Washington Square apartment. His tie was British regimental. Cain smiled as he remembered Epstein, who'd told him that to succeed in the State Department, one should dress British and think Jewish. Cain backed the tie with an American-styled powder blue, button down shirt. On a whim, he wore black suspenders instead of a belt.

Function, not fashion, dictated his choice of shoes. After the night his knee went out, he'd protected himself with cautious steps and surreptitious aspirins. The pain was gone, but such a recovery could never be trusted as it would never be complete. Shoes with a narrow heel taxed his balance and thus strained his knees; he needed a solid base for his feet. His hand passed over his chic loafers and lifted the pair of heavy, plain-toed black brogues from the closet floor.

Judson had barbered Cain's hair to within an inch of his scalp. Time's retreat from his temples now showed more clearly, and its toll on his countenance was easier to tally. His hands smoothed the hair against his head: *another new image.* After a last inspection in the mirror, he turned off the light and stepped from his room.

Two great Danes loped down the hall toward him. Cain stood still. The dogs' mouths came to his chest; their hot panting breaths beat against his shirt. One of them drooled on his hand. They sniffed him, then trotted on: he'd been accepted as part of the kennel.

Cain checked his watch as he started down the stairs: 7:24.

In a deserted parking lot across town, Frank Peterzell lifted his eyes from his wristwatch at the sound of a high-powered car racing toward him. A black Thunderbird swooped into the parking lot, slid to a stop ten feet away. The driver's smoked glass window electronically hummed down. Danny Layten, six-feet-two of postadolescent muscular charm, grinned at him from behind the steering wheel.

"Hey! Frank! Wait'll you see my new suit!"

The interior light blinked on as the driver's door opened.

"Forget it," snapped Peterzell as he walked to the car. "I can stare at you all night."

"What's your hurry?" asked Danny as his passenger buckled his seat belt. "Your guy said ten o'clock, right?"

"Right."

"So it's like seven-thirty. It ain't that long a ride."

Peterzell shook his head: "If you don't know enough to show up early, you don't know enough."

"Franky, don't be like that!" Danny grinned at his burned-out companion in the terrible plaid sports jacket. Who impatiently flicked his hand toward the windshield. Danny stepped on the gas and peeled out of the parking lot.

Cain paused on the third-floor landing: Kimmett's door stood open. No guard or nurse waited at the desk. Cain stepped into the room and heard the low intonations of network television news:

"... Tel Aviv reported no losses in the raid, although Palestinian guerrilla sources claim they shot down *two* Israeli warplanes. On the economic front, Wall Street analysts today concurred with the Commerce Department's figures showing ..."

From the floor by the bed, the master's favorite great Dane *whoofed*: an uncharacteristically subdued announcement. The dog kept his head on his paws.

"There you are, Cain!" Kimmett stood to Cain's left, facing a full-length mirror. The old man wore spit-shined black shoes, black trousers, and suspenders. His shirt was white; he adjusted a black bow tie. Judson stood nearby, holding a tuxedo jacket. Kimmett's hair was fluffed like a cloud. He used an electronic control wand to silence the TV, then shot his green eyes at Cain's business suit.

"This is a formal banquet!" he snapped.

"I'm the outside entertainment," answered Cain. The butler entered and awaited orders. Like Judson and Kimmett, he was in classic evening dress. Cain glanced at him: "I don't want anybody mistaking me for a servant."

"Just be sure they believe you're who we tell you you are," hissed Kimmett.

"That's me," said Cain.

"Hmph," said Kimmett. His attention returned to the mirror.

Cain strolled to the table in the window.

"I'm surprised by this," he said.

"By what?" snapped Kimmett, as he adjusted gold cufflinks.

"This dinner—downstairs."

"Don't be deceived by my caution." The old man's reflection grinned. "I leave this room, if I must. The pure air, my secure world, they keep me well, but I can do things that would amaze you."

"Un-huh," replied Cain.

Below the window, one of Nelson's men paced a beat on the veranda. Cain watched him for a moment, then walked back through the room's circle of couches and padded chairs. Something tucked in the corner of a couch caught his eye.

"What have you been doing?" Cain asked. "I haven't seen you since Friday."

"My affairs are none of your concern," said Kimmett. He stood before the mirror, held his arms out from his sides. Judson carefully pulled the tuxedo jacket onto his watchful master.

Which gave Cain a chance to lean over the couch and see what lay tucked in its shadowed corner: A black velvet neck band.

"You're the one who should account for yourself," said Kimmett as he turned from the mirror. Cain stood straight before his gaze. "Nelson told me that you had one of our people drive you off the grounds. To a pay phone. Why not use my phones?"

"Some matters require privacy," answered Cain.

The old man stared at him, but Cain kept his counsel.

"Yes," agreed Kimmett finally. He grinned. "That's true.

"Time to go downstairs," he said.

Cain led the way.

"I don't see why we gotta go out to *nowhere*," groused Danny as he piloted the Thunderbird away from the center of town.

"What you don't see isn't nothing," Peterzell told him.

"What's that supposed to mean?"

"It means what it means," said Peterzell. He was tired, shaky, overdue for a little blow. "Nothing more."

"Yeah," said Danny, pouting. "Well . . . well."

They rode in silence for a moment.

"So," said Danny as they cruised passed a McDonald's. He leered at his companion. "What do you think?"

"Think about what?"

"The suit! Ain't it great!"

Danny hooked a thumb under the lapel of his new fawn-colored three-piece suit.

Frank closed his eyes. His head began to throb.

"You know," Danny told him, "you should dress right."

"Yes," said Frank. "That must be my problem."

"You need any help, just let me know."

"I'll be sure to do that."

"I mean," said Danny, coyly. "I can rig you up with something real special."

Frank sighed.

"I mean," said Danny again, "this suit is *specially* custom cut. For a guy like me. Or you."

Still, Frank didn't take the bait.

"I mean, it's cut for more than a regular suit."

Frank turned his full attention to the man behind the wheel.

Danny grinned and opened the suit coat; a black machine pistol in a swing-out shoulder rig lay against his chest.

"Jesus Christ!" yelled Frank.

"Miami special," Danny gleefully explained. "A MAC-10. Takes a silencer, which I got on order. Don't you love it?! Thousand rounds a minute.

"I only got two spare clips," he apologized.

"You schmuck!" whispered Frank. "Thing like that gets excited, you end up killing the wrong person!"

They looked like a parade descending the stairs: Cain, Kimmett, Judson, and the butler. Nelson met them on the first floor.

"We're ready." He glanced at his watch: 7:45.

"Pen all the dogs," ordered Kimmett. "We've had enough unpleasantries."

"Have an accident?" asked Cain as Judson left to obey.

"They're an excitable breed," said Nelson.

Kimmett scowled: "You've taken care of everything?"

"All but the seating arrangements," answered Nelson. "I thought you might want to do that."

The Thunderbird followed its headlights through the hills on a winding, paved county road.

"In the trunk, right?" asked Peterzell.

"Just like you said."

"What else you got?"

"Meaning what?"

"Meaning they can see your eyes all the way to Denver."

From ahead in the night, a pair of headlights bore down on the Thunderbird. In silence, the men watched them draw closer, closer . . . rush past—a pickup truck with an unseen driver.

Half a mile more of white-lined highway rolled under their wheels. Danny glanced at himself in the rearview mirror.

"They got a dip bag there," he said. "So I hit a little."

They cruised down the other side of the hills, the outer slope of Steeltown's valley. The forest along the road gave way to open fields. Farm country, thought Frank, though he barely recognized the difference between a crop field and wasteland. The night was clear, a quarter moon, and out here, past the city lights, thousands of stars twinkled in the indigo sky. For all the time he'd spent gazing at stars, he still knew none of their names. He pushed a button on the car door; his window slid down. Cool night air flowed across his face. He recognized the scent of pine from the hills they had left, a hint of sage and moist earth. He shut the window.

"So," Franky asked, "you bring any with you?"

The doorbell rang promptly at 8:00.

"Remember," Cain told Kimmett as the butler marched to answer the door, "no speeches, no nasties. You're a crusader with a conscience, not a candidate."

The man who would be king glared at his knight as the castle door swung open.

Three couples in their sixties swooped into someone else's mansion wearing their fur stoles and quantities of jewels.

The show's angels, on time for good seats, thought Cain as Kimmett clasped their wrinkled hands, assured them his health was excellent, and agreed with them on the evening's terrible importance.

"This is the commission's investigator," Kimmett said, sweeping the old women and their older men to Cain. They cooed at him and tested his grip; their eyes caressed his size, fans assessing the new heavyweight in the ring. He smiled and professionally remembered the names he personally ignored.

"Shall we take cocktails in the drawing room?" said Kimmett.

Cain thought the music floating over the crowd from the drawing room's stereo was either Mozart or Chopin.

"I love Brahms, don't you?" said the governor's young lawyer. Her red silk dress fit loosely. She'd wound her long russet hair into a severe bun, kept all but the necessary hint of makeup off her cheeks and lips. A correct glass of white wine was clenched tightly in her chewed-nail fingers and held out from her chest so she would not create disaster with a stain on her dress. She kept her voice low and dignified, and prayed that she was right about the music because damn it, she really was a Yale graduate, thank you very much.

"Yes," Cain said, "Brahms is nice."

"Ah ..." she said, wondering if he remembered her name was Beth Worby, "we're going to be working quite closely together, and I want you to know that just because I'm an attorney ..."

"I won't hold that against you."

Damn his smile! she thought.

"What I mean is," she said, "we both work for the commission, though I'm on the governor's staff, but we're like partners."

"We'll be fine," said Cain. Her eyes were brown. He scanned the crowd over her head: Nelson was socializing politely as he made sure nothing impeded propriety. The publisher of Hammond's newspaper, a man named Thomas Evans, stood in the center of the room, drinking alone. Three of Kimmett's contemporaries had the host trapped in a corner, biting his tongue as he listened to them prattle. His green eyes met Cain's; Cain winked.

"I want you to know," Beth said, and Cain looked back at her, "I've researched the law, and while there are precedents ..."

"The issues won't be legal," Cain told her.

"Excuse me?" she frowned.

"So you're the hotshot," said a craggy-faced man in a cheap and ill-fitting suit. His left hand imprisoned a large glass of whiskey; he was missing his ring finger.

"I'm Cain."

"Yeah, I heard." The weathered man swallowed half his whiskey. "Me and my big mouth started this damn thing. They say you're good. You'll find I'm a fair man. Think you can fix this damned mess?"

"Yes."

"Christ, I hope so."

He wandered away, glaring at the surrounding walls.
"That's . . ." said Beth, before Cain interrupted:
"I know."

"What now?" asked Danny.

The Thunderbird was parked at a rest stop. Danny'd backed the car up until its taillights were only four feet from the barbwire fence separating this graveled turnout from some farmer's field. Three litter barrels stood sentry twenty feet to the right of the car; the windshield faced the highway thirty feet away. Everywhere else there was nothing but night. When he turned off the lights, it was as though the big dark swallowed them. Frank lowered his window and ordered Danny to do the same; told him to kill the engine. Their exhaust dissolved into the blackness. Danny smelled the dusty gravel beneath the Thunderbird. The air was chilly. A few moments after the engine died, crickets began to chirp.

"What now?" Danny asked again. He realized he was whispering. He didn't know why.

"Now we wait," replied Frank.

"I hate waiting," grumbled Danny. He sniffed.

"Yeah," said Frank.

"What time is it?"

"You got a watch."

"Just trying to . . ."

"It's eight thirty-seven," said Frank. "Twenty-three to nine."

"Ten o'clock, you said?"

"Whenever."

"I hate waiting."

Danny stared out the windshield at the night. Not a damn thing out there but the damn highway, a gray line across his vision that blurred into blackness at both ends.

"Frank?" he asked. "What did you learn in prison?"

His partner didn't reply for what seemed like an eternity (two minutes by Danny's watch), so he whispered, "Frank?"

"What did I learn in prison?" answered the man. His head didn't move, his expression stayed blank. "Nothing."

"I didn't expect to meet you quite like this," Cain heard a man say. Cain and Beth Worby turned to face him: he was short, trim, with sandy hair and smile lines. Behind him stood a petite, brown-haired woman with tight lips and a pretty dress.

"This is . . ." began Beth.

"Russ Boswell," said the man. He shook Cain's hand. "I'm the professor who's agreed to leave the ivory tower and hunt dragons."

His grip was dry and sincere.

"Didn't you know I'd be coming tonight?" Cain asked.

"I didn't even know I'd be here," said Boswell. "When I first talked to the governor, I figured we'd be a week arguing over who was on the commission. But . . ."

Boswell shrugged. He gestured to the crowded room.

"We're off and running," he said.

"Nervous?" asked Cain.

"Of course!" he said, and Cain loved him for it.

"Let me introduce you to my wife," he said, and pulled the brown-haired woman to his side. She smiled, shook Cain's hand.

"This is the man who's going to be taking care of me, dear," Boswell told her.

"I see," she said; her lips twitched. "Please do."

"Where are you staying?" asked Boswell.

"Mr. Kimmett kindly put me up for the night," Cain told him.

"You flew in today?" asked the commission chairman.

"I've found a deal on a kitchen-suite at the Commodore Hotel," said Beth. "There was no problem getting a reduced rate within per diem. You might want to check the place out. It's quite nice."

"Thank you," Cain told her.

"It might be a good idea," she continued, "us staying in the same place."

"Yes," he said, "it might."

"Do you know everybody on the commission yet?" asked Boswell.

"I've talked to the two upstate legislators on the phone," said Cain. "Met the man who started it all a few minutes ago."

"There are two people from the Citizens' League we signed onto the commission who you should get to know," said Boswell. "Art Meadows, who administers the local federal poverty program—he couldn't make it tonight—and . . . *Paul!*"

The angular man in a brown suit loomed over everyone else in the room. He looked like a crane perched in a lily pond, certain that there were fish beneath the rippling surface and just as sure they were quick and had sharp teeth. He swung his long neck and thin-nosed face toward the man who'd called out his name, and stepped to where he'd been bidden.

"This is Paul Borge," said Boswell. "Another one of our commissioners. Paul is a Methodist minister."

Borge's fingers were long and kind. He shook Cain's hand.

"Associate minister, actually," he said. "At least as long as I have a church."

"Some of Paul's parishoners aren't wild about his work with the food bank and the League," explained Boswell.

"No," corrected Borge. "I'd say they *are* wild about it."

They all laughed.

With a powerful blast of its air horn, a semi blared by on the highway. The Thunderbird shook in its wake.

"We've been here a long time," said Danny.

"We'll be here a lot longer," said Frank. "Might as well get used to it."

"What time is—"

"Nine to nine."

"Hey: back to back nines!" said Danny. "Must be lucky."

"Must be," said Frank.

"Yeah."

Danny looked out at the nowhere. The truck was only

the third vehicle to pass by since they'd arrived. He was cold. Even the damn crickets had shut up. They were probably cold too. Crawled back in their holes like sensible bugs. He wished he could put up the window, but that would probably piss Franky off. Wished he could play the radio. Hell, they were *so* early! Nothing was going to happen for a long time.

"Hey, Franky: You got a girl, don't you?"

He didn't reply.

"Come on, who . . ."

"Don't worry about it," said Franky, quickly.

"Hey, I'm not worried, you know? Guys like us don't have any trouble, right?"

Frank said nothing.

"I mean, nothing else, they'll smile at us for the powder, right? We smile at them 'cause of the powder they put *on* their face and they smile at us for the powder we put *in* their face!" Danny laughed uproariously.

"It's the same trick," he insisted. "Same trick."

The two men didn't speak for seventy seconds on Danny's watch.

"I had a girl," said Danny. Franky strained to hear him. "She was . . . It just didn't work out, you know? Like the business. She didn't understand. Had some ideas. And an old man. Churchy type. She said he didn't believe any God stuff, but he was always preaching at me 'bout doing this, doing that. She'd pick it up . . .

"Had the softest hands," whispered Danny.

Twenty seconds ticked by.

"Fuck it," whispered Danny.

"Yeah," agreed Frank. "Fuck it."

"And fuck them!" insisted Danny. "Women! I fuck 'em all the time, believe you me."

"I believe you," said Frank.

"You name it, I fucked 'em. Blondes, so many damn blondes, walkin' down the street, they make you want to cry. I fucked so many of them, and they all loved it. Chink girls, Orientals, all that long black hair and no bullshit. They got tiny tits though. Even blacks, couple times, you know, to see what it's like and it's *something*, believe you me! Everywhere. Dallas, New York, down in New Orleans that time. Kentucky. Seattle.

"And I never once paid for it!" Danny jabbed his finger toward the man with whom he shared this nowhere night. "Never fuckin' once and I never fuckin' will. Anybody asks, you tell 'em Danny never ever fuckin' pays for it!"

"I'll tell them."

"Never!"

"I'll tell them."

Danny settled back in his seat. He could ask him now. Enough time had passed and enough was left. In a minute. He sighed.

"But hell," he said. "There's nothing like a Steeltown woman."

Cain heard a man's pleasant tenor say, "I'm sorry." When Cain turned toward the sound, he saw the handsomest man in town facing the old man who owned this house.

"There's a problem at the boy's boarding school," said the handsome man. His shrug apologized again.

Cain saw him first in profile. His hair was golden, his facial features perfect: regular ears, high cheekbones, and tanned cheeks. His nose was Roman, his mouth full. He wore his tuxedo naturally, moved with grace and restraint. He was tall enough to star at guard on a high school basketball team, trim enough in his forties to catch the crowd's eye when he stepped onto the tennis court in all white. Cain couldn't hear the old man's reply. The crone layed his claw on the handsome man's arm, turned him around. They shared brilliant green eyes—though the old man's burned with the fire of a blast furnace, while the younger man's were like Chinese jade.

The old man led his prize to Cain.

"This," he said, "is my son, Elliot Kimmett the Fourth."

"It's good to meet you," said the son as they shook hands.

"Yes," said Cain, "it is."

"I'm sorry I didn't make it on time," apologized the younger Kimmett. "Family problems."

"Ah," said Cain.

"But, then, I'm not crucial to this crowd." He smiled.

"We waited dinner for you," said the old man.

"Sorry, father. Some things can't be helped."

She wore black, with a string of pearls. Her dress was elegant and costly and fit her lean form perfectly. She parted her ash blond hair on the left and let it curl above her shoulders. Her eyebrows were long and arched lightly above well-spaced denim blue eyes. Her mouth was wide, with perhaps too long an upper lip. She came toward them slowly, with fluid but firm steps, scanned the room without flinching.

"I got through and talked to him," she told the handsome man, then looked at his father: "*Our* family business."

"Sylvia," said the old man, "This is Mister Cain. Our commission's investigator."

"*Our?*" she said as she watched the old man. "Don't you mean *your?*"

"This is my charming daughter-in-law," said the old man.

"Please don't start," whispered his son. His eyes swept the room and saw others turn away.

"How do you do, Mrs. Kimmett?" said Cain.

She let Cain fall into her eyes: "Do what?"

"We don't have to be so formal," interjected her husband, forcing a smile into the group. "I'm Elliot, she's Sylvia."

"And what do we call you?" Sylvia said to Cain.

"When?" he replied.

The old man laughed. He nodded a cue, and the butler announced, "Ladies and gentlemen, if you please."

The butler swept his hand and parted the crowd so their host might lead the way. The old man took the arm of the governor's lawyer.

"You're so lovely, my dear, I can't bear the thought of you dining next to anyone but me."

Those who heard him chuckled; Beth smiled gamely.

"And I think," said Kimmett, smiling to Commission Chairman Boswell, "as host, I should have the honor of having you on my right."

"Don't worry about your wife," Kimmett told him. "My son and she will be right next to us."

The old man led his dinner companions two steps forward, stopped and turned around.

"Cain," he said. "Would you fill up the other end of the table? Perhaps with Reverend Borge. And dear Sylvia. Doesn't that balance you perfectly? A man of God on one side."

He laughed, and led the way.

"Christ," muttered Sylvia under his breath. "Don't you just love family affairs?"

"How'd you get into this?" Danny asked.

"What?" said Frank.

"You know," said Danny. "This."

"That's the dumbest question you've asked all night."

"Fuck you, too," said Danny. He thought that after they did it, they'd feel better. Maybe it was just because it was so close. He checked his watch: 9:14. Looked at Frank. What the hell.

"Me," said Danny, not caring it he was talking to Frank or just throwing words out the window to the great nowhere, "it was the coolest thing I could do. Also the easiest. Also paid the most. Also, once I got started, it made sense. Plus it ain't bad work. Beats the fuckin' mill, like my old man, every day same place, shit pay, and the whole world's a foreman."

"My father was a doctor," said Frank Peterzell.

"Yeah?" asked Danny, eager to hear anything from the man beside him. "So what did he do?"

Franky turned and stared at him.

"I mean . . . you know," stammered Danny.

"He died."

"Oh." Danny swallowed. "Is that why . . ."

"Two years ago."

"Oh," said Danny again. Then, "I gotta pee."

As Sylvia Kimmett settled in her chair, she turned and told the woman in the maid's costume, "I missed drinks. Would you please bring me a scotch on the rocks, right away?"

"I'm sorry," the maid whispered, "but your father-in-law order us not to give you anything but that wine with dinner."

"Bring me a drink! *Please!*" insisted Sylvia.

Cain turned toward the maid, said, "Why don't you get me a double scotch? If Mrs. Kimmett picks up my glass, it's my problem."

The maid retreated. Sylvia Kimmett stared at the man she'd just met.

"Where are you from, Mr. Cain?" asked Reverend Borge.

Cain turned to his right, smiled at the clerical crane and let the minister watch the sweep of his eyes encompass the mansion.

"Light years from here," said Cain. "How's the business of saving souls?"

"I wouldn't know," said Borge. "There are too many crises of the body in Steeltown to worry abut men's spirits."

"Hand in hand," muttered Sylvia.

"In these hard times, aren't people flocking to you seeking redemption?" Cain asked the minister.

"People seldom seek redemption," said the minister, "hard times or not. If things get rough, they look for a savior, they look for someone to blame, they look for some forgiving act of purification—but redemption? Aligning oneself with what's right regardless of the rest of the world? That's too lonely and abstract a battle for most souls."

"For want of a nail," said Cain.

"What are you talking about?" said Sylvia.

"All the forbidden topics," answered Cain.

"Steeltown," said the minister.

The maid placed a large tumbler of ice and amber liquid between Cain and the woman in black.

Sylvia gently seized the maid's wrist, held her there.

"Genie," whispered Sylvia, "I'm sorry I'm such a bitch. It's been an awful day, then all this too, I . . ."

"Don't worry about it, honey," said Genie. She patted Sylvia's hand. "We all get a little crazy when we come up here."

She pulled back so the butler could serve the soup; he was three stations away and the master of the house was leering at Beth Worby's breasts, so Genie risked leaning forward to whisper, "But it ain't such a bad idea for you to go easy on the booze."

Sylvia nodded.

Cain drank from the tumbler.

"Smooth," he said. "But I've had enough."

He set the glass between them; Sylvia shook her head.

"How's the crisis with your son?" asked Cain.

She snorted, shook her head.

"At least this school didn't have him arrested, too."

"What time is it?" whispered Danny.

"Twenty after," Frank whispered back. "Forty before."

"I've only done this part a couple times," said Danny. "And never with guys I didn't know. You know these guys?"

"I guess," said Frank. "At least one of them." He glanced at Danny, saw the young man lick his lips.

"I know them enough," said Frank.

"I ain't worried about any rough stuff," said Danny. "I mean, that's what my job is, right? Rough stuff. And I can handle it."

"There won't be any rough stuff. This is business."

"Yeah, but if there is, don't you worry about it, hear? I hold up my end. Everybody knows, Danny doesn't let you down. You just ask. They'll tell you."

"I know."

"Fuckin' A." Danny's lips set into a hard line. "Fuckin' A."

A car glided by on the highway. Its tail lights faded off to the left, toward the hills surrounding Steeltown.

"Where *did* you come from?" Sylvia Kimmett asked Cain after the entrée plates were cleared away. "Where are you going and how are you planning on getting there?"

"As you know," Cain told her, "when the commission was formed, the feeling was an outside investigator would be crucial to . . ."

She shook her head.

"Don't hand me the party line. I know my father-in-law. You're in *his* house."

Her eyes flicked toward the head of the table where the man she'd married sat. Cain saw her face cloud, then her lips pressed into a thin line. Her whisper was harsh.

"My husband doesn't need your game, whatever it is. He doesn't want it and he doesn't need it."

"My understanding is his work with the Chamber's development committee to facilitate the Japanese—"

"The Japanese," she interrupted. Shook her head. "Today's good deed to do. Move forward. Nothing undone. Nothing . . .

"Surprise me, Cain," she said suddenly. "Don't be like everybody else."

Her smile was lame: "*All* of us.

"Don't you do it to him, too," she said.

"Do what?"

"You know," she said. "You know."

"At least the Japanese aren't as horrendous as the last great failed idea to save Steeltown," interjected Reverend Borge, speaking more loudly than necessary.

"What was that?" asked Cain, turning toward Borge and away from Sylvia's glare; her trembling hand raised the scotch to her lips.

"A nuclear waste dump," said Borge. "They wanted to turn the Pit into a storage facility for radioactive waste.

"Imagine," said the minister. "The city always used to glow in the dark, with the mills and smelters and factories banging away in the night. They wanted us to glow again, only quietly, and forever. Life's fundamental poison power invisibly flickering out of the Pit. Wouldn't that have been something to see?"

"You know what will be something to see?" said Sylvia. She drank from the scotch tumbler. "Jackson Cain, in action. You know what I think?"

Cain shook his head.

"I think I better sign on for that show. I think it's one I don't dare miss." Her finger pointed at him. "I'll get a seat right behind you. Watch where you're going and what you're doing."

She trailed off, set her jaw.

"That's a promise, Cain," she said.

"No," came the murmur from the head of the table, "that's not necessary."

Cain checked his watch: 9:47.

"But it is." Professor Boswell held up his hand against

Kimmett's protests. The old man flushed, then paled. Boswell cleared his throat to gain the room's attention. Kimmett swallowed and forced a smile toward the man privileged to rise and speak.

"Excuse me, ladies and gentlemen," said Boswell. On the table, his wife's right hand curled around her linen napkin. The handsome son smiled encouragement. Beth Worby took mental transcription. The crowd fell silent. Cain saw everyone turn to watch Boswell except Sylvia. She faced the wall-length windows, her eyes vacant and far away.

"First," said Boswell, "I'd like to thank you for coming, and for all that you've done to get us here. Especially Mr. Kimmett, who graciously hosted this dinner so supporters, commission members, and staff could gather under one roof.

"We've all come here out of tragedy, for a common cause.

"I grew up here, though in the last few years I've begun to feel like I led the life of the blind, not seeing what was before me every day. Maybe not wanting to see it. Maybe not being able to. Maybe that's what Josh Hammond's murder will do for the town, make it face what we all know but ignore, make this city willing to be what it says it is, a place for people to live and work and be free. I have no illusions about this commission curing all the evils of the world, or of even this one hard-luck town. I became a lawyer because I thought I could serve justice, discovered lawyering was about using rules to get things for clients. I became a professor hoping to learn more and teach what I knew. Most of my students don't care what their lessons mean, as long as they get credit for having had them.

"I'd like to tell you justice will come out of what we do, but I can't. I can only promise you that I'll try, and that just maybe, we can make life in Steeltown a little fairer for everybody."

Boswell sat down.

The crowd applauded politely.

"It's time," said Frank.

"What!" Danny felt like he'd been shaken from a deep sleep, though his nerves had never been on a keener edge.

"Ten o'clock," said Frank. "A couple minutes to."

"Look!" hissed Danny.

A pair of headlights shown in the hills to their left. Danny and Frank watched the glow sail over the highway toward them, closer, closer.

"Do you think . . ."

"Shut up!" said Frank.

He wrapped his fingers around the door handle. Danny gripped the steering wheel with both hands.

The headlights slowed. The right turn blinker came on, and the car whipped into the rest stop.

"He's going too damn fast!" said Danny.

The car's brights were on. The machine skidded across the gravel until its grill was only five feet from the Thunderbird's hood.

A river of glaring yellow light engulfed the Thunderbird.

"Can't see!" swore Danny. He raised one hand against the glare of the car's high beams. Both front doors on the car swung open. Through his squint, Frank noticed no dome light came on in the machine.

"I don't like this!" he whispered.

Two more cars swooped in with their lights out until they turned off the highway, one from each direction. Frank saw brake lights flicker as the drivers made the turn, then they hit all their lights: their twin-beam headlights, spots mounted on their side, their whirling red cherries.

"It's a rip!" yelled Danny as a loudspeaker demanded *"Don't move!"*

"Sons o' bitches!" screamed Danny. He leaped from the car, stumbling on the gravel as he groped under his new suit.

"No!" yelled Frank. He dove out the passenger door, tried to burrow face down into the gravel.

Danny squeezed off a burst from the MAC-10 that danced a line of holes up the police cruiser's hood, punched out the windshield, and ripped three tunnels through the chest of the driver, State Trooper Gordon C. Dickinson, whose cheating wife loved him but couldn't help it and didn't want to hurt him or their daughter and would have stopped in a year and gotten over her guilt before menopause and never known he knew all along. Dickinson's partner and a DEA agent who'd bailed out of the first car plus a trooper from the cruiser to the Thunderbird's right returned Danny's fire. Danny crashed to the gravel as five .357 Magnum slugs drilled crimson holes through his brand new suit.

"Don't fuckin' breathe!" bellowed a man as he rammed a shotgun against the back of Frank's head, crushing his face into the gravel. Rocks ground into Frank's mouth. He didn't dare gag. Hands slapped along his body, his legs. Someone bent his arms behind his back. Handcuffs bit his wrists. They jerked him to his feet, bent him across the Thunderbird's hood and searched him again, throwing the stuff they found in his pockets on the T-bird's hood.

Frank saw two troopers lift one of their own from behind the wheel of the blasted cruiser, ease his bloody body into the second cruiser, and speed off through the night, sirens screaming, red lights spinning, as they raced toward the nearest hospital even though everyone knew it was too late. Red lights still spun on the roof of the shot-up cruiser, turning scattered glass beads from the shattered windshield into rubies. Headlights bathed the Thunderbird. Someone read him his rights in a shaky voice. Frank heard someone else yell, "Son of a bitch!" and a boot thunk into a body.

Frank couldn't help himself, yelled, "Who are you guys? We paid!"

They whirled him around and upright, slammed his butt against the T-Bird. A stocky man in a polyester suit and cowboy boots whose baby face now looked like Satan holstered a big revolver under his jacket. He tossed a plastic bag of torn twenty-dollar bills on the hood beside the matching wad from Frank's pocket.

"I'll tell you who the fuck we are, Franky!" growled Bill Wood. "We're your fuckin' doom, and you ain't begun to pay!"

Wood jabbed a meaty forefinger at the torn bills on the hood.

"They snitched out your friend Walter Mathews, too. We nailed him and his bucks hours ago."

He waved a search warrant in front of Frank's face.

"We don't even *need* this anymore, chump! We were going to nail you for possession with intent and you tossed us *death!*"

Wood pushed his face so close to Frank's their noses almost touched.

"Hey, Franky: kiss your life good-bye!"

Sylvia and Elliot Kimmett IV were careful not to be the last ones to leave.

"I'm sure working with you will be a pleasure," said the handsome man as he shook Cain's hand. The butler held the door open to the night.

Cain agreed. His watch said 10:27. Did the television in his room broadcast news at eleven?

"See you around," Sylvia told him. Her eyes were bright.

"That would be nice," said Cain.

"Do you want me to see about a room at the Commodore?" Beth Worby asked him as the golden couple left. Her cheeks were flushed from too much wine.

"Thank you," he told her. "That would be nice."

She nodded, stiffly shook his hand, and joined the departing parade.

Kimmett's contemporaries kept him trapped at the dining room table for another two minutes, then tarried saying their farewells to Cain. By the time he pushed them on their way, cajoling publisher Evans into giving Reverend Borge a ride home, all the nonpermanent staff had been dismissed. Cleanup would wait until tomorrow. Nelson joined him at the door to watch the taillights of the departing cars pass through the front gate.

"I'll lock up," said Nelson.

"Don't forget the dogs," Cain told him as he went inside.

With Judson holding one arm and the nurse who'd been waiting upstairs supporting the other, Kimmett shuffled toward the stairs. He'd never recovered from the pallor triggered by Boswell's speech, but he'd carried on, the genial host. As he walked now, his thin chest labored and his breaths came in rasps. But his green eyes burned bright; he smiled at Cain and said:

"All in all, a terribly *perfect* evening."

His Honor

"MAYOR NASH WILL SEE YOU NOW, Mr. Cain," said the matronly private secretary.

Cain took his time rising from the outer office's leather couch. Two other men waiting their turn glared at him enviously. The blond receptionist gave him a cheerleader's grin as the older woman led him through a door guarded by two human mountains in bulging suits.

"I'm sorry you had to wait so long," she said as they walked down a carpeted hall. From behind closed doors came the sounds of ringing telephones, mumbled voices. "Monday morning is terribly busy."

"Terribly," said Cain.

The windowless corridor wound through City Hall's fifth floor. They passed through an open area where secretaries stared at computer screens, their keyboards clicking like crickets. She led him around a corner. More closed office doors, with no signs or numbers fixed to their dark wood surfaces.

Noise ceased. The carpet absorbed their footsteps. The silence deepened with each step. The air smelled of marble and cement despite the luxurious wood paneling and royal maroon carpet.

At the end of the corridor waited a set of closed double doors. As they neared the doors, the silence magnified Cain's heartbeat. The corridor opened to another reception area. To his left, Cain saw an ornate secretarial desk—undoubtedly his escort's. To his right waited two more human mountains, one sitting in a chair tipped against the wall, the other behind a desk watching TV monitors.

"Hold still," said a man behind Cain.

Hands touched his back, and Cain automatically raised his arms. The man he hadn't seen patted him down.

"No metal detector wand?" said Cain when he turned around. The hands belonged to a gray-haired man in a rumpled two-piece suit who had a whiskey nose and chewed a toothpick.

"I'm an old-fashioned kind of guy," he said, the toothpick bobbing with his words.

"This is Mr. Carson, the mayor's special assistant," explained the secretary. Then she gestured toward the double doors. She waited until Cain grasped the gold handle, then stayed him with her touch.

"Enter softly," she instructed him. "His Honor is working. Sit in the chair beside his desk. No need to greet him. He knows you're here. He'll speak to you when it's time."

The ceiling in Mayor Nash's office curved to a dome twenty feet above the floor. Law books covered half the walls, maps and aerial photographs of the city filled the rest. The flags of Steeltown and the United States flanked curtained windows behind the oak desk. The mayor was working through a stack of papers, scanning each letter, report, or memo, initialing or signing it, sometimes scrawling a note before dropping the finished product in the out basket.

Mayor Richard Nash looked like an egg with a horseshoe of wispy gray hair and bushy eyebrows. His ears and nose were flat, his small mouth curved in a frown. His cheeks were wrinkled, and he had jowls. His gray suit, white shirt, and black tie came from a discount store.

The mayor ignored Cain when he entered. Cain paused, then crossed the thirty feet of empty floor to the chair beside His Honor's desk, sat, and watched the man work.

The stack of papers took another ten minutes. The last sheet was a list of names, brief notations, and phone numbers. Nash scanned it quickly, then picked up the telephone and dialed a number.

"Martha?" The mayor spoke into the receiver, his anemic blue eyes pointed toward the doors but focusing on nothing.

"Mayor Nash. You called the garbage department about trash in the alley . . . Un-huh . . . Behind the Denton place? . . . I've met the people who live there now: the Kiblers, right? . . . Remember when you knocked over those cans sneaking in after that Legion dance? . . . Oh yes I do. . . . How's the boy? . . . Un-huh. . . . Math better? . . . Fine. Tell him we're very proud. He keeps it up, we should have no trouble with West Point next year. . . . How's Mrs. Bailus down the street? . . . You tell her I want to know if she has more trouble with Medicare. Tell her daughter, too. . . . I know, I know. . . . Are you well? . . . Mother's fine, thank you very much. . . . You know me, Martha. . . . Don't worry about the garbage. I'll take care of it."

The Mayor had small, white hands. He pushed a button for another telephone line, poked the numbers for another call.

"Gorton? The mayor. Get a crew and a truck over to the alley behind the eight hundred block of Iron Avenue *now*. Get every damn bit of garbage behind Martha Frye's house, then clean the whole damn block. Put her place on the special list."

Without waiting for a reply, he punched another line on the phone, another number.

"Jules? . . . Mayor Nash. . . . Fine. Thank you. . . . You and a few boys want to make your old shed into a furniture repair place, right? . . . I remember the bar you made for the Elks Club. Fine piece of work. . . . Un-huh . . . I hope so too, we could use their plant. Talked with the zoning commission yet? . . . Un-huh, well, if you square it with their procedures, I'll see they don't dawdle. . . . No problem."

Another line punched, another number called.

"Mother? . . . Okay. . . . How are you? . . . Tell one of the deputies, and he'll be glad to take care of it. . . . Yes. . . . Martha Frye sends her best. . . . The man from that new commission is sitting right here. . . . Yes, I know. . . . Yes, he is. . . . I think so, too. . . . I'll tell him. . . . Good-bye, Mother."

The Mayor hung up the phone. He had almost no neck

between his starched white collar and his chin. As he turned to Cain, his face swung round as though it were part of an assembly line machine.

"Mr. Cain."

The mayor gave Cain his limp hand to shake.

"Your Honor," said Cain.

"Been wondering when you'd come by."

"You're my first official appointment."

"Of course. Courtesy call."

Cain shook his head. The mayor's frown deepened.

"I'm here on business," said Cain.

"As I understand my dear friend the governor's mandate, the commission is investigating a simple murder blocks from here."

"We've got a lot more on our plate than that."

"What does the commission want, Cain?"

"I haven't decided yet."

"You?" The mayor paused. "I see."

"But as long as we're talking about Hammond's murder, do you have any ideas?"

"No."

"Not a one?"

"I'm mayor. I deliver essential services to the people of my city. Ask the chief of police about killers and crime."

"Hammond did some stories on you, didn't he? On problems in City Hall."

"Once he wrote about the dog catcher."

"Other stories, too."

"Probably."

"And you knew him."

"I know most everyone here."

"Did you like what he wrote about you?"

"Do you have a point, Cain?"

"What do you think Hammond did to get himself killed?"

"Perhaps he made himself a pest. That's dangerous. For anyone."

"He probably just didn't know how to be a *real good pest*." Cain drew his last words out slow and easy. He smiled.

"Is that what you do, Cain?"

"I do my best," said Cain. He stood, looked down at the

mayor. "I do it well and I do it right. No need for me to spend any more time here today, is there?"

The mayor frowned.

"Don't worry: we'll see a lot of each other," said Cain.

"I doubt that very much," said Nash. "My subordinates handle matters such as your commission."

"Not anymore," said Cain. He walked away. When he reached the door, Cain turned back to the man perched behind the desk:

"My regards to Mom."

The Badge

"YOU'VE ARRESTED MY SON," the unshaven man in the rumpled suit told the uniformed sergeant behind the elevated booking desk. "I want to see the chief."

Cain halted when he heard those words from the man who'd preceded him through the police department's front doors. Police headquarters was a ten-story stone building around the corner from City Hall. Traditional twin globe lights flanked the front entrance and could be seen from the city square. To the right of the concrete stairs was a garage entrance presided over by a fat cop sitting in a folding chair, reading *The Sporting News* and smoking a cigar. Cain passed through its cloud as he entered the cop shop. The booking sergeant's elevated desk filled the wall to the door's left. A television camera mounted above a steel door with a bulletproof window scanned the room from the wall opposite the front entrance. A long wooden bench bolted to the wall faced the booking desk; Cain stood by it while he waited his turn. A whiff of cigar smoke singed the sour jailhouse scent of dried sweat and urine.

"Your son, huh?" said the desk sergeant. He had a face like a bulldog. "Who's that?"

"Pete Vandross. Peter."

"What did we get him for?"

"Over the phone, he said drugs."

"And Daddy's here to get him out and swear he's an angel done wrong by the bad old cops."

■ 87 ■

"My son's a rat's ass," said Mr. Vandross. "Him being guilty or innocent doesn't change that."

"Well," said the sergeant. "Ain't that something. Where's your lawyer the law lets you have?"

"I didn't come here to see a lawyer, I came to see the chief."

"You did, did you?" The sergeant smiled. "Well now, maybe you will and maybe you won't. First off, you better see the boys in narcotics. Siddown while I call upstairs."

Mr. Vandross glared at the sergeant, but stepped backward until his calves brushed the bench. He sank down, then slumped forward, elbows on his knees, forehead cupped in his hands. Cain took his place in front of the sergeant's desk.

"While you're on the phone, Sergeant," said Cain, "let the chief know Jackson Cain is here to see him."

"What's your problem, Bud?"

"It's Cain, Jackson Cain. Chief investigator for the Special Legislative Commission."

"Pardon me all to hell I'm sure," said the sergeant.

"Pardoning you is the governor's job," said Cain.

He walked to the bench, sat down.

The sergeant picked up his telephone.

"What can you do?" Vandross whispered, speaking to Cain only if he cared.

"Rough night?" asked Cain.

"Rough life."

"Your boy in trouble?"

"My boy *is* trouble," said Vandross. "Has been since the day he was born. Didn't matter: love, discipline, patience, anger . . . I worked harder and did more and didn't do so I'd be an honest example . . . Shrink went crazy over him, didn't do any good. His Mom plumb ran out of tears. She's dried up and hollowed out. Someday she'll crumple up and blow away. He hit her bad once. He's just smart enough never to try that again while I'm alive. His brother and sister are great and had to get that way on their own because we could barely get the time away from him to potty train them and sign their report cards. Middle kid and hell, he's the middle of everything. Like a cancer.

"What can you do?" he asked again.

"I don't know," said Cain.

"Sometimes . . . Sometimes I can't believe he's my seed. Or that the nurses didn't accidentally switch babies when we weren't looking.

"Had a dog when I was a kid," said Vandross, a bad smile on his face. "Dog turned nasty and mean. We knew we had to have it put down and my dad, hell of a man, he wanted to take it to the vet but I said no, it was my dog and my job. So we drove out west of town, down into one of the old mine cuts, dug a hole, pegged the dog down tight. I had my twenty-two rabbit gun I got for my twelfth birthday, put the barrel up close to his head and . . .

"What can you *do?* He's my *son!*"

"Forget him and start over," said Cain.

"He's seventeen," said Vandross. "And that makes him mine."

"Hey, you!" yelled the sergeant. "Vandross! Go through there!" The sergeant pointed to the steel door. "Take the elevator to the fourth floor. Ask for Detective Johansen. He's been expecting you."

"What about the chief?" asked Vandross.

"Talk to Johansen. He'll see what he can work out. And you, Cain: Ride with him, but you go up to the ninth floor."

The sergeant buzzed them through. The elevator was cold and shook. Vandross moved forward when it shuddered to a stop on four. The doors slid open and he stepped out.

"Good luck," said Cain.

"Too late," he replied.

The doors slid shut.

When they opened again, Cain stepped out to face a glass-walled office full of men in shirt-sleeves and ties who sat at littered institutional gray desks, guns on their hips. He felt their eyes swivel to him, like snakes in a glass bowl. The black letters on the door read OFFICE OF THE CHIEF and, below that, SPECIAL DETECTIVES SQUAD. Through the glass, Cain heard phones ringing, typewriters, the men mumbling to each other. He opened the door.

"You Cain?" said the detective closest to the door.

"Yes."

"Come on. Chief's waiting."

He led Cain through the maze of desks, past all the hard eyes who undressed the stranger, weighed his meat, and proclaimed it not so much. Cain's escort knocked on the smoked glass door labeled CHIEF.

"Yeah!" bellowed a voice from inside that room.

"I got the Cain guy!"

"Well so bring him in, bring him in!"

"After you," said the detective, jerking his thumb toward the opening office door.

Chief DiCarlo's office had gray walls, no windows, an institutional steel desk with three scarred wooden captain's chairs scattered in front of it, a dozen pictures on the wall of the chief shaking hands along with a few wanted posters and a cheap fishing print. Cain assumed it once served as an interrogation chamber. He breathed deep, and imagined he could smell fear and dried blood instead of pepperoni and sausage, beer and heavy spices. Two large detectives in shirt-sleeves had obviously stood when they heard the knock; they leaned against the walls as Cain walked to meet the man behind the desk.

"Hey, how you doing?" DiCarlo called out to Cain. "Have a chair, have a sandwich, we were just catching an early lunch. We can bring you a beer, you want? Swenson, get him a beer. Take one of the kielbasas, only place in the whole country that makes them as good as Baltimore."

Police Chief Harry DiCarlo filled an extra-large executive chair behind the standard policeman's desk. Cain figured he'd stand three inches over six feet. His suit coat was draped over the back of the chair. The collar on his blue shirt was open, held against his thick neck by the loose tie. The shirt's custom cut couldn't hide porcine slabs of muscle and fat on his shoulders and chest. His gut was massive. His biceps seemed the size of Cain's thighs, and his forearms and hands were proportionately huge. A diamond pinkie ring adorned his thick fingers. He'd had to order extra links for his gold Rolex watch.

DiCarlo's face was like a pink pumpkin, with a wide grin and squinty, bright blue eyes. A sweat sheen covered his high forehead, and his close-cropped gray hair was matted.

"Sit down, sit down," DiCarlo urged as Cain complied. "Make yourself at home. Welcome to town and all that. You want a sandwich, right? And a beer?"

"No thanks," said Cain. He lied: "I already ate."

"Too bad." DiCarlo's hand swept over the chewed remnants of sandwiches on greasy wax paper. "This is great stuff. The best."

"Some other time."

The two men stared at each other. Behind Cain, one of the detectives coughed.

"So," said DiCarlo, "how you doing?"

"Been busy," said Cain. "Just came from seeing the mayor."

"Oh."

"Not an overly friendly guy."

One of the detectives behind Cain laughed. DiCarlo snorted, said, "Well, His Honor's never exactly been one of the boys."

"So I figured. Not like you, huh, Chief?"

DiCarlo frowned.

"We *are* the boys, Jack."

"I like a team," said Cain. "Yes, I do."

"Whose are you on?"

"Right now, I've got this commission gig," said Cain. He shrugged. "And a job in New York."

"So I understand."

"You were a company man yourself, weren't you, Chief?"

"Only we called it *the Bureau*," said DiCarlo. "The Company were the fools across the Potomac."

Cain chuckled and DiCarlo smiled.

"What brought you to see me?" DiCarlo asked.

"I figure we got a lot in common," Cain told him.

"Like what?"

"We both have the job of chasing Hammond's murderer."

"Oh. That."

"Yes, that. And maybe we got something more in common, too."

"Like what?"

"We'll know when we get to know each other better."

"You plan on sticking around here?"

"Hell, I got a job to do."

"Ain't no trouble finding a killer in Steeltown," said one of the detectives. "We got a lot of people that could fit that bill."

Cain kept his eyes on the chief as he answered the detective behind him.

"Maybe so," said Cain. "Maybe for anybody but this Hammond character. Whoever gets hung with his killing has to be big enough to satisfy everybody. Big enough to justify all this commotion. Maybe that means hanging a lot more than murder on his shoulders, maybe that means hanging a lot more than one trigger-happy schnook."

"That what you're thinking?" asked the police chief.

"That's what I'm thinking."

"Who do you think did it?"

"I don't know," said Cain. "You tell me."

"I have a squad of detectives working on it."

"What have they come up with?"

"Well now, *Jack,*" said DiCarlo. "That's an ongoing investigation. You're a bureaucrat for a temporary political band. I sure can't justify releasing any confidential information to non-law enforcement personnel without a court order."

Cain reached inside his suit pocket, flicked his hand, and a heavy gold badge landed on the chief's desk.

"State trooper," said Cain. "Sergeant, no less. Courtesy of the governor. And my commission has subpoena powers."

"They give you some steel to go with that shiny piece of tin?" said DiCarlo.

"Guns aren't my favorite thing," said Cain, shaking his head.

"But you like the badge, don't you?" said the chief.

Cain shrugged.

"Well now, *Sergeant* Jack," said the chief. "That kind of makes us comrades in arms, doesn't it?"

"It just might, Chief. Now how about Hammond's case jacket?"

"It's in the field. With the investigating officers. Soon as they come in, soon as I get a chance to review it, I'll let you know."

"Sounds fair," said Cain. He put his gold badge back in his pocket. "I figure that's about noon tomorrow, right, Chief?"

"You can call."

"I will." Cain smiled, nodded to the big man. "And I bet you'll be here. I bet you and I won't have any problems between us. We're going to get along swell. That's what I bet."

"You sound like you know what a badge is for."

"Let's say I'm familiar with the apparatus."

They all laughed.

"You guys been having a lot of problems lately, though."

"What do you mean?" asked the chief.

"Well, there's Hammond. Then there's that mess last night when the trooper and coke dealer got killed."

"That happened over the county line. That's not even the sheriff's turf."

"According to the newspaper," said Cain, "the busted fish were Steeltown boys. Odds are, whatever put them out there came from here."

"We don't know anything about that," said the chief.

"*That* would make me nervous," said Cain.

"You're a more excitable guy than me," said the chief.

"Cautious," said Cain. "The kind of guy who likes tidy towns and tidy packages and knows how to make money getting them that way."

"Is that what you're interested in?" said the chief. "Making money?"

"We all gotta eat," said Cain. He leaned back in his chair.

"Speaking of excitable guys," he continued, "I met one downstairs. Fellow name of Vandross. His son threw his ass in the ringer."

"Drug bust, Chief," said a detective. "Clean and righteous. PCP, none of our . . . none of our regular crooks. Some whiz kid with a garbage can."

"You remember Vandross, Chief," said the other detective.

"Oh, yeah!" said DiCarlo. "He was in my office once before. Stolen car. Come to find out, we didn't really have the goods on the kid after all."

"Yeah," said a detective. "Come to find out."

"Sad guy," said Cain. "Good man."

"Drowning in shit if you ask me," said a detective. "He'd pay us to lose the kid in the state pen or worse, but his old lady, she's still got hope and the hubby don't want to turn out her light."

"Seems a shame," Cain continued. "That poor father is jacked out of shape and we all know there's more to come. He can't have many bucks left to bail his kid, buy a lawyer. Whatever. Kid's a creep, but he's a juvie, and the most you can stick him for is what?"

"We can put him upstate in detention for a year," said a detective. "That's worth something."

"Yeah, but to who?" said Cain, world weary. "The kid will do a year in juvie and love it, even if he's somebody's punk. When he walks, he'll be so schooled that next time he'll give you guys real trouble. This trip will probably bust the old man, kill the old lady. Leave a lot of bad feelings. Being unpopular doesn't help you run your streets. We all know that. Besides, he's seventeen. Next time he might be a year older, and then his ass will truly belong to you."

"I don't get it," said the chief. "What do you care about this kid or his old man?"

"I don't," said Cain. "But I got a badge, and a job to clean up this town. This is one more drug bust on the record. I don't want to have to go looking at any more records than necessary."

Cain shrugged. "But I don't give a damn. Suit yourself."

"What the hell, Jack," said the chief finally. "Who knows what can happen? Life's full of weird justice. Maybe this kid will get lucky and we'll discover we forgot to Mirandize him. Hell, maybe the lab will screw up. Maybe he'll skate just because nobody cares. Hard to tell."

"And maybe it might just be one of those free rides," said Cain. "Not for him, but for his old man."

The chief laughed:

"Hey, Jack! This is Steeltown. Anything can happen."

A Place
Not to Hide

CAIN WALKED ACROSS THE CITY square to a stone building named after a dead mining czar. A photocopying business filled the first floor. Lawyers, accountants, and small businesses rented the top seven floors. He rode the old cage elevator to the third floor, had trouble opening the grill, then walked down the hall reading numbers and signs on the office doors' clouded glass.

A workmen in white bib overalls painted black letters on the glass of door 327. He leaned back to admire his barely begun work and Cain stepped around him, opened the door.

"Hey!" yelled the workman.

"You're doing fine," said Cain as he stepped inside.

He entered an empty white-walled office with windows overlooking the town square, open doors leading to other unadorned rooms. The paint smelled fresh.

"We're going to need air conditioners, too," Beth Worby explained to two anxious men in work clothes as the three of them stood in the middle of the room. Her eyes criticized Cain's entrance. "One for each room. They shouldn't get in the way of the file cabinets against the wall, do you think?"

"No, ma'am," said one of the workmen.

A thick black cord snaked out of the gray-tiled floor, coiled a few loops, then connected to a multibuttoned black telephone unit by Cain's feet. In the room to his right, he saw a similar phone system; its black, curlicued receiver

■ 95 ■

cord stretched diagonally across the doorway from the floor to somewhere Cain couldn't see. From that room came the disembodied voice of former professor Boswell:

"... does that mean? ... I realize the commission formed on short notice, but when you agreed to serve on it ... I understand. ... No, some of the others are having difficulty too. ..."

"Start with the desks," Beth told the two men, "then the file cabinets. Try to keep them in the placement we discussed, but if you can't, just get them up and in."

"Yes, ma'am," said the first workman.

"Ah, ma'am?" said his co-worker.

"Please: Ms. Worby."

"What are you suggesting?" said Boswell's voice.

"Miss Worby, thanks for hiring us."

"Yes," said the other workman.

Beth flushed. "I ... That ... sure."

"You know, honestly, Miss Worby, we could do with at least two other guys for all that moving—or it will take us a hell of a lot longer and you said you wanted it done quick as possible."

"You're right," she said. "Know anybody we could hire?"

The two workmen looked at each other.

"... That's, well, that seems to be turning out as the best possibility," said Boswell.

"The town is full of good men, Miss Worby."

"Okay," she said. "Use your judgment. Hire—What? Two more?"

"Okay."

"No, I mean, are two enough?"

"We'll try to make do with two, ma'am. Save you some money."

"Don't worry about that," she said. "Not as long as it's well spent and we get this done as quickly as possible."

"Look," said Boswell, "I appreciate your problems."

The two workmen mumbled their agreement, hurried from the office, leaving Beth Worby and Cain staring at each other.

"All right," said Boswell. "I'll call them and check it out

and if that works for them, I'll set up a conference call for as many of us as I can loop together."

"Nice of you to show up," Beth told Cain. Her words formed like ice crystals. She wore a brown business suit over a white blouse. Her russet hair was in a bun.

"Let's get some lunch," Cain told her.

"It's a little early for that, isn't it?" she said.

He glanced at his watch as Boswell said, "Okay, when?"

"The big hand's on eight and the little hand's on twelve," said Cain. "Just about right."

"For a Monday morning," said Beth. "For the first day of work. Where have you been?"

"Come on," he said, "I'll buy."

"I've been here since eight," she said. "Hiring workmen, planning office space, making sure the phone worked, drawing up lists . . . I'm an attorney, not—"

"Even lawyers need to eat," said Cain. He stepped into the room where Boswell talked on the telephone. The professor had his sports coat heaped on the floor, his tie loosened. He paced back and forth, a yellow pad and a pen clutched in one hand, the receiver held against his ear by the other.

"We'll be back in a while," Cain whispered to him.

Boswell nodded, intent on his conversation.

"And we'll bring you something to eat," Cain said.

Boswell paid him no attention, told the person he was talking to, "I'm afraid that might not be acceptable."

Cain went back to what would become the reception room, smiled at Beth. "You ready?"

She glared at him, but when he walked to the door, she followed.

They said nothing of consequence as Cain led her across Steeltown's city square to a carryout cafe. He ordered coffees and three of the kielbasa sandwiches he'd declined at police headquarters.

"They're great," he said. "You'll love them."

The midday sun warmed the square. He led her to a bench at the far end, one with its back to the river and facing City Hall. There were no trees. Half a dozen pigeons congregated at their feet; a sparrow joined them, but the pigeons quickly drove it away.

"Never trust the office," he told her as she took a sandwich from him.

Her frown softened into puzzlement, then perception. She unwrapped the spicy sausage in a soft roll. They'd put mustard on it.

"Especially never trust the office phones," he continued. "Or the phones in your hotel room. Any phones, for that matter. Not unless you have no other choice."

"Aren't you being a little paranoid?" she said.

"I spent the morning in the mayor's office, shmoozing with the chief of police," said Cain. "I've been those places before and I know this kind of town. Here, paranoia is stamped on your passport."

"What ..." she shook her head, began again as Cain took a bite of his sandwich. "Why did you go there?"

Cain stared at her as he chewed.

"Okay," she said, blushing. "Okay, I'm not stupid, but do you think they know something about Hammond's murder?"

"You know they run this town?" he said.

She took a bite and nodded.

"Then you know this is about a lot more than Hammond."

"What are we doing here, Jack?" she whispered.

A man with sandy hair, black metal glasses, and a tan suede windbreaker crossed the square from the drugstore to a Christian Science Reading Room. The banner welcoming the Hiroshima Auto Works flapped in the breeze.

"Lunch," Cain told her.

"Oh," she said, sighed, then shook her head. *"Yale!"*

Cain laughed.

She joined him. They swallowed coffee from the white Styrofoam cups. A man carrying a briefcase slowly climbed City Hall's steps.

"Where did you ..." she started, then began again: "Did you go to school? I mean, college?"

He laughed again, shook his head.

"Oh, I went to school," he said, laughed again. "Even had a year of college.

"Not Yale," he added.

"Oh," she said. "What do you call home?"

From the corner of the square to their left walked a man wearing an unnecessary raincoat. He headed diagonally across downtown's open zone toward an office supply store, his hands in the raincoat pockets, the coat unbuttoned.

"Home is where you don't need to hide," said Cain. "What do you call it?"

She smiled, shook her head and thought a moment before she said, "Home is where you're wanted."

"I've been wanted a few places," Cain told her.

They both laughed.

"I'm from Wisconsin," she said.

"Small town girl made good?"

"Well," she said, "I'm here."

"What else can you expect?" he asked.

Again, she smiled, shook her head. They finished their coffee, carried a sandwich and a sealed cup back to their office. They saw no one they knew on the way.

What You Know

"THERE YOU ARE," SAID Sylvia Kimmett as Cain and Beth entered the commission's suite, laughing.

They fell silent.

"Hi," said Russell Boswell, who stood next to Sylvia in the middle of the empty front office. "Do you all know each other?"

"We met last night," said Beth.

"Sylvia is coming to work for the commission," said Boswell. "She'll manage the office, which will free you two for substantive work."

"A dollar-a-year volunteer," added Sylvia. She wore a fawn-colored blouse, tan pleated slacks, low-heeled shoes. "We wouldn't want anybody to think this commission was a Kimmett family trough."

"Such a bargain," muttered Beth.

"I've got to go," said Cain. He put the paper sack with Boswell's sandwich and coffee on the floor.

"Me, too," said Sylvia. "There are a few things I need to get straight before I start tomorrow morning. Nine o'clock okay?"

"Sure," said Boswell.

"I'll be here," said Beth.

"Russ told me you've done a great job setting the place up," Sylvia told Beth. "Anything that can wait, why not leave for me to handle?"

The two women smiled at each other.

"Care to walk me to my car, Mr. Cain?" said Sylvia. She headed toward the door, not looking back to see if he followed.

With a smile and a shrug to Beth and Boswell, Cain did.

Sylvia Kimmett took long strides with a quick rhythm. Cain walked half a pace slower, sometimes seeing her face in profile, her ash blond hair curling along her smooth chin line; sometimes watching her square shoulders, the sway of her narrow hips.

They didn't speak in the hall, kept their silence as the caged elevator dropped them down to the main floor. She led the way through the revolving lobby doors without a word.

"You don't waste time, do you?" he said as they crossed the square.

"Who has time to waste, Mister Cain?" she said.

"You don't need to call me mister," he said.

"You're right," she said as they reached the sidewalk.

"What does your husband think of you joining our merry band?"

"Aren't you more concerned about my father-in-law's opinion?"

"You father-in-law isn't on the commission."

She shook her head. They stopped where an American sedan waited at an expired parking meter. She unlocked the car door, then turned and faced him.

"My husband is pleased that I take an interest in his work."

"Yeah," said Cain, "but does he know what you're doing?"

"Do you, *Cain*?" she said. She opened the car door and slid behind the wheel.

He shut her door for her. She started the engine, brushed her hair away from her eyes, and drove off.

Cain dropped quarters into a gas station pay phone.

"Yeah?" said the man who answered his call.

"Do you have Peterzell on ice?"

"We've got a dead trooper on ice. Peterzell is on the execution line."

"And?"

"And his attorney-of-record came to see me. A Steeltown wizard who spent the midnight hour not pulling rabbits out of his hat for me and the U.S. attorney. Wanted bail, wanted a plea."

"What did he get?"

"The wall. He didn't want his client to give. 'Fact, he was more concerned about his client not talking than anything else."

"Whose lawyer was he?"

Wood laughed.

"That's what I asked Peterzell," said Wood. "He decided he should get a second legal opinion. You ever try to find a lawyer at dawn who'll come down to the jail to work quietly and for free?"

"Don't make me pull it out of you," said Cain. "We don't have much time."

"It took Peterzell and his legal aid lawyer about ten seconds to decide that Franky should buy his way off killer's row."

"You held up our deal?"

"Everyone believes Walter Mathews is in protective federal custody."

"What did Peterzell give up?"

"Names, places, and dates, most of which are only leads or confirmations of what we already guessed."

"Who and what?"

"I tell you, and you tell who?"

"Come on, Wood. Why would I set this up as a double-deal?"

"How many reasons do you want, Mr. Drop-A-Dime?"

"It's a two-fifty toll call from here," said Cain, "and I'm out of quarters. You've got to trust me, just like I need to trust you."

"So far," said Wood, "he's only given us enough legally sustainable knowledge for warrants on a stash house and a guy named Wolinsky—who, as you know, is a pal of Johnny Maxx."

"What are you going to do?"

"Take 'em off."

"You're two, two and a half hours away," said Cain. "I figure the first lawyer has realized he's lost and put the word out."

"Yeah, well, tiptoeing around to get warrants from a federal judge because you can't trust the locals in the target zone takes time. Besides, I've been waiting for a call from an anonymous friend."

"Just in case I need to cover my ass, right?"

"Do you?"

"Don't worry about me. Are you telling DiCarlo or the sheriff you're throwing a party in their town?"

"About ten seconds before we kick in the front door. Multiagency cooperation is a keystone of effective law enforcement."

They laughed.

"Will I see you there?" asked Wood.

"Talk to you soon," said Cain, and he hung up.

The security guard at the newspaper building's main doors waved Cain toward the elevator.

"Newsroom's on the second floor," he said. "So are all the rest of you guys."

Thick glass doors separated The *Steeltown Tribune*'s newsroom from the rest of the world. On the other side of their gilt-lettered surface, Cain saw a long room with rows of desks and VDTs. Fluorescent lights hung from the high ceiling. Plastic green partitions made semiprivate offices toward the rear of the room.

Reporters worked at only two desks. A dozen men and women who obviously belonged in the room stood to Cain's right, watching two television crews and a cluster of visitors standing by the switchboard. Evans, the paper's publisher, stood with the visitors.

One TV crew—cameraman, a male lighting and sound technician, a male reporter, and a female producer—surrounded one of the desks. Unlike the other desks, this workplace was free of paper, books, pencils, and pads—free of everything, a scarred metal surface without even a desk pad. The VDT screen next to the desk was blank.

The TV reporter muttered something to the cameraman, who then said something to the producer. She spoke to the *Tribune* reporters huddled against the wall, then shrugged and moved papers, a notebook, three phone books, and a sheet of wire service copy to the empty desk top. She rearranged them several times, exchanged the swivel chair barely visible behind the desk for one with a taller back, then nodded to her on-camera personality and stepped off-camera as he positioned himself in front of the desk. Klieg lights brightened the scene. A red light on the camera glowed. The TV reporter started his spiel. Cain entered the newsroom.

"... of Joshua Hammond," the TV journalist solemnly intoned. He held a microphone; his eyes were focused into the camera, yet could still scan a stack of cue cards held by the producer.

"Hammond was the star investigative reporter for the *Steeltown Tribune* who was brutally gunned down by person or persons unknown. The hunt for Hammond's killer is the focus of intense law enforcement activity here in this industrial city, and has attracted international attention. As with the Bolles case in Arizona more than a decade ago, America's press corpse has—"

"*Cut!*" yelled the woman producer.

The crowd groaned.

"It's *corps*," the producer told her chagrined colleague, "not *corpse*."

"Yeah!" yelled a man standing with the *Tribune* reporters.

"What star?" muttered a woman standing next to him. She shook her head, walked across the newsroom and out a side door.

"Hurry up!" yelled the cameraman for the second TV crew. "We've got to get our tape on the plane, too!"

"Could somebody open the wire room door?" yelled the first crew's sound technician. He wore earphones. "The teletype chatter is too faint."

One of the newspaper's employees complied with the request.

The TV reporter cleared his throat, got the nod from his producer, and began again as Cain leaned against a file cabinet. The publisher turned his eyes away from the film-

ing and noticed Cain. Cain discreetly shook his head, and
Evans looked back at what the world would see.

"Behind me is the desk of Joshua Hammond," the TV
journalist said again. "Hammond was the star investigative
reporter . . ."

The TV crew finished without another mistake. They
gathered their equipment, scurried from the newsroom as
the second crew returned the desk to reality, shot their
story, then quickly left. *Tribune* reporters shuffled back to
their desks, while a half dozen reporters for other newspapers
bombarded Evans with questions. He held up his hands,
said, "That's all I've got, I've already told you!" and retreated to a glass-walled office. He shut the door behind
him. The out-of-town journalists probed each other with
veiled questions, parried the same with noncommittal mum-
bles, then drifted from the newsroom, eyes on each other.

Except for one, a stoop-shouldered man with thinning
curly brown hair who wore a terrible suit and a hangdog
expression that brightened when he noticed Cain. Cain noted
the man's attention and quickly turned away. He casually
walked to the publisher's office, knocked on the glass door,
and stepped inside.

"My God, Cain!" said Evans as his visitor sat across the
desk from him. "Do you realize what's going on?"

Cain shrugged; before he could speak, the publisher
said, "Do you know who I talked to today?"

"No."

"Everybody! Those camera crews are from the networks.
Reporters from Los Angeles and Washington and Chicago.
Sidney Hershfeld called! Two Pulitzer Prizes and he calls
me!"

"Is he in town?"

"No, he's working on some book and a South American
story and he's not sure if he can squeeze us in because the
Times wants the series right away and has already sent a
guy here but for Christsakes: he called!"

"Yeah," said Cain, "he's a good reporter."

"Good?" exclaimed the publisher. "He's famous! The
best!"

Cain glanced into the newsroom through the publisher's

walls. The stoop-shouldered journalist was nowhere to be seen.

"You know who else?" whispered Evans.

Cain shook his head.

"I got a call from a producer of *This Week's Hour!* There's a chance, if they do a story, they'll need to interview me. Imagine: me on TV with *James Bradson!*"

"What about Hammond?" asked Cain.

"Huh? Oh, ah . . . I . . . Ah, what do you mean?"

"What are all the reporters asking? Did you learn anything new from them? You haven't mentioned me or how we're working together with the commission, have you?"

"No! Of course not! I . . . They have all the usual questions: what kind of guy he was, what—"

"What kind of guy was he?"

"Well, I . . . This isn't what I told them, of course . . ."

"Of course."

"I mean, he was a reporter for us, and there's a certain image we must maintain."

"Un-huh."

"He . . . well, he was smart enough, I guess. Ambitious. Cocky. Even though he pushed too hard for stories, he knew when to back off and not make a fool of himself. He knew our policies. When he quarreled with them, I wasn't always sure why."

"What do you mean?"

"Well . . . he was awfully ambitious. And obnoxious."

"Was he a good reporter?"

"His stories were well written."

"You've got editors to help with that. How about his facts?"

"He made the normal number of errors."

"Was he tough? Did he get good dirt and make it stick when he threw it on the front page?"

"We're not that kind of newspaper," said Evans. "We're a family paper in a fine city. We don't go in for cheap sensationalism."

"Un-huh," said Cain. "But did Hammond?"

"If he published an exciting story, he'd enter it in a contest."

"But nothing too ..."

"He didn't ... No. I mean, he was no Sidney Hershfeld."

"Now he's a martyr who'll be cast as one."

"Well ... you've got to respect the dead."

"I want copies of all his stories," said Cain.

"So do all the reporters," answered Evans. "I had to forbid them access to our computer morgue. I'm having all Hammond's stories duplicated so we can distribute them fairly."

"Hold off on that," said Cain. "Get me the first set and stall them until I tell you."

"But we're the press, with a First Amendment right to ..."

"This is a commission request," said Cain. "You don't want to deny an official request that might help catch a murderer, do you?"

"No, no, it's just that ..."

"Don't worry," said Cain. "They'll never know so they'll never mind. By the way, what happened to Hammond's desk?"

"A few hours after his body was found the police came in and took everything from it: scrap paper, phone books, Rolodex, notebooks, emptied his garbage can, cigarette butts and his ashtray, his coffee mug.... They took dozens of pictures of his desk and work area, then scooped everything into black trash bags and carried it out."

"City cops or sheriff's?"

"City officers, though sheriff's deputies showed up later. There wasn't much for them to do here, though, and they left angry. All the cops want copies of his stories too."

"I'll bet. Hold out on them too."

"But ..."

"It's okay," said Cain. "I've already talked to Chief DiCarlo."

"If you're sure."

"I'm sure. Did they have a warrant?"

"What?"

"A search warrant."

"Why ... No. I mean, it's always our policy to cooperate with the authorities."

"Lucky for me, right?" said Cain. He smiled. "Remember: no need to mention me in any of your stories or interviews. I'm nobody. They should all quote Russell Boswell."

"Of course," said Evans. "Whatever you say."

The stoop-shouldered reporter caught Cain as he walked out the newsroom doors.

"I know you," said the reporter.

"We've never met," said Cain. He punched the elevator button.

"Yeah, I know," said the reporter. "I'm Howie Cohn. I work for the Philadelphia *Eagle*."

"Good paper," said Cain. The elevator still hadn't come. "And you're . . ."

Sooner or later, thought Cain. Had to happen.

"My name is Jackson Cain."

"You're a friend of Sid Hershfeld's from Washington."

"What makes you say that?"

"I met him at a reporters' conference in eighty-five. I cover D.C. for my paper and one night about—three months ago, wasn't it?—I saw the two of you at some dingy bar in the Adams Morgan neighborhood, waving arms and yelling."

The elevator doors slid open.

"You know Sid," said Cain as they stepped inside the elevator. He pushed the lobby button. "He gets excited over everything."

"Yeah," said Howie Cohn. "What was he excited about then?"

Cain smiled, looked at the man from Philadelphia. They were about the same age. Cohn wore a wedding ring.

"You ever talk to Sid about women and sex?"

"Ah . . . no," said Cohn.

"Believe me," Cain told him. "It's an experience."

They laughed. The elevator stopped its descent.

"What are you doing here?" asked Cohn.

The doors slid open.

"You mean you don't know?" asked Cain.

"No."

They walked outside.

"I just got hired by the special commission," said Cain. "One of their investigators."

"Is that what you did in Washington?" asked Cohn. He glanced over his shoulder as they walked down the street, saw no one he knew.

"Not like this," said Cain. "I work for a big firm. They got the contract to do this, sent me."

"What firm?"

Cain told him; the reporter could find it on the record.

"I think I've heard of you guys," said Cohn, and Cain guessed he hadn't

"Subcontracting us was faster than going through their state civil service," Cain explained.

"I'll bet." The reporter shook his head. "Bureaucracies."

"Yeah."

"Hard to find your way through them," began Cohn.

"So you wouldn't mind me helping you out on this story, right?" said Cain.

They both laughed.

"How about it?"

"Only if it's totally deep background, no ID to me. And keep me out of the headlines, okay? I'll need a job after this one."

"If I can," said Cohn. He couldn't contain his glee. "Who shot Hammond? Mob? girlfriend? What story was he working?"

"That's what I want to know. If I find anything I can pass along, I will. But right now, I only know this is a hot town."

"What do you mean?"

"You hear about that drug bust just over the county line?"

"Hammond tied into that?"

"I don't know. But I hear it's just the start."

"Start of what? And where can I learn more? The police?"

"Hah!" Cain shook his head. "Watch yourself with them."

"What about the drug bust?"

"I heard the guy to talk to is named Wood, DEA out of the state capital. Don't mention my name, but tell him you know there's a major drug and corruption ring coming apart in Steeltown. Maybe he'll give you background, if nothing else. Since I'm telling you that now, he'd be a second source and you could go with it."

"With what?"

"What you got is better than the rest of the pack."

"And we can keep it that way, right?"

"I can't promise to stay exclusive, but I don't need to be aggressive about talking either. I'd rather be low profile. Maybe you could help us both by nudging your colleagues away from me."

"I'm not their boss."

"Yeah, but they follow the prevailing current. If you're getting good stories, watch what you print and what you say . . ."

"This business," said Howie Cohn. He shook his head. "It stinks, you know?"

"I know."

"What story was Hershfeld working on when I saw you guys? I heard he's got some great South American stuff."

"If that's so, maybe he won't even make it to print."

"Tell me about it," said the reporter from Philadelphia. "It's not what you know, it's what you can prove."

Out of
the Shadows

"WHAT DO YOU WANT?" said the man in grease-stained overalls as he walked out of the shadows, his words resonating
in the dim cavern.

"Just looking around," said Cain.

"You lose your car?" said the man. He wiped his hands
on an oily rag, glanced at the vacant slots and silent auto-
mobiles scattered through the underground garage. "You
got a ticket?"

Cain opened his hand and the attendant saw the badge.

"Oh," said the attendant. He nodded to the left. "Back
there, one level down, third slot from the pillar. Number
sixty-two B."

He wiped his hands on the cloth again, walked away.

Fluorescent lights cut the darkness. Yellow lines di-
vided the concrete floor into numbered parking slots, most
of which were vacant. Slot 62B was one of four empty zones
between two cement pillars. An irregular dark stain just
inside 62B's yellow border marred the gray floor. The stain
was the size of a man's shirt and looked like a Rorschach
blot.

"You need something else?" said the attendant when
Cain stepped into the cashier's booth on level A ten minutes
later. The attendant took his eyes off the quiz show he'd
been watching on the black-and-white television; the TV
volume was off.

"Whose spot is . . ." began Cain.

"Sixty-two B is an open slot," finished the attendant. "All the slots down there are. The monthly renters are all up on the A level."

"So . . ."

"I figure Hammond drove down there, parked in sixty-three B at random, got out of his car, and *Blammo!*"

"That's where they found his car? The next slot over?"

"Hell," said the attendant, "how many times I got to tell you guys this?" His voice held no anger; indeed, Cain thought he enjoyed the attention. "Which are you? City cops or county?"

"State," said Cain. "Double-checking. Anybody see anything?"

"Wasn't nobody here to see nothing," said the man. He nodded to the crossbar. "While back, management decided it was a waste to pay an attendant to sit here and watch how few cars use the place, so they installed that thing. You drop fifty cents in the slot or the tokens the monthly customers get, the crossbar raises, and in you go. The only reason I'm here now is to keep curiosity seekers and reporters and *public officials* from messing the place up."

"Who found the body? It was late for anybody to be here."

"Ten-thirty didn't use to be late downtown. A guy who janitors one of the buildings across the street, 's crazy about his Caddy and don't want it scratched or moon burned, so he parks it here while he works. He walked down to get it and got the thrill."

"Anybody live in this building?"

"Nah. And only about half the offices are rented."

"Anything in the building open that hour of the night?"

The man shook his head. "Ain't no reason for him to have been here. You wanna know what I figure?"

Cain surprised him and said, "Sure."

"Well," said the man with a grin; he wiped his oily hands across his chest to prolong his moment. "I figure Hammond was just a guy in the wrong place at the wrong time."

Cain hailed a taxi outside the underground garage. He made sure the cabby was not the one who'd ferried him from the airport. Even with Cain's new short haircut, that first cabby might remember him. But Cain decided even if the cabby remembered his face, he would want to forget the ride; he'd tell no one.

His watch said five o'clock: rush hour. His cab drifted easily through the streets. Two men with briefcases chatted as they walked toward the town square. A fiftyish woman with stiffly spun gray hair explained something to a twentyish woman whose brown hair was sculpted in the identical style. In the taxi's mirror, Cain saw three, sometimes four, cars behind them: average American sedans with ordinary-looking male drivers whose features he couldn't quite discern.

"This is it," the cabby told him, pulling to the curb.

Cain paid the man and pushed the buzzer beside the glass doors. Swooping gold letters in the glass transom read Commodore Hotel and Apartments.

The desk clerk said Miss Worby had informed him that Mr. Cain would be arriving and would he care to inspect the type of suite she thought he had in mind? He would. The desk clerk gave him a key marked 517.

The suite was an overblown hotel room with a refrigerator and two-burner stove. The furniture included a bed, couch, coffee table, television, two bureaus and a book shelf. The two windows overlooked an artery that fed into Main Street; they opened enough to admit fresh air but not enough to let him jump. They were above the roof across the street, so no one had an easy view—or shot—through them.

At least there'll be no flashing neon lights, he thought.

Someone knocked on the door.

No peephole, noticed Cain.

The someone knocked again, certain that Cain was inside.

Cain's stomach muscles tightened as he touched the knob. He paused, braced himself, then jerked the door open.

"Hi," said Beth. "I just got back from work. The desk clerk told me you were here."

"Come in," said Cain.

"I know it's not much," she said, her hands warding off complaint as her face beamed encouragement. She entered the room. He closed the door. "Nothing like what you're probably used to, but . . ."

"You'd be surprised."

"Did you know there's a sun roof?"

He shook his head and she continued.

"Not much, but it's cute and no one can see you. Not that I plan on using it, but . . . My room is two floors up—and just like this. Not a bad deal, right? We can even walk to work. The desk clerk is on twenty-four hours a day, the phone lines are direct . . ."

"Did he tell you that?"

"I asked. I know a trick or two."

"Good."

"So . . . are you going to take it?"

He nodded. "I'll call Kimmett, have him send over my bags."

"So," she said. She stood between the window and the bed.

"So," he replied. He stood closer to the door.

"Umn . . . what did you do today? After you left?"

"Checked a few things out," he said.

"Anything I should know about?"

"Not really," he said. "Not yet."

"Did . . . Did Sylvia Kimmett come with you?"

"No."

"I wonder what it will be like working with her. I don't even know what experience she's had."

"I wouldn't sell her short."

"Believe me, a woman like her, I . . ."

Someone knocked on the door.

Cain and Beth quickly looked at each other. She shook her head, shrugged.

"Who is it?" Cain yelled.

"You should have done that when I knocked!" she whispered.

"Desk clerk."

She relaxed; Cain didn't.

"Can you let yourself in?" he said.

Beth frowned, blushed, stepped back, her eyes fixed on the door.

The knob rattled and the desk clerk entered.

"Is everything satisfactory, Mr. Cain?" he said. "I see Miss Worby found you."

"Yes," said Cain. "Everything is fine. I'll take this room."

"Excellent."

The desk clerk reached inside his suitcoat and Cain stiffened.

"This came for you," said the clerk, handing Cain an envelope with his name written on it.

"Came? How?"

"A young man dropped it off."

"When?"

"About five minutes ago. After Miss Worby arrived, or I would have asked her to bring it to you. Is everything all right?"

"Fine, thank you," said Cain.

The clerk smiled and left.

"What is it?" asked Beth, nodding to the envelope. She blushed again, said, "Excuse me, I don't mean to pry."

The envelope was thick, cream-colored paper—expensive. "Jackson Cain" was written in flowing, beautiful script and violet ink. He tore the envelope open, shook out the sheet of stationery, and read its message written in the same fashion as the address:

Cain—

Why not drop by my place tonight? I have the penthouse at the Wabash Arms. Say a little after 6.

Johnny Maxx

"Jesus," whispered Beth as she read over Cain's shoulder.

"No," said Cain. He read the note again, turned it over, then carefully refolded it and stuck it back in the envelope.

"What are you going to do?" she asked.

The Third Eye

CAIN RODE THE WABASH Arms's elevator to the top floor. The hands of his watch showed 6:17. The elevator *dinged,* then opened on a long hall leading to a black door with a gold handle. Cain knocked once, waited, then knocked again. The door swung open and the sound of Elvis Presley singing "Heartbreak Hotel" engulfed Cain, along with the scent of musk.

Her golden hair was dyed. She wore a black dress with a slit up the left side, black high heels, and nothing else. The silk clung to her heavy pear breasts. Her nipples were like marbles. Cain wondered if she was excited or if they were that large in repose. She had a sweet mouth, a fine nose and cheekbones, brown eyes with clear whites and black pupils the size of nickels.

"Hi," she said. Her voice was soft and inviting.

"Hi," he replied.

"Come in," she said. "Johnny's getting dressed."

She led Cain into a sunken living room with a leather sofa and chairs. A black baby grand piano stood by the picture window.

"Relax," she said as she walked to a bar where a crushed velvet blue-, silver-, and black-toned portrait of Elvis Presley hung on the wall. The blonde turned a knob and dropped the singer's volume.

"Can I get you something?" she said. "A drink? We were having champagne, but we've got scotch, bourbon"—she ticked off each choice on her fingers, like a meticulous waitress—"gin, vodka, rye, a bunch of brandies, beer, sodas . . ."

"No, thanks," said Cain. "I'm fine."

"Great," she said. Her smile was easy and empty.

"Honey!" boomed a man's voice from another room.

She took several quick steps, stopped close to Cain as she strained to hear and answered: "Yes, Johnny?"

"Who's there?" yelled the voice.

She smiled at Cain and blinked; waited until he told her.

"Jackson Cain, honey!" she yelled.

"Hey, Cain! Come on back!"

"I'll show you the way," she said.

The back of her dress was scooped open to her waist; Cain watched her shoulder blades and spine as he followed her.

"Come on in!" called a man's voice from a bedroom with cobalt blue walls. A matching bedspread had fallen from the disheveled king-size bed to the thick gray carpet. The woman perched on the bed's satin gray sheets so that her smile encompassed both men.

Johnny Maxx stood before a full-length mirror, a tie draped around his neck. He combed his black hair into a modest wave. He had high cheekbones and a dark tan. His black eyes were deep set, and bright. When he smiled—and he often smiled—he showed perfect teeth. His shirt was white, monogrammed; his pants were black, as were his Italian loafers. The clothes fit his muscular frame perfectly. He knotted his tie with well-manicured hands.

"Won't be a minute, Jack," he said, smiling as Cain's reflection entered the mirror. "Make yourself comfortable."

Cain stood halfway between the woman's empty smile and the back of the man he watched in the glass.

"You want anything to drink?" said Johnny Maxx.

"I asked him already," the woman quickly interjected.

"I'm fine," said Cain.

"Great." A wink came with that reply.

"Mind if I finish dressing?" the woman asked.

"No, baby," said Johnny Maxx. "Go ahead."

Her smile flashed gratitude, then she changed it to say

excuse me to Cain, and went into a bathroom. She shut the door.

"Hell of a night, ain't it?" asked Johnny Maxx as he plucked a vest off the bureau. He buttoned all but the bottom button, smoothed the vest across his flat stomach.

"It's nice out," said Cain.

"Yeah? I been inside most of the day."

Johnny Maxx lifted the black leather, double shoulder holster off the bureau. Two long-barreled .38 revolvers identical to those carried by uniformed American policemen since the 1920s weighed down the rig. He slid into the harness with practiced ease. He adjusted the holsters, donned a suitcoat, checked himself in the mirror, then, for the first time, turned to face his visitor.

"How does it look?" asked Johnny Maxx.

"You look good."

"Yeah," he said. "I do, don't I?"

He grinned, gave Cain his hand and a firm shake.

"Nice to know you," said Johnny Maxx. "Glad you could drop by. Come on out here."

Cain followed him to the living room.

"Isn't this a great place?" called his host. He walked quickly, firmly, eager to get where he was going and confident of his pace. Behind the bar, he poured a glass of champagne.

"Sure you don't want one?"

"No, thanks."

"So you got the note. How was it?"

Cain frowned.

"I never saw it," explained Johnny Maxx.

So much for fingerprints, thought Cain, who'd made Beth hide that uncertain evidence.

"Nice note," said Cain. "Could have said a lot more."

Johnny Maxx gestured with his champagne glass:

"That's Debbi for you. A woman of few words, and there are few women like that, believe me."

"I believe you," said Cain. "What do you want?"

"How about dinner? You hungry?"

"I can eat."

"I know the best place in town. How'd you get here?"

"It's an easy walk."

"Great," said Johnny Maxx, stepping out from behind the bar. He left his lone glass on its surface. "We'll take my car."

Debbi strolled into the room. As far as Cain could tell, the only apparel she'd added to her black dress and heels were dangling diamond earrings. Plus a little makeup. She seemed more excited, alert. She descended the steps into the sunken living room one at a time, then curled up on the couch.

"Are you joining us for dinner?" Cain asked her.

"No," said Johnny Maxx.

"Besides," she said, "I'm not very hungry."

On the stereo, Elvis sang "Love Me Tender."

"Stick around, Honey," Johnny Maxx told her as he led Cain to the door. "You can change the tape. Make yourself at home."

"Thanks," she called.

Cain turned for a last look at her smile.

"Nice to meet you, Jack Cain," she said. "Have fun."

He closed the door behind him.

"She's not as dumb as she looks," said Johnny Maxx as he pushed the button for the elevator.

"Does that matter?"

They both laughed.

"Sure," said Johnny Maxx. "What good is a dumb broad? Hard to believe," he said as the elevator doors opened and showed them its emptiness, "but she's had three kids and is pushing thirty. Ain't that something?"

"Yes," said Cain as they started down, "that's something."

The elevator took them to a basement garage much, thought Cain, like the one where Hammond died.

"Too easy to get down here, isn't it?" said Cain as they walked through the well-lit but deserted cavern.

"Two separate steel grate doors to the street," said Johnny Maxx, gesturing toward the far shadows. "One is a combination open, the other is TV monitored and guard controlled. Elevator and stairs open only in front of the desk clerk or on the apartment floors."

"Smart building policy," said Cain.

"I own the building."

Johnny Maxx led Cain to a black Corvette parked away from other cars. A TV camera pointed down from the rafters above the 'Vette.

"Ain't she a beaut!" said Johnny Maxx, like a boy with a new bike. "All American and all *muscle*."

They settled themselves in the car.

"You don't worry about this being Bomb City, U.S.A., do you?" Johnny Maxx asked him, then laughed, and before Cain could reply, turned the ignition key.

The engine roared to life.

"No," said Cain. "Do you?"

The 'Vette's driver laughed again as the car peeled out.

"We'll go to Enzio's on the strip," said Johnny Maxx as they squealed out of the underground garage. "You'll love it."

Cain quickly realized that Johnny Maxx was driving an erratic pattern of random turns and double-back streets. Within five minutes they knew that three sets of headlights followed them.

"My friends or yours?" asked his grinning chauffeur.

"Whoever they are," said Cain, "friends isn't what I'd call them."

"I only have friends, Jack," said Johnny Maxx. "You should remember that."

"Then you're a lucky man."

"Yes sir, that I am." Johnny Maxx glanced in his rearview mirror. "But sometimes a man's luck can crowd him."

He stepped on the gas. The engine roared and the 'Vette shot forward. Cain glanced at the speedometer. Thirty-five, forty, forty-five. Street signs on the corners whizzed by too fast to read. The mirror on his side showed three pairs of headlights.

Forty-five, fifty, and they swung on to the road through the park surrounding the Kimmett family estate. Taillights in front of them drew closer, closer. Johnny Maxx whipped the 'Vette around a Ford with two teenagers searching for a safe place to explore passion.

The 'Vette fishtailed as it swooped back to its own lane.

Cain's stomach churned.

The dashboard lights glowed green on Johnny Maxx's face. His eyes turned from the white lines racing into the 'Vette's headlights, from the dark tunnel through the park trees; glanced at his passenger—who stared at him.

"Mister State Trooper," sang Johnny Maxx, a classic Bruce Springsteen highway ballad, *"Please don't you stop me."*

A car squealed to a stop at a side road, blared its horn at the dark monster that roared past with only inches to spare.

Why didn't I fasten my seat belt? thought Cain. He felt curiously free, like a stone skipping on the river; his throat tightened, burned with bile.

Johnny Maxx shifted from fourth to third. This way and that the 'Vette swayed on the curving park road. Now only two pairs of headlights bobbed in the 'Vette's mirrors.

A quarter of a mile ahead was the traffic light at the park's exit. Cain saw street lights, a movie marquee. High above the pavement glowed a sign for a franchised convenience store. Far ahead in their lane were the red dots of leisurely moving machines. Other cars waited patiently at the traffic light for their turn on the road.

One hundred yards away, the traffic light changed from green to yellow.

Johnny Maxx floorboarded the 'Vette.

Cain wanted to close his eyes; couldn't. He braced himself against the padded dash, knowing the gesture was futile.

The light changed to red.

They blew beneath it at 94 mph. Cain felt and smelled the brakes grab as inertia sucked him toward the windshield. Behind them, horns screamed. Their tires cried for one block, two. A stalled pickup appeared in their headlights as Johnny Maxx frantically downshifted the whining engine. Twenty feet from the pickup, he whipped the wheel to the right. They shot onto a freeway access bridge.

Johnny Maxx took the next exit at the posted 35 mph.

Behind them, the road was dark and empty.

They cruised down Steeltown's beltway strip, parked in a lot next to a low building with a black steel script sign reading Enzio's.

As they walked toward Enzio's door, Cain said, "Nice car."

Johnny Maxx laughed.

"Mr. Maxx!" said the blurry man who greeted them. Waitresses exchanged glances. Customers at the four filled tables turned to *not* stare.

"Hey, Enzio! How many times I got to tell you? *Johnny!*"

"Johnny, Johnny," said Enzio, smiling, shrugging his shoulders to Cain. "Always, I forget."

"But you're a good man, Enzio." The owner tried to protest. "You got a good table for us?"

"Hey! For you, Johnny, only the best."

Perhaps twenty empty tables, all seemingly in positions of equal quality, waited in the dining room. Enzio led them to a table against the far wall. Johnny Maxx took the wall seat.

"Enzio, this is my friend, Jackson Cain. Anytime he comes in, you see he gets good stuff, huh?"

"The best!" said Enzio. He kissed his fingertips. "The best!

"How about some champagne?" said Enzio. "On the house."

"I'll take a scotch rocks," said Cain. "Put it on my tab."

"Hey, no need to . . ." started Enzio, but Johnny Maxx silenced him with a raised hand.

"No problem, right Enzio?" As the owner rapidly smiled and shook his head, Johnny Maxx added, "Me, I'll take the champagne."

Enzio scurried away.

Cain said, "Who were those guys?"

Johnny Maxx shrugged. "Maybe DiCarlo's goons, or the sheriff's deputies."

"You mean, *Mayor Nash's* deputies."

"You know the score," said Johnny Maxx. He beamed, nodded. "I like that. I like that a lot."

"Do you get along with the chief and the mayor?"

"Sure."

"Sure," said Cain. "I'm not sure they'd agree, but let's skip that for now. What I can't figure tonight is what you want."

"That's simple," answered his host; he shrugged. "This commission you work for is investigating Josh Hammond's murder."

"And other things," Cain added.

"So I heard," said his host.

"What about the commission?"

"I want to contribute."

"What?"

"Money," said Johnny Maxx with a sly smile, joking as though Cain had only asked a question.

"I don't get it."

"You will," said Johnny Maxx. "All you have to do is—"

"Cut the crap," said Cain. Johnny Maxx's eyes flashed, but the man said nothing, so Cain continued:

"You're not a prime candidate to support the commission."

"Why not? Isn't my money as good as old man Kimmett's?"

"Hey, guys!" said Enzio, setting down their drinks. "You ready to order yet?"

Cain nodded to his companion and sipped from the oversize glass of ice and scotch: expensive, far beyond bar brand.

"You know me, Enzio," said Johnny Maxx. "Your special steak, medium rare. House salad with your dressing. Baked potato."

Cain ordered steak, medium, salad and a baked potato.

"Money is money," said Cain after Enzio left them. "It doesn't show who it came from and it doesn't care."

"You're smart, Cain. And you probably know a lot. I bet you've heard about me."

"Un-huh."

"I'm a businessman," said Johnny Maxx. "Plain and simple.

"Well," he added with a smile, "maybe not *plain.*"

Cain gave him no smile.

"I've had my wild times," continued Johnny Maxx. "Who hasn't? But check me out"—

"Sure," interrupted Cain.

—"you won't find anything for your commission. If you do, I bet you and I can resolve it, no problems for anyone."

"Really," said Cain.

"Really," said Johnny Maxx.

"After all, Josh was a friend of mine. And the commission is about improving Steeltown. I'm all for that. This is *my* town."

"So I've heard."

"You'll find I'm quite a civic booster. United Way, Boy Scouts. I bought uniforms for the little league, did—"

He suddenly stopped.

"What is it?" asked Cain.

"Something I can't quite remember," said Johnny Maxx. He frowned. "About baseball."

"Are you helping court the Japanese too?" said Cain quickly.

"I gave a little," said Johnny Maxx. Smiled. "I gave enough."

"You want them to come to town?"

"Don't matter to me," said Johnny Maxx. "My business will only get better if they're pumping more dollars into the economy. Most of my enterprises are services. You know, like video games."

"If they come," said Cain, "they'll swing the big weight here."

"Don't bet on it," said Johnny Maxx. "Anyway, what do you care, Cain? You pimping for the Japs?"

"I have a job."

"You want my donation in cash or check?"

"Check."

"You sure?" He laughed. As he wrote the check, Enzio and a waitress brought their dinner. Enzio waited until Johnny Maxx was through with the table before setting the plates down.

"Here we go!" said the restaurateur. "The best!"

Johnny Maxx handed Cain a check over the steaming plates of meat.

"Ten thousand dollars!" said Cain.

Enzio and the waitress pretended not to hear.

"You're giving ten grand to the commission?" Cain said, loudly.

As Enzio and the waitress scurried away, Johnny Maxx

glared at Cain, whispered, "Wouldn't you say that establishes my credibility and . . . lack of conflict with the commission's purpose?"

"You mean you didn't kill Hammond?"

"You fuckin' saying I did, *Jack*?"

Fire burned in Johnny Maxx's eyes. Cain shook his head.

"Just doing my job," he said, quickly.

Johnny Maxx picked up his knife and fork, slashed through the steak laying before him; he thrust a piece of meat in his mouth and chewed it viciously.

"All this is a surprise," said Cain.

"Stick around and you'll find Steeltown is full of surprises, Cain. Where you from?"

"What kind of surprises?"

Cain bit into his steak. The meat tasted musky, smoky, but good. It's juice ran through his mouth.

"Surprises for everybody," Johnny Maxx told him. "Even me. Like, let me tell you about a guy I know. Hell, I know everybody and everybody knows that. This guy is named Wolinsky. You heard of him?"

"No," said Cain.

"Well, to my surprise, it turns out Wolinsky is up *your* alley, Mr. State Trooper. The TV says he and his boys were responsible for your fellow officer getting shot to shit last night."

"Really?"

"That's what I hear on TV. This afternoon, feds from the state capital kicked in Wolinsky's door. Pissed the hell out of DiCarlo and the mayor's guys—they claim they knew squat about it. But the feds didn't give a damn. Seems they're doing their own thing on our turf. Or somebody's thing. And you know what they found?"

"No."

"Nothing. No drugs, no Wolinsky."

"What happened to him?"

"Maybe he left town," said Johnny Maxx. "Maybe after last night he figured he should."

"Now what?"

"You tell me."

"Can't do that, Johnny. I don't know."

"Yeah, you can call me Johnny. That's what friends are for."

"Are we friends, Johnny?"

"Don't you remember what I told you?"

"I wonder," said Cain.

"What do you wonder, Jack?"

"Who pulled the plug on Wolinsky."

"Interesting question."

They finished their meal in silence. They declined Enzio's offer of coffee. When the check came, Cain grabbed it.

"Mind if I keep the receipt? We can split the cost."

Johnny Maxx laughed.

"Sure, kid. You can work the money anyway you want."

"Time to go home," Cain told him. He turned the bill over, and in bold letters wrote down the date, time, and place; that the bill was for dinner with "J. Maxx."

Who laughed as they walked to the car.

"Think there's a bomb?" he asked as he started the 'Vette.

At Cain's building, Johnny Maxx pulled to the curb, kept the Corvette's engine running, and turned to look at his passenger.

"I like you, Jack, even if you are a cagey son of a bitch. This is a tough town. A guy's gotta be sharp, but if he's smart, he doesn't get too cagey. Especially with his friends. Guys who play cagey find it backfires. Hope you ain't one of those guys."

"Me, too," said Cain.

"That's real good, Jack. You be careful to stay good. Not all my friends do. Like Josh Hammond. He was cagey, and that made him think he was a lot smarter than he was."

Johnny Maxx pointed his forefinger and thumb as though his hand were a pistol. He straightened his arm until his fingertip almost touched Cain's forehead. Electricity tingled between their flesh.

"Remember, Jack," whispered Johnny Maxx, "Hammond played cagey and somebody gave him the third eye."

Rats

THE NEXT MORNING FELT more like summer than spring. Cain stood in front of the Commodore. He wore a gray sports coat, blue shirt with no tie, navy slacks, and black loafers. A black Cadillac with blue smoked windows and three antennae on its trunk pulled to the curb.

"Get in!" yelled Chief DiCarlo from the driver's seat.

"Nice day, ain't it?" said DiCarlo as Cain complied.

"I said I'd call you at noon," said Cain.

"What the hell," said DiCarlo. The steering wheel rubbed his stomach. A police radio on the console crackled. "Like I told you on the phone, early bird gets the worm. Did you sleep good?"

"Yes," said Cain, who'd awoken only four times in the night.

"The sleep of the innocent," said DiCarlo, as they pulled away from the curb. He wore a black suit, white shirt, his collar open, but the tie still strained against his thick neck.

"There won't be any accidents, will there?" asked Cain.

"What do you mean?"

"The Hammond evidence," said Cain. "I told you, we want to see all of it: the case jacket plus everything your guys took from his office and house. We'd hate to find something was accidentally lost."

"If you want, you can play with the slug we dug out of his skull. Everything is summarized in the case jacket. You're wasting your time coming down to the station when I could have sent you that file."

"I had quite a night," said Cain.

"Oh yeah?"

"Johnny Maxx took me for a ride."

"You're kidding," said DiCarlo.

"Of course, you already knew about my adventures," said Cain.

The chief shrugged, smiled as he slowed for a traffic light.

"I keep my eyes open," he said.

"Are you curious about what he wanted," said Cain, "or are your ears open enough to know that too?"

The chief glanced to his left at three men in scruffy clothes standing on the corner. The trio quickly averted their faces.

"Whoa now!" said the police chief. As they crossed into the intersection, he abruptly U-turned the Cadillac.

The three men were walking rapidly toward an alley. One of them looked over his shoulder, saw the Caddy bearing down on them, and yelled to his companions. All of them ran down the alley.

The Caddy surged after them. The chief bellowed into the radio microphone as they bounced over chuckholes: "This is DiCarlo! Get me immediate backups in the alley behind Mulligan's warehouse! I got three hot ones!"

A garbage truck filled the far end of alley. Through the Caddy's tinted windshield, Cain watched the hunted men hesitate, then run to the right, down a long brick driveway.

"I got the sons 'o bitches!" roared DiCarlo.

The Caddy reeled around the driveway corner. Fifty feet beyond the car's hood, a warehouse's brick wall blocked the prey's escape. Two men turned to face the Caddy as it skidded to a halt. The third scrambled up a chain link fence.

"Get down from there!" yelled DiCarlo, opening the car door.

The chief leaped from the Caddy, ran half a dozen steps, jumped and grabbed the ankle of the man scaling the chain link fence. Cain bailed out of the car: he glared at the other two men. One of them wore a green Army fatigue jacket, the other was in shirt sleeves. Cain kept his arms pressed against his sports coat so it wouldn't blow open, held his right hand low as though he were ready to draw a weapon.

With all of his weight, DiCarlo jerked the man off the fence. The man screamed before he smacked into the pavement. He moaned, then was silent. DiCarlo whirled toward the two men who'd stood their ground. They retreated as the chief stalked toward them, retreated with their empty hands held wide, retreated until their backs hit the brick wall and DiCarlo loomed in their faces.

The chief grabbed the man in the Army jacket by his lapels and screamed, "What do you think you're doing?"

"N-n-n-nothing, Chief," whimpered the man as DiCarlo lifted him to his tiptoes. "We were just—"

"You were running! You saw me see you and you took off running, Laprado, now don't fuckin' jerk me around!"

"Not me, Chief!"

"We were . . ." began the other man.

"You'll talk when I tell you, maggot!"

"Yes, sir!" said the man in shirt sleeves, who still hadn't felt the chief's hands. He tried to back up a step, but the bricks stopped him. Cain had never seen a live and conscious man so pale.

Sirens screamed closer.

"You were kitty-corner from Issak's liquor store, Laprado!"

"Look, Chief, we weren't doing nothing, we—"

"You're off your turf, fool! You think I don't know that?"

"No, no," said Laprado, "I know you know me." He looked at Cain, who stood only a few steps away. "You know I'm a stand-up guy, I don't give nobody no trouble, not ever. You know that, detective. Hell, you've known me all my life. I wasn't . . ."

"You wasn't doing right is what you wasn't doing!" yelled the chief as two police cruisers parked behind the Caddy. Car doors slammed. Uniformed officers hurried toward their commander. "You were going to take off that liquor store."

"No, really . . ." began Laprado.

"We wouldn't have done anything like that," quickly added his friend, "not without squaring . . ."

"You talk when you're told to!" yelled the chief. "Forty-three years Isaak's been on that corner. He works hard, keeps his nose clean. Kicks into every charity drive, him with a sick old lady and *you* were fuckin' going to take him off! Probably blow him away so he couldn't complain! For pocket change!"

"No, Chief!" insisted Laprado. "It wasn't like that!"

Five uniformed cops formed a half moon behind Cain and the chief. Two of them watched Cain, waiting to be sure which side he was on. Two others stood over the unconscious fence climber.

"Oh no?" said the chief.

"No!" insisted Laprado.

"No!" insisted his companion.

"No?" repeated the chief. "Then why did you run?"

"Ah . . ." began the man in shirt sleeves.

"Laprado, you were never in the Army and it's a beautiful day, so why the hell you wearing this zipped-up coat?" DiCarlo shook the man by his lapels. "What you got underneath it?!"

Laprado tried to speak, but DiCarlo shook him again. The chief braced his feet, hunched his massive shoulders, and shook the man as though he were rag doll. Laprado's arms flopped wildly as he was jerked back and forth; his shoes scraped the pavement as he tried and failed to stand. The chief slammed him against the brick wall, jerked him forward, shook him and slammed him and shook him and slammed him, again and again. Laprado's head thunked against the bricks and Cain's mouth went dry. Laprado slumped in the chief's grip, but still the chief shook him. Metal clanged on pavement. Cain looked down and saw a large black revolver beneath Laprado's dangling feet.

The chief threw Laprado to two of the uniformed cops; he slumped in their arms, moaning.

DiCarlo mopped his brow with a handkerchief.

"Get them out of here!" said DiCarlo.

Two cops grabbed the man in shirtsleeves, who seemed relieved as they bent his arms behind his back and clicked on handcuffs. They led him to the same cruiser his two companions were dragged to.

DiCarlo angled his head, and the other cops walked away.

"Police work," said DiCarlo, grinning as he mopped his brow again. "How do you like it so far?"

"Seems better than the other side," answered Cain.

"Goddamn rats," said DiCarlo. "A town hits hard times and the rats come out the sewers to eat anything that can't fight back. Somebody's gotta stop 'em or they'll eat the whole damn town."

The chief shook his head. He picked up the revolver, swung the cylinder open, and noted the six loaded chambers. Snapped the cylinder shut, half-cocked the gun, and spun the cylinder.

"Quality piece," he said as he lowered the hammer.

He extended the gun to Cain, butt first.

"You want it?" asked the chief of police.

"No, thanks."

"Sure?"

Cain nodded.

"Never know when you'll need a spare."

Cain shook his head.

The chief shrugged, nonchalantly carried the gun as they walked toward the Caddy. "These days, quality pieces are easy to get."

The last cruiser backed out of the dead-end lane.

"What's going to happen to those guys?" asked Cain.

"Law and order," said DiCarlo. He laughed. "I am the law and I give the orders."

"So I gather."

"Is that what Johnny Maxx told you?" said the chief.

"He didn't tell me much of anything," said Cain. "Except that you and he were friends."

"Oh year," said the chief. He leaned on the Caddy's hood. "Johnny and his *friends*."

Cain stood where he could watch the chief's face.

"You a friend of Johnny's?" asked the chief.

"I'm new in town," answered Cain.

"But you fit in real good. Like with that rat: he figured you for one of my boys. You fit in real easy."

"Seemed that way."

"How'd you like it?"

"I didn't give it any thought."

"You should give everything a lot of thought."

"That's what my boss tells me."

"You mean *Professor* Boswell?" asked DiCarlo. "Or you mean some New York pencil pusher who signs your checks?"

"I mean the guy in the mirror," answered Cain.

"Oh," said the chief. "So that's how it is."

"Just a working stiff, Chief. Like you."

"Ain't a lot of us left here."

"There's enough."

The chief chuckled.

"Yes sir," he said, "there are enough. What did Johnny want?"

"He gave ten grand to the commission."

"*Johnny?*"

"Maybe he wants to see I don't go hungry," said Cain. He shrugged. "Maybe he wants to let people know where he stands."

"What did you do?"

"I took his check."

The chief laughed and Cain joined him.

"How come you haven't put him away?" asked Cain.

"Is this state trooper and commission hotshot to chief of police," asked DiCarlo, "or are we talking just-pals?"

"I'm curious."

"Mr. Maxx is a citizen with rights," answered the chief. "Despite numerous allegations and rumors, there's always problems with hard evidence and witnesses. If a guy gets busted for spitting on the sidewalk, maybe he and Johnny are friends but there's nobody who can prove Johnny told him to spit. Mr. Maxx is a businessman who lives in a well-insulated world. So he's innocent until proven guilty."

"Proof doesn't seem hard to acquire in Steeltown," said Cain.

"Well," said the chief, "legal technicalities aren't the only considerations. I know what it's like to be an innocent man persecuted by society, so naturally I have a lot of sympathy for Johnny."

"Naturally."

"What else did he want? He could have mailed a check."

"This Wolinsky business has him stumped," said Cain. "It's got me puzzled too. You told me you didn't know anything about it. Feds and troopers come into your town to kick ass and take names and you don't know anything about it. Doesn't seem right for the chief of police."

DiCarlo's face darkened.

"What about the sheriff?" asked Cain. "What does he say?"

"That no-nuts fool doesn't count. Where you going with this?"

Cain shrugged.

"Two Steeltown guys get bushwacked on a drug bust and the feds take a shot at Wolinsky. They're all friends of Johnny Maxx's."

"So?"

"So maybe the rats aren't the only ones getting restless," said Cain. "Those feds didn't get sicced onto Johnny's friends by coincidence."

"Is that what Johnny thinks?" said the chief.

"What else can he think?"

"Does Johnny think it was me?"

The chief sounded more curious than concerned.

"We don't share secrets," said Cain. "But it's badges that are after him, and you got the biggest one in town."

"But I don't own all of them."

"Tell that to Johnny," said Cain. "You think about it too."

The chief stared at him.

"A rat who'd dare to bite Johnny is a rat with a giant hunger."

"What do you care, Cain? Are you signing up with me?"

"Somebody killed Hammond and I got to find out who," said Cain. "The longer I don't know that, the more that peculiar things keep happening. I don't want to get my business caught in somebody else's fight, and if it's already there, I want to be sure who's who."

The chief mopped his brow. Cain started to say more, thought better of it, and kept his silence.

"Come on," said DiCarlo. "I got better things to do than kick rats around an alley."

Trapped

"GO ON IN," said a cadaverous detective as he opened the door to a dark room. "It's all there."

"The switch is around the corner!" yelled another cop over the mumbled conversations, typewriter clatter, and ringing phones in the squad room behind Cain.

In one hand Cain held a thick manila file folder; with the other, he groped in darkness that smelled of stale smoke and dried coffee. He flicked the switch, entered the room, and shut the door.

A bare bulb glowed over a rickety wooden table. A metal chair waited in the corner by a pile of bulging black plastic garbage bags. The walls were white, the floor gray. There were no windows.

Cain dropped the file on the table. He untied a garbage bag. The black plastic yawned like a mouth. In its gape, Cain saw a Styrofoam cup, a banana peel, a typewriter ribbon, crumpled paper, and notebooks. He nudged another garbage bag with his foot, sighed, and carried the metal chair back to the table.

For an hour he read crudely typed and poorly written police reports on Hammond, Joshua P., a twenty-eight-year-old white male, occupation: newspaper reporter, who died when a .45 caliber bullet pierced his skull three centimeters above the bridge of his nose. Powder burns indicated that the gun barrel was fired as close as an inch and no further than two feet from Hammond's forehead. The autopsy also showed Hammond suffered from herpes and bad lungs.

A twenty-seven-page list of items seized as evidence noted the banana peel, crumpled paper, reporters' notebooks numbered one through seventeen and not summarized, a phone diary–appointment book, a pair of sneakers from Hammond's bottom desk drawer, plus other items great and small, all of which were presumably in the black plastic garbage bags.

The file's stack of eight-by-ten black-and-white photographs showed Hammond on his back in garage slot 62B; his late model German car filled 63B. Close-ups showed Hammond's head in a pool of blood, the third eye distorting his handsome face. Dozens of photos depicted his house. He was an untidy man. Sometimes the photos accidentally included policemen; in one of them, a detective stuck out his tongue at the camera. The last few pictures showed Hammond's desk.

Cain rubbed his eyes, checked his watch: not quite noon.

Don't stop, he thought, ignoring his hunger and headache.

Sorting through the plastic trash bags took Cain another two hours and stained his clothing. When he finished repacking the bags, he flipped through the photographs again, found the one he was looking for, and frowned. Carefully, he tucked the photograph down the back of his pants, then put on his sports jacket.

DiCarlo was laughing with a group of detectives when Cain came out of the small room. The chief mopped his brow with a handkerchief.

"Hey, Jack, you all done?"

"For now," said Cain. He handed the file to DiCarlo. "Don't lose anything, we'll want some of it later."

"Bring a wheelbarrow," said the chief. "And a subpoena."

All the detectives laughed.

"By the way," said Cain, "a few items are already missing."

The laughter stopped.

"What are you talking about?" said the chief of police.

"Hammond's address and appointment book," said Cain.

"Oh yeah," said DiCarlo. "That."

"Where is it?" said Cain.

"We sent it to the FBI lab," said DiCarlo, smiling.

"What about photocopies of the pages?"

"Didn't make any. Didn't want to damage evidence."

"Un-huh. and you took no notes either, right?"

DiCarlo grinned.

"When is it due back?" asked Cain.

"Wheels of justice," said DiCarlo. "How slow they grind."

"Where's the desk blotter?"

"What's that?" asked the cadaverous detective.

"Every desk at the paper has a blotter board, a big calendar with tear-off pages that fills the middle of the desk. You can see Hammond's in the photos, but it isn't in the bags. Where is it?"

"Shit," said a bald black detective, "seven garbage bags full of shit, and he says one thing is missing. The man ain't got no sense of proportion."

"What's there is there," said DiCarlo.

"What officer is in charge of the investigation?" asked Cain. "Who ran the searches?"

"I guess that might be me," said the cadaverous detective. He grinned, slow and easy.

"And I checked him through every step," said the chief.

"Hell of a job," said Cain.

Cain rode the elevator to the first floor. A mimeographed sheet taped above the elevator buttons warned all officers of extra duty due to the coming union rally. At the front desk, the nasty booking sergeant argued with a foul-mouthed woman over unpaid parking tickets.

Summer ruled the streets by the time Cain stepped onto them. His skin beneath his shirt grew warm and sticky, and he feared his sweat might ruin the stolen picture.

Take your time, he thought.

On Cain's side of the town square, an elderly woman listlessly window shopped. Three teenagers, their hair dyed nihilistic black and highlighted green and red, stomped the sidewalk in surplus Army boots. They wore black shirts, torn and safety-pinned jeans. A man and a woman a year or two older than the black-clad trio passed them; the couple was dressed in simple but brightly colored shopping mall shirts and jeans.

Across the square, two men argued in front of a drug

store; they wore scruffy work clothes and shined shoes. A woman walked out of the drug store, counting her change. She passed a sandy-haired man with black metal glasses and a blue blazer who was scrutinizing the window of a camera store with a going-out-of-business sign, and two men in suits who stood in a doorway, eyes averted from everything. She turned the corner, and was gone.

Cain started across the square, stopped before he reached the opposite side, and frowned. He whirled, walked rapidly to a cafe.

"Sit anywhere you ..." began the waitress as Cain entered.

But he was past her, headed to the restrooms before she finished. She sneered at his wake.

The back door beyond the restrooms led to an alley filled with dumpsters, cardboard boxes, and other debris. Cain shut the door behind him, saw no one in the alley. Above his head hung the bottom rung of a black iron ladder leading up to a fire escape's grilled platform.

He jumped.

Fire stabbed his knee. He grabbed the ladder's bottom rung and pulled himself up, wriggling and swaying as he grasped rung after rung until his feet reached the bottom step. In seconds, he was squatting on the fire escape platform three stories above the alley.

Pigeons cooed hostilely at him from a window ledge. An invisible cloud of spoiled food and wet cardboard surrounded Cain's perch. He saw a mangy black cat stalking a path through the crumpled boxes and cartons and heard the fleeing scamper of tiny claws. Cain made himself vanish into this time and this place.

The restaurant's back door flew open. The two men in suits who'd stood in a doorway burst into the alley. With a flick of his hand, the older man sent his companion racing to the left, while he ran to the right. They reached the ends of the alley, scanned the streets, then ran back to the restaurant's door. Through the black grill beneath him, Cain watched the tops of their heads.

"Shit!" yelled the older man. He pushed his companion

inside the restaurant, then turned and again swept the alley with his eyes.

On the black iron grill, Cain withdrew further into himself; thought of nothing, nothing.

Below him, the man kicked a pile of cardboard boxes. The black cat *meowed* and bolted for safety. The kicker swore, then whirled and went back inside the restaurant, slamming the door.

Cain waited twenty-five minutes, then climbed down. The black cat watched him limp out of the alley.

Three blocks away, Cain found a corner bar with a phone booth.

"Commodore Arms," said the man who answered Cain's call.

"This is Mr. Cain. Any messages for me?"

"Miss Worby left word that she is out until late tonight. Howard Cohn called, left a number, and asked you to please call him. A woman at the newspaper called to say the front desk was holding the package you requested and that Mr. Evans will discuss further deliveries with you. And a man called and said to tell you to call your friend with the dogs."

"Your boss called me," Cain told Raymond Nelson a moment later.

"*Our* boss," said Nelson. Kimmett came on the line.

"You haven't been—" snapped Kimmett, but Cain cut him off.

"I haven't been wasting my time or your money," said Cain.

"You've been seen around town with the wrong crowd."

"You picked my playmates. Do you have something besides complaints to give me?"

"Me give *you*? You're supposed to give to me!"

"Don't worry, I will."

Cain hung up before Kimmett could reply. He dropped quarters in the telephone's slots to call New York.

"Ron Com Photo," said the man who answered Cain's call.

"Is Willy there?"

"This is Willy."

"This is Jack Cain. I need a favor."

"Hey, Jack! Long time! What do you need?"

"I've got an eight-by-ten black-and-white I want blown up clear and clean. Poster size. Fast."

"No problem. Your company is a big customer. Happy to—"

"This doesn't go on the company tab. It doesn't get logged and or mentioned to anyone—especially anyone from the company."

"Personal dirty pictures, Jack?" laughed Willy.

"I need it sent back to me the same day you get it."

"We're swamped and—"

"There's a hundred up front and three more when I get it back. Plus a hundred expenses. Cash, straight from me, with no record."

"Deal. When do I get it?"

"I'll American Courier it to you today, you'll have it tomorrow morning. Get it back to me at the courier's office in Steeltown no later than Tuesday."

"Steeltown, Jack? What kind of picture you got there?"

Cain hung up. His fourth call went to Bill Wood.

"I can't come to the phone right now," said DEA Agent Wood's taped voice. "After the tone, please leave . . ."

Cain left no message. Local information gave him the address of the American Courier Services office six blocks away.

His knee hurt. The bartender sold him a packet of aspirin. He washed three of them down with two scotch and waters while on TV movie cowboy Randolph Scott rode toward an ambush. Cain felt his knee stiffen as Scott shot his way clear.

Lucky man, thought Cain. He paid for his drinks, left.

Walking to the courier office kept Cain's knee loose. The newspaper building was another twenty-minute stroll. There, the security guard gave him a thick manila envelope of clippings bearing Josh Hammond's by-line.

The scotch and aspirin dulled his hunger and his pain. The sun hung low above Steeltown's roofs. His rented room waited across town.

Focus, he told himself. Keep going.

His feet took him back to the town square, to the commission's office building. Evening shadows lay on its stone wall. A light burned in the commission's third-floor window.

Laughter echoed down the empty corridor as he walked toward the half-open door with the commission's title freshly painted on its fogged glass. A man's laughter, and a woman's.

"Hey, Jack!" said Russell Boswell when Cain stepped inside the office. "How are you?"

Sylvia Kimmett's eyes were cool and blue.

"You should at least keep the door closed," said Cain.

"We were just about to leave," replied Boswell. He spread his hands to encompass the suite of rooms. "How do you like it?"

Boswell led Cain through their chambers. Sylvia followed them; Cain felt her eyes on his back.

What had been empty rooms was now a workplace. The entry room had a receptionist's desk, complete with a computer and telephone system; behind the desk were file cabinets, a photocopying machine, a coat tree with four empty hooks.

"Two more desks are on order," said Boswell, nodding to the room to the right of the reception area. A desk and chair were crowded into a corner, along with two file cabinets. "You and Beth and I will be cramped, but at least we have a place to sit."

"In here," said Boswell, leading Cain to the room on the other side of the reception area, "is the conference room. Nice bookshelves, huh? Beth drove up to the capital to scrounge a reference library and software programs."

"What have you been doing?" said Sylvia behind Cain.

"I've been busy," he replied.

"Doing what?" she asked.

Cain looked at the bare walls.

"I'll tell you later," he said.

Boswell noted his gaze, said, "Sylvia is getting us something to hang on the walls. Prints, photos, whatever."

"How about some scalps?" said Cain.

A long table surrounded by half a dozen chairs dominated the conference room. By the window was a wooden table, small and scarred. A telephone and yellow legal pad waited on its surface.

"That's Sylvia's spot," said Boswell.

Cain turned to face her.

"A little far from the action, aren't you?" he said.

"Close enough," she said.

"But the surprise addition to our empire is outside," said Boswell, nodding to the street. "The governor assigned us a car from the state motor pool. It's parked around the corner. I figure that solves your transportation needs."

"Let's keep it for general use," said Cain. "If it works out for me, fine, if not, whoever needs it should have access to it."

"One never knows who might be behind its wheel," said Sylvia. "Or what wheel Jack Cain might be behind."

"That's right," said Cain. He noticed Boswell staring at the manila envelope in his hand.

"We've got a lot to talk about," he said, then carefully enunciated his words: "But it's not the best time."

"Time is everybody's trouble," said Boswell. "I'm beginning to think the best victory we can hope for is to find a time when all the commission members can meet."

"Give them the right reason, they'll find the time," said Sylvia.

"What are you two doing now?" said Boswell suddenly.

"Well, I ah . . ." said Sylvia.

"I really don't . . ." began Cain.

"Come for dinner," said Boswell. "I'll call Barbara. If we don't have enough for a fast and easy feed, Johnny Maxx owns the best pizza carryout in town."

They laughed.

"Call Elliot," Boswell told Sylvia. "Tell him to join us."

"He can't," she said. "He's dining with the Japanese tonight, then taking them to the community symphony."

"So you're alone, too," said Boswell. "Too bad Beth isn't here. Come on: you two have nothing better to do."

Driving the orange state car, Cain followed Sylvia's taillights through dark streets. Ahead of her drove Boswell.

Boswell led them to a "new" middle-income housing development built in the early 1970s when the decline in domestic industrial production and demand was perceived as merely another periodic economic slump. These streets had fewer chuckholes than the rest of the city. The homes were pleasant, split-level ranch houses, with big front lawns and driveways, clipped hedges, and picture windows with the curtains drawn tightly shut.

Boswell parked in the driveway of a white house. The porch light glowed.

"Hi, Dad," said the teenage boy with shaggy brown hair and thick glasses who greeted them at the door. Boswell introduced Cain and Sylvia to his son, who shook their hands, told his father nothing was new, then ran upstairs where his younger sister suffered from a spring cold and a radio blared rock music.

"Barbara!" called Boswell. "We're home!"

"She made the pizzas," he told his guests as they walked deeper into his house and the odor of baking cheese, tomatoes, and sausage. "We try not to give Maxx any more money than necessary.

"Barbara!" he called out again as they walked through the living room with its comfortable sofas and chairs. Family photos covered the cabinet for the Japanese-manufactured television and Korean-built VCR unit.

"Hi, honey," said Boswell as his wife met them in the sunken study with bookshelf walls and love seats surrounding a coffee table. They kissed; his wife's lips quickly resumed their cautious rigidity.

"Dinner won't be much," she said.

"Better than I had with Johnny Maxx," said Cain.

He got the shocked looks he expected, so he told them about his night with the gangster, about his day with the chief of police, about Hammond's clips. But nothing about the photograph he'd stolen.

"I don't know about Johnny's blonde," said Cain.

"That's Debbi Dolan," said Sylvia. "A good kid."

"She's no kid," said Cain. "Besides, good kids and Johnny Maxx don't mix. You know her?"

"The whole town knows about her," said Barbara Boswell.

"A dozen years ago," continued her husband, "she was

the high school beauty nobody could forget. I remember seeing her while refereeing basketball games."

"I'll bet," said his wife, and the married couple laughed.

"What's she doing with Johnny Maxx?" asked Cain.

"He's her best choice," said Sylvia. "Last good deal."

"Bullshit," said Cain.

"That's something you probably know a lot about, Cain," said Sylvia. "But all you know about Debbi Dolan is what you want to see. I don't know everything about her, but I like her. We talk in the grocery store, wave on the street. Shock the same old ladies.

"You men eat her with your eyes. She's got that something; she can't shake it anymore than she can shake her smell. So powerful she scares off most of the good men and challenges all the creeps just by being Debbi. Try handling that at twelve years old. Or ten.

"I don't know if it's true, but supposedly one of her uncles raped her about then . . ."

"Jesus!" said Russ Boswell, "I didn't know . . ."

"Father worked in a mill, she worked surviving everybody telling her she was lucky. At seventeen, she married the best of the creeps who'd been pawing her. She probably hoped marriage would protect her from the other creeps. She was pregnant, of course."

Sylvia shook her head:

"A *real* Steeltown romance.

"Three kids and a lot of beatings later she dumped him or he ran away. Maybe he couldn't take being her husband.

"That was about four years ago. All the wolves started biting at her again. She kept them far enough away to keep those three kids alive, but never knew peace.

"Until Johnny. Next to her own gravity and the trouble it means, he is the most powerful thing she's ever met. She knows he's dangerous, bad. But . . .

"It's a bargain," said Sylvia. "You look at the hand you got, what cards could be left in the deck, and you try to keep from losing.

"Johnny's charming, he takes care of her and her kids, doesn't hurt her. Him being there makes sure nobody bothers her. She can relax a little. He probably gives her the first peace she's ever known."

"He doesn't keep her safe from trouble," said Cain, "he *is* trouble. Eventually, somebody will blast or bust him and she'll become what soldiers call a proximity casualty."

"She probably doesn't believe in eventually," said Sylvia.

"What about Johnny?" asked Cain.

"Hey," said Sylvia. "She's Debbi Dolan: even if he wasn't a normal man, he'd figure she was Johnny Maxx's due."

"He keeps her stoned."

"Maybe," shrugged Sylvia. "We all need something to help."

"Is he vulnerable through her?" asked Cain. "Can we . . ."

Sylvia shook her head, brushed her ash blond hair off her forehead.

"They're both too smart for that," she said.

"But . . ." began Cain.

"Leave her alone," said Sylvia.

"The pizzas!" said Barbara Boswell suddenly, and they all smelled burning cheese.

"I'll give you a hand," said Sylvia.

"No," replied the hostess. "If you could clear the table—and Russ, go upstairs and tell the kids to come down in a while to get theirs—Cain will help me."

Cain followed her into the spotless kitchen. The oven blasted them with heat when she opened the door, put two pizzas on platters, turned the dial down, and left a third in there for the children. Her hands suddenly grasped each other, pressed against the counter top as she leaned her weight into them, closed her eyes.

"Barb—" said Cain. "Are you . . ."

Her eyes opened; soft and brown, moist.

"Please!" she said. "Please, Mr. Cain: Don't get my husband killed!"

"Barb!" called Russell Boswell's voice from the other room. "Do you need any help?"

"No!" she yelled back, her eyes hardening but not leaving Cain's face. "I'm fine.

"We're fine," she said, in a quieter tone.

■　　■　　■

"Too bad Beth isn't here," said Russell Boswell as he leaned back in his chair. Pizza crusts and crumpled beer cans covered the table. He sat next to his wife, across from Cain and Sylvia. Hammond's photocopied news stories lay in the middle of the dinner debris.

"Yes," said Sylvia, "she'll be sorry."

"Why?" asked Mrs. Boswell.

Sylvia smiled, shrugged off the question. This wife of Steeltown's most handsome son wore an ivory silk blouse unbuttoned to a modest neckline.

"Do you think we'll get Hammond's appointment book out of the chief?" asked Commission Chairman Boswell.

"He'll fight us, but we expected that," said Cain.

"We did?" said Boswell, smiling.

"This is where the Citizens' League started," he continued. "Four years ago. We were just a bunch of average citizens . . ."

"Honey," corrected his wife.

"Okay," he said, "maybe better educated and mostly white collar, although we had some steelworkers, too. We'd all pretended that the way things were was the way they had to be. But we couldn't handle that anymore, couldn't stand the control corruption had over our lives. For one thing, a corrupt system doesn't work. If something has no integrity, eventually it collapses in on itself."

"So you decided to do something," said Cain.

"Somebody had to," replied Boswell.

"There are a lot of other somebodies out there," said Sylvia.

"We never figured we'd get a chance like this," said Boswell.

"You mean to solve a murder?" asked Cain.

"You know what I mean," said his commission boss. "Got any ideas on who killed Hammond and where to start?"

"No to who," said Cain, "yes to ideas.

"He wasn't that dangerous," said Cain, tapping the news stories. "There's nothing here worth killing him for. But maybe he finally knew something worth putting a bullet in his brain. We find that something, we'll find who killed him."

"There's no shortage of places to look for something big," said Boswell. "He did stories on the mayor, the police chief, Johnny Maxx, the labor unions, the companies, the governor . . ."

"I think Beth would prefer us to start somewhere other than the governor's office," said Sylvia.

"Let's start with the big three," said Cain. "Johnny Maxx is the roughest. Let's leave him alone for awhile. Let's go after the mayor and the chief.

"Hammond did stories on municipal contracting. Competitive bidding means how much the mayor can squeeze out of whoever he wants to get the contract. There's got to be proof there, and even with Nash owning the keys to the file cabinets, we can find some gems."

"Mayor Nash can't stand to be challenged," said Boswell.

"So," said Cain, "jerk his chain and maybe he'll get so mad he'll get crazy stupid and blow up City Hall for us.

"As for DiCarlo, well, he's got a murder to solve and a drug scandal he can't control. Hammond did a few pieces on the boys in blue blowing cases. Let's take a closer look at *why* they did. If they were bribed or bungled, maybe we can bust a few badges, and they might give us the chief, who might give us . . ."

"You looking for a killer," said Sylvia, "or are you looking to kill a town?"

"What we have to do for sure," said Cain, "is keep this hot, keep it in the public eye. Nash, DiCarlo, even Johnny Maxx, they depend on apathy. If they can keep the crowd calm, then all the subpoenas in the world won't help us."

"We already tried that," said Boswell. "The League wore itself out with public awareness campaigns and . . ."

"And they didn't have a juicy bone to keep the audience's interest," said Cain. "We got Hammond's murder."

"Old news," said Sylvia.

"Then let's make it new news. Commission Chairman Russell Boswell should hold a news conference—quickly, before the out-of-town reporters dash off to the next brushfire. Stand up before the cameras and talk about how we're investigating tie-ins between Hammond's murder and civic corruption, racketeering . . ."

"But the commission hasn't decided . . ."

"Damn it!" said Cain. "We are the commission! Us, right here, in this room!"

"And Beth," added Sylvia.

"And Beth," said Cain. "If we wait for the commission, we'll go nowhere. You can't even get them together for a meeting."

"But I'd like to have as many of them on board as possible," said Boswell. "At the press conference, we should at least have the local people—Reverend Borge; your husband, Sylvia; the—"

"No," said Cain.

"No," said Sylvia.

"Look," explained Cain, "one man out front is clean and clear and simple. He can deliver, he can sell. We want you up there throwing body punches, saying there's monsters and saying we're going to get 'em. That's a hot story. That'll give us the public: they like a good fight. And we'll draw out the opposition. They won't be able to ignore us. Once they're in the open, they're vulnerable."

He paused for breath. At the same moment, he and Sylvia turned from watching Russell Boswell frown to look at each other.

"If we don't deliver," said Boswell eventually, "the good people will hang us with our own hype."

"And if we do," said Sylvia, "the bad people will want our heads."

Barbara Boswell slammed her beer can down on the table. Cain impassively returned her glare.

"Don't worry about the payoff," said Cain. "We'll be fine."

"I owe it to the others to tell them what I'm doing and why," said Boswell. "How will Elliot feel about this, Sylvia?"

"I—he would want to do whatever's right," she told him. "Keep him in the background and he'll be happiest.

"We'll all be happiest," she added. "It'll be best."

"Call a few of your closer friends on the commission, if you must," said Cain. "Reverend Borge, Sylvia's husband.

Might be a good idea, cover your ass. But don't give any-body a chance to tell you no."

A minute of silence passed uncomfortably.

"You know," Boswell finally said, "I didn't . . . I'm not . . . This is all starting to sound too much like politics."

"Everything is politics," said Cain. "That's just the way it is—not bad, not good, just the way it is."

Another minute passed. From upstairs came the gunfire of a television drama.

"Okay," Boswell said.

His wife began clearing the dirty plates and crumpled beer cans off the table. They all stood, and Sylvia bent to help. Cain noticed how her slacks pulled taut and her flat hips belled out as she leaned over.

The two women carried the garbage from the room. Cain scanned the crowded book shelves: law books, a few college texts, half a dozen books of poetry, and twice as many novels. Most of the volumes were either classic philo-sophical works or famous histories. Cain ran his fingers over the Durants, over Wells, over Toynbee.

"You know," said Boswell as they stared at the books' spines, "that's why I do it.

"Everything," he said, defining *it*: "History. The past carries us forward into the future. I try to ride that wave, do what's right, and push it where it should go by knowing where it's been and how it got there."

His wife and Sylvia rejoined them.

"The way I see it," said Cain, "we're trapped between yesterday and tomorrow. We need to understand the past, but don't count on yesterday deciding anything. As for to-morrow, we don't have it and never will. We have to make the best of things today, but everything else is just hope. Just dreams."

"That's what guides us," said Boswell. "Keeps us going."

"Guess so," answered Cain.

Sylvia and Cain thanked Barbara for dinner. Her smile was polite, but fleeting; her lips were grim when she shook Cain's hand. Her husband walked them to the door, bid them farewell.

They slowly walked down the sidewalk. Above them,

the moon was heavy, old. The night was warm. Crickets chirped in the freshly mown lawn, lights glowed in the homes around them. Cain noticed she wore no perfume.

"I didn't expect you to be so ... involved," Cain told her.

"You didn't expect me to be so smart," she said.

He couldn't resist smiling. He unconsciously ran his hand over his head.

"Do you always wear your hair so short?" she asked.

"Makes it easier to take care of. Harder to grab."

"I'll bet," she said.

"Do you need a ride home?" he asked before thinking.

"I've got my own car," she said.

"That's right," he said. "I forgot."

Our Time

"YOU'RE A HARD MAN to find," Cain told Paul Borge shortly after dawn. "Why don't you get a telephone?"

"I hate those things," said Borge. "Anybody can call you. Anytime. Besides," said the crane-like minister, "you found me."

The two men sat on a bench in the park surrounding Kimmett's estate. Behind them, trees swayed in the morning breeze; before them lay a field of untended grass.

"The lady at your rooming house said I might find you here. Russ Boswell needs your advice on a commission matter."

"My advice?" Borge smiled. "If Russ needed that, he wouldn't use an intermediary. So maybe it's not my advice he needs, but my approval. Are you here to convince me to give it?"

"He didn't send me, but—" Cain grinned and shrugged.

"I trust Russ to do what's right," said Borge.

"Good," said Cain.

"Why doesn't Sylvia Kimmett trust you?" asked Borge.

"I don't know," said Cain. "Did she tell you anything?"

"She didn't have to. She doesn't trust you, but I expect you two get along fine."

"Why?"

"You have the same eyes," said Borge.

"Not that I mind riddles," said Cain, "but this is Wednesday, not Sunday. And not exactly your pulpit."

"Even if it were Sunday, I wouldn't be in church. My congregation feels I serve them better if I do not intrude. All I have to do to intrude is be there. Be me.

"Can't help it," he shrugged. Sighed.

"Do you miss going to church?"

"Lord, yes!" laughed the minister. "Not the rituals—I'm a Methodist: what rituals we have are benignly simple. And I don't miss giving sermons. These days I have more questions than answers anyway. But you know what I do miss? The singing."

He laughed and Cain laughed with him.

"Even the worst jaw-busting hymns, the ones with no melody or rhythm or rhyme. I love to sing—and sing with a congregation.

"That's what we Methodists are infamous for," said Borge. "Sometimes I believe we come closest to heaven when we sing all together: *Make a joyful noise unto the Lord, all ye lands.*

"I have a terrible voice," he confessed, and Cain laughed. "Now *that* is a good reason to exile me!"

"So you come out here," said Cain.

"Not every day," said Borge. "But I won't hide in my room. So I forsake my private space for public life."

Borge shook his head.

"That's an illusion anyway. There is no more private space. There's TV or fashion or the telephone or zoning laws or ear or nose pollution. Even in your bathroom you can't do anything that won't be scrutinized by strangers. Where is your soul's own space? Where is the touch of God?"

"Do you believe in that stuff?" asked Cain.

"Judge man not by words alone," said Borge.

Somewhere in the city, a car horn honked.

"You know what I have to do today?" asked Borge. "I have to visit the family of a man who hung himself last night.

"Forty-four years old, laid off twenty months with no way to feed his family and be the man he thought he had to be. He lynched himself from a railroad bridge that used to support trains hauling coal to the factory that used to be open and give him a job. Used to be isn't anymore."

"Is there a lot of that?"

"There's two kinds of suicides these days in Steeltown.

"The first kind is the most common, like last night. A man feels he's been locked outside, forgotten, with nowhere left to go. He's beyond desperation and not looking back. Violence becomes casual to a man like that. If the only target he can find is in the mirror . . .

"The other kind of suicide is like Simms, who was treasurer of the SIC, the umbrella union that—"

"I know what the SIC is," said Cain. "I read about Simms. He killed himself . . ."

"Just before you came to town," said Borge.

"That's right," said Cain, remembering that he'd read that newspaper story the day he'd secretly met Kimmett.

"Simms killed himself because he knew things were going to get worse," said Borge. "He wasn't going to be forgotten, he was going to be found out. He couldn't bear that shame.

"Maybe there's only one kind of suicide," said the gaunt man of God. "Shame: shame of being found out and shame of being forgotten. Maybe they're the same. The forgotten man feels he's finally been found out as a fraud, a fake who's lost to his preordained fate of failure."

"What secret of Simms's was going to come out?"

"Can't you guess?" said Borge. "Money. Union money. Where it is and where it isn't. That's what this big rally is about. Simms knew it was coming, so he sat in his car and blew his brains out."

"Can you get me into that rally?" asked Cain.

"Why?"

"Hammond wrote about union trouble. Maybe that killed him."

"Are you sure you aren't just another vulture?"

"Judge man not by others' words or deeds," said Cain. "Have charity. And common sense."

"Common sense is a commodity I'm seldom accused of having," said Borge. He shrugged. "I'll see what I can do for you."

"Thanks," said Cain. "Want a ride somewhere? Anything I can do for you?"

"Care to sing a little?"

Cain shook his head no. He walked back to his car. Behind him, on a park bench, perched a tall gaunt man, like a silent crane.

No one seemed to be following Cain, and that bothered him. He was sure the watchers saw him arrive back at the Commodore the night before. He'd parked the state car smack in front of the hotel. Now when he checked the car's mirrors, they showed him only where he'd been.

Beth met him in the lobby of their apartment building.

"I worried you'd stand me up," she said as they left.

"Just because I got your note doesn't mean I could say yes."

"What better thing do you have to do?"

As they walked to the car, she told him that her trip the day before had been successful; he told her about dinner at the Boswell's.

"Sorry to have missed that," she said.

"That's what Sylvia said you'd say."

They climbed in the orange sedan.

"Really?" said Beth. "What's she like? I mean, socially?"

"Tough," said Cain.

"I'll bet," said Beth. "I know about women like her."

"Know what?"

She shook her head.

And then he understood.

"You like music?" he asked suddenly. He flipped on the radio, found the station that played classics, and turned the volume up. Again they heard four voices from England who'd changed the world.

"Do you like The Beatles?" he yelled to Beth, who stared at him as if he'd gone mad. "You want to sing along?"

Without waiting for a reply, he broke into song; only twice did he get the words wrong. Two songs later, he turned the car into the parking lot of the pancake house opposite St. Anne's Church.

"They bugged the car," he told Beth as he led her inside. "That's why nobody is on my tail. Probably a trace bug and a transmitter so they could hear what we say and know where we are."

"Who are *they*?" she asked.

"I don't know," he told her as they reached the doors.

"We can't work like this," she said.

"We'll fix most of it tomorrow," he told her as they found a booth. They ordered, and he told Beth about Boswell's press conference.

"Reconnaissance by fire," he explained. "We take blind shots and see what pops up."

"Do you always have this much fun?" she asked.

Cain laughed.

"This is where Joey the Blimp ate his last waffles," he told Beth.

She looked out to the parking lot, to the orange state car that had brought them here, across the street to the church.

"You know how to dampen a girl's enthusiasm," she said.

"You're no girl."

"That's right," she told him, and smiled.

"If you were, you wouldn't make it in this job."

"Oh."

A shadow fell across their table.

"Mind if I join you?" boomed Chief DiCarlo. He grinned down at them, slowly extended his heavy paw toward Beth.

"Nice to meet you, Miss Worby," he said. "I'm the chief, but you can call me Harry."

She gave him her hand and felt it disappear in his flesh. Grunting, DiCarlo pushed himself into the booth next to Beth, who wedged herself against the wall to accommodate his bulk. Their sides touched; his massive leg pressed against her thigh.

"Did you a favor, Cain," said DiCarlo.

"What?" said Cain.

"My men saw some undesirables hanging around your hotel. I had them run off, and my men made it clear they shouldn't come back."

"Were they Maxx's boys?"

"Couldn't prove it," said the chief. "But that's a good bet."

"Johnny won't be happy about that."

"Who gives a shit?" said DiCarlo, his eyes gleaming.

"*Excuse me*," said the waitress, and they leaned back so she could put down the plates of pancakes, bacon and eggs.

"I'll let you two enjoy your breakfast," said DiCarlo. He pushed his way out of the booth, sauntered from the restaurant; through the windows they saw him climb into a cruiser and be driven away.

"That's who the bugs belong to," said Cain. "His cops have been on me all along. And probably Maxx's men, somebody from Nash. Now he's cut them off my track—which helps DiCarlo as much as me."

"I hate it when people drop by before I've finished my coffee," said Beth.

They sipped from their mugs.

"Did you go out much for breakfast when you were a kid?" she asked him.

"No," said Cain. "My father worked odd hours and I slept late."

"Dad loved to take us out for Sunday breakfast," she said. "He said it gave Mom a break, but he did it because he loved to. He always made it a big deal, and we always went along. Color comics."

"I read them too," said Cain. "When the old man was done."

"Happy times," she said.

Cain took another sip of coffee.

"What were you like as a boy? A kid?" she asked.

"Do you want a picture?" he teased.

"I'd love one."

"Sorry." He shrugged. "What you see is what was there. Only in high school, with a little more hair."

They laughed.

"I never saw anyone like you then," she said.

"You just didn't notice."

"Well, none of you ever noticed me!"

"Yes we did," said Cain. He shrugged. "If a girl like you had noticed me then, maybe I wouldn't be here today."

Beth flushed.

"Where did you go to high school?" she asked.

"Doesn't matter," he told her, "it's all the same."

"What about now?" she asked.

"Now we're here," he said.

The Way
Things Are Done

THE WOMAN PRESIDING BEHIND the commission's reception desk the next morning looked like a giant bulldog. She had gray hair, a square jaw, and wore a khaki suit. Her black eyes glared at Cain as he closed the door.

"My name," she barked, "is Catherine Rose Wagner. You're Jack Cain. I've taken two messages for you. It's six and a half after nine."

"Where did you come from?" asked Cain as he closed the door.

"Marines," she said. "Sergeant major, retired."

"Catherine will handle the front office for us," said Sylvia from the door leading to her desk in the conference room.

"I'll bet," he said. "Come on," he said to Sylvia, and to Catherine: "Call the state police commander for me."

"Can you manage the receiver yourself or do you want me to switch it on speaker?" snapped Catherine.

Cain hesitated at the door to his office, looked back and said, "Please? And I hate speaker phones."

"That's better," she said.

Sylvia followed Cain to his office.

"What was her listing in the Yellow Pages?" he asked, nodding *hello* to Boswell, who sat behind a desk, telephone pressed against his ear. A light flashed on Cain's desk telephone. He answered it and Sylvia leaned against the door jam.

"Commander? This is Jack Cain of the Steeltown commission. . . . We need our phones and office swept for bugs. . . . Yes, I'm calling from there . . . I know they'll know. . . . That's fine. And I want it done at least three times a week, unannounced and unscheduled, always the same technicians, and I'll call you to verify them. . . . Yes, I hope so too."

Cain hung up. Boswell shook his head, resumed concentrating on his phone call.

Sylvia smiled. She wore a simple blue dress that cost more than the average steelworker drew for a week's unemployment; the color matched her eyes perfectly.

Catherine marched into the room.

"You forgot your messages," she snapped, handing Cain two pink slips.

"What do I call you?" asked Cain.

"Anything reasonable, sir," she said.

"Don't call me sir. Jack is fine. And no need to salute."

"Get smart with me," she said, with a camouflaging smile, "and you'll be jack shit."

She turned sharply and withdrew to the outer office.

"I'm going to love her," he told Sylvia, and they laughed. Boswell waved for them to be quiet.

"Let's go to your office," said Cain. Sylvia led him there.

"He's still trying to get the commission members scheduled into a meeting," she said. "He's nervous about his press conference."

"No need to be," said Cain as he looked at the message slips: publisher Evans (wanting to know if he could release Hammond's clips) and reporter Cohn (wanting anything). "They'll take what he gives them."

The office door opened and closed.

"Sorry I'm late," said Beth. She marched into the conference room. "I had to load my car with the law books and computer. I thought I'd catch a ride with you, Jack, but . . ."

"Good morning, Beth," said Sylvia.

"Sylvia, can you and Russ set up the press conference for this afternoon?" said Cain.

"Sure."

"And call these two back. Tell the publisher to release Hammond's clips and tell Cohn to go to the press conference."

"Do I get to unload the car?" said Beth; her tone was droll.

"You and I have more important things to do," he said. She smiled, then her eyes flicked beyond him to Sylvia.

"Have fun, kids," said Sylvia.

"I don't understand," said the clerk behind the counter at City Hall. "You need to check with someone else."

"The sign on the door reads Office of Records and Contracts, right?" said Cain.

"Of course it does," snapped the clerk.

"Then we're where we want to be," said Cain.

"You want copies of all the city's requests for proposals, the bids and contracts for the last *ten years*?"

"Yes," he told her.

"We can't do that," replied the clerk.

"This state has an open records law," Beth told her. "Any member of the public can look at those documents during business hours. We can also get copies, provided we're willing to pay the copying fee, which must be minimal and is set by state regulation.

"Ten cents a page," she added.

"Well," said Cain, "we're the public, our pockets are full of dimes, and . . ." he nodded to the clock on the wall above the door: nine-forty-seven. ". . . we're here."

"That's . . ." began the clerk. She bit her lip, glanced over her shoulder to the other clerks pretending to be busy at their desks or the gray file cabinets filling the room. "That's not our job."

"If we're in the records and contracts office," said Cain, "that's your job."

"It's the law," said Beth.

"I don't think so," replied the clerk. She looked over her shoulder again; again found no help.

"I'm an attorney," said Beth. "With the governor's office. Assigned to the Steeltown investigatory commission. And a citizen."

"But that's not the way things are done!" said the clerk.

Cain and Beth smiled.

"Look . . . just . . . wait a minute."

She scurried to the desk farthest from the counter, conferred briefly with a man who wore a bow tie; he peered around her to stare at Cain and Beth. They smiled. He picked up the telephone, dialed.

"Here we go," whispered Cain.

"The timely response of appropriate agencies," replied Beth.

The man in the bow tie hung up, walked to the counter.

"Mr. Cain," he said. "Ms. Worby. I'm afraid your request is more complicated than it seems."

"Ah," said Cain.

"How's that?" asked Beth.

"Simply . . . simply put," said the bow tie, "it requires an extraordinary effort on our part to process and . . . to . . . to . . ."

"To comply with the law?" asked Beth.

"It's not a question of compliance," said the man, "it's . . ."

"Then what is it a question of?" asked Cain.

"Well . . . procedure. That's it. Procedure. We want to be sure we're proceeding correctly."

"Should I read you the statutes?" said Beth.

"That's certainly not necessary. We've checked with the mayor's assistant, and he promised the mayor's office will get right on this and will work everything out."

The man smiled, relieved to have found an answer.

"We'll be back for the documents in the morning," said Cain.

"But . . ." said the man, then stopped, and watched them leave.

"And what will we get?" Beth asked Cain as the bureaucracy's glass door clicked shut behind them.

"Doesn't matter," he said. "If they give us nothing, we can nail them for that. If they give us anything, we'll find something in it to nail them."

"What do you think Hammond found?" asked Beth.

"Who cares about Hammond?" said Cain as they walked down the musty corridor of City Hall.

■   ■   ■

"More secrets?" said Beth as Cain slid into the booth at the cafe on the square. She sipped her third cup of coffee while the waitress strolled over to fill Cain's cup for the first time.

"Just personal business," he told her.

He'd called Bill Wood from a pay phone, but the DEA agent had nothing new. Cain gave him vague promises of more to come, and pressured him to force a federal grand jury to chase Johnny Maxx.

"What do you think we've been doing for the last few years?" said Wood.

Cain called the courier service, but no package had arrived for him from New York. His last call arranged that night's rendezvous.

"Like I said," repeated Beth, "more secrets."

"You're an inquisitive woman," Cain told her.

"It's my job," she said.

They laughed.

"Why did you leave the bugs in the car?" she asked.

"If DiCarlo thinks we don't know about them, maybe we can jerk him around."

"So what personal business do you have in town?" said Beth.

"Don't you ever give up?"

"Not if it's worth it."

"Come on," he said, dropping a dollar bill on the table, "let's get back to work while I still have some secrets."

Cain and Beth were half a block from the commission office when four men walked out of a building ahead of them to a Cadillac parked at the curb.

"Well," said Johnny Maxx, when he saw Cain and Beth, "look who's out in daylight."

"Speak of the devil," said Cain.

Cain stepped ahead of Beth as he walked toward Johnny Maxx's smile. One of Maxx's companions, a dumpy, fiftyish man wearing a rumpled suit, averted his droopy eyes from Cain and Beth; his other two companions riveted their gaze on them. One man was stocky like a jackknife; the other looked like a bear in a three-piece, pinstripe blue suit.

Cut in the stone archway of the building the quartet had left were the words *Steeltown Industrial Coalition*.

"Meaning me?" said Johnny Maxx, his smile steady.

"Actually," said Cain, "we were talking about Chief DiCarlo."

"Really?"

"Seems he steamrolled some friends of yours."

"Is that right?"

"He seemed to enjoy it," said Cain. "Of course, I'm not telling you anything you don't already know."

"But you could," said the smiling man. He stepped around Cain. "For instance, you haven't introduced me to this lovely lady."

He held out his hand. A flush crept out of Beth's white blouse and colored her face. Her breaths became shallow, yet they moved her shoulders and breasts with a quick, exaggerated rhythm. Beth hesitated, but that hand didn't go away.

"Johnny Maxx," he said softly.

She met his grip. His eyes danced.

"Beth Worby," she said softly.

"It's a pleasure," he said, finally releasing her hand.

"Forgetting your manners, Johnny?" said Cain. He nodded to the three men behind Johnny Maxx.

"Miss Worby, I can see my worries about Jack are wasted. With you, he's in marvelous hands. And a lucky man."

"I . . ." began Beth; she stopped, uncertain.

"What brings you here, Johnny?" asked Cain.

"Business," he said. He smiled. "Friends."

"Working on the grand jury stuff?" said Cain.

"What grand jury?!"

"I was hoping you could tell me," said Cain. "The local law hasn't said word one about it to me or anybody on the commission."

"Then what are you talking about?"

"Something I heard," said Cain. "Maybe you heard something, too. You being a fine citizen with a badge and friends everywhere."

"My friends," said Johnny Maxx, "aren't the kind to have anything to do with grand juries."

"Is that right, fellows?" said Cain to the three men who stood behind Johnny Maxx.

The jackknife man and the bear turned to Johnny Maxx; the dumpy older man turned his back, shuffled his feet.

"Hey, Johnny," said Cain. "You heard any more about the feds and your friend Wolinsky? Anybody know what he's doing these days?"

"Nice to see you, Jack," said Johnny Maxx. His smile didn't waver. He headed toward the Cadillac, the other three men eagerly preceding him. They climbed in the car, drove off.

"I feel like I should wash my hand," said Beth.

"To clean it," said Cain, "or to cool it off?"

She glared at Cain, her eyes wide, her lips parted as if to speak. She blushed, but said nothing. He led her down the sidewalk.

Artificial light fell gently on their small circle in the mayor's office: Beth, Cain, and Nash, seated on wooden chairs. The afternoon sun burned around the edges of the heavy curtains behind the mayor's desk and sent shadows toward them like dark fingers reaching across the bare wooden floor.

"We seem to be caught up in a chain of misunderstandings," said Mayor Richard Nash. His pale hand rose from his lap, turned palm up. A shrug tilted his egg-shaped head to one side; he frowned.

"For instance," he continued, "my invitation was for Mr. Cain—though I'm pleased to meet you, Miss Worby."

"I thought it might be wise to have the commission counsel in our meeting," said Cain. "I assumed from your assistant's call that you wanted to talk about commission business."

"There's no need to be so formal," said Nash.

"Un-huh," said Cain, who with Beth had passed through the same gauntlet of secretaries, aides, and sheriff's deputies he'd met when he came alone to the mayor's office. But in this visit, the mayor came from behind his desk to greet them, then led them to these three wooden chairs, which would be whisked away as soon as they left.

"Steeltown works," continued the Mayor. "Despite the experts' doomsaying, despite the politicians, my city works. I see to it. And it works well. Because we have a way of getting things done here.

"That way," he continued, "does not include government by press conference. Calling people corrupt and crooks and other baseless innuendos."

"Mr. Boswell called no one corrupt," said Beth. She'd stood at the back of the commission office next to Cain and Sylvia while Russell Boswell read the carefully prepared text to the dozen reporters and TV cameras. "He said that based on Hammond's stories and persistent rumors the commission has heard, we must investigate the possibility that a pattern of corruption and gangsterism exists within the city and that Hammond was killed because he . . ."

"I'm a lawyer, too, Miss Worby," said the mayor. "And I watched the television show. Another afternoon soap opera."

"Like the Watergate hearings?" said Cain.

"Don't overreach yourself, Mr. Cain," said the mayor. "You and Commissioner Boswell must be careful about that."

"Why didn't you ask to see him?" said Cain.

"There is no need for me to explain my reasoning," said Nash.

Cain wondered what would have transpired if he'd come alone to meet the mayor.

"Forget about the press conference," said Cain. "Boswell did what he had to do. Maybe he made you uncomfortable and your enemies happy. The question is what you're going to do about it now."

"I'm sure you have some suggestions," said His Honor.

"Nope," said Cain. "But I've got questions. Like Hammond."

"He found no crimes."

"Maybe he wasn't a good looker. Or maybe he hadn't gotten around to printing them yet."

"Running a city is a big business, Mr. Cain."

"It's a public business, and we're being unwisely stymied on our end of it. Just like Hammond."

"Yes," said the mayor. "I heard about your visit to the clerk's office."

A loud *buzz* sounded, the office door clicked, and the seedy aide named Carson stepped into the room.

"Sorry to disturb you, Mr. Mayor," said Carson, "but we're having some trouble with the Dearborne project, and . . ."

The mayor's egg face turned bright crimson and seemed to swell; his tiny hands rose a few inches from his lap and twisted into trembling claws. He turned, shouted to Carson:

"*I . . . told . . . them . . . how . . . to . . . handle . . . it! Tell . . . them . . . to . . . DO IT!*"

"Yes, sir!" said Carson. He quickly backed from the room.

The mayor sighed deeply. The claws settled back to his lap and rearranged themselves into hands. The blood withdrew from his face.

"About the city contracts, your Honor," said Cain.

"What are you after?" said the mayor. "And why?"

"What you have is a mess," said Cain. "And we're the ones supposed to clean it up. You've got a dead reporter who wrote about trouble in your administration. You got the feds' drug busts and grand juries, all being egged on by the national media. You got everybody looking for a target with a loaded gun."

"It's a circus," said Nash.

"Then there's gotta be a show," Cain told him.

"This is government!" insisted Beth. "Public policy and administration of law! The political process! This isn't . . ."

"Hammond wrote about a lot besides me," said the mayor.

"Sure," said Cain, "but we started here because we thought we'd find no problems, but instead what we . . ."

"This is not acceptable, Mr. Cain."

Who replied to the mayor with a shrug.

The shadows on the floor drew closer as they sat in silence.

"Mr. Cain, Miss Worby," the mayor said finally, "as chief city executive, I am dependent on a large and complex bureaucracy, much of which I inherited. And while I exercise a great deal of oversight in my administration, I cannot control everything."

"Of course," said Cain.

Beth frowned. She sensed a rhythm between the two men in the room, one which made her uncomfortable.

"Some processes take time," said the mayor. "I understand your impatience. Russ Boswell has always been destined for fine things. I'm sure your futures are also promising. The Hammond murder is a blight on my city which I want wiped away. I wish you God speed in that endeavor, and will do what I can to help.

"Including," he said, "offering constructive criticism when you wander astray.

"Now, if you'll excuse me, I must get ready for another interminable dinner with our Japanese guests."

He stood. So did Cain and Beth. She stared at Cain, her eyes full of questions. Cain's face lacked expression. The mayor gave them each his small right hand for a limp shake.

"Good-bye," he told them. "Good luck."

First Blood

THE BOW-TIED RECORDS CLERK smiled when Beth and Cain entered his office at 9:02 the next day.

"Hello," he said from behind the counter. "Nice to see you."

"Looks like you were expecting us," said Cain.

"You said you'd be back first thing in the morning."

From beneath the counter, the clerk took a fist-thick file folder, plunked it down before them.

"What's that?" asked Beth.

"The first batch of city contracts you requested. Actually, copies of them. The mayor instructed us to waive the copying fee. The law allows us to do that for the public good.

"We'll continue processing the rest of your request as quickly as possible," added the clerk. "Although the mayor's task force complicates matters."

"What mayor's task force?" asked Cain.

"Why . . . didn't you see the paper this morning?" said the clerk. "Small item, back page?

"The mayor has an in-house task force to review all city contracts to be sure the law had been fully complied with. Yesterday they issued their latest report—a routine notice that they expect to be done by the end of the year."

"How long has this task force existed?" asked Cain.

"Quite some time," said the clerk. "I'm sure the mayor's office could provide you with its paperwork."

"I'm sure," said Cain. "How does this task force compli-
cate our request?"

"Well, they are wading through all the records, which
has generated an abnormal amount of chaos—understandably
so."

"Understandably," said Beth.

"And since they have historical priority, your request
will be processed by us as they complete their task and
return the records to our control."

"This file has been through the mayor's people?" said
Beth. "And who else?"

"Funny you should ask that," said the clerk. His bow tie
wiggled. "I'm sure I'd have mentioned it to you, if you
hadn't asked."

"Really," said Cain.

"What's funny about these contracts," said the clerk, "is
that we found copies of them. I *think* that the reason we
have the extra copies is that we duplicated them for Mr.
Hammond."

"What are we looking for?" asked Sylvia as she, Beth,
and Cain sat around the commission conference table, each
of them reading documents from the contracts file.

"We'll know when we find it," answered Cain. He glanced
at his watch: 3:10 in the afternoon; they'd been working
thus since mid-morning, pausing only as three state police
technicians poked around the office rooms with electronic
wands, then wired black boxes to the telephones and watched
dials spin.

"If bugs were here," said the commanding technician,
"they've been turned off."

"Why did Nash order this released to us?" asked Beth.

Sylvia smiled as Cain said, "We'll know . . ."

"I know," Beth finished for him, "when we find it.

"It's a grab bag," she continued. "Contracts from twelve
years ago, bids from last week, some records incomplete,
some photocopies unreadable. . . . If this is how they give us
everything, we'll never know what we've got."

Beth flipped the page of the stapled papers she was

reading, grumbled beneath her breath. Cain and Sylvia smiled at her anger—and noticed each other's reaction.

"Wait a minute," said Beth.

She quickly flipped pages back and forth.

"Listen," Beth said finally: "This is a complete filing. Notice of bid proposal, submitted bids, contract, the works. Eight years old. For police cars. Contract controlled by something called the PPRB—Police Procurement Review Board.

"The city wanted thirty new police cars. Got bids from a few local dealers and three elsewhere in the state. All the bids but one were between five and six thousand per car. Some man named Jeffrey Meyers bid seventy two hundred dollars per car. And he got the contract!"

"Meyers?" said Sylvia. She frowned. "The only Jeff Meyers I know of was a harmless old guy who my husband said used to run favors for Olson, hung around city hall, the cops.

"He's dead now," she added.

"So is Olson," said Cain. "Who's on that Review Board?"

Beth flipped through the pages.

"Doesn't say, but for approval, the contract had to be signed by the board chairman and secretary and they're . . . Chief Harry DiCarlo and Mimi Grossman," said Beth.

The three of them stared at each other.

"Mimi Grossman is dead too," said Sylvia. "She'd worked in City Hall forever."

"Wait a minute!" yelled Beth. She ran her finger down a list of invoices. "The bid called for thirty cars. Meyers delivered them plus one more—a quote command use vehicle.' And . . ."

She shook her head.

"There's a photocopy of a car registration stapled on the back of the invoice. One fully equipped Cadillac sedan, bought by General Equipment Fund, Steeltown Police Department. Title signed over by the review board to Harry DiCarlo, chief of police.

"He got a car," she whispered.

"It's all there!" cried Beth. "In black and white! He got a car! On a phony low bid contract he regulated, he got a car for . . ."

"For maybe departmental use," said Cain. He held up his hand: "I know, but let's be sure. Besides," he said, "this doesn't make sense."

"What do you mean?" yelled Beth.

Sylvia watched Cain.

"Of course it makes sense!" insisted Beth. "DiCarlo rigged the contract for Meyers, who was a friend of Olson's, who I guess was once a heavy in this town. God knows why Olson wanted the contract rigged—maybe to pay off his buddy or maybe just to be a nice guy and spread the sugar around; who knows, who cares, he's dead. And DiCarlo's piece was a Cadillac! It makes perfect sense!"

"It's penny ante," said Cain. "That makes sense. Lots of crooks who wash their dollars are careless about covering how they get their pennies. DiCarlo was new to being a chief with a license to steal. Olson was the big man then. DiCarlo would love to please him and profit, so DiCarlo wouldn't worry too much about his tracks.

"What doesn't make sense is Nash feeding us DiCarlo. He should have fed us Johnny Maxx. That's the smart move for the mayor, the least risky and the easiest, probably the best long-term gain. Johnny is ripe for a fall. If we take him for anything, people will assume it's for Hammond's murder, too. Everybody will be satisfied and the commission will have to go away.

"This," said Cain, waving his hand at the contracts file, "this doesn't make sense."

"So what?" said Beth. "Being smart and making sense isn't always what people do."

"You think this is a phantom?" asked Sylvia.

"I think it's a shot at three dead people and DiCarlo," said Cain. "But it's something that can wound, not kill."

"Maybe that's all Nash had," said Beth.

"Or all he had that wouldn't backfire," said Sylvia.

The door to the conference room suddenly opened.

"You guys got anything yet?" said Russell Boswell.

The women glanced at Cain.

"We're not sure," Cain told his commission boss.

"Keep at it," said Boswell. "I've got to dash around town soothing ruffled feathers."

He left.

"What are you—*we* going to do?" asked Beth as the echo of the closing door faded.

"Do you think Hammond knew about all this?" asked Sylvia.

Cain looked at his watch: 3:31, ninety minutes left in the business day, four hours before his next scheduled move.

"Beth," he said, "in the bowels of state government are all the old motor vehicle records. Drive up to the capital tonight. You'll need to bully your way in because tomorrow is Saturday. Track these vehicles, especially the Caddy. Have at least one unimpeachable witness with you, photocopy and certify everything, make notes, make the officials you work with do the same. And lock them into secrecy."

"I know what to do," she said.

"Remember," he cautioned her, "you're still in Steeltown up there."

"Sylvia," continued Cain, "on your way home *now*, stop by the newspaper. Be low key. Nobody should know exactly what you're doing. Have Evans let you personally check their files and copy clips about that 'car dealer' Meyers, the little old lady from city hall, the review board ... and Olson."

"But not Chief DiCarlo?" asked Sylvia.

"Not yet," said Cain. "Let's stay subtle and unseen."

"See you in the morning," said Sylvia. She picked up her purse, left the office.

" 'Bye, Jack," said Beth.

"Good luck," he said.

She smiled, hesitated, then she too left the conference room. A minute later, he heard the outer office door open and close.

Jackson Cain leaned back, then sank forward, his weight filling his arms as they pressed against the table. His head hung down until his chin almost touched his chest; his eyes were closed and for ten, for twenty minutes, he was nowhere.

There was a knock on the conference room door; Catherine entered.

"Chairman Boswell gave me permission to leave early

today, as soon as I finished my work," she announced. "Do you want anything?"

"If I do," he said, "looks like I'll have to get it myself."

"That's right," she said. "I'll lock the outer door."

She left.

The afternoon sun warmed the room with yellow light. Cain loosened his tie, called the courier service, and learned that his package from New York had arrived; they agreed to deliver it to him immediately. He hung up, walked to the window overlooking the square. After two sharp blows to break the paint seal, the window opened enough to admit a refreshing dry breeze. He leaned against the wall, looked outside. In the doorway of a building across the city square a man in a tan Windbreaker and black metal glasses checked his watch, and Cain felt his memory stir.

"Well," said Cain as the man moved deeper into the doorway shadows, "I'll be damned."

Twenty minutes later, a courier brought him a yard-long tube. The New York photo lab had done a fine job; Willy had returned the print Cain stole and included the negative he'd made. Cain unrolled the poster-size photograph and laid it on the conference table, weighing down the edges with law books.

"Why was this so important to DiCarlo?" he asked himself as he stared at the black-and-white magnified image of Josh Hammond's 'lost' desk blotter sheet, a soiled calendar covered with doodles, crude drawings, numbers, coffee stains, and barely recognizable scrawls.

The glass in the door to the hall rattled as someone tried the knob; rattled again. Someone knocked.

Cain quickly rerolled the photographs, thrust them in their tube. He tossed the tube to the top of the bookshelf—a seemingly careless storage of an unimportant item.

Again came a knock.

Through the door's black-lettered, clouded glass Cain saw the shape of a man. Cain stood at an angle from the door and called out, "Who is it?"

"Hello?" answered a baritone voice in the hall. "It's Elliot Kimmett. Is anybody in there?"

Cain unlocked the door and admitted Sylvia's husband.

"Nice office," said the Kimmett heir as he walked through the commission rooms. "This is the first chance I've had to visit."

"That busy?" said Cain to the commissioner he'd created.

"Mostly with the Japanese delegation."

"How's that going?"

"Hard to say," said Kimmett. He smiled, but the shake of his head said he was frowning. "To tell you the truth, I'm not sure it's going well. They're polite, inquisitive, interested . . . But we're running out of things to show them and ways to keep them busy."

"When do they leave?"

"A few days. I wish this afternoon. I'd like them out of town before tonight's union rally—just in case."

"In case . . ."

"Never mind me," said Kimmett. "Perhaps I worry too much. These times are so hard, we're straining to put on such a proper show, and the SIC gathering tonight to air their dirty laundry . . ."

He shrugged, said: "Those poor men."

"The Japanese?"

"No." Kimmett frowned. "Is Sylvia here? I haven't really talked to her since yesterday, and tonight there's the mayor's banquet and I'm not sure if she's . . . Is she here?"

"She should be home by now," said Cain.

"May I?" said Kimmett. They stood in the conference room; Kimmett pointed toward his wife's phone.

"Of course," said Cain. "It's your office."

Kimmett dialed a number, listened to it ring for more than a minute. Cain shifted his feet, careful to not watch the husband.

"Well," said Kimmett, "she's not there."

"She was on a commission errand," said Cain. "Probably took longer than we thought."

"Probably," said Kimmett. "Yes, probably."

He nodded to the yellow legal pads and photocopied contracts.

"How is it going?" he asked.

"Fine," answered Cain.

"Is there anything I can do to help?"

"Well . . . I think Mr. Boswell could probably use you."

"Russ is a good man," said Kimmett.

"Yes," answered Cain. "By the way: Sylv—your wife has done a great job setting us up and . . . You know."

"She's a wonderful woman," said her husband.

"Yes," agreed Cain.

"Perhaps I'll try her again," said Kimmett.

As he did, Cain perched on a corner of the conference table.

Again, the husband got no answer. He hung up, frowned, and then he, too, sat on a corner of the table.

"Still not home."

"Oh."

"She's probably busy," said Kimmett. "Our son comes home tomorrow."

"I didn't know that."

"He's been away at school. She's probably quite busy getting ready for that." Kimmett smiled. "He's not your usual teenager."

"Ah."

"Do you have any children, Cain?"

"No."

"Funny thing about children. You think you're creating a piece of tomorrow and you wind up enmeshed in today."

"I wouldn't know."

"Well," said the handsome scion of Steeltown, "we all get through life—in one fashion or another.

"The trick is," he added, after a pause, "to do it well."

Cain shrugged.

"How did you find my father?" asked Kimmett.

"What do you mean?"

"Never mind," said the son, shaking his head. "I shouldn't put you on the spot. Anyway, he's little business of yours. But . . .

"My father . . . He is a difficult man, Cain. You must not let him . . . *Corrupt* isn't the right word, nor is *control*, but . . . You must always remember to follow your own course with my father."

"I'll remember," said Cain.

"It's nowhere near as easy as it sounds," confided Kimmett.

The two men said nothing for more than a minute. Cain grew restless, but the other man seemed comfortable with silence.

"Well," said Kimmett finally, "third time is the charm."

He walked to the telephone and called his home again.

"No one's there," he announced when he put down the receiver.

"Three strikes," he joked. He walked to the outer office and Cain followed him.

"Still light out," said Kimmett, glancing out the windows. "Summer is here."

"Looks like it," said Cain.

"The banquet is at Enzio's," said Kimmett. He glanced at his watch. "I have to be sure everything there is ready and Sylvia . . .

"If you see her, say hello. Tell her where I am, what I'm doing."

"I will," promised Cain.

"Thanks, old sport," said Kimmett, with boyish camaraderie. He left.

From the window, Cain watched him emerge on the street, disappear to his duties. Cain stayed at the window for half a hour, his gaze locked on the doorway across the square. The man with black metal glasses didn't show himself.

Soon enough, thought Cain.

He hid the tube of photographs behind the bookcase, flipped through the documents on the table as he put them in folders. When he was about to lock them in the reception room's file cabinet, a key rattled in the hall door. It swung open, and Sylvia stepped inside. For a moment she didn't see him in the shadows, then her eyes widened.

"Oh!" she exclaimed. "I didn't think anybody would be here."

"Killing time," said Cain.

"Well," she replied with a nasty grin, "that makes two of us."

She shut the office door and walked into the conference room. Cain closed the file cabinet, followed her and found her standing in the west window, arms crossed, staring at the sunset.

Red light bathed her. Her blue dress draped her listlessly. In that light, her blond hair looked like stiff copper wire. She wore more makeup than when she'd left. Her eye shadow was smudged and the rouge on her cheek was spotty. Her lipstick was bright red. From across the table, Cain smelled that she'd absorbed a stubborn cloud of stale cigarette smoke, processed air, and liquor.

"Your husband was here a little while ago," he said.

She didn't reply.

"He called your house, but you weren't there. He had the mayor's dinner to go to, he said. I don't know if he went home first."

"Neither do I," she said.

Cain sat on the same corner of the table as before, and tried to sound casual.

"Where you been?" he asked.

"Finishing some business I didn't care about anymore," she said. Her words went into the window glass.

"Did you get the news clips?"

"That too."

She turned from the window without facing him, gave him her back as she walked to her desk. As she opened her drawer, she said, "The clips are in that envelope."

A white envelope lay on the table.

"Tomorrow," he said.

"Whatever," she replied.

She turned to face him, a bottle of scotch in her hand.

"Well, Jackson Cain," she said, "care to join me?"

"Why not?" he replied.

"Why not?" she repeated, and he fetched coffee cups from the outer office.

"This one's got water in it," he said as he sat three tan mugs on the table. "No ice, but . . ."

"You want it cut?" she asked.

"Makes it smoother," he replied.

She splashed straight scotch in one cup, a mixture in the other, and handed the adulterated one to him.

"Cheers," she said.

They drank and watched each other. He moved to the middle of the table, sat on it. She perched on the corner, dangled one leg over the edge and kept the other on the floor. Her knee was nicely shaped, her calf and ankle trim.

"So," she said, "what did you and my husband talk about?"

"The Japanese," he replied.

"Of course."

"How busy he is, the comm—"

"Always," she interrupted.

"Your son coming home."

She stared into her cup and swirled the amber fluid, then took a long drink.

"Ah, yes. Our son."

"Is he your only child?"

"Isn't he enough?"

"I don't know him," said Cain.

"He's not my baby anymore. He's a Kimmett. Somehow."

"I don't know much about all that."

"One night," she said, "one night you lose a little bit of blood and the next thing you know there's a whole new world."

Cain took a long drink.

"You know what I used to think?" she said.

He shook his head.

"I used to think that if I could just bake a great cherry pie, then everything else'd be fine.

"Turns out," she said a second later, "I must be a lousy cook."

"That's not everything."

"Oh," she said, her face drawing down in mock seriousness, "no, it sure isn't.

"But what do you care, Cain? What do you care about me and my husband and the kid who was once my little boy and my hometown and all that? You're not going to tell me, are you?"

"Would you believe me if I did?"

"Probably not," she said, shaking her head. She smiled, and gently shook her cup at him. "Probably not."

"Why do you drink so much?"

"You mean *too* much, don't you?"

"I guess I do."

"What do you know about all that?"

"I've had my days."

She looked at him over the mug's rim.

"Yes," she said, "I'll bet you have. Well, I'll be damned."

"You ought to go home," he told her.

"Ought to, ought to, *ought to!* You and my husban' and your damn *ought to*'s! What about *can*'s and *want to*'s? And *can't*'s and *don't dare*'s and *don't know*'s? What about them?"

He didn't reply. She suddenly stood, leaned closer to him. He smelled scotch on her breath, powder on her skin. She said, "Do I make you nervous, Mr. Cain?"

"No," he said quietly.

She leaned back.

"You know just where you're going and jus' what you're doing, but you only think you do." She shook her head. "I know about that."

"I know you do," he said. "But it's time for you to go home."

"What kind of man are you, Cain? You know what I see when I look at you?"

"No."

She shook her head, wrinkled her brow as she stared at the floor.

"I don't either," she said. "Funny. I don't either."

He moved toward her and she jerked back, her eyes wide with defiance and fear. He slowly circled around her and she backed up until the conference table pressed against her hips and she could retreat no further. Her crimson lips parted and her breath came in quick gasps.

Their gaze didn't break as he fumbled for, found the phone on her desk. He called information, asked for the taxi company's number, then punched the proper buttons. He ordered a cab.

"Come on," he said, reaching toward her. This time she didn't shy away. His fingers touched her thin arm. She trembled. "You can't drive and you have to go home."

"I don't want to," she said.

"It's the only place," he told her.

He led her from the office to the elevator, rode down to the ground with her. The cage filled with her scent that had become warm and salty like the sea in summer. He kept his hand on her arm, led her from the square to a curb just as a taxi pulled up. Evening's gray light was fading to black; streetlights came on. Cain put her in the back seat, started to ask her for her home address, but the cabby said he knew where she lived and would have her there in five minutes. For safety, Cain lied and said he'd call to check on her. As he stepped back to close the door, she parted her lips to say something, then closed them and stared at him with misted blue eyes. He shut the door and she looked away.

The cab drove off. Cain watched its taillights turn the corner, disappear. He looked back to the square and the doorway where the man in black metal glasses had stood; it was empty.

Buddha

DUSK BECAME DARKNESS in the blink of an eye as Cain walked to his rendezvous. His path led him through Steeltown's deserted square, where the surviving businesses had locked their doors until tomorrow; down the side street toward the adult bookstore, the Palace Hotel, and the Cairo nightclub, where once he'd been someone else. He'd begun his journey in a dream; the Palace's blue neon sign pulled him from his trance, and he started to turn away, circle around this risky history for safer ground. Then he saw a fat woman in a miniskirt and purple stockings standing on the corner.

He had to know.

"Looking for company, mister?" she whined. Black roots showed under her white hair. She smelled of cheap musk and tobacco.

"Information," said Cain.

"The library is back thataway," she said, "and closed."

He held his trooper badge toward her like a priest brandishing a crucifix to a vampire.

"Come on! You got no beef with me, I'm iced and everybody . . ."

"Talk when you're told to and you'll stay on the street," said Cain. "Mouth off or make up tales, I'll put you away forever."

"Sure," she said, an insolent drawl she could claim meant whatever was necessary for her to have said.

"There used to be a girl who worked the Stroll, brown hair, wore a black velvet neckband."

"She don't come around much anymore."

"Why?"

"I heard maybe she got herself into trouble."

"What kind of trouble?"

"Maybe she took a job she couldn't handle."

"Is she hurt? Is she alive?"

"Who knows, who cares? It's all the same. She'll be back or she won't."

"Know anybody who knows any more?"

"There isn't any more to know. And what do you care?"

"Forget about everything," Cain told her.

"You're the Man, baby," she sneered.

Cain turned his back and left the neon light.

Twenty minutes and five blocks later, a well-tended Chevy pulled to the curb by the boarded-up bowling alley where Cain waited.

"How you doing, Jack?" said the Reverend Paul Borge from the car's front passenger seat. "Ready for a ride?"

Cain climbed in the back seat.

"This is Arty," said Borge, nodding to the driver, who turned and gave Cain his strong and calloused hand.

"Pleasure," said Arty. "You want a beer?"

"Sure," said Cain.

He and Arty popped cold cans together.

"Paul here don't drink," teased Arty. "Did'ja know his church don't even use wine for communion? Goddamn grape juice."

"It is what you make it," said Paul.

"Yeah, well, let's make the meeting," said Arty. He let out the clutch and they surged forward into the night.

The wheels lulled Cain back to dreams. His heart told him to *look back;* his mind said *don't bother.* If someone followed, he couldn't be seen. Through the windshield, between the driver and the man of God, Cain watched the street roll out in their headlights.

The high school parking lot overflowed with tightly packed cars and pickups; Arty barely found space for the Chevy. Red lights spun on dozens of police cars parked at strategic junctures. Hundreds of murmuring men and women surged toward the glass doors past lines of city cops who tapped riot clubs into their free hands and wore white helmets with Plexiglas face visors.

"They wanted this just for the membership, you know?" said Arty as they walked toward the school. "But there's widows with pension rights, kids whose old man is racked up in the hospital, husbands and wives who won't sit home and wait meek-mouthed for bad news, so it got opened up. But no press, no public, so you guys ain't supposed to be here. Make yourselves invisible, huh?"

"In the gym!" chanted ushers wearing SIC-logoed jackets. "Go through to the gym!"

The shoulder-to-shoulder crowd swept Cain down the locker-lined hall. Arty steered him to the gym's busiest entrance, where men with anxious eyes scanned for unwelcome faces. Cain ducked his head between two strangers, and the crowd carried him through.

Arty laughed as the three of them stumbled inside: "Ain't no sign-in tonight!"

Folding chairs covered the shiny wood floor, and bleachers encircled it like a horseshoe. Paul found them three floor seats on an outside aisle. Their chairs straddled the court's halfway line. Beneath the far basketball hoop was a makeshift stage, with a long table, some chairs, a lectern with a microphone. On stage, the man with droopy eyes who Cain had seen with Johnny Maxx huddled with three other men.

"Who's that?" he asked Arty.

"The Steeltown Industrial Coalition president," said Arty.

The air was thick and clammy. High above the crowd, amidst the exposed orange steel rafters and dangling lights, air conditioning units labored to cool the gym and clean its smoke- and sweat-filled air. By 8:20, every chair on the floor and every seat in the bleachers was filled; people stood three deep along all the walls except the far one with the stage, where a line of muscular men kept the crowd at a distance. Cain recognized one husky usher as the bear who'd been with Johnny Maxx and the SIC president.

"How about him?" asked Cain.

"Organizer," said Arty, who held one of the few factory jobs in town. "With the SIC, not a local. Also strong-arms for some bug runners. You know about our numbers game?"

"I know about the bug," said Cain.

Someone started a chorus of foot stomping that half the crowd joined for five minutes. Catcalls, whistles and shouts of "Let's go!" "Come on!" "Get started!" cut through the thick air. The crowd squirmed in its seats and shifted along the wall, ripples of motion flowing back and forth through the gym.

At 8:31, all the lights except the spot on the stage mike blinked out. The crowd hushed. Cain heard a commotion toward the back of the gym, and like everyone else who could, he turned to look.

A powerful spotlight hit a cluster of men at the main door. They marched down the middle aisle, a determined processional plowing through the masses. Cain stood with the crowd. All he could see was a phalanx of jacketed men grimly pressing forward to the stage. An inarticulate roar shook the room. The foot stomping began again, and loud, prolonged applause.

The phalanx reached the stage. The jackknife-looking friend of Johnny Maxx's bounded up the stairs toward the SIC president and his companions, who were on their feet applauding and smiling. The jackknife made a show of standing firm and scanning the stage before he turned, and nodded into the phalanx.

Out of the phalanx came only a man. He climbed the stairs slowly, the applause increasing with each step he took. He'd clothed himself in the coal black suit of Big Bill Haywood, John Lewis, and Samuel Gompers, cut modern and styled to compliment his bulk, which *The New York Times* claimed topped 350 pounds. He was bald, with a moon head and huge dragon ears. He swayed as he walked, let the SIC President and the other men on the stage grasp his hand or touch his coat sleeve. He waved to the crowd. The spotlight glinted off his gold Swiss watch. The crowd responded with an even louder roar and more applause as other spotlights skimmed shafts of light over their heads. He basked in attention for a minute, then he motioned the SIC president to the microphone.

"Brothers and sisters," said the president, "fellow family members. Honored guest . . ."

Again the crowd roared.

"Let us rise for the Pledge of Allegiance."

A spotlight zeroed the red, white, and blue banner hanging from the gym wall behind the stage. The men on the stage, including the icon in the coal black suit, turned, put their hands over their hearts, and like most of their fellow citizens in the crowd, recited words they'd memorized in grade school.

When the oath ended, the merely important people on the platform looked to the man in the black suit. Paying them no heed, he lumbered to a giant wooden chair and sat down; arms curved around his rotund belly to rest his hands on his knees. His countenance was smooth and wise, beneficent; his eyes peered into the very hearts of the crowd. He was bathed in golden light.

The droopy-eyed SIC president waited until everyone on the platform found seats, until those in the crowd with chairs occupied them; then his amplified voice echoed through the gym.

"Welcome to this special meeting of the Steeltown Industrial Coalition," he said. "I'm glad so many of you could make it, because tonight is a very important meeting."

Someone shouted in the crowd, but the words were inaudible.

The president held up his hand; the jackknife man whispered to an usher, who in turn moved a few steps deeper into the crowd.

"I remind everybody," said the president, "that though this is a special meeting, rules still apply. We got order, we got principles, and we're going to follow them tonight—just like always."

A spattering of applause interrupted the president, and was encouraged by the men sitting on the platform—except for the honored guest in the black suit, who remained impassive, immobile.

"You see who's with us tonight." Again came applause, but the president didn't stop. "He's the man who talks for us with the politicians in Washington and the bankers in New York and the men who run the companies, he's the chief executive of the best union in America, and we at the

SIC are lucky to be affiliated with it and luckier still to have him running the Teamsters!"

This time, polite and tired applause refused to be cheerleaded into enthusiasm.

"Now, to business," said the president.

"Anybody care if we skip the reading of the minutes?"

"*No!*" roared the crowd.

"How about committee reports?"

"*No!*"

"Old business?"

"*No!*"

"Okay," said the president. He wiped his brow. "I know what's on your minds. But first we're going to have a minute of silence for our dear departed Brother Simms, by your vote, SIC treasurer for the last seventeen years, who died and deserves our respect and remembrance for all the good he did our union."

The murmuring "silence" lasted less than thirty seconds.

"Okay," said the president, "now . . ."

Someone in the crowd shouted. Without thinking, the president leaned into the microphone and said, "What?" and the crowd quieted.

"*What about the money?*" The words echoed through the gym, faint but finally heard, and the crowd roared.

"Now that's enough!" yelled the president. "We got a lot of business and an honored guest with an important message. We got one mike. You want to talk, fine: when it's time, we'll open the floor and you raise your hand like everybody else and I'll recognize you and one of the ushers will lead you to the mike so you can say your piece, as long as we got time and as long as you aren't just spouting words to hear yourself talk. This is a union, not a damn debating society.

"I know what you want. You want to hear your money is safe."

Catcalls, whistles, and some applause interrupted him.

"Well it is," said the president. "We got all the answers to your questions. We did everything by the books . . ."

"*Who kept those books?*" boomed an unexpectedly amplified voice. The president's jaw fell; spotlights searched the crowd and the jackknife man hurried off the stage. *"Let us see the books!"*

A spotlight suddenly zeroed a man in the crowd holding a small microphone, a $12.95, battery-operated child's toy that could amplify a kid's fantasies about being a rock star or TV game show host.

"Sit down!" said the president. "You aren't supposed to interrupt and ask questions now!"

"Where are our SIC Special Unemployment Benefits checks?" boomed an amplified woman's voice from a different part of the gym.

"What the hell . . ." began the president.

"How come we bargained into the unemployment line?" echoed another amplified male voice from the bleachers.

The crowd muttered, people turning and twisting, uncertainly searching out each new voice. Beside Cain, Arty shook his head, grinned, and whispered to him: "Fucking radical troublemakers."

Then Arty reached under his Steelworker-logoed blue Windbreaker and pulled out one of the child's microphones.

"Duck down, would ya?" he said to Cain and Paul Borge. They complied as Arty stood:

"How come only one in ten guys make it into SIC retraining programs and they get taught jobs for monkeys that nobody hires 'em to do when they get out?" Arty said into his mike.

"Now, look!" said the president.

Bent over, his face between his knees, Cain and those around him were abruptly flooded by a spotlight.

"How come only the locals could come up with the cash to help the food bank?" bellowed an amplified voice on the other side of the gym. The spotlight left Cain, and he looked up.

On stage, the man in the black suit slowly got to his feet. The crowd roared as he moved to the lectern and waved the SIC president away from the official microphone. All lights centered on him. He jerked the microphone off its pole and walked around the lectern to the edge of the stage. His moon face glared at the crowd; they grew restless, then quiet, still. Slowly, he reached a hand out to them.

"WHAT IS THIS BULLSHIT?" he bellowed.

The walls echoed: *bullshit, bullshit, bullshit.*

"You know who I am!" he yelled. "You know what I stand for and how I got here! You put me up here because I can kick more ass than anybody you ever met, and you know that's what this union needs!

"I got you good deals, right? More money than the fat cats wanted to give you. I took care of you, right? And I'm still takin' care of you and you damn well better believe it!

"So I come here because you got trouble and what do I get? I get whiny bullshit and dumb questions when I should be hearing solidarity and how we're all gonna put our shoulder to the wheel and hang tough.

"You got a beef, then you got a beef with me, and I'm saying you ain't got no beef. You wanna know where your SIC benefit money is, I'll tell you where it is. It's where it belongs, it's right where you put it. It's invested, for all of you."

Cain looked around him at the faces of the men and women of Steeltown. They were absolutely still, waiting for the leader in the black suit to let them breathe.

"These things aren't easy to understand," he told them. "That's why you got us, that's why I got lawyers and accountants. I'll give you what you already know and I'll give it to you in a nutshell.

"Half your SUB fund is invested in a regular Teamsters pension and profit plan system. Most of it is tied up in Atlantic City casinos, where the real, long-term money is made, and let me tell you, we ain't putting it on the crap tables."

Someone laughed, and the tension eased. Slightly.

"The rest of the money is invested for you, by you, with you, right here in Steeltown, in city bonds, helping buy you a better place to live. How you could complain about that, I don't know.

"You wanna know why your checks are late?"

Several voices in the crowd yelled "Yes."

"I'll tell you why," he said. He stepped back, nodded, and drew them with him as they waited for his answer. "I'll tell you why:

"The government.

"Yeah, that's why: the government. They dick with us every chance they get. And all that dickin', well, we gotta deal with it and that means we can't get our system to work as fast as we want. But they ain't gonna stop us!"

Scattered applause greeted his promise. And puzzled faces.

"So what are you worrying about? Forget it, I tell you! We've beaten everything they've thrown at us and we always will. And we ain't never lost a dime of your money doing it!"

"What about the Penesquitos pension fund in California?" interrupted an outlaw-miked voice. The spotlights found the questioner, a thin, fiftyish man standing amidst the chairs on the gym floor: *"They went belly-up for about two hundred million 'cause they were . . ."*

And he was jerked off balance by the jackknife man, who pulled the mike from his hand. An usher jumped the man from behind and threw him into the aisle. The jackknife man shoved the rebel; he stumbled into two ushers, who hustled him toward the rear of the gym as the spotlight on their battle blinked out.

"I believe," boomed the giant on the stage, "that man has just been ruled out of order."

He chuckled, but only the men on stage joined his mirth.

"And I know he's definitely out of his mind. He's got some beef 'bout something that ain't about Steeltown and ain't about us. Let him write his congressman."

Again he laughed, and again he laughed alone.

"Why did Simms blow his brains out?" boomed another rebel mike.

Before the spotlights and ushers could find it, the honored guest held up his hand:

"You wanna know why Brother Simms killed himself?"

In the silence that overpowered the gym, Cain swore he heard his heart beat.

"Simms killed himself because he lost his balls," said the national labor leader as he moved back behind the lectern. "Now any of the rest of you got that problem?"

"Oh Lord," whispered Borge.

"Remember," boomed the nation's most powerful labor

czar: "This is Steeltown! You people are the blast furnace of America, and how you make it is how it goes, so we gotta make it right. Now I gotta go kick some ass and get all of you back to work again!"

As he turned from the lectern, the other men on the stage leaped to their feet, applauding. Within seconds, many people in the crowd were clapping, too.

Many.

The SIC president took the microphone to thank their guest, but few people paid him any mind. The leader who'd given them his message from the big world walked off the stage and was immediately surrounded by the guardian phalanx and led out a side door. Chairs scraped on the gym floor and drowned out the president's farewell words. Thousands of feet shuffled to the exits. Cain drifted with the crowd as strangers' words floated past him:

". . . way I look at it is you buy it or you don't. If you don't buy it, what choice you got? We already bought it."

". . . wonder how much his suit . . ."

"Did I tell you I won fifty bucks on the bug?"

"Hell, then at least somethin's working in this damn town. Here, lay off a buck for me, might as well keep Johnny in a job."

". . . to Arizona, 'cause I figure the oil and construction jobs in Texas are already taken. My old lady's sister is there. We can stay in her trailer until we find somebody to buy our house here."

"It's all just gotta work out. It's been bad before, but it always works out. This is America and this is Steeltown and that sure as shit ain't going to ever change!"

". . . read he was at the White House last week . . ."

". . . that son of a bitch didn't have to throw him around like that, all of them and just . . ."

". . . if something don't come through soon, what the hell we gonna do?"

Cain bumped against Arty, who was watching the faces in the crowd avoid his.

"I was told this town had no guys like you," said Cain.

"Town's full of guys like me," said Arty. "They just don't know it yet."

"But . . ." said Cain.

"Hell, nobody'd know it if they depended on the big shots who know what's what. Those people can't see us, don't talk about it much if they do. Maybe it scares 'em. That Josh Hammond guy you're so interested in? He couldn't be bothered with us."

"What about . . ." began Cain, and Arty grabbed his arm to steer him through the crowd and out of the school.

"This ain't a good place for answers to your questions," said Arty. "We can talk on the way home."

When the wheel of the night spun them to that journey, talk they did.

"What are you guys?" Cain asked from the back seat. "Are you organized or . . ."

"We're just tired of the crap," Arty told Cain as they drove through the city. "We had jobs, we had unions, we had the SIC and America and Congressmen and wars we got shot to shit in so it would all stay safe and it seemed to work great, just as long as nothing changed and you didn't ask the wrong questions.

"Most of our folks fought their way up out of *poor*. We're middle class now. Maybe you think mill work isn't much, but hey, you have to be just as sharp to keep a blast furnace running as clerkin' in a bank. We remade this country since the Depression, and that wasn't just big buildings and beating the Japs and Nazis. We bled our way out of the slums and into the suburbs.

"Now middle class is a crumbling block. We're the first ones fallin' off it. I used to worry about being sentenced back to the Southside. Now the Southside is creeping toward me. My wife, a grandmother, works at a Roy Rogers hamburger stand next to high school kids. Wears a cowgirl uniform. She's lucky to have a job. My plant will close soon, the last one to go. If I get anything, that's the kind of work it'll be. Every year, takes less people to make what we need while we get more people who need to work. Maybe we'll end up manufacturing junk we'll all need to buy so we can pretend we got something worth doing."

"But here and now in Steeltown," said Cain, "are you guys organized to . . ."

"Organized to what?" said Arty. "This town's already lousy with *organizations*. Where the hell would we start and what the hell would we do? Where would we aim to go?"

"It's never too late," said Paul Borge in the front seat.

"Reverend," said Arty, "maybe all your *believin'* makes you blind."

"Or lets you see," argued Borge.

"But tonight . . ." interjected Cain.

"Tonight was just a wild hair idea some of us had," said Arty. "Shake our fist. Hell, the big man should be proud of us: we ain't sold all our balls to those goons. But the mikes was just a craziness that shook us until we turned it loose."

"You think they'll let it slide?" said Cain.

Arty drove silently for a few blocks.

"What are they going to do about it, Arty?" asked Cain.

"We all know where each other lives," he replied after another long pause.

"What does that mean?" said Cain.

Arty shook his head.

Cain stared at the passing city streets, remembering what everyone who'd streamed out of the gym had seen before the wheel of the night spun them on their way: red lights swirling in the indigo air. Half a dozen city cops laughing and joking with the jackknife man as they stood beside the open back doors of a paddy wagon casually parked in front of the school exit. Inside that shiny metal box, his hands cuffed behind his back, slumped the heretic who'd been ruled out of order. Blood dripped from his nose and mouth. His face was pale, his eyes were clouded glass.

Midnight

CHIEF HARRY DICARLO sat at a long table, playing solitaire. His giant hands hid the deck while he shuffled the cards and laid them out in seven precise piles. He dealt the remaining cards slowly, turning them face up in their own pile while carefully considering their value. A worn black notebook and pen waited at the edge of the game, and resting on the table within easy reach of his right hand was a pearl-handled Magnum revolver.

"This is a funny place for you to show up tonight," DiCarlo said when the two cops who'd searched Cain in the living room brought him to their boss. DiCarlo's eyes didn't leave the cards. "Sit down."

"I was in the neighborhood," said Cain. He'd parked the state car in front of the house, been buzzed through the iron picket fence to the steel-backed front door. DiCarlo watched the cards as he talked—though Cain knew the Chief saw him at the edge of his vision. The revolver's black bore stared at Cain.

"Lucky for you I was up," said DiCarlo.

He turned up a black six, found a home for it on a red seven.

"I got hooked on this game in the Bureau," he said. "Not much else to do on a stakeout when it isn't your turn at the window. I play it pro style, Vegas rules. You lay 'em out light, go through the deck one card at a time, try to fill the aces' row. Fifty-two cents a game, nickel back each card you get up there. You get one pass, then it's tally time."

The ace of clubs flipped out of the deck; he smiled, and laid it above the seven piles.

"There's a nickel," he told Cain.

"How's your record?"

"Long haul, I owe myself a little." DiCarlo shrugged, nodded to the worn black notebook. "These days I seem to be winning."

"What little wet dream brings you here?" said DiCarlo.

"What I started to wonder," said Cain, "is why you're so tight with Johnny Maxx."

"Whatever gave you that idea?" said the Chief as he turned up the jack of hearts.

"I keep my eyes open," Cain told him. "When things heat up around here—and they will—I wonder what people will think of that."

"What makes you think they care?"

"They aren't stupid."

"They're scared. Makes the same difference."

"You can't trust fear," said Cain.

"Maybe," shrugged the Chief. He turned over a deuce of diamonds, hesitated, then laid it down on the three of clubs.

"What is it you want, Cain?" said DiCarlo. "And don't give me that bull about your job and Josh Hammond."

"I'm just turning over the cards I get, Chief. And I gotta get 'em from somewhere."

"So you come to me."

"I go everywhere, Chief. You know that."

"You're a resourceful guy, Cain."

"The Mayor thinks so."

"Does he now," said DiCarlo, turning up a ten of diamonds, which he put on a jack of spades, then moved the stack headed by a nine of clubs onto the new red ten, which created a gap in the game.

"Nash passed me a card with your name on it," said Cain.

"So you slink over here at midnight to tell me. To warn me? To trade? What?"

"To let you know, that's all."

"Out of the goodness of your heart?"

"My heart's got nothing to do with it. My head does.

"Look where you're sitting, DiCarlo. The Mayor's nudged you out front. You can either do the same to him, or push Johnny out there. The Feds already want Johnny, and officially, you're supposed to, too. Whatever the Mayor hangs on you, if you walk with Johnny, then that's against you too."

The king of spades turned up; DiCarlo used it to fill the blank space.

"You need to rack up some points on your side, Chief. And you got to score them against somebody."

"What's this card you say the Mayor gave you?"

Cain shook his head.

"Can't tell you," he said. "Don't worry, you'll find out."

Steeltown's chief of police laughed. "I don't need to worry, Cain. Even the Feds couldn't make the play on me."

"Different days," Cain told him.

"Why are you so hot for me to take on Johnny?"

"Somebody has to go."

DiCarlo turned up a useless five of spades.

"Johnny, me, Nash, you don't care, do you Cain?"

"Nope." He shrugged. "Johnny's crazy."

"But with a lot of out-of-town friends," said the Chief.

"We're in Steeltown," replied Cain. "If it's your turf, that shouldn't matter.

"And the Mayor," continued Cain, "is not an easy man to work with."

"Tell me something I don't know."

"But he's wrapped real tight in city hall. Won't be easy to unroll him."

"There's ways," said DiCarlo, his eyes scanning the cards. "And there's time."

"We're talking now," said Cain. "Now it's shaping up that you're on front street—right out there with Johnny, who's the biggest target in town. Mayor Nash is behind you, everybody's looking, it's getting hotter, and you're sitting here, playing solitaire."

Cain paused, waited for DiCarlo to speak. The Chief slowly turned over one, two, three cards, all without finding a play or saying a word. Cain stood, shook his head.

"I figured you for a smarter player than this," he said.

The queen of hearts turned up. DiCarlo placed her on

the king of spades, then moved the stack headed by the jack of spades on top of her. The card under that jack proved to be the ace of diamonds, which he moved up top. The card under the ace was the deuce of clubs. The deuce of diamonds went to its ace, as did the the deuce of clubs—followed by its now-uncovered three.

"I'll get by," said DiCarlo when the play had settled. "But you're getting to be more bother than you're worth."

"See you around," said Cain. He nodded to the table with its gun and cards, shook his head and said, "Lots of luck."

Thirty minutes later, Cain flicked on the light in the Commission's conference room. All seemed as he'd left it—except that night now filled the windows. He retrieved the tube from behind the bookcase, spread the blown-up photograph of Josh Hammond's desk blotter on the conference table.

What makes this so important? thought Cain as he scanned the black and white image: a half moon smudge trailing drips that were probably a coffee stain; a doodle of a stick man peering over a ledge; dozens of nonsense geometric drawings; phone numbers Cain later linked to women, a pizza parlor, a friend's house, Hammond's doctor; the notation, "b-bll, 8, Y"; a scrawl reading, "lose 65 jbs, keep 12."

And in the bottom right hand corner, on the line between two dates Hammond hadn't lived to see, *"N's man, 5th St. grg. 10p."*

"As in Nash," whispered Cain. He stared at the inscription for ten minutes, running its permutations through his mind, then put the photo back in its tube and again hid it behind the bookcase. He turned out the conference room light.

In darkness, Cain crept back to the window overlooking the square. He counted to thirty. By then, he reasonably should have left the office and its view for the elevator.

Across the street, in the shadows of the doorway, something moved. Streetlights—or maybe it was the moon—glinted off something shiny, perhaps something like black metal-framed glasses. Then the shadows were still and dark again.

The Limp

"GOOD MORNING, MR. CAIN," said Kimmett's butler on Monday as he bowed the visitor into the mansion. "We weren't expecting you. Mr. Kimmett and Mr. Nelson are walking in the garden."

"I'll wait in his rooms," said Cain, climbing the stairs.

The butler raised his hand to protest, but then thought better of an effort possibly beyond his duties.

No one sat at the nurse's station outside Kimmett's doors. Cain tried the knob: locked. A great Dane trotted down the hallway, sniffed at Cain, and won a pet. Cain pressed a button under the desk. A buzz sounded in the door lock for fifteen seconds—enough time for Cain to reach the knob and admit himself to Kimmett's private lair.

He closed the door behind him.

Sunlight streaming into the room fell on the rumpled bed and softened the sickroom scent. Cain scanned the wall of blank television screens, the bedstand with its silent black telephone. Breakfast dishes waited on the window table. As Cain walked through the cluster of sofas and overstuffed chairs, the smell of coffee grew stronger. He touched the pewter coffee pot: cold. Outside the window, Cain saw empty green lawns and lush trees.

The rolltop desk in the corner was unlocked.

In its top right-hand drawer, Cain found a thick black address book with phone numbers for Mayor Nash, Chief DiCarlo, the governor, state legislators, publisher Evans, the

state's congressmen and senators and a dozen national legislators from other states, a few celebrities like the male
singer who'd been a legend since World War II, the White
House, the national headquarters of both major political
parties, law firms, and banks around the world. The book had
Kimmett's son's business and home numbers, as well as his
grandson's. Boswell's numbers were there as were those for
Cain's firm including private numbers of the firm's president.
The ledger had listings for the SIC's president and that union's
recent honored guest. And two numbers for Johnny Maxx.

The middle drawer held a black automatic pistol Cain
didn't touch. The massive business checkbook he pulled out
and opened.

The check stubs dated back to the first of the year. Cain
flipped through hundreds of checks covering the routine
expenditures of Kimmett's empire. He found the check for
his firm's consultation, the check for the half million fee.
Throughout the year, there were checks made out to cash or
to Kimmett's secretary Nelson with the notation of "ad-
vance against expenses," "necessary draws," or other am-
biguous descriptions. The amounts for such checks varied—
$5,000, $1,000, $15,000, and, five days earlier, $10,000. The
money seemed to flow into the checking account from trust
funds, stock sales, savings accounts, liquidations of unspeci-
fied assets.

The buzzer in the door shattered Cain's search.

Quickly, he thrust the checkbook back in its drawer and
scrambled toward the window table. In his dash, he twisted
his knee and barely stifled a scream. He had to drag his left
leg the last few steps to the table; reached it just as the door
swung open.

Judson stalked into the room. Like the butler, this giant
wore a black tux, though the collar on his white shirt was
open, as if he hadn't had time to finish dressing. His head
swiveled, and his eyes found Cain.

"The coffee's cold," said Cain, touching the pewter pot.
His weight rested safely on his right leg. He tried to make
that stance look casual. "Hell of a way to treat a guest."

"You're not supposed to be here," said Judson. He came
toward Cain with steady, lumbering strides.

"Don't worry," said Cain. Had he closed the middle desk drawer all the way? He dared not look away from Judson to check. "We work for the same man, though I'll be damned if I can figure you for the team."

Cain's words slowed the giant; he stopped, looked down at the man he could smother with his bulk like a child hugging a doll.

"I mean," continued Cain, concealing his anxiety with a rush of ad-libbed ideas and fast-found words, "look at you: where did you come from and why did he hire you—and he makes you wear those ridiculous monkey suits."

The torrent of ideas and questions pulled Judson's face to a frown. He stepped back, and Cain breathed easier.

"Everybody wears a uniform for work," said Judson.

"Is that what you are?" asked Cain. "Just another worker?"

"Mr. Kimmett's good to me. Nobody else ever was. He gave me a place 'fore I even left school. Gives me what I need and takes care of me."

"So you do what he says," said Cain. "And he decides what you need. You don't even know what wanting something else is, because he keeps you . . . When was the last time you were off these grounds?"

Judson blinked.

"You're a strong man, Judson. You're not stupid, though he's got you dressed up and fitted for that role. You don't need him. He's got you tricked into thinking you do. You could make it on your own. It'd be hard, you'd have to remember you are somebody, you wouldn't have him riding on your shoulders, making the decisions, but . . ."

"What do you want here?" snarled Judson. "Everything was fine and you come here and . . ."

"I'm doing my job," said Cain. "Just like you."

"No you're not," said Judson. "You're right. I'm not stupid, and you're not . . ."

"*Cain!*" barked old man Kimmett from the doorway. He wore his terrycloth bathrobe over ivory silk pajamas, blue slippers on his feet. Banker-suited Nelson stood beside him.

"What are you doing here?" wheezed the old man as Nelson helped him to the bed.

Kimmett lay back against the pillows. Nelson moved to a control panel on the wall, turned a dial. The air grew sweeter. A red light glowed above the door.

"Judson and I have been having a chat," said Cain as he strolled toward the bed. His gait seemed arrogant, controlled—but really hid his limp and the pain each step cost him. He turned with his words to look at the giant standing by the window table—and swung his eyes over the desk: The middle drawer was safely shut. "He kept me company while I waited for you."

"I can't imagine what you two have in common," said Kimmett. His eyes were closed. Nelson watched Cain approach the bed. "Except that you both work for me."

"About that," said Cain, gazing down on the withered old man, "it's time for you to do something."

"The question is," said Kimmett, his eyes still closed, "what have *you* done?"

"Never mind. What we need ..."

The old man's eyes opened.

"Sit down!" he commanded. "I don't like looking up at you."

"I won't squat on your floor," said Cain.

"Judson! Bring them chairs!"

As easily as an ordinary man might pick up books, Judson lifted two chairs from the window table, carried them across the room, and placed them beside the bed for Nelson and Cain.

"Go," Kimmett told the big man as the two higher ranked employees sat down. "Finish dressing. Take care of the dogs.

"And be sure to close the door behind you!" Kimmett yelled to the giant's departing back.

Judson obeyed.

"Are you going to be around to see this through?" Cain asked the old man propped up by satin-cased pillows.

"What's the date?" asked Kimmett.

"June seventh," Cain told him.

"I don't plan on giving you a Christmas bonus," said Kimmett, "but only because you better be long gone and

long done by then. I'll be here long after I celebrate New
Year's in my new town."

"Not if we aren't careful now," Cain told him. "They're
going to try to dismantle the commission, or at least hobble
it more than we've managed to."

"Who's they?" said Kimmett. "And why?"

"*Who* is an open contest," said Cain. "*Why* is because
we're about to make it extremely uncomfortable for everyone in town—including you if you're not prepared."

"Don't worry about me!" snapped the old man. "Worry
about yourself! All I've seen from you is a bunch of talk and
Mickey Mouse tiptoeing around and if you don't—"

"You're damn right, you haven't seen!" snapped Cain.
"And you won't see until I'm ready, and if you're busy
gawking where you're not supposed to be, you'll get run
over!"

"Mr. Kimmett appreciates your concern," said Nelson.
"However, we are more interested in results."

Cain told the old man: "You have to be patient."

"Being *patient* is for somebody who has no other choice,"
answered Kimmett.

"Revise your philosophy—or at least your rap," said
Cain. "Because patience is what you need to sell the fence-
sitters on the commission and the governor and anybody
else you can think of who our targets can pressure. They
haven't started yet, but they will."

"When?" said Kimmett.

"Start making your pep calls this morning," said Cain.

With as much caution as he could conceal, Cain stood.

"And for the record," he said, "I haven't been here."

"The difference that makes is not apparent," said Nelson.

Cain rubbed his left thigh.

"My leg fell asleep in your cheap chair," he lied. He
limped to the door. "I'll be in touch."

"Wait a minute!" Kimmett yelled to his back. "You
can't . . ."

But Cain was out the door.

One of Nelson's thugs gave Cain a ride to a half-deserted
shopping mall. Cain waited until the thug drove away, then

limped to a pay phone by the sliding glass doors of a discount drug store.

"Commission," snapped Catherine when she answered Cain's call.

"It's Cain," he said, "is—"

"So nice to finally hear from you. We've all been here since the office opened at eight. It's nine-thirty-three. We've been wondering."

"Let me speak to Beth."

"Certainly."

Beth agreed to drive across town and pick Cain up.

"Bring the state car," he told her.

When Beth arrived, he waved her out of the driver's seat.

"What's the matter?" she joked as he settled behind the wheel. "Don't you trust me?"

"Sure," said Cain. He tapped his ear with his forefinger, and she nodded, stuck out her tongue at the dashboard.

He laughed. Turned on the radio to a lonesome highway ballad.

"Too bad there's not an all-news station," she said.

"You like that?" he asked as the car rolled through the parking lot.

"Ah . . . sure. I guess. Don't . . . don't you?"

"I used to love the radio. The surprise of hearing a song that I loved. Like they played it just for me."

"I love music, too," Beth said quickly.

"The talk stuff," said Cain, shaking his head. "I don't need another voice from nowhere telling me this is true and what to do."

"Oh."

Cain took a left off the commercial strip, a right through a tree-lined neighborhood.

"You seen much of this town?" he asked Beth.

"Enough," she replied. "Everything there is to see."

"I doubt that." He smiled at her. "I've got something to show you."

He drove through streets she didn't know. She expected him to check the mirrors for hidden watchers, but he never looked back; indeed, he seemed not to notice the vacant lots and old buildings flowing past them—yet he navigated a true and steady course while on the radio, Roy Orbison sang "Running Scared."

"How's Sylvia seem this morning?" he asked.

Beth turned from him, looked out the window in time to see a boy throw a baseball to his brother.

"Fine," said Beth. She sighed, then in a voice of obligation, said, "She asked about you, too."

"She had a rough weekend," said Cain.

Beth watched the houses roll by.

"Were you with her?" she asked.

"No."

"Oh," she said. Then smiled. "Oh."

The road ended at a chain link fence, beyond which Beth saw a big nothing. She looked more closely, discerned the sky curving down to meet a distant rim of brown hills.

"Come on," said Cain as he parked the car in front of a weather-beaten house. "It's only a few steps."

She said nothing about his limp. They walked to the fence. Cain grabbed the links. Beth pressed her face against the steel bands: they were cool, and dug into her flesh. She stared into a crater vast beyond her mind's measure.

"The Pit," said Cain. "Not counting what's eroded around the lip of the rim, it's just under a mile and a half wide.

"See that pickup truck at the bottom? On the mud flats? Looks like a toy? Probably some old miner listening to ghosts. The Pit has nothing left to salvage, and now it's too expensive to mine. See those dark spots on the dirt walls? Look: follow that scar. That's a road. Follow its zigzags almost to the top and . . . Yes, you see it now. That's the mouth of an abandoned mine shaft. Hundreds of miles of tunnels burrowed under Steeltown. No map of 'em. Now and then a chunk of road or somebody's house sinks a few dozen feet when a tunnel collapses. The mills illegally dumped toxic wastes in them. Now the deep shafts are useless and empty, just like the Pit. Unless you honor them as graves for the trapped miners."

"Why did you have me lead our friends to that shopping mall?" asked Beth.

"I needed a ride," Cain whispered, not concentrating on her question. He blinked, refocused; said: "That seemed like as good a place as any to keep them guessing."

"And why here?" she asked.

"I was pretty sure you'd never seen the Pit close up."

"It's lovely," she drolled.

"You'd have loved the mountain," he told her. "You really would."

"What are you doing?"

"Did you read the paper about Friday night's union rally?"

"Not much to that—was there?"

"Don't count on a Steeltown newspaper to tell you what you need to know," he said. "We need a subpoena."

"For what?"

"All records concerning city bonds purchased with SIC funds. Everything: where the money went and where it is now, who signed for it, who touched it."

"The wording will be tricky, but . . . Who are we serving it on?"

"Mayor Nash."

"Nash thinks he already gave at the office."

"This is a needy town," said Cain. He smiled.

"Might take a day, two," she said. Shrugged. "What else?"

He shook his head, scowled, and she felt suddenly anxious.

"What's . . ." she began.

"Let's go," he told her, and started toward the car.

An old man in a black suit shuffled toward them. He met them before they reached the car. The cuffs on his white shirt were frayed. Stains dotted his black tie. He had wispy white hair, sunken cheeks, and misted blue eyes. As he shuffled, he held his twisted hands out before him, ready for a beach ball that seemed to elude his trembling grasp.

"Hey!" called out the old man when Cain and Beth were only a few paces from him, "I know you!"

Beth felt Cain grab her elbow; he'd been limping: perhaps he needed to steady himself. But he propelled her toward their car, like an insistent partner in a dance.

"Wait!" said the old man. Beth stopped, pushed back against Cain's pressure, and made him stop too. The old man raised his hand, his arthritic fingers unable to point, yet his gesture unmistakably meant for Cain. "I know you!"

"Maybe," said Cain, feeling all the eyes of the world on him as he tried to steer Beth past this ancient apparition. He turned—and twisted his knee. He winced, needed to lean into her for balance.

The old man stared curiously at him; Beth's face showed concern.

"Are you . . ." she started to say.

"Okay," Cain quickly replied, remembering: the old man had been in the hotel lobby when Cain checked in as John Reston. Cain smiled disarmingly. "I've been in town for a few days. You've probably seen me on the street."

"I get around, really I do! Nothing else to do, but . . . No, I *know* you: you're Pete Cainelli's boy."

Beth stared at the thunderstruck man who gripped her elbow.

"I know'd you from your limp!" the old man said proudly. "You look different, but I remember and I remember your limp. I remember when you got hurt playing baseball and all that next year you limped, and old Pete, why, he'd go around town just as proud of you as if you'd got a war wound like all those other boys."

Cain pushed Beth toward the car. They brushed past the old man.

"Jimmy!" he called after them as Cain unlocked Beth's door. "That's it, isn't it? Jimmy Cainelli! I'm . . ."

"You're mistaken," said the man with the limp. He practically threw Beth into the front seat, slammed the door behind her. She quickly rolled down her window.

"No," said the old man as Beth's companion limped around to the driver's door. "No, I know things. I know many things. I haven't forgotten. You've been gone a long time, though. Where you been? Why did you come back?"

Cain climbed behind the wheel, ground the engine to life.

"Is that your wife?" called the old man.

The engine roared. Tires crunched, power steering whined

as Cain turned the car from the curb, forced it into a winding, full-curve turn headed back the way they'd come.

Behind them, the old man waved good-bye.

"What ..." Beth started to say, but her companion
frantically chopped his hand, flipped the radio on as loudly
as he could stand it.

They drove without speaking. The radio played songs
they ignored. Cain parked on a side street leading to the
town square and the commission office building. Beth waited
for him to speak, but he limped grimly toward their office.
When they reached the square and were alone on the sidewalk, she yelled at him:

"Stop!"

He kept walking.

*"Want to do this in the office with everybody listening and
watching?"* she said. The urgency in her words made her
whisper seem like a shout.

He stopped.

Beth circled him slowly, her eyes soaking in every detail
of his image as though this were the first and not the thou-
sandth time she'd considered what she saw. She blocked his
path to the refuge of his workplace.

"You've got to trust me," she said fervently. "I want
you to trust me. I know that—"

"You don't know anything."

"Yes I do. That old man and I, we know. He knows who
you were and I know who you are. I look at you and I see—"

"You think you see a mountain, but you're only seeing
your own pit," he told her.

"I want—"

"You want something you think you don't have and you
think I do, something you feel is powerful. That phantom
pulls at you and you want it but it isn't there and it's no
good if it is. That's what you see in me. That's what you saw
in Johnny Maxx too. Same fire, only ..."

"How can you ... How dare you ..." She glared at
him, sputtered. Shook her head. He tried to brush past her.
Again she stopped him, this time with her hand on his arm.

"What happened to Jimmy Cainelli?"

"Jim Cainelli is gone. He left town and he's dead."

"What about his parents, his family? What about his father?"

"They're dead and buried."

"You can't—"

"I can do what I have to! And you have to, too."

He grabbed her shoulders.

"Listen," he said. "Whatever you think, forget it. Don't talk about it. Don't tell anyone *anything*, or everybody will pay for your mistake because this is something you can't understand."

"Teach me," she said.

"No time," he told her. "Learning takes time and telling wouldn't work anyway. You're . . . Beth, you're a good person, but you—"

"You know that I—"

"*I* know that we've got a chance to do something good here, we got a bigger chance to fail, and you can destroy it all, just by mentioning what you only *think* you know!"

"That's why you're here, isn't it? Because you're Jimmy Cainelli."

He paused, said, "The firm knew my background could help on this job."

She shook her head.

"Don't give me that," she said. "I'm not stupid."

"Then play this smart," he told her. "This is what it is, and nothing more."

"You can tell me, you can trust me, I'll help you, I—"

His shaking head stopped her.

"It's because of—" she began.

"It's because of nothing," he said. "It's because there's no other choice."

His eyes had been locked on hers; he blinked, refocused— and she saw his vision suddenly hooked by something over her shoulder.

Beth turned, looked across the square and saw nothing unusual: a few ordinary downtown pedestrians. Opposite the commission building, innocently sitting on a bench in the wide-open town square, was a man in a tan sports coat who watched them impassively through his black steel-rimmed glasses.

"I have to go," Cain whispered.

She turned, saw him staring at the man in black glasses. Her head swiveled back toward the square. The man on the bench stood, regarded the two of them with an easy, confident patience. He slowly walked away.

"Get inside," Cain told her. "I'll be there soon. Don't say anything about—"

"I won't! I wouldn't!"

Cain nodded, his mind letting go of her. He patted her arm, stepped around her, his eyes focused on the departing back of the man in the black glasses.

"Jack, who—"

"Everything's fine," he mumbled. "Everything will be all right."

Beth watched him as he limped across the town square, bright summer sun all around and Cain like the shadow of the stranger he followed.

That side-street Steeltown bar opened early for anyone who stumbled through its doors. Two scruffy men of indeterminate age and undeniable status slumped beside each other at the bar, one before a mug of beer, the other before a glass of wine, each lost in his private version of the same song, each indifferent to the other; to the bartender who moved his lips as he read a national tabloid spread out on the bar; to the man in black glasses who sat at one of the tables pushed against the wall behind them, his face toward the door that opened with a tingling bell as Cain stepped inside.

The bar smelled: of sawdust and grease from the grill in the back, of cigarettes and cheap pipe tobacco, of pine-scented urine from the restrooms, of stale booze and fresh coffee from the pot on the burner behind the bar and the tan mug on the table in front of the man in black glasses.

Some woman sang a country and western lament from the cheap radio in front of the blue-lit backbar mirror. Cain limped toward the man in black glasses, who kept his hands resting on the table and with seeming indifference watched Cain approach.

Cain looked down at the black glasses, called out to the bartender, "I'll have coffee, too."

"Nice to see you're temperate," said the man as Cain sat down across from him. "These days."

"You're Nick Malone," said Cain.

"We've never met," he replied.

"You fit the description."

The bartender brought over a mug of coffee and walked away, told the wine drinker to shut up.

"This your kind of place?" he said.

Nick Malone shrugged. The lenses of his glasses were clear protective plastic; no refraction distorted Cain's view of the man's eyes: one was blue, one was green.

"I don't mind it," said Malone.

"How long you been in town?"

"Long enough." Malone smiled. "Long before you knew."

"My company hires you only for special jobs," said Cain. "Mostly . . . wet work."

"Your company never uses me," said Malone. "Remember?"

"Who are you working for here?"

"Your company," said Malone. He smiled again.

"Doing what?"

"They thought you might need a little help. Of one kind or another."

"So they gave you a contract," said Cain. "How big is your franchise?"

"That's a question decided by the firm. Consider me . . ." he paused, continued: "Consider me your backup nobody knows about. I'm behind you all the time, all the way. In case."

"I'm doing fine, thanks."

The wine drinker growled, snapped his arm back to throw his tumbler at the radio. Red wine sloshed from the glass and he lost his grip just as his arm reached full cock. The glass flew toward the two men at the table. Malone didn't blink or turn his eyes from Cain's face. Malone's left hand floated off the table, caught the hurtling glass back-handed and lowered it gently beside his own steaming cup of coffee as the crimson liquid spray hit Cain.

"You never know," said Malone.

Red drops rolled down Cain's cheeks and soaked into his suit.

The bartender jerked the wine drinker off his stool, muscled him to the door and threw him into the street. The bell tinkled as the door slammed. He wiped his hands on his apron, stomped back toward his post. On the way, he picked the wine glass off the two gents' table.

"Any trouble you make," said Cain, "will double back on you."

"I don't make trouble," answered Malone. "I clean it up."

"Sure you do," said Cain. "As long as you're around, you might as well do some good."

Malone laughed.

"You know who Russell Boswell is?" asked Cain.

Malone nodded.

"I want you to keep him healthy."

Cain's words elicited a shrug from the man whose glasses protected and obscured his eyes of different color.

"As long as that doesn't interfere with ... with what *my* client, *your* firm wants, I see no problem."

"Don't worry," said Cain. "It's what everybody wants."

"Who'll take care of your two women friends?"

"That's not your concern. You worry about Boswell."

Again, Malone smiled.

"I hear your client is grumbling."

"He'll get what he pays for."

"We'll make certain of that," said Malone. He shook his head. "Those guys: they never want to sit back and just let us handle things, do they?"

"Who's here besides us?" asked Cain.

"You mean for the firm or out-of-town talent?"

"Both."

"The firm is satisfied that ... that with my *assistance*, the client will be adequately served. As for other out-of-towners, I've seen nobody I recognize. Besides, from watching the parade you lead around town, I don't think the players here need to import muscle."

"Remember this," said Cain. "Don't get cute or creative

and don't ever—*ever*—forget that this is *my* contract, *my* job. I'm running it. That means I'm running you. You work for the firm and the firm put me in charge of what goes on here."

The two men stared at each other while the radio announced fair summer weather.

"How's your leg?" asked Malone.

"Fine."

"Yesterday's woes." Malone leaned closer to Cain. "We can't let them cripple us now."

City of Rust

CATHERINE ANSWERED THE RINGING PHONE as Cain entered the office.

"Commission," she snapped.

By the time the door closed, Beth had dashed from her desk to the reception room; her eyes were wide, her words quick: "Are you . . ."

"He just arrived," Catherine told the caller. She glared at Cain. "It's for you. Chief DiCarlo."

Cain brushed past Beth as he headed into their office.

"Everything's fine," he told her, not looking at her face.

"This is Cain," he said into his phone.

Beth followed him, anxiously sat at her desk. Boswell was absent. Sylvia appeared in their doorway, her face pale and drawn. Her blouse was blue, her slacks grey.

On the phone, DiCarlo told Cain, "Glad you made it in time."

"In time for what?" Cain replied.

"In time to see what you ought to see and hear what you ought to hear. You know the intersection of Ferris and Broadway?"

"I can find it."

"Fifteen minutes. I'll be waiting."

The phone went dead. Cain hung up.

"Good morning," said Sylvia.

"Good morning," he told her.

Beth watched them.

"I made coffee," said Sylvia. She shrugged. "It's old, but . . ."

"I can't stay," he said.

She smiled, shrugged again, and walked away. Beth and Cain watched her go.

"How are you coming on the subpoena?" he quickly asked Beth.

"I've been worried." Her lips made a hard line, she swallowed. Pressed the bun of her auburn hair to be sure all strands were in place. "The paperwork will be done by this afternoon—*Jack.*"

The intersection of Ferris and Broadway funneled traffic to the river and its seven-mile line of mills and factories. Clapboard two-story bars with neon beer signs in their windows sat on two of the corners. A convenience store occupied the third point, kitty-corner from a boarded-up dry cleaner's. Cain parked a block away. His leg felt better. He walked by an alley in which waited an idling police cruiser. A traffic light dangled from the cross of cables above the designated intersection. The signal changed from orange to red.

DiCarlo waited in an unmarked sedan parked close to the light. Cain passed two parked cars filled with detectives before he reached the chief. As Cain neared the chief's car, the passenger door opened and DiCarlo's cadaverous detective stepped onto the sidewalk. He flashed his ivory grin at Cain and climbed in the back seat.

"Why all the troops?" asked Cain as he settled in the front.

From behind the steering wheel, DiCarlo replied, "Watch."

For twenty minutes, they waited. The car smelled of warm plastic. DiCarlo drummed his thick fingers on the steering wheel. The detective in the back seat wheezed dry breaths on Cain's neck. The police radio crackled with routine calls. The traffic signal cycled between red and green. A dozen obedient cars cruised beneath it.

A battered blue Ford traveling west on Broadway didn't slow down as it rolled beneath a red light.

"There!" yelled DiCarlo, shooting his forefinger at the receding Ford. "Did you see that?

"Been happening all day," continued the chief of police. "My men said they noticed it some last week, but today . . . all over town. Not everybody, but too many."

"Too many what?" asked Cain.

"Too many people here don't believe in traffic lights anymore. Not like the old days when folks tried to get away with one little something so they could get a little something more—home from work quicker, make the movie, win the drag. These days light busters aren't trying for something *more* 'cause there isn't more to get. They've lost faith in traffic lights. They just go."

The chief shook his head, lit a cigarette, blew smoke toward the windshield.

"I've got more important things to do than watch traffic scofflaws," said Cain.

The thin cop behind him made a sound like a snake coiling in dry leaves.

"You're playing in the traffic, Cain," said DiCarlo. "And the old rules are crumbling. Personally, I don't care if you end up smeared on somebody's bumper, but this is my town, and I don't want you making messes for me to clean up."

"Then you should have taken care of business a long time ago."

DiCarlo flicked his cigarette out the window: "I don't take orders—from you or anybody."

"We going to sit and watch cars all day?"

"Open your eyes, Cain. Life is speeding up."

DiCarlo checked his watch.

"Over the past few months, my detectives have become aware of a shocking ring of gambling that's opened up in our fair city. There's a number's game called the bug. We're going to squash it. In twenty-nine minutes, my boys are going to knock over a dozen dealers, a counting house. Plus there's this casino cross town: a couple crap tables, roulette, baccarat and a Turkish game called Barbut, even a hot buffet line and a couple bars. We're gonna kick that door, too. Confiscate a bunch of cash and make arrests."

"Anybody we know going to end up in a paddy wagon?"

"Doubt it," said the chief. He smiled. "At least, not yet."

"Johnny won't take this lying down."

"He'll take what he gets."

"What about the mayor?"

"You think His Honor can bitch about us breaking up crime when he's got an investigating commission parked in his backyard?

"Besides," said DiCarlo, smiling, "if he isn't careful, somebody might jerk His Honor out of City Hall."

"How could that happen?"

DiCarlo merely grinned.

"Why tell me?" asked Cain.

The chief of police seemed to swell with his answer, like a toad full of flies.

"Understand me, Cain," said DiCarlo. "We both got badges, we both got jobs, we both got a life. I don't want to mess with anybody I don't want to mess with, and I don't want to mess with you, unless you mess with me. You need a body to pay for a body to be gone, which is where I want you. You gave me a song about the mayor trying to make me the body you need. Forget about the mayor: I got him covered.

"Now I got a crime war. Maybe there's a bone in there for you. Ask, I'll see what I can do. Or grab what you can on your own.

"But remember: you're playing in traffic, and it ain't safe out there anymore. You don't want to get run over, you better be sure you're in my car."

"Are you going to keep me here so I won't tip Johnny?"

"You want to be a fool," said DiCarlo, "that's your choice."

The city gun behind Cain laughed.

"Hit the bricks, *amigo*," said DiCarlo. "I got police work to do and a town to keep in the law."

The detective in the back seat opened his door, stepped to the sidewalk. Cain did the same, ignoring the cop's ivory grin.

DiCarlo radioed commands. The cruiser in the alley rolled to the intersection and parked where it was visible from all approaches. One car of detectives pulled in front of DiCarlo's sedan, the second car fell in behind. The chief's heavily armed caravan cruised away beneath the traffic light that changed to green.

From his perch on a stepladder, Paul Borge pointed to an open box of canned goods on the concrete floor and said to Cain, "Hand me that, would you?"

Cain lifted the box up to Borge, was surprised by the strength with which the minister swung the weight to the top of the stack. Borge dusted his hands, sat on the ladder's top rung and surveyed the pyramid of boxed food built along the musty warehouse's wall.

"Ought to last us four, maybe five days," he said.

"Then what?" asked Cain.

Borge shrugged, climbed down the ladder.

"Then *is* what," he said. "Why are you here now?"

After DiCarlo's armored column left him, Cain found a pay phone and yelled his way up his firm's New York chain of command.

"Why did you put Malone on my back?" he demanded of the man who'd authorized it.

"You're representing the firm in a hostile environment and need protection," was the reply. "Given my concerns about your potential, we felt it wise to have a second resource on the scene—especially since the client has complained about your pace."

"Kimmett's a spoiled, ignorant fool!" said Cain.

"Perhaps," said the man who was Kimmett's contemporary.

"Malone is a shooter."

"He is a consumate professional. And he's ours."

"You mean mine," said Cain. "My soldier."

"As long as your desires do not interfere with his ultimate objective to maintain the firm's integrity."

"And what about my integrity?"

The firm's president paused, said: "Malone will see to that."

Cain hung up. The noon sun found sweat on his brow.

He dropped quarters in the pay phone and reached the man he sought.

"I thought I'd been kissed off," said DEA agent Wood.

"Now is our chance," Cain said, and relayed DiCarlo's plan. "If you've got anything on any of Johnny's boys, push. *Anything*: even if it eventually gets thrown out of court. Grab 'em, shake 'em. Go for Wolinsky, go for a drug bust, conspiracy, go for . . ."

"Go for *who?*" snapped Wood. "You want us to fetch and carry and go and do for *you?*"

"So far, you've got nothing to complain about," said Cain. He hung up before Wood could reply.

An hour later in the warehouse by the river, Cain turned to Borge and said, "I need your help."

"Theological counseling, no doubt," said the minister.

Their laughter echoed through the warehouse. Dust floated in shafts of sunshine from skylights four stories above the concrete floor. Dozens of lights dangled from black cords secured in the beams, but only a few of those lights were lit. Borge and Cain strolled through the shadows.

"Do you know where you are?" asked Borge.

Cain shrugged.

"This used to be the warehouse for Butwin Trucking," said Borge. "They hauled steel, oil, ore, they hauled finished goods. They had a hundred-truck fleet in the 1960s, and this place"—he swept his hand toward the almost empty vastness— "this place was crammed to the roof with everything you can imagine."

"Who owns it now?"

"Everybody and nobody," said Borge. "When Butwin went belly up, they owed the world. The city ended up with this place. Nobody wants to buy it. Accountants claim it's a valuable piece of property, but it's worth nothing. Maybe that's why Nash lets us use it for the food bank."

He nodded to other stacks of boxes.

"Forgotten refuse of forgotten people.

The minister shrugged. "What can I do for you?"

"What happened to the guy who got arrested at the rally?" asked Cain.

"The cops threw him in jail overnight," Borge told him.

"They bounced him around some. His buddies came up with a hundred, and they let him walk. Lesson paid for, lesson learned."

"Would he give the commission a formal complaint?"

"And stand up to DiCarlo and the SIC all by himself?"

"No. The cops have busted hundreds of people, shaken them down, and let them walk. There'll be tracks of that in their bureaucracy. With that evidence, plus you fishing around quietly, we can come up with dozens of cases of police brutality or corruption to nail on DiCarlo."

"Why are you going after the chief?"

"Everybody is going after somebody," said Cain. "Di-Carlo's taking on Johnny Maxx."

"Why?"

"War is inevitable and DiCarlo has two enemies. Johnny is the most vulnerable, so the chief will attack him first, whip him until he's out or at least too weak to fight. DiCarlo is grabbing cash from Johnny today—which will make the chief stronger while Johnny gets a taste of hunger. When he's got Johnny where he wants him, DiCarlo can turn and take on the mayor."

"What's keeping the mayor out of the fight?"

"Don't know," said Cain. "He's taken a pot shot at the chief, but that was just to get us off his back and keep DiCarlo on his toes. I've got an idea why the mayor won't take on Johnny now, but . . ."

Cain shook his head, frowned.

"So why do you want to help Johnny and take on the chief?"

"I'm helping nobody. I'm helping us."

"Where does Josh Hammond fit into this sound and fury?"

"He's why we're here."

"All right," said Borge after a moment's thought. "I'll find you victims. That's easy enough here.

"Do you *really* know where you are?" asked Borge again.

"Steeltown," said Cain.

The minister shook his head.

"Come on." He led Cain to the parking lot, to the edge of a bluff overlooking the river and its seven miles of rusted factories and mills and power plants. On the far horizon was the Pit.

"This could be Youngstown, Ohio, or Butte, Montana. Birmingham. Allentown. Detroit. Pittsburgh. Maybe Houston. Anywhere in what they call America's rust belt.

"Only our red isn't rust. You make a town like you make steel—purify raw ore with fire and honest sweat, pour it into a clean straight, mold. Do that, and you get a beam that'll last forever. But if you cheat, cut corners, do less than the best ... what you get is weak. Vulnerable. When it rains, it rusts. So that's what you really made.

"That mess down there?" Borge nodded to the river. "That mess in town? Foreign competition or bad luck didn't make them, we did. What looked so good for so long turned out to be no better than what we put into it. We are what we make, and what we made ... that isn't rust."

Home

THE STATE CAR TOOK JACKSON CAIN off warehouse hill, along the river, past Bushmaster's mill, where his father labored in blast furnace number 3 for twenty-six years until 4:47 A.M. on October 3, 1965, when a load of quarter-inch steel slid off its dolly. Pete Cainelli jumped clear. Hit the thereafter eternally damned guard rail—"company should have replaced it long before." The rail tore loose and spun him off the catwalk, a fourteen-foot fall to his back that left him healthy to the eye but broken inside, weak, unfit for "honest work."

As Cain drove out of the gorge, he glanced at the dirt side road leading to a bluff. There, on a March Friday night in 1967, seventeen-year-old Jim Cainelli stared down at Linda Lombardi as she lay on the back seat of his family's Chevy, her white blouse open, her bra somewhere in the front, her skirt shoved up around her waist, her panties under his feet. He wore his socks and sneakers, his underpants and blue jeans bunched around his virgin ankles. She was all-over pale, like he imagined ivory or silk must be, only warm and moist, moaning or crying or maybe both. Electric guitars throbbed in the car's radio. Power and joy and terror surged through him; all the famous, overdue promises would come true *now!* Then he heard the whistles and clangs of the mills, smelled their stench beyond her flesh. Her thighs were smooth and strong and ready to close tightly around him, capture his seed and trap him forever. He rolled away.

Newhouse Road led to Ferris Street. That artery took Cain
to its intersection with Broadway where the two cops in the
parked cruiser caressed his car with their sunglassed-vision.
He obeyed the red light, escaped the black holes of their eyes.

Two miles down Broadway was Rat Man's house.

On Jimmy Cainelli's eleventh birthday, Rat Man didn't
show up for work. A foreman dispatched Cain's father and
two other mill workers coming off-shift to check on the man
who threw a fit whenever they tapped the blast furnace and
a belch of flame turned unlucky rats into squealing, skitter-
ing balls of fire.

Cain's father had often told his son how the unions and
the company had taken pity on a lost soul, made him rat
catcher for the mill, given him traps, cages and a club, kept
him out of Warm Springs, where the mad went.

Everyone joked about Rat Man, avoided his touch. He
haunted the works, more sensed than seen. Once Jimmy
Cainelli visited the mill, a boy led through the locker room
where his father and *real* men put on their steel-toed boots,
hard hats, goggles, and gloves. Father took son to Old Number 3, pointed out this and that, whispered to the boy *secret
truths* about how much harder one job was than another,
about how the son shouldn't repeat what the father said
about anyone over dinner, about where the son could expect
to start when it came his turn to work in this inevitable
inferno that burned your nostrils, soaked your clothes with
sweat, and blistered your skin beneath the grime. The boy
shook hands with men who shared his father's sentence—
with everyone except a gaunt figure in the shadows with
eyes as white and hot as Old Number 3's heart.

The morning when Jimmy was eleven was the first time
anyone visited the Rat Man's house, a shack set back off
the street, well away from *real* homes.

Cain's father knocked on the Rat Man's door. No answer. He looked at his two comrades. Good men. Hard
working, courageous men. Knocked again. Behind the door,
a radio played German polka music. The door knob turned in
his hand—unlocked: who would steal from such a person?
The door swung inward.

Rat Man sat in an easy chair in a living room decorated

with cast-off finery. An elaborate art deco lamp with a swooping blue glass maiden holding a crystal moon glowed on the table. One of Rat Man's friends he'd rescued from the mill sat beneath the lamp's moon, flicking his skinny tail; another sat on the shoulder of the man's corpse. Half a dozen more danced freely on the carpet to the radio's polka. Steeltown legend says cops sent to close down the house did so with blazing guns and bandannas tied over their faces; the legend tells of a terribly gnawed body.

"Don't know if that's fact," father always told his son. "I saw what I saw in that chair and running all over and I *slammed* that door. We flew off that porch like the devil was after us."

Even now, Cain shuddered as he passed Rat Man's shack.

Cain drove by his high school, where priests had taught patriotism and he'd sought the perfect pitch, learned to run the bases, look over his shoulder for the pickoff throw or Ralph Suda's fist. Or for Beverly Turner's miniskirt sliding further up her legs as she sat at her study hall desk, watching the clock. Or for the smile Allison Handley always gave some other guy.

The Italian cemetery on Garibaldi Street had surrendered its ethnic segregation before Cain was born, but natives still knew it by its past. Cain glanced at the iron bar gate as he drove by. Inside waited two grass patches and marble stones with words carved into them that time would erase: one grave was for a mother who discovered that the cigarettes she smoked to calm her Steeltown nerves and make her feel beautiful had eaten her lungs. Another grave dug three years later belonged to a father who drowned in his heart's bitter blackness, certain he knew the truth and angry that everyone around him made such fatal mistakes.

"I live at One-Thirteen Turin Street," whispered the ghost of Jimmy Cainelli, a boy proud and certain of his navigatory catechism. "My Dad works for Bushmaster and my Mom stays home while I go to school. She bakes chocolate chip cookies. She coughs, but it's okay. My bedroom is at the top of the stairs, our toilet runs, and I have seventy-three comic books plus all the Hardy Boys and I read them under the covers at night with a flashlight. I don't have a sister or a brother and my parents are sorry but I don't mind. We live in Steeltown, United States of America, and there isn't a better place in the whole world."

The white picket fence he'd had to keep painted was peeling and broken, its gate dangling from one hinge. Yellow grass and brown dirt were now the front yard. Someone had grafted an ugly bulge that looked like a dining room extension onto the left side of the house. The once-white walls were now what hardware stores called salmon—or had been, before that cheap paint job started to crack and peel. The aluminum screen door was new. As Cain sat in his car parked across the street, that door swung open. A stranger in a soiled white tank top and cutoff blue jeans shuffled onto the porch. His greasy hair was askew, he needed a shave. Cain saw a tattoo on the man's right arm. The man lit a cigarette, casually threw the empty pack into the yard, leaned against the porch post, scratched his sagging belly and smoked.

An old woman came out of a tidy house two doors away from Cain. Memories flooded over him. He ached to touch them. Cain couldn't stop himself; he climbed out of his car and hurried after the old woman.

"Mrs. Kincheloe!" yelled Cain.

She turned, frowned. She was shorter, much shorter, with miles more wrinkles, white hair and a tremble.

"Do you remember me?" he said as he drew near, unable to keep the eagerness off his face. "Do you remember? I'm Jim Cainelli."

"Oh my Lord!" She drew back, her hand touching her chest. She shook her head. "I didn't recognize . . . I thought you were dead, too."

"Not quite yet," he said.

"You never came back," she said. "Your father . . . You never came back."

"I couldn't."

"What are you doing?"

"I'm just passing through. How are you?"

"So many years." She frowned, shook her head, and he saw that same smart light in her eyes. "What do you want?"

He turned away from her, looked around the neighborhood.

"I have some things to do," he said. "Private things. And if anybody finds out I'm here, it'll be bad trouble."

"They why tell me anything?" she said. "Why come back at all?"

Again she shook her head. Stared at this person she'd met the day his parents carried him home from the hospital.

"All those smarts," she said before she turned and walked away, "and you still don't understand, do you?"

The Hand in the Glove

"HOW SOON WILL WE BE READY?" Cain asked Beth when he arrived at the office.

"Catherine is typing the subpoena now," Beth answered from behind her desk. Cain heard the clicking of the computer keyboard in the outer office. "Probably another half hour. Where have you been?"

On the way to the office, Cain surreptitiously visited the bus depot.

Twenty thousand, he thought as he stared at the suitcase from Chicago in his locker. Plus a few thousand in the briefcase in his room. Maybe enough.

At the commission, Boswell was out. In her office, Sylvia argued over the phone with a stationery company. Cain picked up his telephone.

"Get me DiCarlo," he told the cop who answered his call.

Cain and Beth stared at each other as he waited on hold. The computer keyboard clicked outside their office.

"Why are you bothering me?" said DiCarlo.

"I need some beef to help serve a subpoena," said Cain. "The commission is officially asking your department for backup."

"Serve what subpoena on who?" asked DiCarlo.

"As you know, Chief," said Cain, "especially over the phone, I can't divulge such information until the process is adequately—"

"Don't mumbo jumbo me," said DiCarlo.

"Call it something for a friend," said Cain. "Something that blends in nicely with your current operations."

"You're doing that, I better send a whole squad."

"Two uniforms will be enough," said Cain. "This isn't war."

"Un-huh," said DiCarlo.

They hung up.

"I have to file notice of the subpoena with district court," said Beth. "To keep them honest, I'd better have a witness."

"Sylvia!" yelled Cain. "Could you come here a minute?"

She finished her phone call, joined Beth and Cain.

"Can you help Beth?" asked Cain as Sylvia perched on the edge of Boswell's desk. She'd watched Cain from the time she entered the room. Now she nodded yes to Beth; turned back to Cain.

The three of them heard the outer office door open, close. A high-speed computer printer began to whine.

"Good afternoon, Commissioner Kimmett," said Catherine.

"Hello. Is my wife here?"

He walked into the room where Cain and the women sat, and announced, "The oddest, most wonderful thing has happened!"

"What's that, dear?" asked his wife.

"The Japanese gave ten thousand dollars to the United Way campaign!" he told them.

"That's good—isn't it?" asked Sylvia.

"Well the charities certainly can use the money," said her husband. "Nobody has much to give these days, but . . ."

"But what?" asked Cain.

"But we never mentioned that to them," said the heir to the throne Cain was hired to build. "We didn't hide the town's problems, but we certainly never put them in the spotlight.

"The most peculiar thing," he said, "was that they gave the check to *me*. I'm just one of the hospitality delegation, not a public official, and I'm not on the United Way's board!

Right after lunch, they took me aside, gave me the envelope. But no gracious speech, no mention of why, or what or . . .

"I asked Mr. Nakusonna about it," continued Kimmett. "You remember him, dear."

"Yes," said Sylvia.

"Tanaka's reply was just as puzzling," said Kimmett. "He mumbled something about, 'appropriate way of handling the matter.' Then bowed slightly, and walked away."

Kimmett shook his head.

"What have they said about the auto plant?" asked Sylvia.

"Nothing," said Kimmett. "If we were impolite enough to press the question, they'd politely let it slide to the floor.

"But this has to be a good sign!" he insisted. "They wouldn't invest in a community they were going to leave, right?"

Sylvia said nothing.

Cain said nothing.

"I'm sure it's a positive step," said Beth.

Catherine marched into the room, placed a pile of papers on Beth's desk, and announced: "Finished."

"Sorry to interrupt your work," said Kimmett.

"I need to proof these," said Beth.

"We'll give you some privacy," said Cain, leading the Kimmetts to Sylvia's office.

When the three of them were alone, Kimmett lowered his voice:

"I didn't want to say anything in front of Miss Worby or Catherine, because they're not included. My father has asked us to dinner. You, too, Cain. He said it would be good for our son to get to know Cain—which, of course, it would. The boy should meet all types of . . ."

Kimmett stuttered to a halt, blushed slightly.

". . . of people in various occupations, and . . ."

"That's fine," said Cain. On the edge of his vision, he saw Sylvia maintain her composure.

"Well," continued her husband, "good, that's settled."

Husband turned to wife:

"I called the house. Woke Elliot. He's not happy about it, but he'll come. I'll be with a client until six at least, so ..." He frowned, and both Cain and his wife knew the thought was not spontaneous.

"I know," said Kimmett. "Sylvia, why don't you pick Elliot up at the house, and I'll give Jack a ride?"

The commissioner smiled to the commission's hired hand. The outer office door opened and closed.

"It'll give us a chance to talk," said Kimmett.

"Mr. Cain," called Catherine from the reception room, "the police are here."

"Yes," he replied, "I know."

"What are we doing here?" said the biggest of the two uniformed cops as they followed Cain up the cement steps. "This is City Hall!"

"That's right," said Cain.

"But the chief said you were going to serve a subpoena and we had to make sure you didn't get whacked."

"Loosely speaking," said Cain, opening the door and stepping inside the marble halls.

"Nobody said anything about hitting City Hall!" said the cop.

Cain kept walking, his momentum pulling the policemen along.

"Just doing our job, right guys?" he told them.

"This is not good," muttered one of the cops. "This is definitely not good."

But they followed Cain through the rotunda's marble columns, down the long institutional green hallway. The cops' heavy shoes echoed through the building. A man in a white shirt and tie and a plump woman in a plum-colored dress stopped gossiping to stare.

The chief clerk in the Office of Records and Contracts wore his customary bow tie. He scurried to the counter when Cain and the cops marched through the door.

"The city treasurer is in that office, right?" said Cain, pointing to a clouded-glass door beyond the maze of clerks' desks.

"That's right, he—Hey!" called out the clerk as Cain led the two red-faced cops through the counter gate, "You can't—"

But Cain was past him, opening the door. Beyond it, a fat man dropped his magazine.

"Are you Steeltown's city treasurer?" snapped Cain.

"Ah . . . Why . . . Yes, but . . . What the hell are you—"

"I've got something for you," said Cain. He held a folded paper toward the treasurer—who automatically took it.

"You've just been served with a subpoena for all records concerning the city's management of funds connected with any purchase by the SIC of city bonds," said Cain. "You have twenty-four hours to comply.

"Service has been duly completed and witnessed," said Cain, nodding to the two policemen—both of whom were staring everywhere but at their fellow city official. "Failure to comply means a contempt charge against both you personally and the city."

"I . . . Just . . . The mayor . . ."

Cain and his escort left. On his way through the maze of clerks' desks, he nodded to the man the bow tie. "Have a nice day."

As soon as the door closed behind them in the hall, one of the cops tapped Cain on the shoulder:

"I ain't signing no witness papers, nowhere, no way," said the blurry officer of the law. His partner nodded agreement.

"Don't worry about it," said Cain. Since leaving the office, he'd slowed to a stroll.

"Come on," urged one of the cops. "Let's get out of here."

"What's your hurry?" asked Cain as they reached the rotunda. Cain walked through the circle of marble columns to a bench facing the floor's inlaid giant Great Seal of Steeltown. He lifted his foot to the bench, examined his shoe lace.

An explosion of slammed-open doors echoed through the building. The city cops turned to look, and Cain raised his head.

From the far end of a long corridor, His Honor Richard Nash stormed toward them. A phalanx of aides and sheriff's deputies hustled behind the egg-shaped mayor.

Nash started yelling before he reached the rotunda:

"Goddamn you, Cain! What do you think you're doing?"

Cain pointed at his shoe.

"This is my Goddamned town!" yelled the mayor. He and his troops reached the rotunda. The aides fanned out in a half-moon with the marble columns at their backs. Nash glowed red.

Cain's escorts stepped away from him; their eyes zeroed the mayor's men, who glared at them. One of Cain's cops unsnapped his holstered revolver.

"No one comes into town and jerks me around!" Mayor Nash tapped Cain's chest with his tiny forefinger. His words sprayed Cain. "No one! Subpoena be damned! No one!"

"How do you think the town is going to react if there's anything fishy in the city's bond deal with the SIC?"

"The people have faith in me!" The mayor took a deep breath; won control of himself. The crimson flush faded from his face, his volume dropped to a conversational tone, and he leaned back from Cain.

"You sure about that?" said Cain.

"Confidence, Cain," said the mayor. "That's how politics works. I've got it because I am who I am. That's why the people have confidence in me, and that's why Steeltown works and you and all the damn legal papers in the world won't make any difference to that!"

"But what if?" asked Cain.

Nash laughed.

"I don't know why I bothered to get mad," he said. "Bad habit. All the strings in my hand, and I let a shadow man like you get me mad. You're not worth it, Cain. You're history waiting to be forgotten.

"Out there," said Nash, sweeping his hand to the invisible city, "they don't care—and if they care, they don't know what to do. I tell them what to do. They let me because they want to *believe*—believe that I'll take care of them and believe that they don't need to worry. They'll choose hard times over having to think for themselves. Thinking scares people, confuses them. They want certainty, and I give it to 'em.

"Do what you think you can, you and your damn subpoenas. Won't matter. You got nothing that can break through the way things are, and even if you did, there's nothing they can do."

Nash turned and glared at Cain's two city cops.

"It won't matter who's on your side, Cain. You won't get me out of the mayor's office!"

"I already did," said Cain. He smiled.

Blood rushed to Nash's face. His lips drew back from his tiny teeth and he snarled. His hands clenched into small fists.

Three of Nash's bodyguards and his chief aide, Carson, moved toward their boss.

Cain gave them his back and slowly walked toward the exit.

DiCarlo's cops sidestepped toward the door behind the man they were supposed to protect, their hands close to their guns, their eyes on Nash's men.

One of the mayor's deputies stepped toward the retreating trio; he spit at their feet.

"What are you doing?" yelled Nash. He cuffed the deputy, pointed to the spittle on the marble floor. "Clean that up!"

The biggest of Cain's cops laughed.

Two of Nash's bodyguards moved forward, and Cain's cops quickened their pace. The deputy who'd offended his boss pulled a handkerchief from his pocket, knelt to wipe the floor. He glared at his retreating fellow Steeltown lawmen.

"Mister," said the cop who laughed as he and his partner followed Cain down City Hall's steps, "you got balls for brains."

"Is that a compliment?" asked Cain.

"Beats me," answered the cop.

Elliot Kimmett IV met Cain at the commission office at 5:00 P.M., sharp. Cain knew the time because as Kimmett walked through the door, Catherine shut off her computer, activated the telephone message machine, bid them good night, and left, her scheduled duties complete. Beth rode the elevator down with the men.

"A busy night, Ms. Worby?" Kimmett inquired politely.

"I've got some things to do," she said, her eyes on Cain.

He'd avoided her since that morning's encounter with the old man.

"I hope it's pleasure, not business," smiled Kimmett.

"Yes," she answered, "me, too."

Cain frowned.

On the street, Beth said good-bye, headed across the city square. She wore a brown-skirted suit over a white blouse. Her auburn bun was in danger of unwinding. She walked with her shoulders well set, emphasizing her narrow waist and her curved hips. She had sleek legs and trim ankles.

"Along with everything else," said Kimmett, mindful that both he and Cain were watching the sway of Beth's hips, "she is a very attractive woman."

"I know," said Cain.

"I'm parked this way," said Kimmett, leading Cain down a side street.

They talked about the weather, the deplorable state of the roads; joked about Catherine, the Commission's nine-to-five Marine.

"My car's there," said Kimmett, pointing to the next block.

Cain looked, and as he did, he saw a parked black Corvette shark. Through its windshield, he saw Debbi Dolan sitting in the passenger's seat, her dyed blond hair brushing her shoulders. She stared through the glass and saw nothing.

"I thought we were friends," said Johnny Maxx, as he stepped out of the evening shadows behind Cain and Kimmett.

They whirled.

"Hello, *Sonny*," Johnny Maxx said to Kimmett.

Kimmett blushed, looked away.

"You've been busy, Cain," said Johnny Maxx. His blue pinstripe suit was rumpled, his tie a millimeter askew. The words he spoke were crisp, parceled out by a tightly set jaw.

"You heard about me taking on the mayor?" was Cain's quick reply.

Johnny Maxx's black eyes narrowed.

"What I see and hear is trouble," he said. "Nothing that won't be handled, but nothing that's gonna make life easier for anybody."

"I heard DiCarlo rousted your boys—your friends," revised Cain quickly. "We're hunting up brutalities and bungles by the chief. If he pulled any today, we can help out you and your people."

Kimmett shifted from foot to foot. He stared at the sidewalk, at parked cars, at the skyline in the distance.

Johnny Maxx shook his head; stepped closer to Cain.

Even Johnny isn't crazy enough to get rough here, in broad daylight, two of us and one of him, his woman sitting a block away, thought Cain. Even Johnny couldn't be *that* crazy.

Then, half a block behind the gangster, Cain saw a man walk across the street for a better angle on the altercation, a man with black metal-framed glasses and quick hands. Cain relaxed.

"What are you worried about?" he said as Johnny Maxx leaned toward him. "The commission hasn't done a thing directed toward . . ."

"Blow it off, Cain: bullshit don't make it on my street."

"I don't bet on it either," said Cain.

"In the Marines," said Johnny Maxx. "I boxed a little. Every guy who ever stepped into the ring knows that it isn't the glove that hits you that matters, it's the hand inside.

"The *commission*," he said, shaking his head, "DiCarlo— Hell, for all I know, the feds: they're just the glove. I get hit by a glove, I look for the hand inside. I'm feeling your hand, *Cain*.

"You know what I do when I get hit? I'm big enough to take a few taps from hotshots and let 'em slide. Let fools dance until they wise up and get out of my face. But sometimes comes a fool who wants to really fight and has to learn.

"You know what I do in a real fight, Cain? I don't just swing back. I rip off the whole fuckin' arm and make you eat it. You want to mix it up with me, you better be goddamned hungry, because you're sure as shit gonna eat it."

Johnny Maxx smiled at Kimmett. "Say hi to your old man, Junior."

Seconds later, Johnny Maxx gunned his black sports car from the curb and roared down the street. His passenger's beautiful face was impassive.

Nick Malone was nowhere to be seen.

Elliot Kimmett stood on the sidewalk of his hometown, his gaze focused far away. Cain turned to him.

"Well," said Cain, "it sounds like he's left us some room to maneuver before he . . ."

"I don't want to know," said Kimmett. "That doesn't matter to me now. Maybe someday, but not now."

He shook his head.

"This sad place," he said.

"I don't get it," said Cain. "With your money, you a lawyer, smart, educated. A big wheel here just by being born."

"A wheel goes round and round, Cain. That doesn't mean it wants the trip."

"You could have gone anywhere else. Done anything else."

"Nobody has that freedom." He smiled. "Even Elliot Kimmett the Fourth. Given the lousy numbers before him, maybe especially Elliot Kimmett the Fourth.

"Steeltown is Sylvia's home," he said. "We married very young. She was fragile. I had obligations to her, to not impose on her life any more than I had, take her away from her family, her friends. Her roots."

"Roots aren't all they're cracked up to be," said Cain.

"They're what hold us to the earth," said Kimmett. "And hold the earth together."

"No," said Cain. "That's our hands."

"Maybe you're right," said Kimmett. "Maybe I just stayed here because this was easiest, this was safest."

"Safe? With guys like Johnny Maxx?"

"And my father?" Kimmett smiled.

"Yeah," said Cain.

"Yes. Him. Well, the Johnny Maxxes are everywhere and your father never leaves you.

"Maybe I should have been a doctor, Cain. Their rule is mine: First, do no harm.

"Do you know how difficult that rule is to follow? It was the only way I could see to keep from becoming . . . First, do no harm. Not to anyone, not to anything. Because once you start, you can never know where the harm stops.

Once you adopt that rule ... Well, harm is easy to find, avoidance is complex and difficult. So few people understand, see what you're really doing ..."

He trailed off to embarrassed silence.

"Come on," he said to Cain. "Let's go see my fine family."

They walked toward his car. After a few steps, Cain said, "What was it you wanted to talk with me about?"

"Oh," said Kimmett as he unlocked the car's passenger door for Cain, "that."

He shook his head. "Nothing you probably don't know."

"But ..."

"Just try not to hurt ..." began Kimmett, then he finished, "I want to be sure everything is all right for ... That you ... All right with Sylvia—and her work for you. On the commission. She worries about it, doesn't say everything she feels ... But she cares about ... about it. And what she wants, what she needs ... that's what she should get."

"Sure," answered Cain. "Fine."

The husband smiled wistfully.

Elliot Kimmett V kept his blond hair chopped short; his inherited green eyes were wild and his mouth habitually curled in a sneer. He wore a wrinkled white shirt he'd outgrown, a faded denim jacket covered with black-inked scrawls—the one across the back read CHAOS. He tapped his heavy silver table knife on the white linen tablecloth with an irregular beat. His fingernails were dirty; his hands were soft, pale. At his grandfather's table, he sat between his parents. Cain and Nelson sat across from them, while the old man presided from the end. None of the adults commented on the youngest Kimmett's unwashed odor.

"And they let you graduate anyway?" said the grandfather.

"They figured they'd get me back if they didn't," said the boy. He shrugged, sneered. "They were wrong. Stupid. So what."

The butler served the vegetable bouillon.

"At least this time," said the grandfather. "We didn't have to buy off some girl."

The old man grinned at Sylvia. She stared off in the distance, her face bloodless.

"You're learning," said the old man to the boy.

"Hey, *Gramps:* I'm a fuckin' high school graduate."

"Son," said the boy's father, "you shouldn't talk to your grandfather that way. Or any adult who—"

"It's a free country," sneered the boy.

"Nothing is free!" snapped the old man. "You always have to pay! Remember that!"

"Hey!" said the teenager. "What are you going to do? Cut off my trust fund allowance? That'll screw up your taxes. And in case you ain't noticed, *Gramps,* you're too wasted to try spanking me."

"Judson!" bellowed the old man.

The giant marched from the kitchen to his master's chair.

The teenager looked at Judson, sized up the old man's leer.

"Looks like you win this one, *Grandfather.*"

The old man laughed.

"You're smart," he said. "With the proper guidance, you'll learn to use it. We'll get you into college . . ."

"What if I don't want to go to college?"

"It never hurts," said the old man. "It's a credential you can wield profitably. You need it, you'll do it—because I say so. And because it will keep you out of the hospital."

The kid smiled a secret to himself; loudly slurped his soup.

"Why do you do this?" said the middle Kimmett. "I don't know why I come and let this happen."

"Because I'm your father," said Cain's secret client. "Because you should.

"And what about you, my dear?" the older Kimmett asked Sylvia. "What do you think should happen?"

She drank the scotch she'd carried to the table, kept her fingers around her glass. "What difference does that make?"

The boy yawned, and filled his water goblet with red wine.

"What do you want, young man?" asked his grandfather.

The boy slowly drank the entire goblet.

"I said," intoned the grandfather, "what do you want?"

"You really want to know what I want?" answered the youngest Kimmett.

His grandfather nodded.

The maid cleared for the next course. Only Cain, Nelson, and the boy had emptied their bowls. The butler served the roast beef, pan-baked potatoes, and fresh asparagus.

"I want what I want," said the youth. "And I want it now."

"Listen," said the oldest Kimmett. "Listen good: Sometimes you must wait, just as sometimes you must seize the moment. If you're not strong *and* patient, you won't beat the crowd. And if you don't have a base for your plans, everything you grab slips through your fingers."

"Sure," said the young man. His reply reeked disdain. He picked up his knife and fork; then gave his grandfather a beatific look and sweetly repeated, *"Sure."*

The grandfather laughed. He eagerly attacked his dinner.

"See, Cain?" he said between rapid, wolfing bites. "See how it is in Steeltown?"

"Yes," replied Cain, his eyes steady on the old man. "I see."

Dessert was cherry pie.

The butler and maid served coffee in the drawing room. Old man Kimmett sat in the grandest easy chair, waved aside a steaming cup, and kept his bright eyes moving from one family member to another; sometimes he chuckled. His son took a cup of coffee from the butler and thanked him, dropped two lumps of sugar in it from the silver bowl on the silver tray carried by the maid, and thanked her; this handsome lawyer in a blue suit carried the cup across the room to the intoxicated teenager slumped on the sofa. Father gently urged son to drink the steaming brew, held the saucer for him. Sylvia stood at the French windows, her arms folded across her chest as she leaned against the glass and stared out at the night.

China clattered as the youth plopped the empty cup on the saucer in his father's hand. The father suggested another cup; the boy mumbled incoherently and waved his hand, slumped farther down on the couch, closed his eyes. His father whispered something none of the others could hear. The boy showed no reaction. The lawyer turned and walked to the serving table, where Nelson and Cain stood. As Kimmett placed the cup and saucer on the silver tray, Nelson walked away.

"I must apologize," Kimmett whispered to Cain, with a glance toward where his father sat straining to overhear their conversation. "For my son. For my father."

"No you don't," Cain told him.

"Blood is its own burden," said Kimmett. His eyes searched the face of this man he barely knew. "Do you understand?"

"Yes," said Cain. "No."

"Look," said Kimmett, with an apologetic shrug. "I have to take my son home. Sylvia will give you a ride. She's had a few, too, but she's fine. Is that all right?"

"Whatever I can do to help."

Kimmett smiled wistfully. Turned and saw his wife staring out the window, the light from outside making her gold hair seem silver. He hesitated, then, with his eyes still on her, said, "After I get him settled ... I ... There's a mountain of work at the office. I'll be there quite late."

The lawyer stared at his wife for a moment, then shifted his gaze to his father. Cain saw the middle Kimmett's eyes narrow.

"Time for us to leave, Father," he said.

At the window, Sylvia turned to watch.

"Why?" the old man told his son. "Wasn't the food good enough?"

"I've had my fill," answered the son. With labored steps he crossed the room to the teenager slumped on the couch.

"That's your problem," drawled the old man. His green eyes blazed. "You've never had enough of an appetite—or maybe your guts just can't take it."

"I'm content with my appetites," said the middle-aged lawyer. "And I've never asked you to satisfy them."

"You don't have enough fire in your belly!" snapped the old man.

"Oh," said Elliot Kimmett IV, with a wistful smile, "I've got plenty of that."

He nodded toward Sylvia. She lowered her eyes as she crossed the room to help her husband gently pull their drunk son off the couch. The boy staggered to his feet with a parent supporting each arm. Together, the three of them started toward the door.

"We're going now." The lawyer's words were an affirmation of faith rather than a statement of intent.

"I'm not through yet!" yelled the old man.

"Sylvia is giving Cain a ride home," announced her husband.

She looked at her spouse, blinked; stared at Cain, then dropped her eyes once more to the floor.

"He has to talk to me!" shouted the master of the house.

"I'll wait in the car," mumbled Sylvia.

She and her husband struggled to keep their son upright and move forward. They almost toppled over at the drawing room doors. As they shuffled into the foyer, the grandfather yelled to their backs, "You can't just walk away! Sooner or later, you'll have to learn! You'll have to deal with . . ."

The front door slammed behind his retreating family.

"Sooner or later," said the grandfather as the door slam echoed. He chuckled: "Sooner.

"See!" he said to Cain. "He does have fire! He just doesn't know how to make it burn."

"I wouldn't know about that," said Cain. "He seems fine to me."

"You're not paid for opinions!" snapped his employer. "You're paid for results, and I'm not happy with what I'm seeing!"

"Get your eyes checked," said Cain. "Johnny Maxx is in DiCarlo's frying pan because I turned on the heat. Mayor Nash has troubles—some of them from DiCarlo, most of them from us. He's shook up. I intend to shake him more."

"Nash is a hard man to get a handle on," said the old man. He stroked his chin. "But once you do . . ."

"Once I do, he's gone. He has to be in total control, and that makes him overextended, vulnerable. Somehow, somewhere."

"What about DiCarlo?" asked Nelson of his fellow FBI alumni.

"When it's time," said Cain. "I'll go after him."

"What about your commission?" said Kimmett. "I never liked that idea. Too risky. You've set Russ Boswell on a track. He's getting noticed. The brave and pure knight. He might get ideas."

"Don't worry about Boswell," said Cain. "He'll never be you."

"I don't *worry* about anyone!" said Kimmett. "But I keep my eye on everyone."

"Is that why you complained to the firm about me?" said Cain.

"You needed reminding who is boss."

"What else is going on in your town?" asked Cain.

"What do you mean?"

"Did you know the Japanese gave ten grand to charity?" said Cain. "Right here in River City?"

"When?" said Nelson. He glanced at the old man.

"Today," Cain told his client. "Via your son."

"The Japanese are my son's business," said Kimmett. "This town is mine."

"They're paying it a lot of attention. They could be a problem for us."

"The Japanese are many things," said the old man, "but they're not stupid. Don't worry about them. And remember: you work for me."

"I know why I'm here," said Cain. "I have to go. I don't want to keep your daughter-in-law waiting."

Kimmett roared with laughter.

"You do that!" he said, between gasps. "You do that!"

His laughter pushed Cain outside.

The summer wind blew through Sylvia's hair as she drove streets Cain knew didn't lead to his hotel. He shared her silence.

She parked the car on a bluff at the dead end of a residential road. The nearest house was two blocks behind them: no one seemed to be home. She turned out the headlights, shut off the engine. Three strands of barbed wire, black lines beyond the windshield, separated them from the long fall into the Pit. The lamps of Steeltown twinkled behind and to the sides of the bluff. The moon hung above it all, fat and luminous with reflected light.

"What did the bastard want with you?" asked Sylvia.

"The bastard wanted to tell me the ways of the world and what I should do about that in Steeltown," answered Cain.

"You're his man, aren't you?" she said. "And not just because he bankrolled the commission."

"He thinks so," said Cain.

"And he's right," said Sylvia.

Cain shrugged. "I know what my job is."

"Want to tell me about it?" Her tone was mocking.

"Want to try believing me?" he replied.

"Never mind," she said. She looked out the windshield.

Crickets silenced by their arrival began to sing again. Cain looked at Sylvia. The breeze mussed her golden hair and brought him a whiff of scotch with her warm scent: he remembered Montana mornings and wheat fields. The gravity of the moon held her face toward the windshield. After a few moments, he, too, turned to face the glass.

"Where are you from?" she asked, her voice soft, gentle.

"Someplace like this," he said. "Lots of places."

"Where that mattered?"

"Last?" he asked. He sensed her answering nod. "El Salvador.

"A few years ago," he told her. Shrugged. "Yesterday.

"My firm sent me there on a contract we had with an American telecommunications company that needed somebody who spoke Spanish and could work the shadows without selling them out."

"Where did you learn Spanish?"

"In jail," he said. "A good base in high school, but—"

"Jail?" She shook her head. "That's one possibility I never imagined. How did that happen?"

He sighed, rolled his head on the back of the car seat. He bent forward, rubbed his neck; shrugged and settled down.

"I'll tell you about jail," he said. "About everything."

He shook his head.

"Everything I can," he amended. "Maybe all this—" He

swept his hand toward the windshield. "Maybe it starts in El Salvador.

"It had been decided however decisions in such a place are made that for national security considerations the telephone company—which had been owned by foreign conglomerates since phones came to that jungle—should be purchased by the Salvadoran government for a few hundred million dollars. The Salvadoran government got most of those dollars from Uncle Sam in an aid package the phone company's lobbyists negotiated through Washington as a patriotic, anticommunist gesture.

"The secret police took over the phone company as soon as the negotiations were on solid footing. My job was to be sure the process wasn't short-circuited—that the right people got paid, that they didn't bog everything down until our client and Uncle Sam were so committed they could be ripped off by the Salvadoran government.

"As soon as the secret police took over the phone system, *Mano Blanco*—"

"The what?" interupted Sylvia.

"*El Mano Blanco*," answered Cain. "The White Hand. The right wing death squads. They're the heart and soul and some say the brains of the official secret police, whether White Hand members carry secret police badges or not. They started using the phone company to track their enemies, political and otherwise. They'd eavesdrop, snoop on all the financial transactions done by wire and use that information to set the price of someone's life by knowing how much to charge."

"What happened?" asked Sylvia.

"To El Salvador?" said Cain. "What always happens to places like that.

"To me?" he shook his head.

"The capital city smells of death. Sweet. Thick. In the morning, there are bodies in the roadside ditches, the parks. Nobody knows how they got there. *El Mano Blanco*, left wing rebels, crooks: they all contribute until it's a meaningless body count suppressed in the local press and abused in the U.S. But I'd smelled death before. And I had a job to do.

"One morning I met with a captain of the secret police

in an outdoor cafe—his meeting, his agenda. Our CIA loved
the guy but never trusted him for a moment. He'd nailed
some rebels in his day. Now he was angling for a *transa*, a
side deal for himself. I don't know what, because if I'd let
him tell me I'd have known too much for an easy no. He got
as far as letting me know he was *Mano Blanco*, that he'd
been squeezing fat cats—left, right, fervently uninvolved,
made no difference to him. Mentioned he knew some cocaine cowboys in Columbia and Kentucky. That was when I
cut him off. Told him I did the business I did and nothing
more.

"I was so tough," said Cain. He shook his head.

"We'd chosen that cafe for its open patio. We had a
corner table, close enough to the traffic to drown out tele-
scope mikes and transitory enough to be safe from routine
bugging. Nobody sat too close to us: in El Salvador, you
must protect your ignorance.

"I dropped money for the coffee on the table. The captain waved as I walked away. Ten, fifteen steps down the
sidewalk, a boy passed me on a motor scooter. Couldn't
have been more than seventeen. He stared at me like he
knew me. Rolled on by.

"The grenade he threw into the cafe exploded just as I
sensed something was wrong. I was starting to turn, when
blammo! Glass and pieces of the waiter's white coat, and
inside, the captain and two old men who'd been playing
chess . . . They'd wanted to make it bloody. An example. An
indulgence."

"My God," said Sylvia, "you must have been . . ."

"I'd seen shit like that before," said Cain. "Been close.

"Four days later, the secret police found the zapper.
Tortured him."

She looked out her side window.

"The kid was a leftist guerrilla, a zealot who worshipped
the fire of revolution and figured to get rid of the captain
and someday walk in his shoes. The secret police gave interrogation transcripts to our CIA. I got to see them.

"The kid's orders were to wait until the well-connected
gringo was clear. The kid didn't know why the rebels wanted
the captain killed. Maybe it was political, maybe personal,

maybe an accommodation for somebody—like those cocaine cowboys in Kentucky or Columbia. Maybe the captain squeezed the wrong capitalists, and they sold him to the reds.

"What hit me, like a bullet in the brain, was that I'd become worth *only* my weight in trouble. And . . . and that was like being worth nothing at all."

"What . . . what did you?" asked Sylvia.

"Finished my job," intoned Cain. "My father . . . he always insisted that no matter what, you *finish the job*.

"And I am my father's son," he whispered. Shook his head.

"What about him?" asked Sylvia.

Cain stared out at the night, thought before answering:

"My dad refused to believe there were places like El Salvador. If there were, they *surely* had nothing to do with him.

"The only times he left his hometown were for his honeymoon in Chicago and World War II. He came back, got a job in the . . . the factory, just like all his buddies. Just like he expected everybody should who wasn't born with a better way—not that there were better ways. Just better jobs. He worked hard, so hard the job and the place broke him. In ways he never even knew. When he couldn't work anymore, when Mom died, he lay down in the grave.

"And he never even *once* saw how it really was!" shouted Cain. "Wouldn't look it square in the face, the whole damn thing, the damn town and the way it was run and what he was in it and what it meant and what it made me and . . ."

"Maybe that was all he could do," said Sylvia. "Maybe that was how he survived."

"Didn't have to be that way," whispered Cain.

"Did you two talk about it?"

Cain shook his head.

"Only a couple times. You didn't talk with my old man about things he believed. You listened, maybe, but . . . otherwise, it was like shouting at stone walls."

"What did he want for you?"

"Part of him wanted me to get something more for myself, lead a better life. Educated, maybe. But he couldn't think of *more* as anything but a better job. If he did, if there was something better, that meant that he . . .

" 'Hell,' he used to tell me, 'don't worry, son. You can always get a good place at the mill—the factory.' "

Sylvia nodded.

"But he wanted me to have a shot," said Cain.

"Then he was a good father," she told him. "What happened?"

Cain shook his head, smiled: "A bad slide on a good steal."

"What?"

"Baseball.

"There were two good ways up and out of . . . my hometown," said Cain. "Education, which was for the lucky who got into it with enough clout behind them, and sports, which could buy you an education or if you were great, a job being a boy until you were a rich man."

"Were you great?" Sylvia smiled.

"No," said Cain. "But I wasn't bad. Had a lot of hustle, according to the coach. Guts. Tough.

"My first error was I played baseball. Not many scholarships for that, and if you don't make the pros out of high school . . . You don't need to know all this."

"I like baseball," she told him.

They turned and looked at each other full face and easy for the first time since she'd parked on the bluff. Smiled.

"I played shortstop," he told her. "Had a fair bat. We were the Catholic high school . . ."

"I went to public," she said.

"I know," he told her; continued: "Our cross-town rival was public. Big game our senior year, first of the spring and I was hustling my heart out, hoping for a scholarship or a minor league contract.

"First at bat, I hit a liner to right, made first and tried to stretch it to a double. Slid into second with a chance, but . . .

"I was too eager, sloppy. I blew out my knee. I remember holding it, screaming and rolling in the dirt, watching the dust float away and knowing, right then, even before the doctors told me. Two surgeries and it still gives me trouble.

"So baseball was over for me. My grades were okay. I never had to study hard. I knew *so much*—"

"We all did," she said.

"Not enough for anybody to give me an academic free ride. We were pretty broke then: my accident, Dad's accident, Mom being sick . . .

"The other way out of town was war. I couldn't even get drafted. All those uniforms crying out for warm bodies to ship to Vietnam, and none of them would take a busted up knee."

"What did you do?"

"What I *wouldn't* do was surrender to the same death shop as my father. God, we fought over that! And I wouldn't stay around, which was maybe the cruelest thing I did back then. He was all alone, and I couldn't wait to get out of . . . that damn graveyard city.

"When he realized I wouldn't stay, he came round enough to help. After graduation, I got a job to hold me over, down in that same damn mill."

"Doing what?"

"Doesn't matter," he said. "Serving short time. I worked every shift they let me. When I wasn't working, I took classes at the local U. Half the time I just walked into classrooms and sat down. Anything. I wanted to know it all, and learn how to escape."

"How did you end up in jail?" asked Sylvia.

"I got away from here," he said.

"From there," he quickly corrected.

Sylvia blinked, but said nothing.

"My dad helped, and I never really thanked him."

"It's not too late."

"He's dead."

"Maybe it's still not too late," she said.

The crickets chirped in the darkness. Somewhere in the city, a siren wailed.

"Maybe," Cain finally replied.

"We did it like you do it in Steeltown," Cain told her. "We used our connections in the union, a guy who knew a guy. Eighteen months after high school, I was a deck hand on a tramp freighter working out of San Diego. Out free in the world at last.

"Made it to Vietnam," he said. "Anchored off Cam Ranh Bay. All I saw was the gray sea, the green crescent of beach line, a jungle blue sky full of jets streaking off on napalm runs, helicopters buzzing back and forth like bees hunting honey.

"It was a bad ship. I knew it and I signed on anyway, so I can't complain. Everybody had some action, from the captain on down. I learned quick how to walk so I wouldn't get tossed over the side.

"In Spain, I took shore leave with a guy my age. Never knew what he was into, don't know what happened to him. But he was dirty, and I knew it. I should have kept my distance, but I didn't.

"Next thing I knew, the Guardia Civil grabbed me off a street in Madrid, beat the shit of me in the van, and threw me into jail.

"It was guilt by association: partially me and that guy off the ship. They'd call me a thief one day, a smuggler the next. They were probably right about my mate, though I was clean.

"But mostly, it was the times: 1969. Franco remembered his civil war in the thirties and the student riots of Paris in 1968. He read about Berkeley, and he didn't want any long-haired American sailor with hoodlum friends corrupting his good Catholic country.

"Thank God I knew enough Catholic and a little Spanish. I've seen worse jails than Spain, but never from the inside."

"Couldn't . . ."

"Could," said Cain. "They could do anything. The only thing that stops people are other people. And I was a nobody on my own. The embassy knew, but even if they cared, wasn't much they could do. My dad . . . he died two weeks after they locked me up."

"Oh, Jack. I'm sorry."

"Me, too," he said. His voice came from far away. "I learned Spanish fast, spent seven months, two weeks and three days practicing. Never even got to a trial, had no faith that I would.

"One morning they took me to the warden's office to meet Mr. Smith."

"Who was he?"

"He was tall and handsome and wore great suits and had gone to Yale. He knew I was innocent, knew all about me, right down to having a transcript of the college classes I'd officially completed. He wasn't from the embassy, he said, though he had friends there. He wanted to know if I was a patriot. And he had a way he might be able to help a young, street-smart guy like me. He had a job, we made a bargain."

"I know about bargains," she said. "He was CIA, wasn't he?"

"Or Navy intelligence or whoever he had to be," said Cain. "I got a great deal: out of jail. Two-year commitment, some money. All I had to do was bum around Europe, Scandinavia, France, hang out with the American deserters, identify them. Keep an eye on the drifters and self-styled exiles from the land of the free and the home of the brave. Blend in and betray. All that talk of revolution. German terrorist gangs, the Japanese Red Army. Mr. Smith was right to be nervous.

"The sixties were going to change the world," he said. "Remember?"

"I missed all that," she said. "What did you do?"

"I got stoned a lot, met a lot of educated, naive kids, played at being one of them. Read the chic books and learned the right music. There were villains, but they fed on the kids instead of turning them into monsters. I fabricated reports, lived a good life.

"After two years, they wanted to send me . . . where I didn't want to go. I said no. Resigned.

"One of their friends in the private sector worked for a firm that need an extra hand in Chile. He asked the Mr. Smith who bossed me then if he knew anybody who was available, and the next thing you know, I started working for who I work for."

"And ended up here," said Sylvia.

"Yes," said Cain. "I finally made it to Steeltown."

"What happened after El Salvador?"

"After I finished the job? Just like my father said?"

"He never told you to do stuff like that."

Cain looked at the floor; nodded.

"I'd always been a drinker," he said. "Other stuff. Nothing I thought I couldn't handle until I couldn't handle myself anymore. After the grenade, what I figured out, the firm and I agreed on a leave of absence. A guy I knew had retired to a fishing camp in the Michigan woods. Another had retreated to his family farm in Montana. I spent some time with them. Dried out and regained my balance. Mostly. Went back to work. In New York. Little traveling, a few dirty little jobs. Spent some time with a woman."

"I wondered about a woman," said Sylvia.

"She was another one who didn't work out," he said. "Close, but only close. She couldn't handle who I was and how I got there even if I could have handled all she wanted."

"Too bad," whispered Sylvia.

"She's better off."

"Maybe," said Sylvia. "Maybe not. Why did you take the commission job?"

"My firm figured I was perfect for this place."

"Steeltown," she said, shaking her head, staring beyond the glass. "I hate this shithole."

"It's what you got."

"You don't know what I got," she said.

He kept his silence. The moonlight streaming into the car colored them the same shade of pale.

"I know what you think of me," she said.

"No," she said after a moment, "I guess I don't."

"What do you have?" he asked.

"What did I get?" she said. "I got a deal."

She nodded to the night.

"You should have seen this place when I was growing up," she told him. "Alive, vibrant, bigger than I could imagine. This was the heart of the world. Or so I thought."

"What is it really?" he asked.

"You tell me, Cain." she said. "You're the man with all the answers. I'd *love* some answers!"

"I think you know them already," he said.

She ignored that.

"Suppose you're seventeen and a friend fixes you up with Prince Charming, a town god who's a senior at Harvard but who turns out to be shyer than the high school boys who fumble at you in cars? Suppose that you're so nervous you ask him a thousand questions and for the first time he realizes someone will listen? One thing leads to another. During Christmas vacation when your parents are out, the two of you are in your pink bedroom with stuffed animals on the bed. It's night, with a blizzard shaking the house and your legs tremble, the heat . . .

"So surpise," she said, "you're pregnant. You want to tell the teacher fitting you for a graduation gown to cut it bigger, but it's all you can do to call that boy in Boston. He flies back, and . . .

"And the next night his father, the lord of the city, summons you to his castle bedroom where he sits at his desk with his dogs. He accuses you of trying to destroy his son, of being a whore, laughs when you cry and claim you're a virgin: *'Then that must be Jesus in there,'* he says. Suppose all that Cain. What do you do?"

"I don't know," he said.

"You take the best deal you can get."

"We discussed my father, an assistant manager of a supermarket the Kimmetts could buy with their spare change. Our home was mortgaged by a bank he partially owned. He mentioned my little brother.

"He let me know I was lucky I fit into his plans. How his son would stand by me because he's a sentimentalist. How fatherhood would check Elliot's youthful rebellion. How now the Kimmett heir would go to law school at the state university, as planned. How I'd be polished there, too. How after Elliot graduated, I'd want to live in my hometown to be close to my family, to see that they stayed safe and happy. How foolish it would be to ever oppose him and the laws of nature that already had me set on the right course.

"It's not a . . . a bad dream he laid out," she said. Smiled. "It's life in Steeltown. Me. Debbi Dolan. A thousand others. I liked Elliot, cared about him, knew he cared about me and would never hurt me! And with new magic growing inside my stomach, I felt scared but special. I'd never felt special before. And I believed so desperately that everything would work out!"

"But," said Cain.

She looked at him. Shook her head.

" 'But's' don't have much power when you're seventeen and pregnant and have to deal with the devil.

"What do you know about love, Cain?"

"Not much," he whispered.

"I thought so," she said. "Lot of people in this town, they think . . . I love my husband, I really do. I love him for what he's done: he's given his life to shelter me, tried never to hurt anybody—not me, not our son, not even his father who he won't let himself hate so he won't become like him. How can you not love a man like that?"

"How do *you* not love him?" said Cain.

"Enough," she said, "not enough.

"Did you know our son isn't our only child?" she asked suddenly.

"No," said Cain.

"We graduated—Elliot from Harvard, me from high school. A small wedding at the mansion. My father got a promotion. Elliot and I moved to the state university, as ordained. My high school girlfriends who went to the U were worried about sorority rush and good professors. Should they take birth control pills and smoke marijuana and be in antiwar demonstrations. I was shopping for cribs and strollers and babysitters to watch our child during my classes.

"My baby . . . she was born dead."

"I'm sorry," said Cain.

Sylvia shook her head, closed her eyes.

"I came apart. Elliot took a leave from law school, defied his father to stay home and take care of a wife who'd sit and stare at the walls. There was this oh-so-polite California clinic, with shatterproof windows and white walls and all sorts of pills and doctors to help me adjust to life. To my deal.

"And I did," she said. "I'm cured. Elliot finished law school. We came back here because he was sure it was best for me. I, of course, had my deal. We made a son. I think we both wanted to atone for . . . for the little girl who never was, for each other. We gave ourselves safe and unquestioning roles and our boy . . ."

She sighed.

"Oh, Cain. I watch my son and more and more I see *him!* And I don't know what to do!"

"You never told Elliot about his father, did you?"

"You know what would have happened if I did?"

"No, and neither do you."

She paused, sighed and whispered: "It's too late for that. Too late for regrets and what-might-have-been's."

"What about now? What about you?"

"I'm the best cared for wife in the world. Elliot loves me in his way that never pushes or interferes. He . . ."

"You need someone to push you," said Cain. "Somebody to . . ."

Then he trailed off.

"Who I have is Elliot," she said. "He indulges my . . . eccentricities. My diversions. I try not to hurt him, we keep going—"

"Going where?" said Cain.

"Going through with it," she said. "That's what marriages are all about, isn't it? Going through with it."

"I've never been married," he said. "Besides, what you're going through with is a bad deal beaten out of a scared kid. You're worth more than that. You don't have to do that anymore."

"Really?" she said. "You mean I'm safe and free because my parents are retired in Arizona and my brother lives in Ohio, a doctor no less? Because my husband is as happy here . . ."

". . . as he can be," said Cain. "Here."

"My son . . ."

"He's on his own now."

"So it's just me," she said; smiled insincerely. "Is that what you mean? But it's never just you. We're tied to our past, our inertia. Ghosts. Ghosts haunt you, too, don't they, Cain?"

"Maybe," he said, looking away. "Maybe."

"Sure they do," she said.

"Your deal is over," he told her.

"But I owe a lot," she said. "To Elliot. I've never made him happy. I can't seem to do that. But I can protect him, help him, not let him lose what he's sacrificed for. Maybe I can't help my son, maybe he's . . . callow, lost. But he's my son and I can't write him off."

"You'd be surprised what you can do. You can go after what you want."

"What I want!" She made a sound somewhere between a laugh and a sob. "That's never been a clear or easy path, has it?"

They didn't speak for a long time.

"How much of what you told me was true?" she finally asked.

"Everything I told you was true."

"How much more is there?"

He didn't answer.

"What do you want from my husband?" she asked.

"I don't want anything from him."

"Except to move him around like a chess piece. You and his father."

"I'm not that old man."

"But you've got some deal with him," she said. "I'm no fool. Be careful, Cain: it's dangerous to be his partner."

"I'm not like him," insisted Cain. "And I won't be."

"You're not like my husband, either. You're not like anybody in this town."

"Don't be so sure," he said softly.

Their silence filled the night.

"What do you want, Cain?" she finally asked.

They stared at each other.

"I thought I could beat you," she told him. "I knew you were trouble the moment we met. I could feel your push on the whole world. I don't know what you're doing here. I thought I could protect Elliot from you, but I don't think so anymore. You're tougher and smarter and know what you're doing. You know me too well. I can't hide from you, pretend and pull off some . . . You see right through me. I can't stop you—from anything, no matter what it is. But please, Cain, don't hurt Elliot. I couldn't live with that."

"That's not what I want," he told her.

"But that's what might happen, isn't it?" she said.

He didn't reply.

"I'm glad you didn't lie to me," she said a moment later. "I know too many lies."

She closed her eyes, then opened them and stared straight into his eyes.

"Do you want me?" she asked.

"You didn't when you came here," she quickly added. "At least, you didn't want *me*. You won't admit you want anybody, but that hunger cries in you like the wind. You look at me and I can feel your hunger. Maybe because I understand it. Maybe more than that."

Quickly, she said, "This isn't . . . I'm not just trying a trade."

"What?" he whispered.

"You know," she told him. The breeze ruffled her blond hair. "A trade for . . . for Elliot's safety. I'd have done that at the start, but . . . not now. Not with you. I don't want . . . I can't . . .

"Hell," she continued, forcing humor into her words, "I'm not worth that much. I'm no Beth, not young and sexy and smart. I'm no bargain."

"Damn you!" He grabbed the steering wheel and lunged close to her. His scream startled Sylvia, but she didn't pull away.

"I don't want you in any damn bargain! No more bargains! No more half ways or pretending and . . ."

Anger overpowered his words. He glared at her. Strands of blond hair fell across her forehead, her blue eyes were wide upon him, and her lips were parted. He smelled her warmth, the tang of her sweat and a sweetness over her perfume. His knuckles turned white on the steering wheel.

His eyes closed, his head dropped. She touched his cheek; he slumped back against the far door. When his eyes opened, they looked out the windshield.

"This damn town," he whispered. Swallowed. And told her, "Take me home."

Rope

"ARE YOU SURE YOU KNOW WHAT you're doing?" asked Russell Boswell.

"You don't think so," answered Cain.

Boswell leaned back in his chair. Cain sat on the other side of the desk. They'd met at seven the next morning outside the commission building.

"That's why you called last night," said Cain. "That's why we're here before anyone else."

"I'm not questioning your ability, Jack," said Boswell.

"Just my intent."

"I have this nagging feeling that you're running your own program."

"I don't believe in programs," said Cain.

"What do you believe in?"

"People," said Cain. "They're what we're doing here."

"What we're doing here is investigating a murder."

"This isn't about *a* murder," said Cain. "This is about fighting killers. Hammond was just one casualty."

"This is about justice," said Boswell.

"That's right," replied Cain.

"Most of my time for the commission is spent keeping our supposed supporters from sweeping us off the streets," continued Boswell. "I expected that. But what I don't expect and won't allow is for us—any of us—to engage in self-destruction. What we're about is too important for that kind of indulgence."

"I've never been the suicidal type," said Cain.

"How about homicidal?"

After a long pause, Cain said, "What are you worried about?"

"Like you said, we're about fighting killers. Not playing their game."

"I'm not playing at anything," Cain told him.

"Then we understand each other?"

"Yes."

Silence filled the room.

"Why do you want to hit the SIC with a subpoena?" Boswell finally asked.

"Nash will fight his subpoena," said Cain. "If the city attorney can't get it squashed in court, the mayor will use the time that legal battle takes to hide all the dirty laundry he can. If we hit the SIC with a subpoena, too, *now*, before everybody has a chance to get together on a cover-up, we might find enough rope to hang them or get them so tangled up they'll hang themselves."

"We'll also be fighting the biggest labor organization in the state *and* city hall," said Boswell.

"We'll be fighting *people*," said Cain. "Institutions like labor unions and political parties or buildings like the White House and City Hall matter only because of the people in them. We've got a lot of those people running scared. Or we will have soon."

"Speaking of scared," said Boswell, "half the businessmen in town are calling me, trying to get the commission to lay off the bond issue. These are independent guys—scared of Nash and DiCarlo and Johnny Maxx, sure, but not tied to them. I thought they'd keep quiet."

"It's Nash," said Cain. "Has to be."

"But I don't understand the lever he's using on them."

"We'll know when we know," said Cain.

"Do you think this is what Josh Hammond was after?"

Cain stared at Boswell, who, after a minute, sighed.

"Go ahead with the SIC subpoena," he told Cain. "Tell Beth I want to review all the documents, the filings."

"Thanks," said Cain. He stood and walked toward his desk.

The phone rang.

"I'll get it," said Cain, picking up the receiver.

"Commission," Cain said into the phone. He looked at his watch: 7:37. The others were due in soon.

"I'm glad someone's there!" said the caller—Evans, the publisher of Steeltown's newspaper. His voice was excited, nervous.

Cain glanced at Boswell, said, "Me too."

Across the room, the commission chairman frowned.

Cain kept his face expressionless.

"Something's come up!" Evans whispered. "I need to speak to Russ Boswell right away!"

"I'm sorry," said Cain. He licked his lips, looked away from Boswell's stare.

"Damn!" said Evans.

"We better see each other now," said Cain.

"But you're not . . . I mean, thank you, but I need . . ."

"Trust me," said Cain. His brow was moist.

"But . . . all right," agreed a reluctant Evans.

Russ Boswell's chair creaked. Cain kept his eyes from him.

"It might look bad if you came here," said the publisher. "My reporters, editors, they're watching . . . I'll come to your office."

"Let's meet for breakfast," said Cain. He named the cafe where he'd eaten with Beth; where Joey the Blimp ate his last meal.

"That's so public!" protested Evans.

"This isn't something we want to bring into the office," said Cain.

Boswell's chair creaked again. Cain glanced at his companion: Boswell, red-faced, was staring out the window behind his desk, his gaze carefully averted from the partial conversation he couldn't help overhearing.

"Well, I don't know," said Evans. "If you think . . ."

"Twenty minutes," said Cain. "Get us a quiet table."

He hung up.

Boswell stood, made a show of straightening his suit and tie. He walked toward the door, then paused in front of Cain.

"Sorry," said Cain. "That was . . . personal."

"I have to leave, too," said Boswell. "I'm speaking to the Jaycees breakfast meeting—they don't meet at that pancake house.

"Cain, I like you. I have to trust you. Your competence. And your discretion. I don't want to lecture you—or anybody—on personal matters. I understand . . .

"Look, just remember what I said about self-destruction. About the importance of what we're doing. In times like these, people like us don't have a private life separate from our public concerns. We can't mix business and . . . Don't get confused or strung out on your own rope. Maybe over breakfast you should mention all that, our conversation."

He shook his head:

"I probably won't be here when you get back with . . ." He shook his head. ". . . with *whoever.*"

As he left the office, he told Cain, "Good luck. Be careful."

Publisher Evans leaned over his cup of coffee and whispered to Cain, "This is all so confusing!"

Cain spread butter over his pancakes. Steam rose from the scrambled eggs and the sausage patties smelled of pepper. He drained his small glass of orange juice, moved his mug of coffee closer to his plate.

"I understand," he said.

"You don't know how difficult it is!" said Evans.

Their corner booth had a window. A wood-paneled wall rose behind Cain. Behind the publisher was the restaurant's only empty booth. The tables were full, customers lined the counter. A waitress flipped a switch by the front door: the air conditioner above the entrance began to hum.

"Hammond gets killed. Your commission starts up. Everybody wants it but won't stand behind it. Instead of going after the crooks, you serve a subpoena on City Hall—"

"Where's our problem?" asked Cain.

"Our problem?"

Startled by his own volume, Evans jerked back—but Cain grabbed his forearm. The publisher furtively looked over his shoulder, saw no one paying attention, then slumped in his chair. Cain let go of the man's arm, took a bite of pancakes.

"What's to be done?" whispered Evans.

"Our jobs."

"What nonsense are you talking about?"

Cain took a bite of sausage, waited.

"I don't know why I let myself get roped into this commission mess in the first place," grumbled Evans.

"Your reporter got killed," Cain told him. "You had an obligation. And you did the right thing."

"Well it sure hasn't paid off."

"Give it time," said Cain.

"If I give it time, I won't have a newspaper."

Cain lifted a forkful of scrambled eggs to his mouth. Before he put them in, he said, "Your advertisers pressuring you?"

"Understand, Cain, I'm not *The New York Times*. I'm an independent newspaper in a town where business has gone to shit. Our average edition is thirty-four pages, most of which is wire copy. Half our ads are sold cut-rate because if the stores who are losing money have to pay the regular rates, they won't advertise. Circulation is way down: people go to the library to read the want ads for jobs. I'm scraping by on national ads.

"My best buffer is the government ads. City, state, county, even the utilities, they're all required by law to run ads in the local press about bid announcements, meetings, what have you. It's nickels and dimes, but it's dependable nickels and dimes. Nobody's talking dollars in Steeltown anymore.

"Last night I get a call from the city treasurer. He tells me the city is suspending all its advertising. He also allows as how he's heard the county will do the same thing. Says he's heard rumors about the utilities. That's on top of all the other calls I've been getting from the guys I do business with, the—"

"What do they want you to do?"

"Get rid of the commission or get it to lay off the city. Especially the bond issue. Maybe we could turn it around if you just went after Josh's murderer instead of turning this into a crusade.

"See," explained Evans, with the sincerity of a convert, "it's bad for business, and business is already bad enough."

He leaned close to Cain.

"There's been some trouble at the biggest city bank," Evans confided. "Examiners are in there. Hard times everywhere for banks. We already had one savings and loan fold, local people losing their shirts because of that national scandal . . .

"Central Bank, the big one? They cut corners to make some deals, then mills started closing . . . I don't know all the details."

"Did you report any of this in your paper?"

"Of course not! That's private business, not news."

"Uh-huh."

The publisher blushed.

"See," he continued, "Central Bank handles the bond issue for the city. And the SIC. The bank also oversees the pension fund. If there's any hint of trouble about the bonds—which I'm sure is not a crisis in any way, shape, or form other than one of public perception—well, you don't want to kick the walls of a shaky bank."

"No," said Cain, "but you might want to warn the people with their life savings locked inside it."

"That . . ." The publisher licked his lips. "That's a question for reasoned, careful consideration. Responsible journalism.

"And not our problem now!" he insisted.

"Does Central Bank hold a note on your paper?" asked Cain.

Again, the publisher blushed.

"We modernized a few years ago," he said. "New presses, better graphics, keep up with the times so we could . . ."

"It's a nice paper," said Cain. "Pretty. Looks good."

The publisher nodded.

"All the out-of-town reporters who came here to cover Josh Hammond's murder thought so, too," said Cain. "They talked about how proud you must be of it, how proud you must be to be part of the crucial American tradition of a battling free press."

The publisher looked out the window.

"When's your TV interview going to air on that network show?" asked Cain. "You and what's-his-name, the big-time reporter?"

After a long pause, the publisher said, "I don't know."

Evans stared out the window as Cain ate the last bites of his breakfast.

"I noticed you didn't carry a story about the city subpoena in today's paper," said Cain. "Must have been you didn't get it nailed down before press time."

Evans kept his eyes fixed on the parking lot.

"Life's going to change in this city," said Cain. "It's important for a man and his business to be in the right place, doing the right job. You're a journalist, with a paper that's had one of its reporters murdered. Nothing bad for business about that. Your friends, your advertisers: they're confused. Scared. But that will change, too. You got to do what's right and ride it out."

"I could end up losing my paper."

"You've got a short-term problem," said Cain..

"That's enough."

"I understand. I really do.

"You're sliding down the minus line. Your bank debt. Overhead. You can't go to the banks for a new loan: they'll say no, even if you deserve the break. If you go to the other people in town with the money to bail you out—the Kimmetts, Mayor Nash's friends, Johnny Maxx—they'll end up taking your paper away from you. They're already strangling you."

"Tell me something I haven't thought of."

"You got any personal money?" asked Cain.

"I . . . I had some personal habits," said Evans.

"The good life," said Cain. "In good times, it's great."

Evans looked at him, then looked back out the window.

"I need to see Russ Boswell," said the newspaper man. "Where is he?"

"Russ can't help you," said Cain. "Just like you can't stop the commission. I'm not saying you couldn't make it rough, like your enemies want. You can not do your job and quit reporting on what you should. You can pull back your support. You can slam us every day in print. But in the end, that won't matter, and you'll wind up covered with shit."

"I'll have my paper," he said. He glared at Cain. "Besides, I'm not so sure you're doing anything worthwhile to begin with. Let DiCarlo chase the killer. That's his job."

"How you going to explain all this to your new buddies, your heroes in the national press?"

"I don't have to explain anything."

"But you like standing tall in the limelight, doing what's right, don't you?"

"Fuck you, Cain."

The publisher started to slide out of the booth. Cain grabbed his arm again. His grip was steel.

"You leave now, you lose everything!" snapped Cain.

Evans tried to pull away, but Cain held tight. The warrior of the First Amendment struggled briefly, then slumped back in the booth. Cain kept his grip.

"Don't be stupid," said Cain. "You're not a stupid man. You're a good man. What you think is a crisis is really your good luck."

The publisher raised his eyes, frowned.

"You need money," said Cain. "Clean money for the job that will keep you a hero and give you a paper worth having. Right?"

Without losing his frown, the publisher nodded.

"What's the weekly shortfall on your nut?"

"About four thousand dollars," said Evans. "I'm behind a little, but . . ."

"I'll get you five grand tomorrow morning," said Cain. "Four a week later, which should be enough to tide you over until . . ."

"*What!*"

"I'm bailing you out," said Cain. "Me—not the commission, not the bank, not old man Kimmett or his buddies, not DiCarlo or Johnny Maxx or Mayor Nash, not my New York boss. Not anybody but me."

"Why are you doing this? How? What's in it for you?"

"Let's say I lead a hard enough life without having your troubles dogging my back," Cain told him. "You doing what you should keeps me walking easier—and gets me out of town faster."

"You plan on leaving soon?"

"Always," said Cain.

"When?"

"When I'm ready. When I'm done."

Evans stared at the man across from him. Cain smiled.

"I'm enough of a journalist to wonder what your story is," the publisher finally said.

"That isn't our kind of relationship."

"What is our kind of relationship?"

"That's up to you."

Again, the publisher hesitated, then asked, "What's this loan going to cost me?"

"Flat payback. No interest. Payments spread out over a year, starting in six months."

"You're a generous man, Cain."

"Don't make that mistake."

"You two want some more coffee?" called a waitress from behind the counter.

Without looking at her, Cain yelled back, "We're fine."

"You get to keep what you've got," Cain told Evans. "Plus a good shot at a lot more down the road."

"Nobody could know about this," said the publisher.

"That's right," Cain told him.

Evans drummed his fingers on the table. He looked out the window, stared at Cain, looked back out the window. Drummed his fingers on the side of his coffee mug.

"It's the . . . the best possible choice, isn't it?" he said.

"Uh-huh," answered Cain.

The journalist drummed his fingers on the table.

"Okay," he finally said. He sighed away a great weight.

Cain smiled, nodded.

"Want to shake?" asked the man across the table from him.

"That won't change anything," said Cain. "And you don't want to do that out in public."

"Oh. Right."

"What other news besides the bank being shaky and the subpoena being served haven't I read in your newspaper?" asked Cain.

"You mean about the, ah . . ."

Cain nodded.

The publisher leaned close again.

"Two of the deputies are in the hospital," he told Cain. "The cops could probably plead self-defense, from what my reporter got out of a witness who won't go public. The deputies jumped the cops coming out of that bar, but they misjudged the meat they were tangling with. The cops may have started clean, but when they got the upper hand . . . Using their blackjacks like that . . . Nobody's going to press charges."

"How many on each side?" asked Cain.

"Six of Nash's deputies, four cops."

"Who had you kill the story?"

The publisher looked over his shoulder, saw no one.

"DiCarlo called me just before press time," he said. "I had to agree: one gang of law fighting another, the facts unclear . . ."

"The night's over," said Cain. "There's been time enough for the truth to sort out. Your reporters ought to be able to get a just-the-facts story in tomorrow's edition."

The publisher blinked.

"It'll be a good story," said Cain. "Sell a lot of papers. Responsible journalism.

"There's a lot of good stories out there today," continued Cain. "Take the city deciding to suspend its advertising. One phone call to the mayor, getting comment on why he's breaking the law . . ."

"He'll be furious!"

"What's he going to do? He's already made his play."

The publisher frowned; Cain shrugged.

"And I agree with you," he continued. "Too soon to do the bank story. Don't want to be reckless."

A slow, hesitant nod was his answer.

"You realize, of course," said Cain, "if you can hold out long enough, show you're tough, the bank will come round. If they don't and if the pressure against them keeps building, maybe they'll collapse. If that happens, maybe your debt to them will dissolve, too."

A new light shone in Evans's eyes.

"This isn't what they taught in business school," he said.

"That's what friends are for," said Cain. "They share information, teach each other new ways out of old trouble. Besides, you're not a businessman, you're a journalist."

"Right!" said the publisher.

"About the City Hall subpoena story," continued Cain. "Got an update from an unnamed source, news you'll want to be ready for so the out-of-town papers and the wires won't scoop you, make you look stupid. The commission is subpoenaing the SIC records on the bond sale."

"Oh Christ!" exclaimed Evans.

"He's not named in the subpoena," said Cain. "You'll be able to give your boys a jump. The kind of thing a publisher who gets national recognition is famous for.

"By the way," said Cain. "Did you hear about the Japanese giving ten grand to the United Way campaign?"

"What!"

"Now there's a nice, positive, cheerful story. Steeltown could use a few of those in the next few days. Going to get rough before it gets better. Lucky you got something good to hang on to."

Cain stood, looked down at the man in the booth.

"I'll bring five grand by your office first thing tomorrow," he said. "Cash. After I've had my morning coffee and a chance to digest the morning news."

Beth ran into the commission building after Cain and grabbed his arm before he could get on the elevator.

"Don't go up there!" she whispered.

She spun him back through the revolving doors, her eyes scanning the city square, the sidewalks, side streets. She clutched her briefcase under one arm, held Cain with the other. She led him around the corner, down the block. Midway down an alley, he muscled her between two green dumpsters.

"Good morning, Beth," he said.

"Where have you been? I saw you leave over an hour ago! I've been waiting in the drug store across the square, never sure who was watching and . . ."

"I went to breakfast," he told her.

"Johnny Maxx came to see me last night!" she said.

Cain looked both ways down the rubbish-strewn alley. The dumpsters smelled of rotten oranges and exhausted disinfectant.

"Where?" he asked.

"My hotel room. My . . . my bedroom."

"Did he hurt you?"

"No! It wasn't like that, but he . . . This was there."

She pulled a large book from her briefcase and passed it to Cain. Embossed on its black vinyl cover in gold letters was:

CENTRAL HIGH SAINTS 1967

"Where did you get this?" whispered Cain.

"I stole it from the public library," she said. "I called and they had all of the high school yearbooks. I looked until I found . . ."

"All of a sudden, you're leading a wild life."

"I know you're mad," she said, "but don't you understand . . ."

"What about Johnny Maxx?"

She swallowed, looked at the cracked pavement; faced him.

"He knocked on my door a little after eight last night and I never thought . . . I thought it might be you. When I opened the door, it was too late."

"It was too late when you called the library," said Cain.

"He walked into my room so cool and casual, like he owned it," said Beth. "Walked past the bed, looked out the window. The yearbook was on the table by the window and . . ."

"What did he want?" asked Cain.

"I . . . I don't know," she said, frowning. She bit her lower lip.

"What did he say?"

"When he talked he . . . he stood right in front of me. At the foot of the bed. Said he only did things for business or for pleasure, and that he'd have gotten neither from killing Josh Hammond. He says you are out to get him for no good reason, that that wasn't why the governor sent me here. He told me he liked me. Thought I was ... *all right*. Smart. And special."

"So?"

Her brow wrinkled at Cain's response.

"I asked him what he wanted, why he'd come, what ... He told me to do my job. To be careful. He said he wasn't any kind of saint ..."

"Was he refering to this?" said Cain, lifting the book with the name of his school team on its cover.

"I can't be sure," she said. "He ... he said he wasn't a saint, but that he was honest about that. That he skimmed his living off other people's hypocrisies and if the governor wanted us to nail some sinner, why didn't we go after DiCarlo? Johnny said nailing a crooked cop always makes better headlines for a politician than bothering another hustler."

"Did he give you any details?"

"He stood so close I could smell his after-shave," said Beth. Her eyes fogged with the memory. "Leather."

"What else did he say about DiCarlo?"

"Nothing. He said it was a shame business stood between us. Said he'd ... see me around. Make special time for it.

"Then ... Jack, he ... I swear, before he left, slowly, he ... he leaned over and ... *kissed* me. On the mouth."

In the alley, her fingers touched her lips; her eyes glazed.

"And you liked it," said Cain.

Beth paled, then turned crimson. She glared at Cain, and sputtered: "Wha—How dare you ..."

"It's all right," said Cain. "Nothing unexpected."

"How could you say that?!" she asked.

"That you liked it when Johnny Maxx kissed you? It's the truth. Saying or not saying it won't make any difference. Admitting it might, if you don't shy away from what you must do."

She pushed past him, stepped from between the two dumpsters and furiously whirled back to yell, "Goddamn you, Jack!"

They circled each other in the alley.

"What right do you have to be mad?!" He fought to keep his volume low. "About what?! That you suddenly discovered you like fire, the edge, the steel in guys like Johnny Maxx? And me? After all these years, you up there, all the good stuff, smart and pretty and knowing just how and where to stand, all the breaks and you took them for all they were worth and tracked *straight ahead*, right to the top. Sometimes a glance for a back street boy, but just for fun, right? And if they were too committed to something, *anything*, forgot about fashion, talked about passion, something that wasn't safe and acceptable, well, then, just too bad, because all that fire is bound to explode and we wouldn't want you to risk being a cinder. So it was just the cool boys for you. Then when it comes time for more than fun and games, you move your eyes from their zipper to their hip pocket!"

Beth stopped circling. Cain's back was to the dumpsters, his eyes blazed toward her. She shook her head.

"What are you talking about?" she asked softly.

He didn't answer.

"That's not me," she said. "It's not you. I'm Beth Worby. And you're Jim Cainelli."

"Jim Cainelli is in here," said Cain. He tossed the high school yearbook back to Beth. "He's a long-gone boy."

"Then act like it," she told him. "You talk about truth, about shying away . . ."

He shook his head. "It's not your fault."

"What *it*?" she asked. "Don't you see . . ."

"Why did you take that book?" he said, his voice sharp again.

"You know why! I . . . I care about you, Jack—or Jim. Any name. All of you. You know that—and don't ask me why or try to analyze it and pull it apart until it's tawdry pieces that don't make sense because that's not how it is, it's one big thing, and I . . ."

"You only care about what you think you see," he said, "and you can't see enough."

"So I went to the library," she said; smiled. "Hey! all those years of college taught me *something*. And I found a book with you in it. Baseball and letterman's club. Key Club. The debate team."

"You shouldn't have done it," said Cain. "We aren't a book, and those are just facts. You can't add them up to make the total you want. You shouldn't have done it."

"I had to," she told him. "And when you care about someone, you have rights."

"Wrong," he said. "You have responsibilities. To yourself. To everybody. What or how you care doesn't change that. Rights have to be given or earned."

"Or won," she said. Smiled. "Never argue with a lawyer."

"The job doesn't make you the law." He closed his eyes.

"I'm sorry!" said Beth. "I know I exposed you to some sort of risk, but . . ."

"If he knows now, he knows. Can't let that matter."

"Jack, everything else . . . All I want is a chance."

"You want more," he said. "And you can't be who you need to be to get it."

"Spare me riddles, Jack."

He smiled ruefully. "Where were you ten years ago?"

"Graduating from high school," she said. "Where were you?"

"Too late," he said. "Too bad."

"No, damn you!"

Down the alley, a door opened. A fat man wearing a greasy white shirt and green pants emptied an aluminum garbage can into a green dumpster. A cigarette dangled from his mouth. He stared at them.

"Come on," said Cain. "We've got work to do."

As he turned to walk away, she held the yearbook toward him, said, "Don't you want to look at this?"

"You stole it," he said, "you keep it."

A Simple
Kind of Guy

JACKSON CAIN STOOD STARING out his hotel room window, a cup of steaming coffee in his hand. The sun had been up less than an hour, but already the pane was warm. He wore a white shirt, a dark blue tie, suspenders and his navy suit. He'd had his black shoes shined.

The morning newspaper lay on the nearby table. The lead story on page 1 told about the subpoenas to City Hall and the SIC. Officials in those institutions had declined to comment. Commission Chairman Boswell said the subpoenas were generated by reports of irregularities in the SIC purchase of city bonds and the possibility that Josh Hammond had been killed because he was investigating such rumors. The Japanese gift to Steeltown also made page 1. Page 2 had a story about the city canceling its advertising. The mayor's comment was a jumble of cliches about economy moves. Page 3 had a story claiming that county deputies were hospitalized following an "altercation" with city policemen.

Cain's suit coat was draped over a chair at the table. An envelope containing five thousand dollars in cash retrieved from the bus depot the night before filled its inside pocket.

Someone knocked on his door: *one two; one two; three.*

Cain moved out of line with the doorway and called out, "Who is it?"

"Nick," came the muffled reply.

Cain admitted the man in black metal glasses.

"You're alone, aren't you?" whispered Nick.

Cain nodded.

"That was my knock," whispered Nick. He took a black box from his jacket pocket. Holding the instrument like a geiger counter, Nick circled through Cain's quarters and held the box over the telephone. He flipped a switch on his device, left it by the phone.

"Nothing," he said. "The scrambler will electronically garble most transmitting signals, just in case there is something here my box didn't pick up. Doubt it, though: your company uses the best shit. How come nobody's wired your room?"

"They figure anything I say to myself isn't worth hearing," answered Cain.

"These people who won't take advantage of modern technology," said Malone, shaking his head. "Got any more coffee?"

"Help yourself," said Cain. He returned to his perch against the window, stared back out at the city.

Malone fetched a cup of coffee from the kitchenette. He sat in the chair opposite the one that held the suit coat, looked at Cain silhouetted against the glass, and shook his head.

"You know better than that," said Malone.

"Nice to know you care," said Cain. He didn't move.

Nick loudly slurped his coffee.

"You know why I never wanted your job?" he asked Cain.

"No."

"It's a stupid way to make a living," answered Nick.

Cain laughed. "I won't argue."

"Not that you gotta be stupid to do it," said Malone. "You gotta be Goddamned smart. And the smarter you are, the more likely you are to get yourself into places where one way or the other you need to deal with guys like me—and that's stupid.

"Not that I'm complaining," he added. "That means I get work and I like what I do."

"Lucky man."

"My luck isn't the question," said Nick. "The question is, are *you* smart *enough?*"

Cain looked at him. The morning light streaming through the window turned Nick's chameleon glass lenses gray and hid his two-color eyes.

"Actually," said Cain, "you don't give a shit."

"Actually," said Nick, "I don't give a shit."

"The firm pressuring you again?"

"They never pressure *me*. They're your problem. And ain't that like it always is? One old man pushing another, both of 'em pushing our buttons. But I ain't heard from them since we met up."

"Then why did you drop by? My coffee's not that good."

Again, Nick slurped from his cup.

"Actually," he said, "your coffee is for shit. But I figured if your room were clean, this would be the best place for us to jaw. About what I read in the morning paper. And your friend Johnny Maxx.

"You ever notice Johnny move? Slick and quick. The chief, he's a lotta beef, but he'll use his boys and none of them seem cagey. The mayor's got an army, but they're all muscle and mouth. Not that all that law with their guns aren't tough, but they ain't like Johnny."

"I thought you liked challenges."

"If I didn't, why would I do what I do?" Nick grinned, shook his head. "But I like to play the game with an edge, and you aren't giving me all I could have."

"I didn't ask for you," said Cain.

"So you weren't a genius," said Nick, turning his hand up in a forgiving gesture. "Doesn't mean you can't get smart now."

"What are you proposing?"

"Well," said Nick, frowning and making a show of thought, "you're ass-deep in trouble, that's why you're here. And I'm here to help, like it or not. If you gave me more notice, more idea of what you were doing, I could be better prepared."

He looked at Cain, who returned his stare.

"But you're the kind of guy who won't do that. Don't

worry: my feelings aren't hurt. Maybe you could do it, maybe you can't, but the plain truth is, you won't. So forget it.

"Now you could bring me in close. Out in the open. Put me on the commission as your out-front backup, which would put everybody on notice, including Johnny. Make things more difficult for them. Might make it easier for me. Might not. I like it in the shadows, where they can't see me while they're looking at you.

"But I don't figure you to like me close. Cuts down on your privacy."

"What do you figure?"

"Johnny's your big trouble," said Nick. "Let me take care of him. Now."

Cain stared at the man sitting before him.

Nick drained his coffee cup. Smiled. Waited patiently.

"You know what I mean," Nick finally said.

"I know what you mean," said Cain. "Is this what one of the old men suggested?"

"The old men," said Nick, shaking his head. "They always speak shit. That way it never sticks to them."

"That's how they get to be old men," said Cain.

"What a gutless way to live. No class. No integrity."

"So you came up with this on your own."

"Hey, they knew who they sent to help you. You think they don't know? Bullshit. They know. They don't care. They play the game so we have to use our guts and they don't need to use theirs. That's how it always is: you and me, the soldiers in the field. That's how they like it, the assholes. At least Johnny, he stayed a soldier and kept his guts after he became a big man. You gotta admire him for that.

"Hell," he added, "it's what Johnny'd do. 'Fact, I'm surprised he ain't tried it already."

"Maybe he got smarter as he got bigger and older," said Cain.

"No fuckin' way," argued Nick. "Not a chance. Besides, that ain't smarter, that's losing your guts. He's still got his."

"How come you're so eager?"

"It's the smart play," answered Nick.

Cain blinked; said, "And?"

Nick shrugged. Smiled.

"I didn't ask for you, Malone. But since you're here, since they told you to make contact, they turned you over to me. I'm your boss, you'll do what I say."

"My orders are to help you," said Malone. "And to make sure you don't end up in the gutter before you finish the job."

"I told you what to do. You're to keep Russell Boswell alive. If he doesn't make it, then this whole thing falls apart."

"So you say."

"So I say—and what I say goes. You know what I say about your idea to whack Johnny cold? I say no. Forget it, I don't work that way. If he doesn't fall into your program the way it's set up, then you don't squeeze his trigger.

"And when you forget your idea, remember this: If you ever try anything like it, then you become part of the problem I came here to solve. Which I *will* do."

"How come you love Johnny so much, Cain?"

"I don't love Johnny."

"Oh yeah!" said Malone, malice curling his lips to a smile. "I forgot: you already got your hands *full* of loving."

"That isn't your business, Nick," said Cain.

"Guess not, cowboy."

"You got any questions? Any more ideas?"

"You know me, Jack: just a simple kind of guy. I don't have many questions or ideas. If I ask something, make a little suggestion, it's just my way of trying to help. You're the smart one, remember?"

"And the boss," said Cain. *"Your* boss. Now get out of here; we're got work to do."

"Sure," said Malone, standing. He pointed to the device by the phone. "You want that? No? Okay. I'll keep it. Hell, you must have one from the firm. Your boss wouldn't send you out less than fully prepared and equipped to do the job and do it right, now would he?"

Before he walked out the door, he turned to Cain, grinned, and said, "See you around."

Feeding the Wolves

HIS TIE LOOSE, HIS SUIT COAT hanging from the coat tree in the corner, Jackson Cain daydreamed in the afternoon sun as Boswell and Beth huddled at her desk.

"The SIC and the city attorney's motions complement each other," said Boswell. "The primary thrust of one is the secondary thrust of the other. One wants outright dismissal, another wants relief from the subpoena pending a hearing on our jurisdiction."

"If we keep the judge who granted the temporary injunctions," said Beth, "they'll win one of the arguments. If either argument is upheld, both subpoenas become worthless. We need to ditch that judge."

"I sense suspicion of more than His Honor's legal acumen, Miss Worby," said Boswell, smiling. "Whatever happened to your faith in the purity of the judicial process?"

They laughed.

The phone rang.

"I'll get it," said Cain.

He'd spent the day with the two attorneys as they went from courtroom to courtroom defending the commission's subpoenas. The front desk was vacant while Catherine photocopied and filed documents generated by the day's efforts.

"Commission," said Cain into the phone, "how can I help you?"

"Do you know who this is?" replied Kimmett's aide Raymond Nelson.

"Sure. How are you?"

"Our equipment shows your line is secure. Can you talk?"

"Sort of."

"Hold on.'"

As he waited on hold, Cain smiled at Beth and Boswell.

"An old friend," he whispered. His colleagues nodded, lowered their voices.

"Cain," said Kimmett on the phone, "lay off Nash."

"Really?" Cain frowned, though neither Boswell or Beth noticed. "I'm surprised."

"You heard me: back off. Leave him alone. Don't worry about him anymore. Nail DiCarlo—and Johnny Maxx, if you can do it cleanly, completely. But forget about the mayor. And . . ."

"Why?" interrupted Cain.

"Don't worry about why. Just do it. Keep the commission off his back."

"I'm not sure that will be possible."

"It damn well better be! You're getting paid to do what I want, and I want—"

"You know the job I took."

The edge in Cain's tone attracted Beth's attention. When she looked, he was smiling.

"Don't make me jerk your chain again!" hissed Kimmett.

"I'm sorry I won't get a chance to see you, too," said Cain.

"What? Cain, what are you—"

"Good-bye," said Cain, and he hung up the phone.

"Who was that?" asked Beth, frowning.

"Just a guy I knew," answered Cain. "Passing through town."

From the outer office came the sound of footsteps; the *ding!* of the glass coffee pot against its hot plate; Sylvia's whispered *"Damn!"*

As quickly and gracefully as he could, Cain grabbed the empty mug on his desk and left his shared office for the reception room.

Sylvia stood at the coffee maker, her back to Cain.

"I'll take some before you throw it out," he said, loudly.

She turned and he walked toward her.

"Did you burn yourself?" he asked as he drew close.

"I'll live," she said.

Cain glanced toward the office he'd left; saw no one behind him in the doorway. He could hear Catherine, still busy in the conference room where Sylvia had been. Cain dropped his voice.

"I haven't seen you—not alone, not since . . ." he shrugged.

"I've been around," she said. Her tone was even, but Cain sensed the secret curl of a smile in the corners of her mouth.

"I'm sorry I was hard on you the other night," said Cain.

"No you're not," said Sylvia. Her smile gave up its secrecy and brightened her face. "Maybe you're sorry you had to be, but you're not sorry you were."

Cain didn't know what to say.

"Nice suspenders," said Sylvia, brushing the back of her nails down one strap, letting the pressure of her hand linger on his chest.

Heels clicked behind Cain. He turned, saw Beth standing in the opening between the two offices. Beth saw Sylvia's hand on his chest, paled, and forgot what pretext that carried her away from her work.

Something *thunked* loudly against the hall door. The fogged glass rattled. Footsteps ran away in the outer corridor.

"What? . . ." said Sylvia.

Beth flicked her eyes to the office door.

Catherine emerged from the conference room; shook her head.

"The damn mailmen are getting lazier every day," she said, heading toward the door. "In the Corps, we would never have allowed—"

Cain grabbed her arm.

"I'll get it," he said, stepping around her.

"What's going on?" called Boswell from the other room.

Standing off to the side, Cain turned the doorknob. The door swung inward half a foot.

Nothing happened.

Cain peered through the gap: the hall was empty. On the floor, leaning against the door, was a thick manila envelope. He swung the door open, stepped into the hall, and looked both directions: empty.

"What is it?" called out Sylvia.

Without answering, Cain ran back into the office, stared out the window at the city square. He saw no one hurrying away from the building, no one in the square who seemed unusual. When he turned from the window, Boswell had joined the others and Catherine was bending over to pick up the manila packet.

"Let me!" said Cain. He crouched over the packet, let his eyes soak in its contours.

"Shall we call the police?" said Beth.

"No," said Cain. "This is ours."

He slowly reached down.

Beth clutched Boswell's arm.

Cain picked up the packet; nothing happened.

"In here," he said, carrying it to conference room.

"What's in it?" said Boswell as Catherine closed the outer door, then followed the rest of them into the conference room.

"Feels like papers," said Cain, "documents."

There was no label or writing on the manila envelope.

"Shouldn't we worry about fingerprints?" said Beth.

Cain ripped open the envelope.

"Guess not," said Beth.

Bent over the table, Cain shuffled through the documents for half a minute until Boswell could contain himself no longer:

"What is it?" he said.

"An anonymous gift from someone with a modest soul and gutsy conscience," said Cain. "Could be out of City Hall, could be out of the SIC, maybe the bank. It's photocopies: ledgers, a couple spread sheets, some jumbled notes, typed reports—here's one from Central Bank."

Cain stood, grinned at his colleagues.

"It's what they never wanted anybody to know," he said.

"Whistle blowers," added Cain. "Where would we be without them?"

Forty minutes later, Cain, Beth, and Sylvia sat at the conference table watching Boswell finish with the documents they'd already read. Boswell scribbled notes on a yellow legal pad. The phone rang. In the outer office, Catherine answered it, then called out, "It's for you, Cain."

"Hello," he said, using Sylvia's phone.

"It's Paul Borge," said the minister on the other end of the call. "I've got five people willing to testify about bad treatment they received from DiCarlo's cops. Three of them refused to volunteer a bribe and got adjudicated hell, one was beaten when they arrested him for public drunkenness, and the other is the man they nailed at the rally."

"That's great!" said Cain.

"It's weird," said Borge. "Normally, everybody would have run away rather than make trouble. Now . . . there's a new mood in town. A *why not* attitude."

"Maybe times are changing."

"Maybe," said Borge. In his mind's eye, Cain saw the minister frown. "There's something out there I don't like. Some . . . spirit."

"Spirits are your business," said Cain.

"People are enough trouble," grumbled Borge.

"Can you get those people here today to make a statement?"

"Probably."

"Great," said Cain. He thanked the minister, hung up.

"What was all that about?" asked Boswell.

"In a minute," said Cain. He nodded to the documents spread across the table. "Is all that's in there what I think?"

"Well, I don't know what you think," said Boswell, shaking his head, "but in there, unless I'm reading them wrong . . .

"First off, you got the pension fund report that shows that ninety percent of the SIC's Special Unemployment Benefits fund has been *invested.*

"Forty-five percent of it is in an interest-free, unsecured loan to an Atlantic City consortium for God knows what. Johnny Maxx got a twenty-grand commission for arranging the loan to people who are probably his buddies or bosses. You can bet those boys won't rig a bankruptcy or walk away on their multimillion dollar debt, *no*, they'd never do that.

"The other half of the SUB money is sunk in city bonds—and sunk is the right word. That money went into the general revenue accounts, probably to make up for the shortfall in taxes since the mills started closing. Cronies of the mayor got special fees in the transaction, and I'm betting the skim off the money once it hit city hall was terrific. All the bonds bought Steeltown is the propping up of Mayor Nash's machine."

"Nobody figured business to stay bad," said Beth. "Nobody figured anybody would ask questions, or be able to find out any answers. If the mills had reopened, the regular tax money would have flowed to cover the bonds' redemption. In fact, if the mills had reopened, nobody might ever have known what was in the SUB fund because nobody would have needed it."

"And then there's Central Bank," said Boswell, "The city's oldest and finest financial institution—which, luckily, does not hold my meager savings. If those jumbled notes our friend enclosed are right, half a dozen bank officers have gotten sweetheart loans or outside fees or some sort of goodies from the SIC, City Hall, or Johnny Maxx so the deal could come together."

"Will it come apart?" asked Cain.

"You figure it," said Boswell. "SIC covers all mill and mine workers and Teamsters in town. Many of them are out of work. They've been making it on government unemployment—which eventually runs out; on their individual union benefits programs—which is tapped, from what I hear; and on charity. Forget about charity. These guys have paid into the SIC SUB fund as their last umbrella against the storm.

"But their umbrella is 'invested.' Even if the trustees at the Central Bank could redeem the city bonds right away, before maturity, they'd have to ask Nash for the money. I'm betting it's long gone. Nor is there much chance for it to return without a major economic turnaround. Which leaves the other half of their invested umbrella, the racket boys in Atlantic City, a town famous for paying off."

"They broke them," said Sylvia. "All those steel hands, the miners, the industry and service and craft unions under the SIC, they're broke. And they don't even know it."

"Yet," said Cain.

"Whatever the SIC has been paying out," said Boswell, "probably isn't their money. Bank funds, maybe, loans to the union. The bank is loaning depositors' money to cover up the bank's trusteeship errors with other depositors' money. Which means the bank's deposits . . ."

"If this is what Hammond found," said Beth, "no wonder they killed him."

The four of them looked at each other.

"What the hell are we going to do with this?" whispered Beth.

No one spoke for over a minute.

Then, Cain said, "Use it."

"What are you talking about?" said Boswell.

"Here it is!" said Cain. "What we're after, what we issued the subpoenas for. It doesn't matter what any judge does, not if we got it already!"

"Cain," explained Boswell, "all we have is a bunch of paper. We don't know these documents—which are mere photostats—We don't know if they're genuine, if what is on them is true, if—"

"What do you *think?*" asked Cain.

"What I *think* is immaterial," answered Boswell. "What I can *prove* and what I *should do* with what I can prove are the crucial categories."

"I'm not saying go wild in the streets with this stuff," said Cain. "but—"

"It's too powerful," said Sylvia, shaking her head.

"—it's a chance," said Cain. "A chance to get at the truth. You can't tell me that getting the truth to the people is wrong."

He paused, out of breath.

"Look," he continued after a moment, "if this is what Josh Hammond was on to, then this is what will flush out his killer. And right along with it, we'll be doing extra public service."

"I didn't realize you were so public spirited," said Boswell.

His words were cold, but Cain sensed a lack of weight behind them. More, Cain sensed Boswell's anger at the world that lay sprawled through the papers on the table; anger, and the excitement of being able to do *something* about it.

"I've got a job to do," said Cain. "We all do. This isn't all of it, but it's a great step, if we play it right."

"And how would we do that?" said Boswell.

"We give it to the press," said Cain.

"What!" said Sylvia.

"You can't . . ." said Beth.

"Not the documents," Cain quickly said. "But the truth. We've been presented with certain allegations. That's the truth. And that's all we have to tell the press. The local newspaper. Everybody will eat it up."

"We can't issue press releases about every allegation we receive—or *say* we receive," said Boswell.

"So we leak it," said Cain.

"That's backdoor government," said Boswell.

"That's how this town works," answered Cain.

"The story goes: 'The commission has received allegations that the SIC SUB fund contains a questionable no-interest loan to an Atlantic City casino group. Johnny Maxx, local businessman, may have received a substantial commission for arranging the loan. Regarding the city bond purchase by the SIC, the commission has been told that the city cannot account for the revenue through the process normally followed by most American cities. Allegations have also been received about possible irregularities involving some officers of Central Bank.' The paper lays it all off on a 'source close to the investigation.' "

"There are half a dozen potentially litigious reasons why the paper wouldn't print all that," said Boswell.

"So let them pick and choose," said Cain. "That's their job. Besides, the only person named is Johnny Maxx, and he's not likely to sue for libel."

"What makes you think Evans would print that?" said Sylvia. "He's never been brave before."

"He's never had this good a story before," said Cain.

"I don't like this," said Sylvia.

"This is how it's done," said Cain. "We use this leak to force the SIC and City Hall to play ball. They won't know what we've got. They'll have to respond and deal with us, bring at least some of the truth out. Right now, they're trying to tie us and the truth up in legal red tape until the commission expires. This is our best shot at stopping that."

"What else?" asked Boswell, after a long pause.

"What do you mean?" asked Cain.

"That phone call you took a few minutes ago," he said. "What people? What statements? For what to do what about what?"

"That's another matter: Chief DiCarlo."

"What about him?"

"You know those columns written by Hammond about the cops?"

"Mild stuff. Sarcasm."

"Who knows what else he had? Cops have always been notorious in this town. Since Reverend Borge was on the commission, he checked them out. He's come up with some witnesses. And if we subpoena the arrest records and the central booking log at the station house . . ."

"That's public record," Beth said, speaking quickly before Boswell could interject any angry word. "We don't need a subpoena."

"In Steeltown, what the law says you can have and what you need muscle to get are often the same thing," said Cain. "That's all I'm asking for: a little muscle."

"To go after DiCarlo," said Boswell.

"To investigate irregularities in the police department which were the subject of Josh Hammond's interest," said Cain.

Boswell shook his head, said, "What probable cause do you have for a subpoena—other than your suspicions, which are undeniably part wishful conjecture—and Borge's as yet unfiled complaints?"

"That comes from Beth," said Cain. "Via a confidential source with a solid, reasonable ability to know."

"What are you talking about?" said Beth.

"Who?" asked Boswell.

"Johnny Maxx," said Cain.

Beth blushed, then paled.

"What—" began Boswell.

"He told Beth that DiCarlo was crooked," said Cain. "That qualifies as an informed source reporting legitimate leads worthy of followup investigation. Probable cause."

"That ..." began Beth. She closed her mouth, shook her head.

"Is that true, Beth?" asked Boswell.

"Essentially," Cain said quickly.

Boswell glared at him, turned to the Beth. She nodded.

"Are you okay?" Sylvia whispered to Beth.

Boswell closed his eyes, squeezed the bridge of his nose between his forefinger and thumb. Sighed deeply.

"Beth," he finally said, his tone strong and certain, "by tomorrow, I want an affidavit about this Johnny Maxx matter. Everything. Understand?"

She nodded.

"We're on touchy ground," said Boswell. He shook his head. The air-conditioners in the windows hummed. The room smelled of processed air and sweat its chill couldn't prevent.

"We all know that if we take these questions to the full commission," said Boswell, "assuming we could ever get them in one room, they'd never tell us to go ahead. We're not a democracy on the staff level. Nor any personalized version of anarchy."

He looked straight at Cain—who returned his steady stare.

"I'm in charge," said Boswell. "The decisions are mine, the responsibility is mine. But I trust you people, value your opinions. It's clear what you're proposing, Cain. Hell! What you've been doing.

"Sylvia," said Boswell, "what do you think we should do?"

"All I see is trouble," Sylvia answered quietly. "My husband would say do no harm. So much has already been done.

I can't speak for him, I won't. I don't know who I represent.
Me a 'staff member,' a citizen of Steeltown: all that's jumbled.

"Maybe there's other ways you can figure to do this.
You're the clever ones, the educated and experienced ones. I
signed on to help, for whatever reasons in whatever ways.
Seems to me . . . this is the deal we've got."

"What are you saying?" asked Boswell.

"Do what you have to do. I'll follow the lead. That's as
much as I can give you."

She slumped in her chair as Boswell asked, "Beth?"

"I support Jack," she replied.

"Why?" asked Boswell.

"Sometimes you have to take a chance," she said, halt-
ingly. "If you don't, why are we here at all?"

Again Boswell rubbed the bridge of his nose.

"Okay," he said half a minute later. "We'll do it that
way. But that's as far as we go until we know where we are.
Understood?"

Everyone nodded.

"I'll take it to Evans," said Cain. "Keep you clean, Russ."

"Only the bare bones," said Boswell. "No more than
your example. No details. No attribution to you or the commission. No speculation. Nothing about the cops. Just the
packet. Understood?"

"You got it," said Cain.

"The rest of us will handle the statements from Borge's
people," continued Boswell. "If we work late, we should be
able to serve the DiCarlo subpoena in the morning."

"I'll be back after I go to the paper," said Cain. "Don't
let anybody know where I've gone or where I'll be."

"Dodging your out-of-town friend?" asked Sylvia.

"I've got work to do," he said, and left.

On the way to the newspaper, Cain spotted a pay phone
on the wall outside a laundromat. He parked the state car in
a space down the block, and walked back. Two young men
emerged from a video games arcade when Cain was a few
steps from its door.

"Well," said Elliot Kimmett V, who was the taller and
better looking of the duo, "if it isn't Steeltown's new cop.
My mom send you to check up on me?"

As Cain stopped to confront Sylvia's son, the other young

man turned his face so Cain could see only his profile. The boy's image stirred a memory in Cain, as did his voice when he muttered to Kimmett, "See you around."

Turning his back to Cain, the boy walked away.

"Don't make the mistake of thinking everything in the world centers around you," Cain told the grandson of the man who'd hired him.

"If it doesn't," came the reply, "what good is it?"

"Wasn't that the Vandross boy?" said Cain, recognizing in the departing youth the shadow of the father he'd met at the police station.

"Well, what do you know?" grinned the youngest Kimmett. "Grampa was right: you are pretty sharp."

"What are you doing with him?" asked Cain.

"What do you care?"

"Do you want to eat your dinner minus a few teeth?"

"Tough, too," said Kimmett. "Don't worry, baby-sitter. He and I aren't what you'd call friends. We just hang together."

"Doing what?"

"Just talk." The high school graduate grinned. "For now.

"Do I pass?" he added, with a sneer.

"Never happen," answered Cain, evenly.

The boy laughed, a family cackle Cain first heard in a guarded room of an old mansion.

"Just you watch!" he called out as he backed away, his emerald eyes on the adult in front of him. "Just you wait!"

He turned, hustled down the block. Over his shoulder, he yelled to Cain, "Say hi to my folks!"

Cain watched him disappear. Shook his head. He walked to the pay phone. The evening sun was a red ball burning at him as he dropped a quarter in the phone. The receiver buzzed in his ear. Cain took a pair of sunglasses from his suit coat, slipped them over his eyes. The city saw its reflection in those lens mirrors.

"He ain't here," Chief DiCarlo's cadaverous detective said into the phone when he answered Cain's call.

"Do you know who this is?" asked Cain.

"He still ain't here."

"Then give him this message," said Cain before he hung up and walked away. "I'm out of pocket. Tell him I'm doing the best I can, but to watch out for the wolves."

The Fist of God

THE GRIZZLED POLICE SERGEANT behind the elevated booking desk raised his eyes from the morning's newspaper when Sylvia marched into the station; she held the door open. Behind her came Cain, a plastic-cased machine gripped in each hand. Cain's brow was soaked. He shuffled his burdens inside police headquarters, then set them on the floor while he caught his breath. Next came Catherine, her eyes bright, carrying a cardboard box. Beth entered last, bearing three empty briefcases.

The clock on the wall showed 9:44.

"Well," drawled the booking sergeant, "if it ain't the hot shot. Looking for a permit for your parade?"

Still out of breath, Cain shuffled to the booking desk.

"We want to see the booking logs for the last five years," he said. "Might as well start with the current log."

"Why, sure!" said the sergeant. He lifted the giant ledger off the desk. "There you go!" He dropped it back on the desk. "You've seen it, now you can get out of here."

"We want to *examine* your logs," said Cain.

"The hell you do," was the reply. "And the hell you will."

"Sergeant," called out Beth, "we have the legal right to look at those logs, and you are in personal and professional violation of the law by denying us that access."

"So sue me," he said.

"No," said Cain, "we don't want to do that." He dropped a folded piece of paper on the sergeant's newspaper.

"What's this?" said the cop, picking it up.

"That's a subpoena," said Cain. "You've just been served for all those ledgers. The subpoena calls for immediate compliance with the law, and orders you to immediately turn them over to us."

The sergeant dropped the subpoena as if it were on fire.

"What the hell is this?" he yelled.

Cain slammed his hand on the desk. When he lifted it, his gold trooper badge glistened up at the sergeant.

"It's your ass, *Sergeant*," he yelled. "Unless you comply *right now*, you're going upstate."

"Who's gonna take me there? You and the three musketettes?"

"Hey!" said Catherine, moving next to Cain. Her voice was clear, her hands steady. "We'd love to smear your shit all over these crummy walls."

Even Cain turned to stare at the ex-Marine—who leered into the eyes of the cop sitting above her.

"We can have an army of state troopers here in five minutes," Cain quickly lied.

The cop licked his lips.

Catherine didn't blink.

"I'm calling the chief," the cop finally said.

"Good idea," said Cain. "You got one minute."

The chief wasn't in, but a captain was. He hurried downstairs, studied the subpoena, then told Cain, "The chief is on the way."

"You read today's newspaper, Captain?" said Cain. "Lot of heads rolling these days. We can't wait to pick 'em up. Get those ledgers."

"Look," said the captain, "even if we let you see them, you can't remove them from headquarters. The law . . ."

Cain nodded to the two machines he'd assembled while waiting for the captain.

"Portable copiers, lots of paper," said Cain.

"How do I know this is . . ."

"If you have more questions, call our chairman," said Beth. "He's in the chambers of the judge who issued the subpoena. You can explain to the judge your reluctance to comply with his order."

"It'll take us a while to find . . ." began the captain.

Before he could finish, Cain pulled the heavy ledger off the booking desk.

"We'll start with this one," he said, handing it to Sylvia.

Catherine marched around the side of the desk, climbed the podium stairs, and elbowed the beefy police sergeant out of her way.

"Hey!" she called. "Guess what I found!"

She lifted three more heavy green ledgers from beneath the desk. When she dropped them on its top, a cloud of dust flew into the air. She fanned it away, snarled down at the cop with three stripes on his sleeve. "What jackass taught you how to be a sergeant?"

Cain, Beth, and Sylvia looked at each other, but said nothing.

Catherine grinned, grabbed a ledger, marched off the podium to one of the photocopying machines. Sylvia began work at the other.

When the clock on the wall showed 10:06, DiCarlo charged into his headquarters. The three women kept photocopying while the chief pulled Cain aside.

"You're off base, asshole!" snarled DiCarlo. "This shit—"

"Where were you when I called to warn you?" Cain whispered back. He shook his head. "Later."

"Why should I listen to you again?"

"If you're that stupid," Cain replied, "then don't bother."

He rejoined his co-workers.

The clock on the wall read 10:09.

They finished photocopying the ledgers at 12:07. Packing the photocopies in the boxes and briefcases and disassembling the photocopiers for transport took another fifteen minutes. Cain grabbed the two machines, Beth and Sylvia took the heavy briefcases, and Catherine scooped up the cardboard box.

" 'Bye!" she called to the desk sergeant as they trudged out the front door and staggered down the precinct steps. "Thanks!

"That was great!" she said as they reached the sidewalk. Cain set the machines down. The others rested their burdens, too.

"I was getting bored with this job," Catherine told Cain. He shook his head.

"I never knew," he told her.

"You guys wait here," he told them. The midday sun warmed his brow. He nodded to where the car was parked half a block away and on the other side of the street. "No sense us lugging them to the car. I'll get it and drive here."

"I'll get it," said Catherine.

Cain shrugged, tossed her the keys. He glanced at his watch: 12:25.

"What now?" asked Sylvia as Catherine walked away.

An attractive young mother smiled as she and Catherine passed each other crossing the street.

Cain turned his back toward them, looked at Beth and Sylvia. He relaxed. Leaned against a parking meter.

"You guys hungry?" he asked. "I'll buy lunch."

The young mother reached the curb on Cain's side of the street, frowned: she remembered what she forgot and turned to retrace her steps.

Down the block, across the street, Catherine got in the car.

Beth smiled, said, "That sounds like—"

The fist of God slammed into Cain's back. His arms shot out from his side. He rose off the sidewalk, thrown forward through the air as the world flashed bright orange and a giant *heat* flooded his body. The pressure blast in his ears almost blacked him out. Beth flew backwards, her legs tripping over the wobbling pile of briefcases so she fell on her side. Sylvia whirled on her toes like a ballet dancer gone mad until she bounced off the brick wall of police headquarters and crashed to the sidewalk.

Cain slammed into the concrete steps as an awful, roaring wave rolled over him, echoed off the buildings. Glass shattered. A hunk of smoking metal the size of a typewriter rained down beside him. His broken watch read 12:27. He lived in slow motion, tumbling, rolling to his back, unaware of the bruises and cuts and the shock to his knee. He saw Beth stagger to her feet, saw Sylvia lift herself off the sidewalk as though she were doing push-ups.

"Help me help me help me!" screamed the young mother

as she fled down the street, her hair, blouse, and skirt on fire.

A teenage girl ran from nowhere, knocked the woman to the ground, and began rolling with her, beating at the flames.

Policemen dashed down the steps past Cain.

A siren wailed.

And down the block, across the street, a ball of fire consumed the twisted, mangled outline of the commission's bombed car; sent an angry black cloud mushrooming to heaven and filled Steeltown's streets with the stench of burning gasoline, rubber, metal, and flesh.

The Coin

"LET'S GET ONE THING STRAIGHT," said DiCarlo. Only the desk's snake-neck lamp lit his office. "If I wanted you dead, I'd rig some Southside boy to stick a knife in your ribs."

Cain slumped in a wooden chair opposite the chief. Cain's legs sprawled askew; his bruised hands dangled toward the floor. Green disinfectant stained his scraped palms. His suit was rumpled, his tie unknotted. White surgical tape held gauze against his forehead. His eyes smoldered like the last two embers in a sack of ashes.

Cool air poured down on them from the ceiling vent. The windowless room smelled of singed hair, smoke, and sweat.

"If you didn't," rasped Cain, "who did?"

"I don't know, Jack. You piss anybody off lately?"

The phone rang. DiCarlo answered it, grunted a few times, then hung up.

"The woman in the street died," he said. "The girl who tried to save her will make it, though she ain't gonna be a beauty queen."

"Catherine."

"Yeah, well, we'll be picking up pieces of her for days."

Cain blinked.

"How?" he asked.

"Dynamite," said the chief. "Easy to get in a mining town."

"Funny how easy it is to use," said Cain. "A block away from police headquarters, broad daylight, and somebody rigs a car bomb. The car wasn't the only thing that was wired."

The desk chair creaked as DiCarlo tilted back.

"Maybe," he said. "If so, that wire didn't start with Harry DiCarlo. And if it's in my shop, I'll find it."

"The bomb wasn't just for me," said Cain.

"Somebody didn't like the ladies?"

Cain shook his head.

"They didn't matter," he said, "or it would have been a bullet, not a bomb. No, they figured to get you, too."

"Don't be a jerk. I never ride in anybody else's car."

"Somebody blows up a state car in front of your head-quarters," said Cain. "Kills two people. Could have killed more. Chump, fool, incompetent, crooked, killer—Hell, the only argument is what kind of asshole you are. Somebody wrote a message for Steeltown with that blood. And they wrote a message for you."

"Maybe that was just the first chance they found to hit you."

"*Sure*," sneered Cain.

"Who?"

"I don't know, Harry. You piss anybody off lately?"

"Johnny Maxx," said DiCarlo.

"Or the mayor," said Cain.

"How do you figure him?"

"He's not happy with me. And he fed me a piece of you days ago. Maybe he got tired of waiting for me to chew it up, figured on killing two birds with one stone."

"Maybe," said DiCarlo. He shrugged in grudging agree-ment. "A bomb ain't exactly Johnny's style."

"Bloody Sunday was a bomb," countered Cain. "And that made Johnny cock of the walk. Now you come along and clip his wings."

"Which side of the coin you want?" asked DiCarlo.

"The right one," answered Cain. "And I'm curious: Why are you quick to hang this on Johnny when you got the mayor in your sights?"

Tilted back in his chair, DiCarlo's face was in the shadows.

"What are you talking about?" he whispered.

After the bomb; after the fire trucks and the ambulance

ride; the X-rays and grim emergency room meeting with Russ Boswell; after Sylvia's devastated husband took her home; after Boswell's wife arrived at the hospital and glared at Cain as she led her husband and Beth back to a once-safe middle-class house; after phone consultations with his firm and the governor; Cain stole away from the emergency room, dodged reporters and a gauntlet of police detectives and sheriff's deputies—who were most intent on watching each other. He begged a ride from a charitable florist who dropped him at the city square.

Now, from his suit jacket, Cain took the folded eight-by-ten photograph he'd retrieved from the commission office.

"What's that?" asked DiCarlo.

"It's your lien on the mayor," said Cain.

"You stole this from the case jacket," said DiCarlo after he looked at the picture of Josh Hammond's desk blotter.

"Bust me," said Cain.

"You haven't played that card yet, have you?" continued Cain. "It's not much. So what if Josh Hammond made a note that said he was going to meet N's man at ten in a garage. Maybe he was talking about the rendezvous that killed him, maybe he wasn't. Maybe N stands for Nash and maybe it doesn't. You pull anything out of Hammond's address and appointment book?"

DiCarlo stared at him. "Today you came after me."

"If I don't get who I need to nail, I'll nail who I can get. I warned you days ago. Besides, you know how that works, chief. It's the cop game."

"Give me one good reason to trust you," said DiCarlo.

"No," said Cain.

In the shadows, DiCarlo shrugged.

"There's nothing conclusive in Hammond's appointment book," he said. "Nothing for the date he died. He had all the numbers you'd expect: the mayor's, Johnny's. Mine. The town's movers and shakers."

"The mayor's man," said Cain, "chews a toothpick and dresses cheap. About fifty."

"Carson," said DiCarlo. "When you wall yourself up in a fortress like City Hall, you need someone to walk the streets."

"N's man."

"Why not?"

"So what now, Chief?"

Outside, afternoon turned to evening. The draft of cool air that had been falling on the two men stopped.

"If I take on Nash," said DiCarlo, "out front, in the open— "

"You can't just take him on," said Cain. "You got to take him out."

"I won't do your killing for you, Cain."

"That's not my style, Chief. That's not what I want."

"What do you want?"

"Right now, figure we want the same thing. To nail Nash."

"With what? Hammond's murder? Never happen. If that were possible . . ."

". . . if that were possible," finished Cain, "you'd already have Nash mounted on the wall."

DiCarlo laughed.

"We're not going to get him with one blow," said Cain. "You won't stick him with the Hammond murder, but you can shake him. Does he know you're on to this?"

"I think he knows something," said DiCarlo. "I trust my men, but there's wires in this town you can't always see."

"Which explains why Nash tried to get me to take a bite out of you," said Cain. "Scare you off, weaken you. The bomb was the second message. He won't quit until you're history."

"You think we can do it?"

"Nash is an all-or-nothing guy. He's rigid, *too* strong: his fortress must be perfect. The commission will hit him with the bonds. Every chance you get, push him and push hard. Worry him with Hammond's murder, this bombing. Chip away little pieces, lean on his walls. Knock his authority. He'll get so frenzied he'll blow himself up."

"So you say."

"Where's Johnny Maxx?" said Cain.

DiCarlo leaned forward, rested his arms on the desk; glared at Cain. "Maybe you're the all-or-nothing kind of guy, too."

"I am the kind of guy who doesn't like uncovered angles. Odds are Nash set the bomb, but we can't take chances with Johnny. Besides, he and the mayor are in the same boat in this crooked bond deal. He's going to get burned, and he won't like it. Eventually . . ."

"Yeah, I know. Eventually he's got to go. You cutting a ticket for me, too, Cain?"

"You bet I am, Chief. You buy it, it's yours."

"Too bad about that bomb," drawled the chief of police.

"Where's Johnny?" repeated Cain.

"Seems like he turned to smoke."

"Today?" asked Cain, and DiCarlo nodded.

Cain said, "Go get him. Formally, legally. Wanted for questioning. Do it public."

"And put everybody on notice?"

"That's right."

"Everybody in town is already on edge," said DiCarlo. "You saw."

"I saw. And I see tomorrow."

"Suppose you're wrong about the mayor?"

"About the bombing? Maybe. About him trying to shut you down? No way. If you go after him and block out Johnny, we're set. Besides, it's what you've been waiting for an excuse to do."

"Could be."

Cain shook his head. Slowly, gingerly, he stood.

"The hell with you," he sighed. "I'm going home."

"You can't make it walking. A cruiser'll give you a lift," said DiCarlo. "I'm going to give you a couple boys to guard—"

"No way," said Cain as he headed toward the door, "I said no to trooper shadows from the governor: it's *never* to your goons holding my hands *real* tight."

"I could use a little something," said DiCarlo.

Cain turned, looked back at the chief.

"This subpoena crap you pulled," continued DiCarlo. "Whatever else Nash put up your sleeve. Some guarantee that all that would get lost would help us both get where we want to go."

"Forget it, Harry," said Cain. "You're out of time and out of choices. The bomb flipped the coin. All you can do now is decide whose face is going to come up."

Dog Fight

From the June 11 **Steeltown Tribune:**

... Mayor Richard Nash called yesterday's car bombing, "an outrage against the citizens of this community.

"One must question the competency of Chief DiCarlo's police department," said the mayor, "when an act such as this happens under his nose."

Chief DiCarlo said he was "surprised" by the mayor's criticism.

"Though he's right about the city being outrageous," said DiCarlo. "What Steeltown needs is a clean sweep."

From the June 12 **Steeltown Tribune:**

... and according to an informed source, in addition to being interviewed about the car bombing, Carson was questioned about the death of *Tribune* reporter Josh Hammond.

In an unexpected phone call to the *Tribune* an hour after police released Carson, Mayor Richard Nash said that he was "appalled" by the interrogation of his top aide.

"This is a blatant political move by Chief DiCarlo," said the mayor. "It has nothing to do with the tragedies that have cursed our city—tragedies which would have been prevented had Chief DiCarlo done his job!"

Chief DiCarlo was unavailable for comment on Mayor Nash's charges. A department spokesman said Carson's questioning was "routine investigative procedure."

Meanwhile, the *Tribune* has learned that Chief DiCarlo has issued a warrant for questioning for Johnny Maxx, a prominent Steeltown businessman, whose whereabouts are unknown. The *Tribune* was unable to confirm the specifics of the warrant, or whether the warrant was related to yesterday's wave of police raids on corner stores suspected of involvement in gambling.

From the June 15 **Steeltown Tribune:**

Three deputy sheriffs have filed a million-dollar lawsuit against several Steeltown city policemen, alleging grievous bodily injury as a result of premeditated, illegal assaults.

From the June 18 Philadelphia **Eagle** *story by H. L. Cohn, reprinted in sixteen papers, including the* **Steeltown Tribune:**

Steeltown, already plagued by harsh economic times and uncertainty and fear in the aftermath of the murder of a reporter and car-bombing deaths, may be facing another crisis. The city's major union and city government will soon be accused of improprieties involving a municipal bond program, according to several sources.

The bond sale is the subject of an almost completed report by an independent commission created by the governor to investigate corruption in Steeltown. The report allegedly criticizes a missing local gangster, the mayor, local and national union officials, and officers of the city's largest bank.

The scandal will have repercussions extending from

Steeltown to the boardwalks of Atlantic City and to the boardrooms of several New York banks, as well as in the marble corridors of Washington, D.C.

The Commission report is rumored to be held up in a bitter fight between commissioners and staff over what should be disclosed publicly. The report was hampered by a lack of cooperation from city and union officials, says a source close to the commission.

The mayor and officials of the Steeltown Industrial Coalition, the city's major union, completely deny ...

From the June 19 **Steeltown Tribune:**

Citing reports of random vandalism and violence, the Reverend Paul Borge, associate pastor for the United Methodist Church, called for "a new search for peace.

"There's too many desperate people acting crazy out there," he said. "They're forgetting that if they act crazy, they'll be crazy."

From the June 20 **Steeltown Tribune:**

Mayor Richard Nash today lambasted Police Chief Harry DiCarlo for "failing to provide adequate protection for Steeltown's citizens and an almost criminal ineptitude in the performance of his duties."

Nash said he may demand the chief's resignation or request that the city council terminate DiCarlo's contract. The mayor cited the recent car bombing, which caused the deaths of two people, as well as citizen complaints about street crime, police corruption and brutality, and "general lawlessness."

Mayor Nash has requested that the county sheriff institute regular patrols of deputies through Steeltown. Normally, deputies patrol only outside the city limits and act as a security force for designated public officials.

DiCarlo told the *Tribune* that the mayor "is trying to cover up his own problems with the bond scandal by making reckless and stupid charges."

From the June 22 **Washington Post** *political column:*

... all of which are spelling trouble for one of
the country's most famous and formidable urban
political machines. Several statehouse sources say
Mayor Nash's loyalists in the state legislature are losing
credibility as ominous clouds threaten their mentor.
According to three party officials, the shifting political
winds have brought a slight increase in the governor's
clout, which could escalate into a major realignment
of power during next year's congressional race. All
sources agree that Mayor Nash is still Steeltown's
political czar, but should he fail to demonstrate sig-
nificant popular support, he may create an opening
for an as yet unforeseeable opponent to challenge his
dynasty.

From the June 23 **Steeltown Tribune:**

The *Tribune* has obtained a copy of the final draft of
the Special Investigative Commission's report on the
purchase of city bonds by the Steeltown Industrial
Coalition.

In a secret ballot at a closed meeting yesterday, the
commission members overwhelmingly voted to with-
hold the report from public release and to curtail the
commission probe into the bond sale.

While Commission Chairman Russell Boswell was
not available for comment, one commissioner, who asked
that his name not be used, told the *Tribune* that the
Commission will continue its mandated probe into the
murder of *Tribune* reporter Josh Hammond "until such
time as it becomes appropriate to conclude this auxil-
iary investigative effort."

The suppressed report on the bond sale confirms
earlier press reports of improprieties, and alleges that
the city government has disbursed all the money gained
from the bond sale without performing any document-
able services linked to that spending. The report also

claims redemption of the bonds by the union would be "impossible" unless the state or federal government agrees to bail out the city.

In carefully worded language, the report raises numerous questions about the conduct and roles of . . .

From the June 24 **Steeltown Tribune:**

Federal and state auditors yesterday closed all branches of Steeltown's most prominent financial institution, the Central Bank, citing "discrepancies" in the bank's cash reserve balance and long-term obligations, especially with regard to management of municipal and "private institutional accounts."

Although spokesmen for the auditors and the bank refused further comment, the *Tribune* has learned that the private institutional accounts are mostly accounts of the Steeltown Industrial Coalition.

Word of the closure spread quickly through the city. By 11:00 A.M., a crowd estimated by police as "several hundred strong" gathered outside the chained doors of Central Bank's downtown headquarters branch. Smaller crowds formed at the bank's shopping mall offices.

The day before yesterday, the bank reported unusually large numbers of withdrawal transactions and account closings.

Yesterday's crowd grew hostile when confronted with Central Bank's locked doors. *Tribune* reporters polled more than two dozen people, who unanimously said they wanted to withdraw their money from the bank because they feared for their life savings.

A dozen police cruisers responded to the downtown scene. Standing on the bank steps behind two uniformed officers, Harold D. Stevens, the president of Central Bank, told the crowd that (their) "money is perfectly safe and that the bank will reopen for normal business as soon as adjustments are made to comply with auditors' requests."

The crowd jeered Stevens and ignored his plea to go home.

At noon, the crowd was so large sidewalk traffic was blocked and pedestrian traffic through the city square was obstructed.

The chief of police ordered his officers to disperse the crowd. A dozen arrests for disorderly conduct and unlawful assembly were reported.

Although the police department spokesman said no one was injured, *Tribune* reporters noted numerous individuals who seemed to have been hurt either by the jostling crowd or by police officers. A *Tribune* photographer's film was confiscated by the police. According to the photographer, the film contained a picture of two policemen beating the crowd with billy clubs.

At eight P.M. June 24, the glowing television screen fills with the stern, egglike image of Mayor Richard Nash seated behind his spotless desk. His gray suit is wrinkle free, his tie correctly knotted, his blue shirt spotless:

"My friends," he says, "these are trying times. We've had crises, and worse, rumors of crises. I say worse, because a rumor is more dangerous than any problem we face. Rumors drown out common sense, make us forget who we are and how strong we are. We need none of the fears and lies spread by rumor mongers and politically motivated agitators.

"There are those who want me to rebut certain anonymous innuendos and charges whipped up by the press. There are those who want me to short-circuit the established systems of law and order for personal gain. I will not do so. Mrs. Nash did not raise her boy to throw mud.

"Some of these people are motivated by genuine concerns and charitable intentions. To them, I counsel patience. To the others, the barking dogs of smug self-service, I say this: Bark all you want. Steeltown has nothing to fear from your bite.

"I could now answer their trick questions and half-truths and ignorant assertions, but to do so would demean my high office and sacred trust. You know me: I have worked for you, provided for you, sacrificed for you, and succeeded for you. Tonight, I assure you that I will continue to do so for a long, long time. Let no one make any mistake about that.

"The time has come to move forward, put the past behind us, and get on with the future. To do that means to celebrate what we have, who we are, and what lies ahead.

"It is in this spirt, the true American spirit of courage and integrity in the face of adversity, that, with the help of several fine, public-spirited citizens, I am reviving a Steeltown tradition.

"Ten days hence is the Fourth of July, the anniversary of the founding of our great republic. In bygone years, to show their strength, celebrate their victories, and bolster their tomorrows, the working men and women of Steeltown paraded from the river to the town square. There they were greeted and honored by those fortunate enough to have served them in the year past.

"We let that custom slip away in the last few years, and I can't help thinking that much of our trouble comes from the loss of such traditional values and rituals.

"Well I say *no* to that! And *yes* to Steeltown! Yes to America! Yes to tomorrow! This is a great and glorious country, and a great and glorious city. I'm inviting—No, I'm *urging*—you to celebrate it with me by reinstituting Steeltown's world-famous Fourth of July parade.

"With funds donated by several generous citizens, notably the grand patriarch of Steeltown, Elliot Kimmett the Third, labor donated by the good brothers and sisters of the SIC, and surplus city materials, a bandstand and speakers' platform exactly duplicating the historic models will be built in the town square, right in front of City Hall.

"At ten on the morning of the Fourth of July, officials of the SIC, assisted by volunteers organized by my office, will meet with you and thousands of your friends and neighbors at the gates of Bushmaster Steel. At eleven o'clock, the parade will begin.

"Marching, growing ever stronger, ever greater, you will arrive at the city square at noon, where I and several good citizens will be waiting to greet you. To celebrate you. And,

I have every reason to believe, to share with you some very good, very important, and very welcome news indeed.

"Central High's band will be there to perform a concert of American music. We will construct bleachers. That night, we have a wonderful fireworks display planned.

"This is more than a parade. This is a rally. This is an affirmation. This is a testament—to you, to your belief in your city, and in your country. With our faith, with our courage, with our convictions, I know we will do ourselves, America and Steeltown, proud.

"God bless you, and good night."

From the June 25, Steeltown **Tribune:**

> Chief of Police Harry DiCarlo said last night that he refuses to grant a parade permit for the Fourth of July parade announced by Mayor Richard Nash in a televised address.
>
> "It's the most absurd idea I've ever heard," said DiCarlo. "We almost had a riot a few days ago, we got hotheads acting up all over town, and Nash wants to have a parade. Hell, it's no Fourth of July parade: it's a media show, a political rally for him."
>
> Under city law, the police department issues all parade permits.
>
> Chief DiCarlo informed the press of his decision one hour after the mayor's televised speech. Less than an hour later, Mayor Nash issued a statement to the media attacking the chief as a "negative thinker."
>
> "Chief DiCarlo has no faith in the good people of Steeltown," said Mayor Nash. He noted that the sheriff immediately volunteered his deputy force to assist the parade organizers in "what little crowd control we'll need.
>
> "The people of Steeltown don't need policing," said Nash. "They police themselves."
>
> As for the legality of holding a parade without a police-issued permit, Mayor Nash said: "I have

instructed the city attorney to go to court and force
the chief to issue the permit. If the courts don't
have enough time before the Fourth to rule DiCarlo
illegal, why, we'll just go ahead and have the parade without him."

From the Live At Five *news telecast, July 1, WSTL, Steeltown:*

"This is Kelly McGuinness live from city square!"
proclaims the perky blond woman on the television screen. Her dress is blue.

Behind her looms a large, elevated wooden
stage. The sounds of hammering, occasional shouts
of workmen, punctuate her delivery.

"Workmen are finishing the final touches for
the grand Fourth of July parade. They'll be putting
up over *half a mile* of red, white, and blue bunting,
draping it from the stage you see behind me and
the bleachers, as well as covering those wooden
booths set up in the square and along the parade
route. Won't that be *something!*

"Those booths are an added attraction for our
famous parade, just like on the holidays of years
gone by. And just like back then, they'll be selling
limited quantities of beer at—you guessed it—old-
fashioned prices: a *nickel!* That's right, *five cents* a
mug. Or a plastic cup, rather, since mugs aren't too
disposable. The beer is a special donation of local
distributors and bars and a few public—*er*—spirited
citizens.

"But if beer isn't your brew, don't despair:
some of the booths will be serving lemonade.

"Since so many people are expected, Mayor
Nash's committee has worked up a *dandy* idea.
Beer sales will be by ticket only: your nickel won't
buy you a brewsky! You can get tickets at City
Hall, SIC headquarters, or any mall. And—here's
the great part—buy two tickets for a dime, and get
one *free*, compliments of Mayor Nash. Remember:

only three tickets—that's three beers—per person. We wouldn't want anyone having too much fun on the Fourth!

"That cold stuff will come in handy, because as Dan the Weather Man will tell you in a minute, a major heat wave should arrive in plenty of time to make our parade party a hot one!"

Headline from the July 2 **Steeltown Tribune:**

JAPANESE REJECT STEELTOWN AS AUTO FACTORY LOCATION

The Heart of the World

CAIN RANG THE DOORBELL TWICE; he'd have rung again to make his presence known over the blare of rock music inside the house, but she answered his summons and opened the door.

"Jack," said Sylvia. She swung the door wider and conditioned, cool air poured out into the afternoon heat. "I didn't expect . . ."

"Come out of there," he said softly.

"What?" she replied, though she'd heard his words.

"Come out," he said. "I can't talk to you in there."

Sylvia wore a white blouse and loose blue cotton shorts cut high on her slim thighs. Her blond hair was brushed, but casually so, and she wore no makeup. She'd been moving cups and bowls from one arbitrary place to another, all the while being bombarded by her son's stereo and watched by the bottle of scotch in the cupboard above the sink. Now she glanced back into the shadowed chambers of her well-tended house. Beyond Cain, she saw the closed doors and shuttered windows of her neighbors, their lawns baking under the hot sun. She stepped to the flagstone stoop, pulled the door shut behind her.

They walked down the stone path to the sidewalk, ignored Cain's unmarked state trooper's car, and headed to the left on the quiet residential street.

Cain's tie bulged in the side pocket of his navy blazer; he wanted to discard the jacket, too, but wearing it kept the secret of whether a pistol waited beneath his shoulder or on his hip. None did. His blue shirt was open at the collar and stuck to his back and sides, absorbing trickles of sweat. He wore gray slacks and black shoes overdue for a shine.

"How did it go?" she asked.

"Russ, Beth, your husband, Reverend Borge, the legislator we got to—who started the whole thing, me," answered Cain. "We sat around Boswell's living room. His wife served lemonade and grim looks. You should have been there."

"No I shouldn't," she said. "Then Elliot would have talked for my benefit, not his."

Cain nodded, said, "We decided that while the commission has had its power and purpose severely constrained, it has not outlived its usefulness."

"End it now," she said. "Get it over with quick and clean, before it becomes something ugly. Before more lives are lost."

They had reached the corner. An imported Japanese station wagon driven by a henna-haired housewife rolled past them. The housewife pretended not to see who was on the sidewalk.

"There's still a chance," said Cain.

"For what?" said Sylvia. "To get DiCarlo? That's what Nash wants, that's what he's pushing for. He's co-opted us."

"Not if DiCarlo can help it."

"What can he do?" argued Sylvia. "If Nash pulls off his parade, there isn't a fence sitter in the state—who won't climb down and line up behind Steeltown's 'ratified' mayor. As soon as that happens, Nash will savage DiCarlo. The commission will be right there, doing its job like it should, helping crucify the chief on City Hall. The bond and municipal corruption investigation failed."

"So did the bank," remarked Cain.

"But none of it translated," said Sylvia. "I'm sorry, and it should have, but none of it connected. The truth isn't worth much if it doesn't move people to action, and it didn't and it won't. Everybody's too scared or too ignorant or stupid or too trapped by the whole mess to do anything about it, even if it means their own doom."

"Borge keeps talking about a 'new mood' around town," said Cain, nodding to the locked houses and trees drooping in the heat. "Something waiting to be born. But what I see is a graveyard. The people are zombies. They're walking around in a stupor, and when they wake up, they'll discover they're dead."

"And then they'll go back to sleep again," said Sylvia.

"Maybe," said Cain.

"You can't change that," said Sylvia. "Neither can DiCarlo."

"He'll try."

"He'll fail. What's he going to do? Arrest Nash for the murder of Josh Hammond or killing Catherine? Pulling in Carson was such a transparent ploy."

"There's more to it," said Cain.

"Not enough," said Sylvia.

At the corner they turned, walked toward a park with empty swings and a motionless merry-go-round.

"Give it up, Jack," she said as they crossed the street. "There's nothing left the commission can do except play the same old game. There's nothing left you can do about whatever it is you came here to do."

"Not yet," he said. "There's still a chance."

"For what? Nash will get DiCarlo, nobody will get Nash. Do you think that you can hang on and use the commission to nail Johnny Maxx? Hell, nobody even knows where he is! He might be dead! Nash could have already taken care of that business—it would pay him to: then he could hang the whole bond mess on Johnny! What's left?"

"Just give me time."

"For *what*? To watch the parade tomorrow? To wave to me up there on the reviewing stand?"

"What are you talking about?" said Cain.

"I didn't think Elliot would tell you," she replied, shaking her head. She ran her fingers down one of the swing's chains. "My wise father-in-law persuaded my good husband to accept Mayor Nash's invitation to sit on the reviewing stand with His Honor and a dozen other city luminaries. Like a good wife, I'll be by his side."

"No, I don't . . ." Cain started to say.

"Don't understand?" finished Sylvia. "What do you want? My father-in-law's arguments, or my husband's reasons?"

"The truth," said Cain.

"My father-in-law," she said, "claims we have no choice. That grand patriarch of Steeltown is funding almost the whole dawn show, so he—or his—must be there to wave the family flag. He claims that he had to accede to the mayor's request to back the parade: the Kimmetts are staunch supporters of the commission and if they don't participate in a ceremonial civic chore, then everyone will assume we're merely conniving, political opportunists.

"More power and a salute to the mayor," she said, crisply nodding her head: "He put one over on the old man.

"My husband . . . all he wants to do is stand tall. He put his heart and soul into the Japanese project and they took part of him with them when they left town. Plus, the commission he agreed to serve on covered itself in blood and filled the town with turmoil. He feels responsible. If he can't fix it or atone, he thinks he should at least stand up and be counted and face . . ."

"That's crazy!" yelled Cain.

"Or noble," she said.

"Don't let him do it!" said Cain. "Don't *you* do it!"

"We don't have a choice. Neither do you. We'll all go to the Independence Day parade, and we'll all watch our lives pass by.

"Nash's deputies and ward heelers are beating the bushes," she said. "Coaxing, bullying, getting everybody out. But he doesn't need to convince people. It's not that they believe a parade will do any good or that they'll get some valuable message from him—that hope died when the Japanese left. Yet everybody will come. There's nothing else they can do. So why not? Like you said, they're zombies."

"DiCarlo will try to stop them," said Cain, "you'll—"

"Yeah," she interrupted, "well, wish the chief luck for me. He doesn't have enough troops to hold back the tide. Permits—hah! He didn't give one and that didn't matter. All DiCarlo can do is pray he can grab something out of the parade or make something from it. No, what DiCarlo will watch tomorrow is his funeral procession."

"Stay away."

"Got to say good-bye to the chief, Jack." Her smile

wasn't happy. "So do you. After it's over, we'll bury him. Everybody wants it, even the commission's biggest backer, my father-in-law."

"I know," said Cain.

"Keep up the pressure on DiCarlo," Cain's New York boss had telephoned to him the day of Catherine's funeral. "Don't worry about the mayor. Deal with Johnny Maxx if you can, but he's not the priority. Our client is pleased— though he noted you've been less than cooperative through- out this whole affair."

"You want DiCarlo nailed, too," she told him.

"But not like this," said Cain.

"This is Stealtown, Jack," she said, and he heard how she spelled it. "What did you expect?"

He shook his head, turned his back to her. He reached out to give the merry-go-round a spin; his hand fell away.

"Why did you come here today, Jack?" she asked.

He turned slowly to face her.

"For you," he said.

"You should have gone to Beth," she said, and he winced.

"I want you," he said.

"And Beth wants you," said Sylvia.

"So do you," was his reply.

Sylvia looked away. He saw her blue eyes glisten.

"Beth doesn't come from where we do," said Cain. "She's been lucky. Smart. She's never had to live with a bad bar- gain. She can't understand that, so she can't touch me. When I touch her, there's not enough."

"But she's great. And she's what you can get."

"Damn it!" he yelled. "I'm through taking what I can get and liking it! I'll take it, use it if I have to and . . .

"My whole damn life. No tears. No complaints. No illusions. I took the world on its *real* terms and made it! I wouldn't be part of it, but I did what I had to do. I watched my step, took what they said I could get and now I've got nothing to show for it but that same damn world! For once, I want some illusions, I want some dreams. I want more than the slag the world says I can get."

He paused, out of breath.

Somewhere in the city, a police siren wailed.

"What do you want from me?" asked Sylvia.

"Walk with me."

"As what? Your reward? Your redemption? Your—"

"As you, damn it! Who you really are."

"Because . . ."

"Because we care about each other, because that's the best dream, because it could work, because there's never been enough for you *their* way: Elliot, the booze, the men, the babies. You took the bad bargain, took what they said you could get. Well it was a losing hand all along. There's nothing you can do to make it better."

"Except play it out."

"What'll that get you?"

She shrugged. "Maybe self-respect. What are you promising me?"

"Not a goddamned thing," he said. "Except it won't be this town."

"I owe my husband and son . . ."

"You've *paid*. Elliot paid, too. Call it clean. He's got a better chance without you anyway.

"And your son . . . What he does, he'll do on his own. From what I've seen, he thinks everybody owes him and he'll never stop trying to collect. You give him anything, he'll steal it all."

"I'm responsible for him."

"Maybe for giving him life. But not for what he's doing with it."

"What do you see in me, Jack?"

"We're alike. To our bones. To our dust."

"If that's true, it's worthless."

"It's true," he said, "and it's worth everything.

"This town," continued Cain, "you were right: it's the heart of the world. But there's a flame inside the heart. That's where the good comes from. We spent too many years caught up in the heartbeat without reaching for the flame. We've got to stop, Sylvia. You and me. We have to finish what we have to do, then we got to leave this all behind."

"What do you mean, 'what we have to do'?"

"Survive. And beat this damn town."

"Nobody can do that, Jack."

"We have to try. Or we wasted all those years just being beating hearts. We have to try, or this town keeps us forever."

"There's no place to run to, Jack. No place to hide."

"Don't you understand?" He cupped her shoulders with his hands. "Running and hiding is what we've been doing! I'm through with that. This town is the heart of the world, this is where I have to start, take a stand. Just as soon as . . ."

"Just as soon as *what*, Jack? As soon as a magic tomorrow comes?"

"Yes or no?" he said. "I have to know."

"Who do you want me to hurt?" she cried. "How much? What price . . .

"You want me to run tonight? Yes, I'll go. Now, right now!"

"We can't," he said. "I've got to finish . . ."

"*See!*" she said. "That's right. You've *got to.* Something else. Something more than me. Or you. Or us."

"That's the way it is if it's right!" he said. "If we run away now, what we didn't finish will haunt us."

"So," she said, shaking off his grasp. "Not now. Not until Jack Cain finishes whatever it is he—"

"Just a few days," he interrupted. "We can make it, we can hold on, we can get ready, then . . ."

"Then whatever it is you'll have done will be part of the price, too. Now I can afford a ticket with you. What about then?"

"Then, too."

She slid into his arms, her forehead against his chest. He felt her body sob and her tears soak through his shirt.

"Go now," she said. "Let's go now."

"There'll still be this damn town."

"There always was. There always will be. You said it yourself: it's the heart of the world."

"We've got to fight it. For once."

"It'll never be just for once."

He didn't answer her.

"I don't understand what you're doing here, Jack," she

said. "I don't understand how or why, who you think you owe, but . . ."

"Once I'd have said I owed it to a busted-up guy who wanted decent work and a square deal . . ."

"Who . . ."

". . . but who I really owe is me," said Jack.

"And what will I owe?" she asked. "Not now, but then: what will you cost me then?"

She pushed away, ran back to the house.

Unfinished
Business

LIKE A BLEEDING EYE, the sun hung above the western rim of Steeltown's valley, drenching the city with crimson light and long shadows.

Cain jerked his car to a stop at the curb in front of his apartment building. He slammed the car door shut, ran up the steps.

The desk clerk watched Cain push through the glass doors.

"Messages for me?" snapped Cain.

"No," said the clerk, a pale man in a black suit and tie.

"You sure?" said Cain.

The clerk replied with a disinterested stare.

Cain marched into the elevator and punched his floor button until the doors slid shut. He paced inside the ascending machine.

Fading sunlight gave Cain's room a rosy hue and showed him he was alone. He threw his sports coat on the bed. He switched on the window air-conditioning unit; machinery grumbled and a cool, artificial cloud floated across his chest. On the other side of the glass, he saw the city.

This is where I am, he thought, then words lost their power of focus. He pulled himself away from the glass, stood trembling, hesitant and confused, then stormed from his apartment.

One minute later, he knocked on Beth's door.

Knocked again.

"Who is it?" came her muffled voice from behind the wood.

"Me," he muttered back. "Me."

"Jack?" she asked.

He nodded, then realized she couldn't see him, said, "Yes."

A key turned in the lock; the chain unhooked and dangled against the wood. The door swung inward.

"I didn't expect you," she said as he came inside, as the door shut and locked behind him. She smiled a secret to herself."

She wore a buttoned, faded denim shirt that hung to her naked thighs. Her feet were bare and her auburn hair was wound in a bun. A slick sheen glistened on her long legs, her face. A brown glow colored her skin. She smelled of something sweet and familiar.

"I've been on the roof," she said, apologetically. "After that meeting, there was nothing I could ... I came back here, decided, I don't know ... I couldn't stand the idea of being locked *inside* anymore, it's so hot, and ... sunbathing. Haven't done that in years."

Over her shoulder, on the bed, he saw a bottle of baby oil. And a black bikini top.

"Where ... where did you go?" She asked the question as if she were afraid of the answer. "You left Boswell's so quickly after the meeting I didn't get a chance to ..."

"Unfinished business," he muttered.

"Everywhere," she said, with sarcasm she meant to amuse.

She stepped back, moved deeper into the apartment, suddenly self-conscious as he noticed the sway of her breasts beneath the shirt. She felt the denim brush against her nipples, and she blushed.

"I ... ah ..." she said, then stopped.

Beth glanced out the window. The skyline cut the burning red sun in half. Shadows flowed across her walls. She snapped on a lamp.

"It's getting dark," she said.

Cain's voice was raspy, strained, as he said, "What do you want?"

"Me?" Her tone was light, nervous: again she used sarcasm to amuse and relieve tension. "All I can get."

He shook his head.

Anger and fear walk hand in hand; he heard them both
as she said: "What is this all about?"

He moved toward her, like a mountain commanded by
a force more powerful than its own great weight. Inches
away, he stopped, stared at her face.

"Jack," she whispered, barely able to find the air to
speak; her heart raced.

His hands grabbed her shoulders—so quick, so hard her
breath flew away as he pulled her close and pressed his
mouth against hers, forced his tongue between her lips. She
lost all sense of time until he pushed her away. She gasped
for air. His hands dropped from her shoulders, squeezed her
breasts. He grabbed her shirt lapels and jerked them apart:
the buttons ripped off, flew across the room; one ricocheted
off a wall, the others fell silently to the carpet. He pulled the
shirt open and down off her shoulders, entangling her arms
at her sides. Her breasts were bare, heavy like melons and
slick with sweat and baby oil; her areolas were giant brown
circles with small nipples; when he ran his hands up her
trembling stomach, brushed them with his fingers, they
swelled like crimson pearls.

"Oh!" she whispered. "Please, Jack, I . . ."

His mouth covered hers again, blocking her words into
cries, whimpers. His left hand pressed between her shoulder
blades, his right hand rubbed her breasts, her stomach, her
thighs. She felt him rub her groin: the bikini's black triangle
of cloth separated their flesh. He pushed his fingers under
the strap, jerked; jerked again. The cord dug into her leg
and then the catch ripped free and he threw the bottoms
from her. He kissed her cheeks, her mouth, her hair, her
neck. Cupped her groin. His right hand circled round her
naked buttocks, pulled her hips to his and she felt him hard
and hungry as he ground against her. She struggled to free
her hands from the shirt, twisting and turning as he half-
dragged, half-carried her toward the bed.

The bun in her hair loosened. Auburn strands fell across
her face, down the side of her neck. As her calves brushed

against the edge of the bed, he stopped, leaned back and stared at her. Their chests heaved.

His left hand pressed against her shoulders as his right hand unfastened his belt, undid his pants. Gravity pulled at the weight in his pockets and his pants fell to the floor. She felt him shift from leg to leg, guessed he pushed off his shoes, stepped clear of the trousers.

She freed herself from her shirt just as his right hand floated toward her head. He hesitated; then brushed the hair from her face.

She stared at him; her eyes cooled, cleared.

Then she shook her head from side to side and her hair came completely free; it swung out, great floating waves of reddish brown. Her scent mingled with the baby oil and sweat and the tang from her loins.

She nervously unbuttoned his shirt as his hands stroked her groin, her thighs, squeezed and pressed her breasts, her nipples tickling his palms; as his fingers buried themselves in her hair. She got his shirt off and kissed him as he lifted her up, back, down, to the bed.

He was on her, his knees spreading her legs apart, his weight riding her as she arched her hips up to meet him.

Words and images and desires rolled through her like waves, jumbling up until all she could do was moan, call his name as he kissed her neck, rose up above her, her breasts overflowing his kneading hands. He pressed his mouth to her right nipple, sucked it between his lips and she thought her breast would explode.

She was slick and slippery with baby oil, so her skin slid beneath his touch, lubricating his flesh, too. Her stomach quivered against his cheek. He crawled back along the bed, down it and off, pulling her with him as he kissed her navel, the line of hair she kept waxed low for her bikini. He twisted to kneel on the floor as he lifted her hips and kissed her fire, her dampness.

"Jack!"

She lost track of time—a minute, an hour, she didn't know. She shuddered, lost herself, shuddered again. He pushed her back up on the bed, spread her thighs wide and she felt him thrust inside her. Again and again and again, a steady, demanding rhythm, his weight propelling them up and down with the bed.

"Please! Yes! Jack!"

Again, she shuddered. Again.

And then he pulled out of her, away. Panic filled her but he straddled her stomach, hard and erect as he rubbed against her breasts. She slid down the bed to meet him, took him in her mouth; his fingers twisted in her hair.

His breaths came in harsh, rasping gasps. She held him close with her hands, her lips, caressed him with her tongue. She set the motion, the touch.

He pulled back, away; her eyes opened wide, but before she could speak, he rolled her to her stomach, pressed himself flat along her back, rubbed himself over her oil-slick skin, moved down until he knelt behind her. He guided her knees forward until her legs were tucked up beneath her stomach and she knelt with her rounded hips high in the air.

"Oh God! Oh Jack!"

At first, she thought she would rip apart as he pushed himself inside where she'd never had any man and it hurt and then it didn't and she was full and he was draped over her, his hands cupped round her body, lifting her breasts from the bed, reaching down and seeking—finding her where she was wet and empty and she shuddered and she didn't know why or how.

"Jack!" she cried; then, from someplace far away: *"Jimmy!"*

He rose, his hands sliding up her flanks, cupping her buttocks as he looked down at her curved back, her auburn hair billowed across the bed; he looked down at her and at them.

And suddenly he was free; it took him and he let go, faster, deeper. He exploded, cried out, and sent his seed where it could spawn no sons to inherit unfinished business.

"At least you weren't thinking of her," said Beth, finally.

She lay across Cain's chest, both of them naked. Except for the lamp she'd turned on earlier, the room was dark with the night. Their shelter was close, the air hot and thick.

"You couldn't have been," continued Beth. "At least, not this time."

Afterward, he'd rolled away. She'd turned and pulled herself across him, whispered *Jack!* and mouthed endearments she dared not speak. Her hair covered them like a shawl. His arm draped casually over her shoulder. She felt her flesh rapidly cool as the sweat evaporated. Then the heat of the room warmed them again, and her skin grew sticky. With her ear pressed against his chest, she heard his heart slow to a steady beat. His breath come in easy, deep draws that moved his rib cage against the swell of her breasts. Twice she heard car horns in the street, once the elevator in the hall. After what must have been half an hour, she was overwhelmed by his silence; only then had she spoken.

When she finished those last words, a trapdoor fell open beneath her; she dropped through the hole, tumbled. She was trying to decided whether she could or should get off the bed, what else to say, when Cain finally spoke.

"You're right," he said.

"Why . . ." She bit her lip, let it go and asked, "Why did you do this?"

Even after all his silence, he needed a few moments to find his answer.

"Because I could," he told her. "Because I wanted to. Because I had to."

"What . . . what about me?"

"You, too," he said.

"That's . . ." she started, then couldn't hold her thesis.

Warm tears rolled from her eyes, lightly tapped his chest. They mingled with his sweat, with the oil smears from her.

"It wasn't going to be like this," she whispered.

"It could be worse," he said.

Beth sobbed.

Gained control of herself—enough to force quiet and calm for then and there, for now.

"It's time for you to go," she said. "Isn't it."

"Yes," he said.

Nothing changed for five minutes.

Then Cain slid his arm from beneath her, eased away. Her head settled on the mattress. Her hair clung to him as he slid off the bed, crackled with static electricity, then fell back, beautiful and long and auburn.

He dressed quietly.

She lay curled on the bed, still, silent.

Cain glanced out to the street-lit city, checked his watch: 8:47.

The air was so thick he had trouble breathing. He touched the aluminum-boxed window unit.

Staring out the window, Cain said, "Do you want me to put the air-conditioner on?"

On the bed, she didn't move.

A car honked in the street below.

"Don't say anything else," she whispered, her face hidden beneath her hair.

Cain hesitated, then flipped the switch on the machine. The motor chugged to life, cool air filtered into the room. She would feel the chill within minutes. He turned on his heel, forced himself to walk slowly, resolutely past the bed, his eyes intent on the door. He checked the lock, turned the knob, and stepped through the portal to the world. He closed the door behind him and heard the lock click.

A dozen steps down the carpeted hall brought him to the elevator with its shiny aluminum doors. Swinging doors of the stairwell filled the opposite wall, beneath the red EXIT sign. Cain punched the button to summon the machine that promised to take him anywhere it could go. He stood slumped in his shoes, his eyes glazed, his shoulders and chest heavy, his head hanging low. In the smudged aluminum elevator doors, he saw a blurry reflection he barely recognized and cared for not at all.

Clanging and groaning, the elevator started its climb to where he waited.

Too late Cain heard the *whirr* of the hinge on the fire door. Too late he felt the rush of wind as behind him the door swung open. As he started to turn, the sap smashed into the back of his head.

And all was fire and blackness.

Hell

TERRIBLE SWEET SMELL: PUTRID HAM, damp rocks. World spinning. Hot. Throbbing head starting to clear. Cain felt pinching on his wrists, his arms rising.

Laying down, he thought: Flat on my face on bumpy, wet hardness, my arms floating up . . .

Bracelets of fire pulled at his wrists. His arms strained above his prone body. His shoulders ached. His chest came off the ground, then his stomach. Inches at a time, he was jerked upright. As his waist scraped off the earth, he realized he could see.

A skeleton wearing a woman's dusty red wig lay on a bed of rocks four feet from Cain's face. The bones wore a crusted black bikini.

Vomit and bile surged through Cain and he was sick.

His mind reeled as his body rose, his knees dragging across rocks. The aching pull on his arms eased as he staggered upright. He breathed deep and tried to lower his hands but *something* held them to the sky.

Only there was no sky.

A stone womb surrounded Cain. He stood in a sphere of gold light made by flickering candles. The carved rock walls were tattooed with the veins of time. Thousands of stones ranging from boulders to pebbles made the floor. Handcuffs secured his wrists; a white cord tied to their chain passed over a wooden ceiling beam as thick as a man's body. The cord angled down and to his rear. In the blackness beyond the light, he heard water dripping, the scamper of claws on stone, a squeak.

"Welcome to hell, Cain," said a man behind him.

Cain turned toward the voice.

Johnny Maxx.

His expensive black suit was filthy. The knot in his tie dangled above the top button of his open vest. Sweat and dust matted his shirt. Johnny pulled on the white line tied to the handcuffs, sidestepped along the stone floor. Cain slid down the length of the beam.

"Come on," said Johnny. "I ain't gonna stand in your puke."

Johnny pulled Cain to the middle of the thirty-foot beam, then tied the cord around a boulder. Cain hung, unable to slide either direction, his toes grazing the floor enough to take only some of his weight. His wrists, arms, shoulder joints, ankles—all ached.

Sweat covered Johnny's face. He gingerly touched his left side. Cain wondered if it was the light that made him seem pale.

"You know what hell is, Cain?" rasped Johnny. "Hell is where there's only truth."

Johnny shuffled toward Cain. When their faces were a foot apart, Johnny smiled.

Then smashed his fist into Cain's stomach.

"We're gonna make sure you fit right in," said Johnny as Cain retched and gasped for air.

When he could speak, Cain nodded toward the bikini-clad skeleton.

"Who's that?" he asked.

"That's Vera." Johnny's grin matched the skeleton's. "A real good friend of mine. Helped out on a big deal a few years ago. She did her part just fine, but she was the nervous kind. Inclined to talk 'bout what was on her mind.

"Guess who else is here!" cried Johnny. He spun Cain to the right.

Against the rock wall slumped the body of a man. The corpse wore its moldy business suit like a tent. What flesh remained on the face was leathery, tattered and torn. The

eyes were gone. A rifled briefcase lay close to the corpse's
twisted hand.

"Why, it's Wolinsky!" said Johnny Maxx. "Everybody
has been looking for him since the feds raided his house—
and here he is, just waiting for them to search hell.

"He could talk, too," said Johnny Maxx, "though he'd
have been smarter about it than Vera. He'd have made a
deal—if he'd been found by people who make talkin' the
lesser of two troubles.

"He was a pal of mine who worked for me, a guy who
could have told about my business. He promised me that
wasn't what he wanted, and I believed him. But I knew him,
too. So I promised I'd take him where he could hide out
until it was all clear. Told him Vera'd be there, too."

With a shrug and a coy grin, Johnny Maxx continued.

" 'Course, I didn't 'splain quite how she looks these
days. I figured that wouldn't matter to Wolinsky. He was
never picky. He liked being taken care of. I promised him I'd
do that. Johnny Maxx keeps his promises."

Johnny closed his black eyes. Cain couldn't tell if the
gesture came from Johnny's body or his soul.

Those black eyes opened again.

"Hell's a cozy place, isn't it?" said Johnny.

"Mine shaft," said Cain. His mouth was dry.

"That's right!" cried Johnny, genuinely pleased. "That's
the truth, just like I said is what is spoken in hell. It's a
mine shaft.

"Deep one, too," he continued. "There's thousands of
miles of shafts and tunnels honeycombing under Steeltown.
But there ain't no worker bees any more. There ain't no
queen—'less you count Vera. There's just you and me.

"Look thataway," said Johnny, pointing off to Cain's
right.

Cain turned his head. In the blackness beyond this cavern, he saw a distant, baseball-size glow of white light.

"Lots of shafts lead out of this room," said Johnny.
"Only one of them goes to the world. I played in these
places as a kid. More'n once I spent a day lost. Nobody
would have looked for me here, even if there'd 've been

somebody who cared. These places aren't safe, but that's never worried me. Does it worry you?"

Cain didn't answer.

"That's right," continued Johnny. "Don't worry. Not now, 'cause this is where you live, with Vera and Wolinsky. And the others.

"You weigh a hell of a lot more than you look," said Johnny, shaking his head. " 'Course, this isn't my best time for carryin'. Had to drag you part of the way. Lucky most of it was downhill."

He grinned. Cain kept his face impassive.

Johnny nodded to the distant light. "Electric beacon, so I won't take a wrong turn on the way out. No wrong turns for Johnny. He don't go where he don't want to."

"So I see," said Cain.

"Not yet," said Johnny, "because you're thinking that that's how you're gonna leave. Or that that's the way some angel'll sneak down here to rescue you. But you're wrong, Cain, you're wrong and you shouldn't be wrong because you've already passed through the shadows of the valley. This is hell where only truth is allowed."

Johnny's right hand fumbled beneath his left lapel, then emerged as a fist carefully wrapped around a fragile treasure. The fist turned palm up a foot from Cain's face. The fingers opened.

In Johnny's hand Cain saw a pair of bent black metal frame glasses. A jagged, marble-size hole marred the plastic left lens; a hole and dried reddish scum.

"He was quick," whispered Johnny Maxx. "And he was good. He was your shadow, Cain. All men like you got to have a shadow. I looked for him, found him. Now you're in hell and you've lost your shadow."

Carefully, Johnny bent the glasses' hooked bows around Cain's ears, adjusted the mangled frame on his face.

"Now you can see the truth," said Johnny as Cain stared at him through the smudged plastic and jagged hole. "Now you know."

He smiled, then slammed his knee into Cain's groin.

Johnny stumbled backward as Cain twisted and whirled

on the beam. Johnny regained his footing first. As Cain raised his head, gasped, Johnny said:

"Aren't you glad I waited until you had your turn with Beth?"

No vomit remained in Cain. His wrists were slick inside the handcuffs' steel bite. He blinked, and through the mangled glasses watched Johnny walk backward, lean against a boulder.

"Is Beth as good as she looks?" asked Johnny. He laughed. "She throws off a lot of heat, don't she? Soon as things settle down, I'll have to find out what she's really like."

Again, Johnny's right hand slid beneath his left lapel. This time his fist emerged wrapped around the butt of a .38 Police Special revolver. Johnny laid the pistol on the boulder, reached around to his hip pocket, brought out a blackjack, and laid it beside the gun.

"Yeah," said Johnny again. He wiped his brow. "He was quick, and he was good."

With his left hand, Johnny pulled aside his coat and vest. A sticky, rusty streak soiled his shirt between his ribs and his kidney.

"But not smart enough," said Johnny. "Did he cost a lot?"

"Wasn't my tab," replied Cain.

"But your team," said Johnny.

"Guess so."

"Know so," Johnny told him. "Know so.

"Don't worry about my side," he added. "Bullet made a clean scrape. I've had to carry a lot bigger hurts. I was in the Marines."

"*Semper fi*," whispered Cain.

"That's right!" said Johnny. "You in the Corps, too?"

"No."

"Army? Navy?"

Cain shook his head to each question, tried to slow his breathing, relax, save his strength.

"Hell, boy," said Johnny. "How'd you serve your country?"

"I flunked."

Johnny laughed. His pleasure echoed off the stone walls.

"What time is it?" asked Cain.

"It's now," Johnny told him. "It's now."

"Is this where Debbi will end up, too?" said Cain.

Johnny picked up the blackjack and marched across the stones.

"Debbi is my woman," he said, his breath hot on Cain's face. "She ain't my business. She ain't yours, either. No way, no how. You even *mention* her again, you're gonna be in a world of trouble. Understand me, Cain?"

The blackjack smashed into Cain's thigh; on the back-swing, Johnny smashed Cain's other leg. Cain's legs turned to rubber and he screamed.

"Yeah, you understand me," said Johnny. He stepped back.

"God, you got awful breath!" complained Johnny. He dropped the blackjack in his suit jacket pocket. "You thirsty?"

Cain nodded.

Johnny shuffled across the lit cavern. Near the edge of the light, he abruptly stopped, hunched over in wary antici-pation. Quietly, with his eyes aimed into the darkness, he bent to pick up a rock. He listened intently, then whipped the stone into the black void.

"Rats," he said to Cain, though his eyes watched the flight path of his missle. Johnny chuckled. "There used to be this guy . . ."

"Rat Man," said Cain. "Lived over on Broadway."

Slowly, carefully, Johnny turned to stare at the man he'd hung from a mine beam.

"Well now," said Johnny. "How'd you know that?"

He lifted a whiskey bottle from behind a boulder.

"Seems we got a whole lot more to talk about than I figured," he said, walking toward Cain, unscrewing the bot-tle cap.

"Here," he said, tilting the bottle to Cain's lips. "Rinse first—and spit over there: don't hit the suit.

"Sorry it's cheap bourbon," he said as he trickled brown liquid into Cain's mouth. "It's Wolinsky's, and he had lousy taste.

"Course," he said, smiling as Cain rinsed, "it's had a chance to age since he brought it down here."

Johnny Maxx laughed, tilted the bottle so Cain could drink.

"Is that okay?" asked Johnny.

The bourbon stung Cain's mouth, burned when it hit his empty stomach. Johnny took a pull from the bottle and walked back to sit next to the gun on the boulder.

Before Johnny could speak, Cain said, "I don't get your deal here. You're too smart for this."

"You *are* a piece of work, aren't you, Jack? We aren't here to talk about *my* deal."

He'll never cut me down alive, thought Cain.

"You come to town" said Johnny, "and next thing, I got trouble and so do my friends Harry and His Honor. Took me ten seconds to figure your game, set us against each other and you pick off the last one standing."

"So you went bush-league and tried to bomb me," said Cain; thought to himself, got to get him close.

Johnny rubbed his side and took a drink from the bottle.

"When I want you dead," he said, "you're dead."

"What do you want, Johnny?"

"I"m gonna get it all, thanks to you," he said; pointed the bottle to the rock ceiling. "Up there, everybody's fighting everybody. Doesn't matter why anymore. Doesn't matter who. The only way to keep from getting shot is to not be in the war at all.

"Me and Wolinsky: everybody wants to hang something on us, but we're not around. If I'm not there, they can't get me, so they'll get each other. After everybody else is down— and after you and me sort out who's done what to who and why—I'll come back, square what they've forgotten, and sweep 'em up. Then it'll be back to business as usual.

"Thanks a lot, Cain," he said. "Here's to you."

Johnny Maxx drank from the whiskey bottle, rubbed his side.

"And you figure Debbi is gonna be up there just waiting for you," said Cain.

The bottle slowly lowered from Johnny's face. He pointed the fifth at Cain.

"I told you once: don't mention her. Not much time left

to learn how the world works, Cain. Don't waste it making mistakes."

"No mistakes," said Cain, praying that was true. "She went to Central High, didn't she?"

He let that truth soak in; paused to let the power surge into his next assertion.

"So did I," said Cain. "So did you, before me."

"Wait a minute," said Johnny. He passed his hand across his brow, stared at the man dangling before him. "That night at dinner, I remember . . . You reminded me of baseball. Do I know you?"

"Us guys from Central," said Cain, "we all know about Debbi."

Johnny stretched his neck. He set the bottle on the ground and walked toward Cain.

Take the pain, thought Cain. Through Nick Malone's gunshot lenses, he watched Johnny draw closer. Take the pain and . . .

Johnny's right jab to Cain's stomach blew his breath away. A left hook hit the same place.

The gangster's fists were sledgehammers. Dangling from the cord, Cain would twist one way with a blow, then its companion twisted him the other, like a spinning puppet. The smack of fist against flesh, Cain's cries that became whimpers, all were echos lost down dark mine shafts.

Up from the stomach to the ribs, to the chest: Johnny Maxx used Cain like a punching bag. A blow like lightning above Cain's heart blacked him out. He came to just before Johnny hit his face. That punch grazed Cain's jaw and expended most of its force on his breastbone. Johnny danced back, fists high, then stepped forward and flicked out two quick left jabs. The first jab snapped Cain's face upright. The second landed in the hollow beneath Cain's right cheekbone. The black metal glasses had slipped: Johnny's fist drove the metal into Cain's flesh—and gouged his own knuckles. Blood spurted from Cain. Johnny danced back, dodged the spray.

As Cain fought to stay conscious, Johnny examined his left fist: he sucked the bruised and cut knuckle.

For a minute, Cain knew nothing other than swirling

black pain. Jackhammers dug inside his skull. He opened his eyes.

Saw Johnny Maxx standing a yard away, the bottle of bourbon tilted up to his lips. The bottle lowered. Cain made his eyes droop.

"Wake up!" yelled Johnny. He swirled bourbon in his mouth, spit it in Cain's face.

The alcohol hit Cain's cuts; he jerked from the sting.

Saw Johnny standing just that same yard away, the bottle slowly tilting up again; the black eyes automatically closing.

One chance.

Keeping as still as possible, Cain settled as much of his weight as he could in his feet. His fingers flexed as he saw Johnny's Adam's apple bob.

Cain grabbed the cord, pulled with all the strength in his arms and pushed off the ground. As he sprang, Cain curled his knees toward his chest, then kicked out, his heels aimed at the astonished face behind the lowering bottle of bourbon.

The bottle crashed to the floor. Johnny's hands parted Cain's feet and the gangster twisted between them. Cain's momentum carried him forward. His crotch hit the wedge of Johnny's upper right arm. Cain locked his legs around Johnny in a scissors vice just as he reached the limit of flight allowed by the cord and the ceiling beam.

When physics jerked Cain back, he pulled Johnny off his feet. The weight of the two men against the cord tore at Cain's shoulders and arms. The handcuffs cut deeper into his wrists. But Cain kept his legs locked tightly around Johnny's upper body.

Johnny's hands couldn't reach the blackjack in his pocket, couldn't reach his second revolver in its shoulder holster under his right arm, couldn't find a grip on the legs that trapped him.

With a bellow, Johnny scrambled to his feet. He was beyond thought, beyond strategy, or he would have let Cain hold him until the man's arms pulled out of their sockets or his legs lost their grip. By standing, he settled Cain lower over his arms. When Johnny tried to rip Cain's legs with his teeth, his mouth couldn't reach Cain's flesh.

Back and forth, Johnny staggered, Cain angling out from him like a twisting, cruelly joined Siamese twin.

The cord held the stress of the two fighting men. But the loop, worked and worried by the struggle, shifted on the rock. The line went slack as Johnny staggered one way. When Johnny jerked back the other direction, the loop slid off the rock.

They crashed to the ground, Cain astraddle Johnny. Cain's knees hit the stones. He screamed. His hips slammed into Johnny's side, over the gunshot wound. The shock knocked Johnny's breath away; pain blurred his mind.

Cain thrust his manacled hands toward Johnny's face: thumbs for his eyes, hands for his throat, Cain didn't care.

But Johnny's hands caught the chain between Cain's wrist. Cain's palms slapped shut as though in prayer, trapping Johnny's fingers and pinching his flesh with police metal. Johnny yelled, pushed up at the madman reaching for his face.

As Cain's fingers brushed his nose, Johnny kicked: his right leg slammed into Cain's back. He kicked again. The third time, he kicked with both legs and curled at his hips. His ankles thudded into Cain's shoulders, his heels gripped Cain's face.

Johnny snapped his legs down. Cain flew backwards, a somersault that sent him sprawling across the cavern. The jerk tore at Johnny's stomach muscles, at his wound.

The stones pulled at Cain as he scrambled, his back to Johnny. He sprawled forward: up to his feet and manacled hands, to a staggered run as he heard Johnny yell.

Ahead was the boulder where Johnny'd sat.

Where Johnny laid his pistol.

Behind Cain came a madman, a fury, who charged his prey only ten feet away. The madman saw Cain lunge forward, bend, and whirl. Cain cocked the revolver and fired all six rounds: two hit Johnny in the chest, one tore through his stomach. The momentum of his charge kept him on his feet and he slammed into Cain, knocking him down. Johnny fell on Cain, pinned him on his back so they lay like lovers,

the empty gun useless in Cain's hand, Johnny's blood streaming between them. Johnny shuddered, gasped. Something in
his chest gurgled and his weight sank through Cain.

For thirty seconds Cain lay frozen beneath his burden;
for another thirty he struggled to push it off him, then rolled
away.

How long he lay on the floor, he didn't know. When he
realized where he was, he tore the glasses from his face and
hurled them into the darkness. He crawled to Johnny's body,
searched the pockets until he found the handcuff key. His
fingers were numb, weak. Blood covered his hands. It took
him a minute to unlock the handcuffs.

Standing proved difficult. The fall from the beam, the
fight, the beating, whatever had happened when Johnny
dragged his unconscious form: his knee suffered from all
that. But he could stand, limp.

Cain glanced at his new watch: guaranteed unbreakable
and waterproof, it's crystal was shattered, its hands were
bent and frozen, its digital display blank.

"It's now," Cain said aloud. "It's now."

A whirlpool of dizziness almost sucked him to the floor.
He tripped over Vera's skeleton. The bones rattled as the
body curled into a new position. The red wig fell from the
skull. As he staggered back, Cain glanced beyond her bones.
Propped on a boulder, he saw the rotting soles of a man's
shoes.

Cain fled toward the white glow at the end of the tunnel. Behind him, paws scurried over stone.

The first beacon led him to another, the second to a
third. The path rolled like a wave, only it was jagged rocks
he scrambled over and the ultimate angle was uphill. The
air was thick, hot. Damp yet dusty. The third beacon put
him in a tunnel that emptied into a cavern lit by electric
candles. Cain found a cot, a flashlight, cases of batteries and
candles, a cooking stove, camping supplies, a case of beer,
boxes with men's clothes. In a first aid tin he found a bottle
of aspirin, took seven, washing them down with warm bot-
tled water. He picked up a monogrammed shirt: *J.M.*

But he found no clock, and cursed himself for not taking

Johnny's watch. He grabbed the flashlight, followed the one shaft leading out of that cavern.

He imagined that twisting, turning journey on a rocky uphill slope as lasting a half hour or a lifetime: time lost its measure in that tunnel.

Then suddenly he smelled it: earth—not the stones all around him, not underground dampness and heat, but *earth*, dirt, green life and the surface of the world. Clean, fresh air.

He stumbled; found he could shuffle faster. Through the tunnel, watch out for that stone, left, left again, right . . .

Ahead, filtering down like falling snow, a shaft of white light. *Sunlight.* Leaning against the wall, a wooden ladder.

He grabbed the rungs. The wood was strong and solid in his grasp. When he looked up, he saw sunlight streaming through the cracks of wood planking.

Cain started to climb.

Independence
Day

THE LADDER LED TO A TRAPDOOR that opened into a cluttered
shed behind a ramshackle house. The shed had a solid lock.
Cain cursed himself for not searching Johnny for more keys.
He rummaged through the shed, found an old claw hammer
and beat and pried the door open.

No one looked out of the house's broken windows.

No one peered out of the other homes on the block.

He staggered to the street, knocked over an aluminum
garbage can that clattered down the road. Cars lined the
curb: a key he hadn't taken from Johnny might have commanded one of them. Cain limped to the first house that
looked inhabited, banged on the front door.

No one answered his knock.

Despite the clamor he made, no one looked out of the
other houses. No sounds of television or radio drifted from
these homes. Doors were locked, shades pulled down.

The sun beat on him from what he remembered as the east.

Morning, he decided. Must be morning. July fourth.

The street he was on led toward the center of town.
With all the speed he could muster, he shuffled forward.

No traffic on the street, cars parked and locked. Dogs
cowering behind white picket fences. Cats hiding. Empty
swing sets. And silence—no breeze disturbed the trees. Sweat
soaked through his shirt before he'd gone two blocks. The
air was thick and wet, the light glaring. Summer's greenery
smelled baked.

Five blocks later he saw a tow truck pull away from a service station. Cain waved his arms frantically, but either the driver didn't look in his mirrors or he didn't care to stop for what he saw.

The white-walled gas station was locked. A hand-inked sign taped to the glass door read, Closed for the Parade.

His reflection stared at him from the blue-toned, plate glass windows: Dark blotches of Johnny's gore stained his rumpled blue shirt, his pants. His own blood crusted on his cheek where Nick's glasses had cut him. Cain couldn't stand erect; his hands trembled.

A pay phone hung on the service station's side.

Cain searched his pockets. So had Johnny. All that remained in Cain's pants was a handkerchief.

The receiver buzzed in his ear and a sigh of gratitude escaped him. He dialed zero.

"Operator," said the woman's voice.

"Help me," whispered Cain.

"Operator," intoned the woman again.

"I need to, I need, Sylvia . . . I need ' talk to . . . Help me."

"Is this an emergency, sir?"

"I . . . Yes, I need to . . ."

"I can connect you to the police emergency number or you may dial 911 yourself, sir."

"No, I don't need . . ."

"Is this an emergency, sir?"

"Yes. No. I don't want the cops or . . ."

"What is the nature of this emergency, sir?"

"I need to talk to Sylvia Kimmett, please get me . . ."

"Sir, have you been drinking?"

Cain sighed; the taste of bourbon and bile filled his mouth.

"I need to talk to Sylvia Kimmett and . . ."

"How are you billing this call? What is the number, please?"

"I don't know her number," said Cain, "I . . ."

"Sir, this is the Operator. You want Directory Assistance. That number is 411."

"Can you connect me?"

"No," said the Operator. "Have a nice day."

The line went dead.

Cain dialed 411.

"Directory Assistance," said another woman's voice.

"Please don't hang up on me," pleaded Cain. "And don't switch me to a computer."

"Sir, this *is* Directory Assistance."

"I know. Help me. I need . . . What's Elliot Kimmett's phone number?"

"One moment please."

A second later she said, "Sir, we have three Elliot Kimmetts listed in Steeltown."

"The son," said Cain. "I want the son. Sylvia."

"There is no Sylvia Kimmett listed, sir."

"Her husband, he'd be the middle one."

"Elliot Kimmett Eye-Vee?"

"The Fourth, yes, that's him."

"Hold for the—"

"Don't!" cried Cain. "Don't give me to the machine!"

"Sir, I . . . Very well. Please note: that number is five-five-five, four-seven-three-four."

"Four-seven-three-four," repeated Cain.

"Thank you for . . ."

"Wait!" yelled Cain. "What time is it?"

"Sir, this is Directory Assistance. Time of day is eight-four-four, two-five-two-five."

"Please," he pleaded. "Can't you just look at your watch?"

She paused, then whispered low so her co-workers and supervisor wouldn't hear her: "It's eleven-oh-seven."

"Thank you! Could you, would you connect me to that number?"

"Sir," she replied, once more with her official voice, "This is Directory Assistance. You're at a pay phone."

"I don't have any money."

"You could make a collect local call," she told him.

"Yes! Let's do that! Collect call!"

"To make a collect call, you must dial zero and speak to the Operator."

Cain hung up.

He slapped the pay phone, hurt his hand and nothing

else. His eyes searched the oil-stained blacktop, the grass at the edge of the service station lot. Found nothing. He staggered to the front of the station, stared at the blue tinted windows. Through them to the steel-plated cash register. An oil barrel used as a garbage can stood between two gas pumps. Cain dumped the trash on the blacktop, then threw the barrel through the plate glass windows.

Blue glass shattered; great chunks fell from the window frame and exploded on the blacktop and inside on the linoleum floor. Cain covered his face with his arms, expected but did not hear gonging alarms. When he stepped through the window's giant hole, diamonds crunched under his shoes. He kicked the barrel out of his way.

He punched keys on the cash register dozens of times before a bell dinged and the drawer slid open. He ignored three stacks of bills, filled his pockets with silver coins. A local phone book lay on a shelf under the cash register: Cain took it.

A black telephone waited on a counter beneath a display advertising snow tires. Cain stared at that free device, then stepped through the shattered window to the pay phone.

He'd forgotten Sylvia's number, looked it up in the book. Fed the pay phone a stolen quarter, dialed.

The phone buzzed. Buzzed again. And again. He let it ring twenty, thirty times, then once for every year he'd lived. He imagined the phones in the Kimmett household: there'd be one mounted on the wall in the kitchen, one stationed in the living room and a business model in the study. One on a nightstand in the master bedroom.

And no one there who answered his call.

Cain hung up, checked a number in the phone book, spent another stolen quarter.

"Good morning," said the man who answered Cain's call. "Commodore Hotel."

"Beth Worby," said Cain.

"I'm sorry, Ms. Worby is no longer with us."

Cain leaned against the whitewashed gas station wall.

"What?" he said.

"Ms. Worby has checked out."

"When?"

"I'm not at liberty to—"

"This is Cain!"

"Ah yes, Mr. Cain. I thought that might be you."

"What do you mean, Beth's checked out?"

"First thing this morning."

"Did she go someplace or . . ."

"It's my impression she has left us permanently," said the desk clerk. "We loaded her belongings into her car. The maids have already finished cleaning her room."

"Did she . . . Was she all right?"

"She seemed somewhat tired."

"Was she . . . Did she go with someone? Anyone?"

"Quite alone."

"Did she say anything?"

"She said good-bye."

"Was there . . . Did she leave anything?"

"She left a letter for Mr. Boswell. Of course, since it's a national holiday, the mailman has not picked it up."

"What about me?"

"She left no letter for you, Mr. Cain."

"What about a note?"

"I'll check your box."

While Cain waited on hold, a five-year-old Chevy cruised past the vandalized gas station. The car didn't slow.

"Mr. Cain?" said the clerk. "There's nothing in your box. I took the liberty of inquiring with the maid. No note was left under your door or otherwise in your quarters."

"Where did she go?"

"I'm sure I don't know."

"She must have said *something*."

The man on the other end of the phone hesitated.

"Well?" demanded Cain. "What did she say? Anything!"

"Nothing, really," said the clerk. "And I'm sure she did not mean it in any impolite or disrespectful fashion. She was, as I may have mentioned, very tired. As I was helping her with her bags, I said that I hoped her stay here had been pleasant and worthwhile. She told me—muttered more to herself, really—that she'd 'gotten all Steeltown had to offer.' "

"And that's all?" asked Cain.

"Yes," said the clerk. "She actually didn't even *say* good-bye. Just drove off."

"The letter to Boswell," said Cain. "Read it to me."

"Really, Mr. Cain: Opening someone else's mail would be against the law, and one simply can't do that."

Cain slammed the phone down. He broke the connection, but missed hooking the receiver in its cradle. The receiver dropped to the earth, dangled from its cord as Cain slumped against the white walls.

Someone else had broken the lock on the men's room door. Cain flipped on the ceiling's bare bulb. The room reeked of urine and insufficient pine deodorizer. There were no paper towels, and the stopper on the filthy sink didn't work. The mirror was spotted. The toilet ran. Only the cold water tap worked. Cain washed his face as best he could with the cool stream of water, swallowed four handfuls. He dried his face with his handkerchief and stared in the cloudy mirror at a face that terrified him.

Four blocks from the gas station, he rested against a street light. He'd seen no one, not a kid, not a car, not a loose dog. The birds were silent, and clung to the trees. The sky was clear, though gray.

A new royal blue station wagon glided toward him from the direction of a shopping mall. Although the sun glistened off its windshield, he knew a woman sat behind the steering wheel. Grocery sacks filled the front and back seats. She stopped at the red light, and looked his way.

Debbi Dolan.

She looked at him with casual curiosity—he being the only person she'd seen on the back streets since she'd finished her shopping. Inside her air-conditioned comfort, she wore dark sunglasses, her dyed blond hair brushed back. The smile on her face was polite. Then she focused on Cain. On his battered face, his rust-blotted shirt, matted trousers. On what she could guess. She slumped. Her forehead dropped to the steering wheel. The light changed to green, back to red. The cycle repeated itself. She raised her head when the light was red, waited until she had permission to proceed, then drove away, without another glance at the man on the corner.

As her car disappeared over a hill, Cain trudged forward.

He heard the parade before he saw it: the murmur of a thousand voices; the tramp of thousands of work boots and sneakers and sandals on a road pockmarked with chuckholes. Invisible dust thickened the air as he moved forward, turned a corner . . .

At the end of the block, a river of men and women and children marched beneath a July sun. The sidewalk that paralleled the parade was empty. Today there were no spectators.

He'd found the tail of the parade; its head was blocks away, snaking toward the city square. Behind the marchers rolled a black-and-white sheriff's department cruiser, red lights spinning. Inside the sheriff's car, Cain saw Joe and his partner. The deputies who'd shaken him down the day he arrived in the city kept glancing over their shoulders at the city police cruiser piloted by DiCarlo's men that crept behind them, shotgun poking up from the dash, emergency lights off, siren silent, driver and partner ready and waiting.

Cain ran along the empty sidewalk; his stumbling gait was faster than the crowd tramping toward the same destination.

In the crowd a woman laughed. Cain saw the whore with albino hair, with a man on each arm. The crowd shifted; she was gone.

He heard the distant band. If they played a tune, it had no name or its name had been lost in the playing. Sometimes Cain heard horns, sometimes cymbals or bells, but over all came the steady, marching beat of drums. He ran faster.

A Mets cap caught Cain's eye; beneath it marched the cabby who'd driven Cain into town and warned him how to spell *Stealtown*.

Exhaustion and pain overwhelmed Cain. He stumbled, slowed, stopped, leaned against the brick wall of a boarded-up building.

His legs shook, acid ate at his knee. His head throbbed so much he could barely hold a thought. The sun sealed his eyes and baked his front, bricks pushed against his back. Grit choked him. There was nothing for his hands to grasp.

As he sucked in a deep breath, his eyes fluttered open. In the sun's glare and dirty air, he saw the grizzled steelworker who'd delivered more money than he'd earn in years to a stranger's hotel room. That honest man marched forward, faithfully part of the parade.

Cain pushed off the wall, ran again.

Though he was bloodstained, battered, and clearly possessed of a purpose beyond their shared direction, no one in the crowd cared about Cain. Those who looked at him saw what they wanted. Some people laughed as he passed them by, pointed but with a gesture that lacked authority. Some people turned away. Since he didn't impede their progress, most of the crowd ignored him, like the bow-tied city clerk who stared at him as though Cain were made of glass.

Two blocks from the city square the crowd slowed to a crawl and overflowed to the sidewalks. Cain twisted his way through mingling bodies.

And then he was in the square, pressed against a building. A child called, "Mommy!" Someone cursed. A man laughed. Cain made his way toward a beer stand where hands reached from the crowd to grab sloppily filled cups and never mind any nonsense about tickets. The crowd surged against the wooden booth and it collapsed. Lumber crashed. Someone cried out in pain and someone else swore. A girl giggled; mirth rippled through the crowd. Cain stepped over the debris. He brushed against a brown-shirted sheriff's deputy who had one fearful eye on the crowd, the other on two of DiCarlo's blue-shirted city cops standing ten feet away.

The reviewing stand waited at the far end of the crowd. Two thousand, five thousand, six thousand people jostled between Cain and that platform, blocking his view of who was on the stand. In the middle of the crowd, a television crew stood on scaffolding a foot above the heads of their audience and actors. Around that tower, hands waved frantically at the cameras; others grasped for the ankles of the blond woman reporter. She smiled, kept her back pressed against those of her cameraman and producer.

The crowd stank: beer, sweat, soaked clothes, a hint of urine. The sun beat down on them, and a sea of humidity floated above their heads. The band played, brass and drums. There was the *rat-a-tat-tat* of firecrackers, shrieks, more laughter. Still, marchers funneled into the city square.

A gap appeared in the crowd: Cain scurried through it. He wormed his way between stone walls and people to the revolving glass doors of the building where the commission had its office.

The doors were locked.

Frantically, he pushed against the brass plate in the middle of the glass door. The lock in the old building shook in its sockets. He glanced to his right, saw a city cop watching him. The cop yawned.

A dozen hands joined Cain's on the door, more pressed against his shoulders, pushing and rocking back, pushing again. Someone cheered their sport. The lock broke with a loud *crack!* The glass doors spun Cain inside. Staggering away from his entrance, he looked back at the whirling doors. No one in the crowd followed the weird guy they'd casually helped. The cop turned to watch the parade and await orders.

Cain stumbled up the stairs, his footsteps echoing in the stairwell above the rolling murmur outside the building.

The two state troopers guarding the commission's door jumped from their chairs when Cain came out of the fire exit.

"Who the hell are you?" yelled one, reaching for his gun.

"Open it!" Cain yelled, pointing to the commission door as he staggered toward them, the door that led to high ground.

"Jesus Christ!" said the other trooper, recognizing Cain.

One trooper fumbled with his key chain. Within seconds, Cain stood at the window overlooking the city square.

"What time is it?" he asked.

" 'Bout ten after noon," answered a trooper.

"Mr. Cain," said the other trooper, "you need . . ."

When he realized his words made no difference, he stopped talking.

The troopers helped Cain lift the air-conditioner out of the way, open the window for a better view. The heat rolled in with the sea roar of people pressed together in the square below.

Another beer stand collapsed below the window. Those

in the crowd near that calamity yelled—with approval, with
anguish, Cain couldn't tell. In bleachers to his left, Cain
read anxiety on the faces of hundreds of elderly people,
people with wheelchairs or carrying crutches who'd been
ferried to their seats in school buses organized by the mayor
and driven by dragooned SIC members. Cain saw Mrs.
Kincheloe, who'd always expected *more* of neighbor Jimmy
Cainelli. The old man in the black suit, who'd remembered
his limp, sat atop a bleacher seat like a crow.

Mack Jensen, the bartender from the Cairo, leaned against
a doorway by the bleachers, beefy arms crossed over his
white apron.

Not far from the TV scaffolding Cain spotted young Pete
Vandross. The teenager wore a black T-shirt. Two carefully
rough-styled young men stood with him, as did someone's
blond teenage daughter, who laughed at Vandross's ges-
tures, glowed with eagerness and energy and the thrill of
the moment. Nowhere did Cain see the Vandross boy's father.

On the right side of the square, Reverand Borge's
crane-like form towered above the heads around him. Standing with Borge was Arty, the unionist who'd sneaked Cain
into Steeltown's last major rally. A hundred bodies away
from them stood Russell Boswell.

Closer to the reviewing stand, Cain saw DiCarlo. The
chief wore his dress blue uniform, stood on a platform of
barrels and boards whose construction he'd personally over-
seen. The chief looked like a gorilla on a pedestal, his sunglasses sweeping over the crowd. Beside him stood the
cadaverous detective. Behind them waited three blue-shirted
city policemen with visored white helmets and shotguns.

The reviewing stand filled City Hall's steps, a wooden
stage draped with red, white, and blue bunting. A banner
stretched across the platform's front and in six-foot-high
black letters proclaimed:

STEELTOWN

The top half of the letters was visible over the heads of
the crowd. The stage floor began above the banner. On

stage, rising above the banner's *L*, was a lectern with a microphone.

To the left of the lectern sat the high school band, red-faced and sweating in their maroon-and-gold uniforms and white-plumed hats. Their teacher-director wore white livery.

To the right of the lectern, in two rows of folding chairs, sat Steeltown's anointed aristocracy. Two chairs were set apart and stationed closer to the lectern. Mayor Richard Nash sat in the first chair, an egg in a gray suit, his pudgy white hands fiddling on his knees. Beside him sat his mother wrapped in a widow's black shawl, despite the heat.

Mere mortal royalty filled the two rows of chairs to their left: in the first row sat Publisher Evans; the pudgy SIC president; a gray-haired gentleman identified in newspaper photos as the president of Central Bank; the three state legislators indebted to Nash's machine; the sheriff. Next came immaculately dressed Elliot Kimmett IV, and to his left, his slouching son, constrained in a blue blazer, white shirt and tie, and khaki pants.

Sylvia sat at the far end of the front row. She wore a skirted, white linen suit.

Ministers, priests, rabbis, city councilmen, and lesser stars sat in the back row.

Standing behind the chairs were the mayor's aide, Carson; patriarch Kimmett's lieutenant, Nelson; half a dozen thugs.

A giant American flag made the bandstand's backdrop.

Along the crowd's perimeter stood clusters of DiCarlo's blue-suited, white-helmeted cops and the sheriff's brown-shirted deputies. Men with Special Deputy badges pinned to SIC red Windbreakers swelled the deputies' ranks. Among those special officers of the law Cain recognized Johnny Maxx's jackknife-looking lackey.

With a glance to his mother, the mayor stood, walked to the microphone.

"Ladies and gentlemen!" boomed Nash's amplified voice.

The sound system squawked.

Enthused, excited by their own existence, their own *presence*, few in the crowd paid attention to their mayor.

"Ladies and gentlemen," he said again.

But the crowd merely swayed, shifting as more bodies pushed into the square.

Nash's mother spoke sharply to her son, words only those on the stage could hear. Her hand flicked toward him.

The mayor blushed; stepped away from the microphone and barked an order to the band director.

The band played Sousa's "The Stars and Stripes Forever!"

As the crowd began to bounce and sway to the familiar rhythm, Cain saw Pete Vandross hand *something* to the blond girl. She took it, hesitated. The other two boys encouraged her. Vandross pointed through the dancing crowd to the reviewing stand. Still she hesitated. Then, slowly, as her friends urged her on, she started forward.

And Cain knew he had to stop her. He dashed toward the door.

"Where are you going?" yelled a trooper.

"You stay on post!" ordered the other trooper, who, like his partner who obeyed him, would be cited for meritorious performance.

"Central Dispatch!" he barked into his hand-held radio as he chased Cain down the fire stairs. "This is Delta 7! We have a situation!"

"Delta 7," radioed the dispatcher in the state capital, connected to the troopers by the miracle of microwave relay stations. "What kind of situation?"

"I don't know!" replied the trooper; then he slid the radio in its belt pouch and jumped behind Cain into the revolving glass doors.

Like a tidal wave, the heat and mass and noise hit them as they spun clear of the building. Cain stumbled into a man waving a tiny American flag, bounced off him and between two women who were trying to light cigarettes. Over the band music he heard them curse him, sensed the state trooper trying to follow in his wake as he charged through the crowd, ignored the fire in his knee, the aches in his body. Between bobbing heads he caught glimpses of the reviewing stand, of Sylvia. He couldn't see the blond girl, but he charged blindly after her.

A fat man stepped on his toes. A boy banged against his shin. Someone spilled gin on his back and an elbow he never saw thudded into his chest. Dizziness and nausea seized Cain, but he stumbled forward. He was panting, crying, his arms flopping and his legs trembling as he pushed forward, fighting for speed but winning only jerky progress through a sea with a thousand currents and endless debris. The trooper became lost in his wake.

The Sousa march ended. Before the crowd could settle back into its own rhythm, Cain heard Mayor Nash's crafty, amplified voice:

"Ladies and gentlemen, 'The Star-Spangled Banner'!"

A whiff of piety swirled through the crowd. Those elderly and infirm in the bleachers who could, stood; faced the flag draped behind the bandstand. Everyone on the bandstand rose, turned to face that giant banner. Many of those in the square placed their hands over their hearts. Most of the crowd stood still, at least faced the bandstand, slowly coming under the spell of reverence ordered from the cradle and yearned for to the grave.

Cain pushed through the crowd, closer, ever closer to the bandstand. He was a hundred, he was ninety yards away.

But the girl was much closer.

Was there.

As her peers on the platform struck the first chord of the national anthem, she jumped on a crowd control sawhorse on the ground in front of the stage, pranced down it like the balance beam in her gym class, and with the aerosol can sprayed a crude but quick crimson *A* over the second E in the city banner:

STEALTOWN

She leapt back into the crowd before anyone standing in the front lines realized what she'd done.

Red drips began to roll down the banner. Three brownshirted deputies and Johnny Maxx's jackknife man dashed after the vandal.

The girl wove through the crowd like a fox, dodging around people with their eyes on the banner. She was young, graceful, lithe; propelled by the thrills of rebellion and fear.

Hunters chased her, not as swift but twice as strong. They knocked aside citizens who got in their way like horses crashing through brush.

Ten feet behind the girl, the lead deputy tripped. The other two deputies fell over his tumbling form.

Those in the crowd who saw the melee laughed.

It's me! thought the girl, triumphantly. It's me!

Behind her, Johnny's jackknife man pulled a police baton from his Windbreaker's sleeve. He was six feet from the girl's fleeing back. Five. Four. He swung the baton across her skull, knocked her hair sideways in the thick, breezeless air.

She staggered forward. Merciful hands kept her from falling, passed her to kind hands who hadn't witnessed the blow but knew her dazed face meant trouble. Her momentum and the support from strangers kept her moving, kept her on her feet and took her deeper into the crowd, her mind a blank, a stickiness forming beneath her gold locks. Kind hands passed her to friendly hands who hadn't seen and didn't know but accepted the kid they assumed drunk then passed her on to indifferent hands who shoved her away to hands that brushed her without thought to the hands of two men who'd seen and knew and read the power of the daze on the girl's face, the ignorance of those around them, the opportunity. They led her away from the square to a side street. To an alley.

Before she reached the kind hands, the jackknife man started after her.

But an ex-miner with kids of his own grabbed his arm, yelled: "You son of a bitch!"

Jackknife man broke free, swung his billy club, and nicked the miner's nose.

Blood flecked the crowd.

The band played, "... *and the rockets' red glare* ..."

The miner had been hit before. In bars, on picket lines, by cops, by crooks. He knew who hit him now. The miner stepped forward, blocked jackknife man's next swing, and smashed his gnarled fist into the face of the hood with a badge.

The deputies jumped the miner from behind. His friends yelled at them as jackknife man fell to the cobblestones.

And DiCarlo saw his chance.

He barked an order to the cadaverous detective, who in turn radioed commands to city cops stationed around the edge of the square. As the detective issued orders, the chief of police sprang from his command post to *take charge* in front of *the whole damn town.*

By the time DiCarlo bulled his way through the crowd, the jackknife man had regained his feet. He cocked his arm to club the struggling miner. DiCarlo knocked the deputized hood back down to the cobblestones.

On the crowd's perimeter, DiCarlo's force moved in, pushing their way toward their chief, ordering the crowd to break up, move on. When they met resistance, they used the butts of their shotguns and their billy clubs to show who was boss.

The band reached "... *does that star-spangled banner yet wave* ..."

Most of the jam-packed crowd couldn't see what had started where, or indeed, what was happening even a few feet from them. There was commotion near the reviewing stand where the band wound up its song, where the mayor faced the flag and savored his hour of triumph. For a while, most of the crowd only knew another wave of jostling, another series of whoops and hollers. The day was hot. Everyone felt the push of their friends and neighbors who grew to look more like strangers with each rude jostle, each nasty elbow.

When DiCarlo's cops made their move, Nash's troops hesitated. All their commanders stood on the reviewing stand, their backs to the crisis. No orders came over the deputies' radios.

But they saw the men with whom they competed for the trough swing into action. Fists and batons and shotgun butts flew with unasked permission in this, *their* town.

The mayor's men surged into the crowd. When one went, all followed. Deputies yelled at cops, who yelled back.

A city cop grabbed a citizen who swung at him and a sheriff's deputy pulled the cop away and the citizen hit the deputy: brown-shirted county man, blue-shirted city badge, hired-hood-turned-lawman, they all had money, guns, and power; labels suddenly made no difference to the citizens of Stealtown.

In the bleachers, the old people who could see some of what was happening frantically tried to climb down, get away.

The brawling along the perimeter of the crowd pushed everyone in the square closer together.

As the band struck the anthem's final chords, the jack-knife man rolled to his back, saw DiCarlo looming over him, bellowing, reaching for him with massive paws. The jack knifeman thrust his hand into his windbreaker.

But DiCarlo was quicker. He pumped all six rounds from his silver-plated Magnum into the man on the cobblestones.

DiCarlo's last round sounded after the band's final chord. Its report echoed off the downtown buildings and hushed the crowd. Almost everyone knew that sound. From radios on lawmen's belts crackled:

"Shots fired!"

Mayor Nash turned to his triumph and found disaster.

"People of Steeltown!" cried his amplified voice. "What are you doing?"

Most of them didn't know what *anyone* was doing. Battling cops and deputies, citizens swept up into those wars: they all ceased to *know*, began only to *do*.

"Stop this!" cried the mayor.

He gripped the sides of the lectern so violently the wood splintered.

"Stop this!" commanded the mayor's microphoned voice.

When DiCarlo raised his eyes from the man he'd killed, he found a hundred frightened and angry faces surrounding him. He waved his revolver at them—empty, but they might not know it.

"Get outta here!" he bellowed. "Move!"

But even if the people around him had wanted to move, they could go but a few steps, and then only slowly. Against the force of the crowd, they could go nowhere by the power of will alone.

Band members began jumping off the back of the stage.

Mayor Nash bellowed into the microphone: *"I order you to stop! This is my town! My town! Stop!"*

Behind DiCarlo, the miner's friends fought the deputies who were trying to handcuff him. A dozen fists smashed the deputies to the ground. Hands robbed them of their clubs, their guns.

Though the citizens in the crowd needed no guns snatched from officers of the law. This was Steeltown, a city in a country where private handguns outnumbered the national population of children. This was Stealtown, where bombs exploded, bosses beat complainers, only gangsters profited, and hope had moved on.

"STOP IT!!!" screamed the mayor.

No one ever knew where the first wild shot came from, or who fired it. As he struggled toward the reviewing stand, Cain thought he heard it come from behind him, back toward the commission's building.

But fired it was. First one round. Then, quickly, three more.

Everyone who had a gun, drew it.

And the volleys began.

Targets weren't chosen, they occurred. Few knew who they shot at; few knew why. Someone was shooting, they shot back. Forty, fifty, a hundred gunshots rang out. Screams filled the air. Some people dove to the ground. Most people could only sway with the mindless mass of humanity that gripped them, sway and panic as their neighbors, friends, and public servants spat death from their hands.

The volleys lasted only a few moments.

Blood sprayed the air, flowed over the cobblestones.

"YOU'VE—GOT—TO—STOP—I—" screamed Mayor Nash.

Abruptly, his words turned to a gurgle, as though the devil swirling through the crowd reached up to the platform to strangle him. The crimson glow that had flushed his head vanished. He paled, turned more translucent than white. A purplish red lightning bolt flashed from his temple to the top of his skull, throbbed, and stood out, like a scar. His mother stared at him. Carson ran to his side, yelling for an ambulance. Nash's hands wouldn't release the fractured lectern. The stroke glazed his eyes and he saw no more of his city.

In the crowd, DiCarlo swung his pistol back and forth. The volleys of gunfire had stopped as quickly and mindlessly as they'd begun. Electricity ruled the mob surging around him as he tried to push his way toward his troops— wherever they might be. He whirled this way and that, saw only faces of fear and hate for one of the men who'd ruled them and led them to this fury.

Through the crowd slipped Laprado, who'd been a rat in an alley to the mighty Steeltown chief of police. He bent as he scurried, snatched the fallen jackknife man's police baton. DiCarlo's back was to him. The crowd parted as Laprado ran, leaped high, smashed the billy club down on DiCarlo's head. Laprado vanished behind people who didn't know him, who didn't care.

DiCarlo staggered, dropped his gun. His sunglasses fell off. When his hand touched his head, it came back covered with blood. He didn't look behind him, didn't know who hit him, and knew that didn't matter. He grabbed the closest man and threw him to one side.

"Clear this area!" he yelled. "Get out of here! I'm the chief of police and I'm ordering you to leave!"

But the crowd had heard enough orders. Besides, there was nowhere they could go. The chief had blood on his hands. Old blood and new blood. His blood. So red, so bright, the people could smell it.

DiCarlo swung at a man who moved too slowly. The chief's punch connected, the man stumbled, but he swung back. A woman grabbed DiCarlo's other arm. A child pushed him from behind. Suddenly the gorilla became a beach ball, battered and pushed from all sides. He roared, he bellowed, finally screamed as his nose blossomed crimson, as hands tore off his badge, ripped his shirt, as he tripped and fell into the frenzy of a punching, kicking, stomping mob that until far too late did not realize who they were and what they did.

The bullets missed Cain. He kept his feet in the panic, and none of the crazed lawmen swung their weapons at him. The crowd swirled him, tossed and turned him, but somehow he slid through their current toward City Hall and the reviewing stand.

In panic, the crowd rolled away from the reviewing stand, knocked over barricades and ran down side streets leading from the square. A police car was overturned. Spectators cheered. Emotions swung from one extreme to the other, merged and evolved so rapidly they could not be recognized by those who experienced them; they could only be lived.

The mob shattered the last downtown department store's showroom window. A dozen people were cut by the glass. One of them, ignoring the blood trickling down his arm, pulled a winter jacket off a mannequin, ran. A bolder soul jumped through the window and dashed into the store, an example emulated by a dozen witnesses.

Two twelve-year-old boys found the municipal fireworks cached beneath the bleachers for that night's planned display. With juvenile glee, they appropriated a string of firecrackers that they thought were just like the kind their dads bought them each year. They lit the fuse with matches taken from one of their mother's purses.

The fuse burned faster than they'd believed possible.

"Look out, Billy!" cried his buddy.

Billy flipped the string of firecrackers back toward where he'd gotten them and they ran. Rolling explosions shook the bleachers, ignited bunting and the cheap, untreated wood used to construct the stands.

Gas trickling from the overturned police cruiser touched a dropped cigarette. With a flash, a roar, that vehicle turned to a ball of flame. Tendrils of fire reached out to the city.

As the burning police car belched black smoke, Cain tripped, grabbed a sawhorse in front of the reviewing stand. Behind him, most of the crowd fled the square; some of them looted. Reverend Borge and a dozen others ran from one fallen body to the next, helping those who were wounded, skipping the dead. Deputies and city cops shuffled about in a daze, their weapons useless, their hearts stunned and

confused as they tried to sort out their loyalties and priorities with no one to lead them. One deputy fired his pistol
into the air; everyone ignored him, and he sheepishly wandered away. Fire sirens sounded in the distance.

Leaning on the sawhorse, Cain raised his eyes to the
stage.

Carson and two deputies were half-dragging, half-carrying
Mayor Nash toward the rear exit. His rigid hand clenched a
jagged piece of the wooden lectern. Nash's black-shawled
mother sat slumped in her chair, unhurt, uncaring, unneeded.

Sylvia.

Her face was stone as she stood watching her son shout
at Raymond Nelson. They and two thugs employed by the
Kimmett family were circled around a handsome man collapsed in a folding chair: he'd turned from pledging his
allegiance to his country's flag and faced the obligation he'd
assumed. A ricocheted bullet from a rogue gun cracked
through his forehead and splattered his brains on the flag.
His blood covered Sylvia's white linen suit. She looked toward
the crowd, and her eyes found Cain's.

In that instant, she saw all of him; his pain, his promise. Saw the gore that covered them both like a price scrawled
over a package.

The youngest living Kimmett yelled an order to Nelson.

Like a good soldier, Nelson accepted succession of command. He directed his men to do the boy's bidding.

Suddenly, Cain knew almost everything.

As ordered, Nelson's men picked up Elliot Kimmett IV,
carried him toward the rear of the stage for a useless and
frantic ride to the hospital. The heir led the way.

Nelson reached for Sylvia's arm, but she shook off the
hand of the Kimmett man. He glanced to where she looked,
saw Cain. Shrugged and hurried after his duty.

Sylvia turned her back to Cain, walked away.

Going, gone.

Cain turned, stumbled back through the square.

"Help me! Help me!" moaned a woman curled on the
ground to his left. In a voice racked with pain, an unseen
man chanted, "God! God! God!" Dozens merely sobbed.
"Over here! Get a doctor over here!" Flames crackled as the

fire consumed a collapsed beer stand. Someone smashed another window. Cain stepped over a woman whose face was shotgunned off; his shoes slid through the pool of blood, and he left sticky red footprints on the cobblestones.

There, straightening up over a dead man: Russell Boswell.

"Come with me!" cried Cain, grabbing Boswell's arm.

"What are you doing here?" said Boswell.

"Come with me," said Cain, his mind racing furiously through dark smoke. "There's still a chance! We can . . ."

"What are you talking about?"

"There's nobody left," said Cain. "There's nobody else who can do it. Nobody else who should. Just you. The governor, we can get him to set it up, you can step in. I've got money, we can . . ."

Boswell pushed him.

"You did this!" he said; pushed Cain's chest again. "You did this!"

"No, no!" Cain waved his hand to deny, to plead. "I didn't! Don't you . . . I didn't know what . . . This wasn't what I planned!"

"What you planned?"

"You," said Cain, "it's been you. Not from the first, not from the start, I didn't know, wasn't sure till I met you. Had to hope, assume, somebody . . . couldn't be me. Couldn't ever be me, knew that.

"This damn town," said Cain. "Only way to beat it was to take them all out, the hell with everything else. Once and for all, clean sweep. Only way to give it a chance is with one man. One good man. One just man. Honest. Take it over and let him run it and . . ."

"You're crazy!"

"You," repeated Cain. "Not Nash or Johnny Maxx or DiCarlo or Kimmett or his son who couldn't and wouldn't, not anybody but you. You can do it. I'll help you. That's why I came. Saw the chance. Gotta beat this town. For once. Or we all lose. We can do it!"

"You're not crazy," said Boswell, stepping back, shaking his head. "You're a fool."

"Come on," urged Cain. "Or we lose everything!"

"I won't play your savior," said Boswell. "Or your saint.

Don't you get it? Even if . . . You want to make me into a Nash or one of the others, into what they were trying to become."

"No, that's not what . . ."

"But that's *how*," said Boswell. "And *how* makes *what*."

He shook at head. Pity replaced his anger toward Cain.

"Go on," said Boswell. "Get out of here: this isn't your town."

Tendrils of flame reached out through the city. Boswell left Cain standing on bloody cobblestones.

Cain leaned against the buzzer, ignored the closed-circuit TV camera mounted on the pillar above the black iron gate.

"Mr. Cain?" said the butler's voice in the intercom box.

"Let me in," said Cain.

Slowly, the iron gates to the Kimmett estate swung open.

As Cain shuffled through them, a steady *whump-whump-whump* droned across the sky: five olive green helicopters chopped their way toward the smoky city square, the first of the National Guard soldiers requested by the state troopers, commanded by the governor, armed by Congress and the President, and authorized by the Constitution to restore order to Steeltown.

Eight months later, the official federal investigatory commission's report on "the disorder" would say 17 people died of gunshot wounds, 30 were wounded, 11 were trampled to death, 5 died of "miscellaneous causes," and 391 were injured through rape, fire, assault and "related events."

Kimmett's gates clanged shut behind Cain.

He'd walked to the Kimmett mansion through streets he'd known forever. The town that had seemed deserted that morning seemed teeming with deserters that afternoon. People ran pell-mell past him, stood on their porches, and wrung their hands. Dogs barked, children cried. Every neighborhood he limped through buzzed with individual excitements and collective woe. Black smoke billowed to the sky from the heart of their city; filled their own hearts. As he climbed the hills, the electronic and human babble in the streets behind him wore away, replaced by the steady sound of weeping, of silence, of shame and grim anticipation. He recognized everyone and saw no one he knew, unless he chose to count the royal blue station wagon loaded with suitcases he'd seen headed toward the highway with less forewarned cars; a boy stared out of the station wagon's rear door window.

"Mr. Cain!" said the butler as he bowed Cain inside the mansion. "We heard the terrible news! Mr. Nelson called from the hospital and . . ."

"Where is he?" said Cain. His voice was hoarse. He leaned against the oak-paneled wall, closed his eyes.

"It's been frightful! All Mr. Nelson's men volunteered to be parade deputies and left the cook and I with only Judson and— "

"Where is he?" rasped Cain, his eyes still closed.

"Judson?" said the butler. "Well, there's been trouble with the dogs. Something in the air has them frightfully upset. Judson is around the house, getting them all penned up."

"He's in his room," said Cain, pushing off the wall. He shuffled past the butler and said, "Get out."

The butler scurried toward the kitchen.

Cain collapsed on the first flight of stairs. A weak grasp on the bottom pole of the banister kept him from sliding to the foyer's floor. How long he lay there, he wasn't sure. The patter of feet on the hardwood floor below him brought his senses back. He rolled over in time to see the butler and a fat woman scurrying toward the door. The butler spoke without looking to where Cain lay.

"We shall lock the gate behind us," he said.

Then they were out the front door, closing it, gone.

And Cain crawled. Up the first flight, around the landing to the second story. He struggled to his feet halfway up the second set of stairs, stumbled his way to the third flight, rested, then climbed: slow, shuffling steps, both hands grasping the rail.

No one sat at the nurse's desk outside Kimmett's room. The red light glowed above his door. Cain fumbled under the desk, pressed the release button, and staggered inside.

The oxygen-saturated atmosphere overwhelmed him as

he crossed Kimmett's threshold. Cain didn't shut the door, so the rich, life-giving gas spilled out into the hall, floated through the house. Sensors in the bedroom noted the leak in the controlled environment and triggered the giant tanks stored in the wall cabinet to maximum pumping.

Elliot Kimmett III sat alone at his window table, staring at the rising mountain of gray smoke on the horizon. He wore his terrycloth bathrobe, ivory silk pajamas. His wispy white hair was a mess and his skin was yellow.

"What have you done?" Kimmett whispered to the man at the far end of his room.

Three television screens flickered silently on the electronic wall behind Cain. He shuffled past the four-poster bed, through the stuffed chairs of the salon sitting area, toward the old man.

"What have you done?" cried Kimmett.

"Funny," said Cain. The overgenerous oxygen supply revitalized him, but still he stumbled and had to grab the white gauze window drapes to keep from falling. Cain lowered himself into the other chair at the table, told Kimmett:

"Everybody wants to know what I've done. Maybe even me.

"I kept our bargain. Remember? I told you I'd take this town away from who had it, but that it was up to you to get it then. The plan was always to keep my bargain, but the rest . . ."

Cain shook his head. "So clever, we were both suckers."

"What you've . . ." began Kimmett, but Cain interupted him:

"It was you," he told Kimmett. "All along, it was you. I should have known. I should have been smarter. The only one in town more desperate than me was you. Everybody else was just hungry.

"You killed Josh Hammond," said Cain. "Me and DiCarlo, we thought we were so smart: 'Meet N's man.' Should've remembered that Nash wasn't the only 'N' in town. Nelson takes your orders. He's a good bureaucrat and a smart ex-cop. He knew better than to pull the trigger himself. The Kimmetts have a lot of soldiers. Hammond was too dumb to know he was being set up. You knew what I meant when I first came here, 'bout needing a reason to be. You knew I was right and you couldn't keep your hands off, didn't trust me and wanted it your way. Always, your way."

"Hammond was a piddly little shit!" snapped Kimmett.

"Yeah, he didn't matter to anybody," said Cain. "But he sure could be made into something, couldn't he? A match. We did that, you and me. Just like you knew we could.

"You did the bomb, too," continued Cain. "Didn't you?"

Kimmett looked out the window.

"Yeah," said Cain, "you did. How'd that work? You saw Boswell getting big, never trusted me and maybe learned a reason or two why you shouldn't. Things were happening, things were moving, and you couldn't keep your hands off.

"But you did more than the bomb. Who approached who about the deal? Did you go to the mayor or did he come to you?"

"What difference does it make," mumbled Kimmett.

"He came to you," said Cain. "Nash was no fool. He smelled you behind the commission all the time. He never thought we could hurt him until we latched on to the SIC bond mess. Johnny Maxx, the chief, he knew they were waiting to snipe him. Alone, he figured he might not make it. He had to make a deal with someone—which is why you took it: if it wasn't with you, it would be against you.

"So he came to you and offered what? To be your boy like he was Olson's? No, he wouldn't go that far. Partners, maybe. The both of you figuring that once you got the chief and Johnny Maxx out of the way, you could outlast or outscrew the other, come out on top. That's why you told me to lay off Nash. That's why when we didn't, you had to make us. Besides, I'd annoyed you, just like Josh Hammond.

"But a bomb! Boswell, who could have become a rival. Your daughter-in-law, who you hated and who even after all these years might have someday been able to grab your son away, steal your immortality. Beth and Catherine. They didn't matter, they didn't count. Me. A bomb, something horrendous that would translate into the commission seeming out of hand, out of control. Just like you wanted, just like you arranged, it got reined in for its own good. You didn't care who you killed, did you?"

"You're not so smart, Cain."

"You're right," said Cain. "Not then. Not even now."

His eyes closed, he deeply breathed the strong air. When his eyes opened again, he stared at Kimmett and said:

"What was the ten-grand bribe to the Japanese for? For them to bring their business to Steeltown or to stay out?

"You remember," continued Cain when Kimmett didn't answer. Cain nodded to the rolltop desk. "Ten thousand dollars from the checkbook in that drawer. To cash, of course. Did Nelson handle that or did you do it direct? Doesn't matter. The Japanese knew where it came from, and they didn't play. They threw it right back at you, only they did it by taking your money in a way you couldn't squawk. Corruption perverted to charity. They used your son to do it, never knowing if he was as sleazy as his father or an innocent dupe they turned into a pawn carrying a message he didn't understand. My guess is the bribe was for them to stay out of Steeltown. You want this place all to yourself."

"Doesn't matter," answered Kimmett.

"That's right," said Cain. "It doesn't matter. Want to know something? Your money probably made no difference. The Japanese probably wouldn't have come here anyway. Nobody wants Steeltown, not anymore. Besides, the Japanese don't make their moves just because someone pushes them one way or another. You know what the saddest part of that is? Your son. He died not knowing how many times and how many ways you betrayed him.

"Maybe that's just as well," said Cain. His voice grew cold. Kimmett's eyes flashed up at him. "Maybe dying was the only way he could get free of all you did and what you had planned."

"What do you want, Cain?" whispered Kimmett. "Why did you come here?"

"I wanted to be the one to tell you you lost."

"Damn you!" shouted Kimmett. His eyes blazed and his frail hand twisted to a fist, smashed down on the table. "I've still got . . ."

"Got *nothing!*" snapped Cain. He shook his head. "Maybe I lost, too, but for me, that's not a bad start. For you, its the end.

"Your town is burning itself down. Your *heritage!* You've got a grandson and damned if he isn't you in his bones. He's worse than nothing, because he'll take what's left away from you, not be what you want. He'll blow his inheritance, just like you have. Oh he'll try to reign over this gutted city: there's no place else he can go and get away with so much. But even if his Johnny Maxxes weren't already out there, he'd fail, and fail fast. Just like you did. Because he's weak and petty and a bully, because he's too smart by half and 's got nothing in his soul but mirrors."

"I'll kill you!" screamed Kimmett.

"You're already dead," Cain told him. "And you know what's even better? You're not only dead, you're forgotten."

With a cry, Kimmett sprang at Cain. Grabbed the arms that Cain lifted to block the old man's charge and had his arms grabbed back. Their chairs fell over, the table wobbled, and they stumbled to their feet.

One man was old, the other wounded. They pushed and pulled at each other like children quarreling while they danced.

Cain rooted his feet, sank his weight and rolled back with Kimmett's force. The old man reached the limit of his push, felt himself being pulled off-balance and jerked back with all his energy. Cain rolled forward with him, only faster. When Kimmett was off-center, Cain blended the power of his push with Kimmett's own retreating energy. The old man flew backwards, crashed to the carpet.

A last look at the old man in his bathrobe sprawled on the floor, then Cain turned, headed toward the door.

He heard Kimmett scramble on the carpet, the *whurr* of an opening desk drawer, and remembered the black automatic.

Cain dove over a sofa, rolled to the floor as Kimmett fired. Three bullets smashed into the hardwood wall beyond the bed. A loud hissing filled the room. Cain pushed himself up from his hands and knees as though he meant to stand, drew Kimmett's aim then ducked as the old man jerked off three more shots. Those bullets smashed into his wall of electronics. A television screen exploded. Sparks flew as wires were cut, tubes shattered. Escaping electricity crackled. Cain tried to fake a forward dive then cut back, but his knee gave out. Kimmett fired as Cain slipped to the ground. That bullet nicked Cain's turning chest, buried itself in Kimmett's mattress. An acrid singe and the smell of gunpowder cut the sweet air. On the carpet, Cain closed his eyes, wondered if he'd hear the gunshot that killed him.

"Damn it!" screamed Kimmett.

Cain blinked, saw Kimmett frantically pulling at the empty automatic's blown-back slide. Slowly, Cain stood.

Kimmett threw the pistol at him. Cain ducked, and the gun bounced off the open door. Kimmett froze in his place, trembling.

Judson marched into the room.

"Get him!" Screamed Kimmett. "Kill him!"

The giant in the tuxedo lumbered forward.

"Wrong man," Cain mumbled to the giant reaching for him with hands like catcher's mitts. "You've got the wrong man."

Judson grabbed Cain around the rib cage, lifted him like a rag doll.

A spark from a gunshot, smoldering electrical wire crackled back along the stream of pure oxygen escaping from the bullet-damaged valve on the tank behind the wall. The tank exploded.

Judson and Cain flew apart. Cain crashed into the cushioned front of the couch, knocking it over as Judson sailed past him.

Most of the explosion's force blew into the hall. The heat and pressure combined with the pure gas. A mushroom of blue flame roared out from the center of the blast. Burning chunks of wall tumbled down the stairwell, sparking random islands of fire in a house primed to burn. When Cain raised his head, flames were devouring the curtains, the bed was ablaze. The ceiling paper was curling.

"Unnhh," called a weak voice close to the window. " 'elp me. Help me!"

Beneath an overturned stuffed chair, Cain saw Kimmett's bare feet, his spindly white legs and ivory silk pajamas, the bottom of his bathrobe.

Amidst the crackle of flames, the sounds of the mansion's wood snapping, Cain heard *dragging;* gurgling, rasping breaths. He looked to his left.

Judson's massive bulk had shielded Cain from the wall that hid the oxygen tank. When that tank exploded, most of the blast went through the thinner hall wall. But the force that ripped through the bedroom wall turned its oak paneling into shrapnel.

Judson crawled on his stomach, one mighty arm pulling after the other. A dozen, two dozen jagged splinters of wood stuck like porcupine quills out of the oozing back of his tuxedo.

"Help me!" cried the master of the mansion. "Help me!"

And Judson crawled to do his bidding.

Cain stumbled out the burning doorway. He more fell than walked down the stairs, dodging patches of fire. The smoke grew thick and gray. Bitter.

Part of the third floor balcony had crashed down to the main floor. The Oriental rug in the foyer quickly conducted flames to the front door; by the time Cain got there, that exit was a sheet of fire.

Coughing, choking, his eyes tearing so badly he could barely see, Cain felt his way down the hall. The locked library door shook as heavy bodies threw themselves against it. From inside came the crazed baying and snarling of half a dozen trapped great Danes. Cain stumbled to the drawing room; through the smoke, he saw what looked like a shimmering plane of soft white light.

Floor to ceiling windows.

Holding a sofa cushion in front of him, Cain charged the light. Glass and window molding shattered as he fell outside to the lawn.

He never remembered running to the front gate; never knew how he managed. When he realized where he was, he punched the exit code into the lock monitor. Nothing happened. The fire at the house had cut the circuits, switched off all power to the fence and jammed the lock. Cain used the crossbars and lock box for footholds, slowly climbed the gate. He pulled himself over the top, dangled above the ground. Dropped.

Was lucky, and took the shock almost completely in his good leg. He grabbed the iron bars to keep from falling. As he did, he looked back.

Orange light shimmered through the mansion, black smoke billowed out the roof. Silhouetted against the flames in a third-floor room stood a giant cradling a limp body. Flames swallowed them.

The park surrounded Cain; ahead was the stream, the river. As the city drifted toward night, Cain left walking, uncertain of his destination but sure of his step.